PRAISE FOR FI

'Fiona Lowe has expertly crafted a world that's easy to spend time in ... If you're looking to lose yourself in a cosy new novel that shines a spotlight on women's lives and stories, then *A Home Like Ours* by Fiona Lowe deserves a spot on your bookshelf.'

—*Mamamia*

'Rich, thought-provoking, and extremely absorbing, *A Home Like Ours* is yet another incredible read from the very talented Fiona Lowe.'

—*Better Reading*

'An insightful, warm and engaging story, *A Home Like Ours* is another fabulous novel from award-winning Australian author Fiona Lowe.'

—*Book'd Out*

'Fiona Lowe's ability to create atmosphere and tension and real relationship dynamics is a gift.'

—Sally Hepworth, bestselling author of
The Mother-in-Law, on *Home Fires*

'Lowe breathes real life into her characters ... a profoundly hopeful tale, one of re-generation, of the strength gained from women supporting women, and of a community pulling together, one that acts as a powerful reminder of the resilience of the human spirit ... a deeply Australian story that brilliantly captures our own life and times.'

—*Better Reading* on *Home Fires*

'Distinctly Australian with its power to evoke grit and tenderness, joy and bleakness, tragedy and comedy, all at once.'

'Lowe is a master at painting believable characters with heart and soul that contribute to creating such an addictive read.'

ABOUT THE AUTHOR

FIONA LOWE has been a midwife, a sexual health counsellor and a family support worker; an ideal career for an author who writes novels about family, community and relationships. She spent her early years in Papua New Guinea where, without television, reading was the entertainment and it set up a lifelong love of books. Although she often re-wrote the endings of books in her head, it was the birth of her first child that prompted her to write her first novel. A recipient of the prestigious USA RITA® award and the Australian RuBY award, Fiona writes books that are set in small country towns. They feature real people facing difficult choices and explore how family ties and relationships impact on their decisions.

When she's not writing stories, she's a distracted wife, mother of two 'ginger' sons, a volunteer in her community, guardian of eighty rose bushes, a slave to a cat, and is often found collapsed on the couch with wine. You can find her at her website, fionalowe.com, and on Facebook, Twitter, Instagram and Goodreads.

Also by Fiona Lowe

Daughter of Mine
Birthright
Home Fires
Just an Ordinary Family
A Family of Strangers

FIONA LOWE

A Home Like Ours

FICTION

HQ

First Published 2021
Second Australian Paperback Edition 2022
ISBN 9781867244509

This is a work of fiction. Names, characters, places, and incidents are either the product of the author's imagination or are used fictitiously, and any resemblance to actual persons, living or dead, business establishments, events, or locales is entirely coincidental.

Published by
HQ Fiction
An imprint of Harlequin Enterprises (Australia) Pty Limited (ABN 47 001 180 918), a subsidiary of HarperCollins Publishers Australia Pty Limited (ABN 36 009 913 517)
Level 13, 201 Elizabeth St
SYDNEY NSW 2000
AUSTRALIA

® and TM (apart from those relating to FSC®) are trademarks of Harlequin Enterprises (Australia) Pty Limited or its corporate affiliates. Trademarks indicated with ® are registered in Australia, New Zealand and in other countries.

A catalogue record for this book is available from the National Library of Australia
www.librariesaustralia.nla.gov.au

Printed and bound in Australia by McPherson's Printing Group

To Amy
A beautiful person, a wonderful mother and
a fabulous publicist.
Rest in Peace

If you have a garden in your library, everything will be complete.

Cicero

'Tis an unweeded garden that grows to seed. Things rank and gross in nature possess it merely.

William Shakespeare, *Hamlet*

A society grows great when old men plant trees whose shade they know they shall never sit in.

Greek Proverb

PROLOGUE

The clear night sky offered no insulation from the insidious cold that curled around Helen with long icy fingers. Despite the jeans, jumper and woolly hat she was wearing, and being snuggled under a sparsely feathered doona, the chill penetrated the layers like a stealth bomber finding its target. Her car could double as a cool room. Shivering, she urged herself to look for something positive in the situation, but her weary sleep-deprived mind struggled to cough up one thing. Eventually it settled on the milk for her cornflakes. Unlike earlier in the year, it wouldn't be curdled in the morning.

A vicious 'hah!' twisted sharp and harsh in her laugh, scaring her almost as much as sleeping in her car did. People believed homelessness meant sleeping on a park bench or in the doorway of a city office building. No one associated it with the wholesome countryside or with people who owned a car. In six months, Helen had learned every rule about how to sleep rough in her car. During the day, her age gave her an invisibility she railed against, but after dark, when she wanted to fade into the inky night, she became visible. Spending more than two nights parked anywhere risked her being noticed by the local police who told her to move on. Even free camping sites weren't harassment-free. She'd lost count of the times she'd been told, 'This is for real campers'. Apparently, the tiny sink in a Kombi or the mattress in a Hiace van made them far more acceptable places to sleep than her car.

Tonight, she was parked in the shadows of ironbarks in an abandoned worksite she assumed had been created for gravel piles when Vic Roads widened the highway. On her self-created scale of safety, the spot scored highly and she'd anticipated a deeper than usual sleep, but the frigid night put paid to that. Perhaps she should run the car for ten minutes and blast herself in heat? She scotched the idea immediately, unable to afford wasting precious fuel.

Her phone, now four days out of credit, suddenly beeped at her. She glanced at the reminder: *JobSeeker form.* Bugger! Before she could lodge it, she needed to apply for ten jobs. It was the game she played to receive a 'looking for work' allowance—aka 'go directly to poverty' allowance. The government thought she should work until she was sixty-five. Helen wanted to work beyond sixty-five, but employers in the real world only wanted to employ people under fifty-five. Over the course of a year, her optimism had morphed into realism before settling on jagged disillusionment. Filling in the form was a fortnightly farce, only no one who received the allowance was laughing. Helen had long ceased applying for jobs she was qualified to do, instead applying for anything to keep the bureaucrats happy. Anything to eat and keep petrol in her car.

Over the previous two hours, the noise of passing traffic had changed from a constant thrum to the occasional whoosh. Helen curled her knees to her chin, pulled the doona over her head and silently recited the opening paragraphs of Elizabeth Gaskell's *Cranford*. It was as much a memory challenge as it was to block out the cold and encourage sleep.

She woke with a start, jerked to consciousness by the whoops and yells of male voices. A hot flush raced across her skin, sweat beaded and she lay rigid, assessing the risk. She hadn't heard a car, but after months on the road she was less attuned to vehicle noise than to human and animal sounds. It was hard to tell how many men or how close they were. Had they noticed her car? Holding her breath, she listened with acute intensity.

The haunting hoot of an owl echoed around her but no voices. Relief rushed air back into her lungs, easing the burn of fear. It lasted five seconds. Then the sky lit up with the brilliant white of spotlights, arcing like searchlights seeking enemy planes.

She shrank under the doona. *Don't find me, don't find me. Dear God, please don't let them find me.*

The crack of a gun shocked the air, vibrating around her in brutal and terrifying waves. Her fist flew to her mouth so fast it bruised her teeth and her stifled scream pooled in the back of her throat, choking her. Voices cheered. More shots rang out—each one coalescing dread. Seconds elongated to minutes as her mind grappled with her best course of action. Stay or go? Both choices were precarious. Definitely dangerous.

The car provided shelter but it offered scant more security than a park bench. She weighed up the fact the hoons hadn't noticed her versus the attention she'd draw if she started the engine. Although reasonably reliable, it hated cold weather and always took a few turns of the key before it kicked over.

Helen eased herself up, keeping her head low, and peered out the window into the dark. Two utes were parked haphazardly across the road, their positions creating a rally-driving obstacle course for her if she left. She swivelled to look out the back window, hoping an easier exit lay behind her.

The car suddenly flooded with light so bright she saw the white scars on the backs of her hands.

'Hey, someone's here.'

Before she had time to dive under the doona, a man's jowly cheek was pressed against the window. His slack mouth leered at her.

'G'day,' he slurred. 'You want some company, sweetheart?'

How drunk was he? Very drunk, because she was old enough to be his mother—possibly even his grandmother if she'd started early.

'No, thanks,' she said lightly. 'I'm pretty tired.'

'I know how to wake ya up.' He tried the locked door. 'Hey, Ricky. Bray! I've got a live one here.'

A live one? Panic exploded.

She scrambled between the bucket seats, banging her head on the central light and scraping her knees on the console. Her hips screamed as she hauled her legs through the tiny space and forced them under the steering wheel.

'Come and have a drink with us, love.'

'You're not planning on going, are ya?' a new voice said. 'Not when Stu's being all hospitable, like.'

The spotlight swung straight at her. Blinded, all she saw were a haze of dancing red spots and black splotches. Her arms rose instinctively and she dropped her head, protecting her eyes.

A series of clicks and thwacks detonated around her as the men tried all five locked doors.

'Open the door!'

She shook her head.

'Playing hard to get, eh? We can play along, can't we, boys?'

The car suddenly lurched to the left and then to the right, its suspension rocking wildly. Would they tip it over? Did it matter?

They had more than one gun between them and they could shoot out the windows.

Still blinded by the brilliant light, Helen shoved her foot forward and found the accelerator. She pumped it twice and fumbled for the key, feeling the plastic head scrape against her palm.

Come on, car.

She turned the key. The ignition clicked and whirred.

Dread dug deep and she tried again. The rocking car gained momentum, then lurched so violently she slid sideways. Her right shoulder slammed hard into the door. The pain barely registered.

Third time lucky. Please.

The clicking and whirring of the ignition was suddenly drowned by the throb of the engine. She had no time for gratitude—the spotlight was still blinding and two utes stood between her and the road. Gripping the gearstick, she moved it into reverse, pressed the accelerator and shot backwards. There was no ominous thud, only outraged yells.

Pulling hard on the wheel, she turned the car away from the light, miraculously avoiding colliding with a tree. Blinking frantically against dancing silver spots, she gunned it. The tyres spun on the gravel, making the car fishtail wildly and she had a split second to decide which was the lesser evil—slowing down and risking being caught or slamming into a tree.

Light cast long shadows as she raced towards the official exit. Her already dry mouth parched further. Would one of the utes try to overtake her and block her in? Or would they use the other exit and get out onto the highway before her, then ram her and push her off the road?

A glimpse in the rear-view mirror offered no answers, only darkness. She veered right, floored the accelerator and hit the welcome bitumen of the highway.

Her eyes flickered between the rear-view mirror and the road in front of her, both fraught with danger. Headlights appeared in the distance behind her and fear's long fingers sank deeper. Was it traffic or were they following her?

The low fuel light glowed orange. Her chest cramped. Had she escaped only to fall prey to them when she ran out of petrol?

Her belief in God was almost non-existent, but heaven rose out of the night like a rising golden sun in the form of a roadhouse. *Thank you.*

She pulled in, killed the ignition, then slumped over the steering wheel, shaking hard. *Move!*

She rubbed her eyes, then glanced around, testing if this reprieve from a starring role in a horror movie was actually real. The reassuring presence of a cop car steadied her—thank God for coppers' coffee addiction.

She made it inside on unsteady legs and headed straight for the toilet, where she vomited into a bowl that was long overdue for a date with bleach and a brush. After rinsing her mouth, she parted with a few precious dollars for a sugar-laden coffee. By the time the glucose hit and she was capable of cogent thought, the police car had left. Not that she had any numberplates to report.

Nursing her coffee, she leaned back on the banquette and closed her eyes, absorbing the warmth of the heated restaurant.

'Hey, lady.'

Helen startled. She had no idea how long she'd been asleep and she blinked a few times, bringing her eyesight into focus. A gold name badge with black writing declared she was being addressed by Sam. 'Yes?'

'You buying more coffee? Something to eat?'

'No. I'm heading out.'

He nodded and walked away. Helen closed her eyes again.

'Hey!' This time he jostled her arm. 'We're not a motel. It's time to go or we'll call the police.'

Once Helen would have argued, but tonight she barely had enough energy to breathe. Rising under his unsympathetic glare, she walked slowly and warily back to the car. It was four o'clock. In less than two hours, light would filter into the sky, bringing with it comparative safety from terrorising morons.

Not prepared to risk sleep, Helen drove. When she saw *Welcome to Boolanga. Home of the Brolgas* and an accompanying blue road sign with the white symbols for a picnic table and toilets, she took the exit.

Riverbend picnic ground greeted her in a spectacular sherbet dawn with myriad shades of pink, purple and peach splaying across the sky in long graceful strands. The Murray River, wide at this bend, glinted violet in the light and a lone pelican glided towards her. Cockatiels shrieked and wheeled above, bursting yet another myth that the country was a quiet and peaceful place.

The wide sandy beach with its tall over-hanging trees—perfect for swinging and bombing into deep water—provided Helen with the real gift. Its existence meant the shire had spent the big bucks installing a boat ramp, gas barbecues, an instant hot-water tap, picnic tables and a playground. There was also a state-of-the-art amenities block complete with a toilet for people with a disability, a sink, baby-change area and, miracle of miracles, a shower.

Despite her exhaustion, Helen whooped with delight. She lathered up and washed her hair, herself and then her clothes. After-wards, she fired up a barbecue, cooked an egg in bread and ate it sitting in the folding camping chair she'd found on a roadside collection weeks before. Soaking up the view, she pretended she was living in one of the impressive riverside homes, enjoying her custom-built outdoor kitchen on her deck.

Daylight meant no one would ask her to move on; she had a few hours' reprieve. A few hours to luxuriate in normalcy and ignore her homelessness. Then the sun would inevitably sink, giving carte blanche to the insidious march of inky darkness and all the dangers that lurked within.

CHAPTER

1

Tara Hooper stood in her bedroom, blinking at the unfamiliar but glamorous woman in the mirror. She swayed a little, admiring the way the crystals on the dress caught the light and threw it back to her in a rainbow of dancing colours. Was it really her?

It wasn't just the dress—she'd also treated herself to a professional hair and make-up session. She usually wore her hair down or tied back in a quick and easy ponytail, but Ebony had swept Tara's long blonde tresses into an up-do, accentuating her long neck. Then she'd blushed her cheeks and smoked her eyes in a way that enlarged and darkened them to an arresting come-hither blue. An altogether sexy blue, which had been the brief. Tara intended to knock Jon's socks off.

She slid some ibuprofen, lipstick and tissues into her evening bag and was looking for her phone when she caught the time on the bedside clock: 6:30 pm. How had it got so late and where on earth was Jon? The babysitter had arrived half an hour earlier to settle the kids and give her and Jon time to dress. They were supposed to be leaving for the Boolanga Chamber of Commerce business awards in five minutes. Hoopers Hardware, Timber and Steel was up for an award and after all Jon's hard work—their hard work—they deserved a win. They needed a win, in more ways than one.

Tara found her phone and called Jon.

'Don't stress,' he answered, pre-empting her. 'I'm just turning into the drive now.'

'You still have to shower and dress! Why have you cut it so fine?'

'Denny North finally turned up just as I was leaving. Apparently we're not the only business in town being graffitied.'

Tara stifled a sigh. 'Please hurry.'

Why had the new police sergeant chosen tonight to talk to Jon when he'd had all week? Tonight was supposed to be a night off from the problems at the store. Hopefully a night of celebration and a chance to reboot and haul them out of the rut she believed they'd tumbled into without really noticing. People talked about the seven-year slump but she and Jon had weathered that. It was the ten-year mark that was proving tricky.

Unlike other couples, they hadn't faltered when they'd become parents; instead they'd embraced the change. From the outside, it appeared that she and Jon had fairly traditional weekday roles—he worked full-time at the store and, apart from one day a week, she'd been at home with the under-fives. In the evenings and on the weekends, Jon was—had been—a hands-on dad. They'd prided themselves on their mixed skill set; how they each played to their strengths and together juggled the many balls demanded by family life. Privately, they'd congratulated themselves on how they appeared to be doing a better job of marriage, work and family than many of their friends.

But lately, Tara wasn't sure they were doing better. This year, things felt different between them—everything was slightly off.

She was missing the chaotic early years when Jon would walk in after work and, with a kid hanging off each leg, grab her around the waist, kiss her and ask, 'How's Team Hooper?'

Initially she'd assumed it was because Clementine had joined Flynn at school. Change always came with adjustment, but all the roles within Team Hooper that she'd happily occupied for years now seemed like chores. It felt like she was the housekeeper, laundress, chef, taxi driver, childcare worker, sports coach, art and craft teacher, and the personal assistant to Mr Hooper instead of a beloved wife. The tight-knit team of four they'd been so proud of felt as if it had fractured into three very separate parts.

Jon was different too. After work and on the weekends, his concentration was always elsewhere—far away from home. Whenever she asked him what he was thinking about, he'd say, 'Just work'. Was it though? Their sex life, which had always been healthy, was deep in the doldrums. Jon had stopped touching her and she couldn't shake the feeling that maybe he wasn't distracted by work, but by something—someone—else.

Tara desperately wanted things to return to normal and tonight was the first step in making that happen. The few times they'd attempted sex recently, Jon had been so preoccupied with work he hadn't come. Once, he'd been so tired he'd gone soft. But winning an award would get his blood pumping to all the right places. And so would this dress. It was so tight she'd forgone underwear, so when Jon peeled it off her she'd be naked and—

Her pelvic floor instinctively twitched, her cheeks flushed pink and her pupils spread like ink across the blue. God, she was as ready to ignite as the tinder-dry paddocks surrounding the town. All it would take was the spark of one deep kiss, one trace of his hand down her spine and she'd go up in a ball of flames.

'Daddy!' Clementine's excited shriek floated up the stairs.

Tara rushed onto the landing, not wanting Jon waylaid by demands to read a story.

'Mummy's a princess.' Wonder and delight rounded Clementine's eyes. 'Isn't she, Daddy?'

'Does that make me her frog?' Jon said, bounding up the stairs towards Tara. 'I'll hit the shower and be ready in six. Promise.'

He disappeared into the bedroom, barely glancing at the silver and gold frock. Or the way it hugged her newly toned body like a second skin, emphasising curves in all the right places.

Disappointment formed a lump in Tara's throat. She swallowed, pushing it down. The only reason he hadn't commented on her and the dress was because they were running late. When they were finally alone in the car, he'd acknowledge that all her hard work with the personal trainer had paid off and tell her she looked a million dollars.

It had taken months, but Tara had finally banished the baby fat deposited by two pregnancies and hitting thirty-five. She was back to the size ten she'd been when she'd met Jon. Back when life stretched out in front of her, full of endless and exciting possibilities. Back when Jon looked at her with hungry eyes that devoured her and a secret smile that said *you complete me*.

By the end of tonight, that look would be back. Tara was sure of it.

The awards night dragged on. As usual, too many people went over the allotted ninety seconds for their acceptance speech.

When Jon asked the waiter for another beer, Tara lost her internal battle to stay silent. She placed her manicured hand lightly on his thigh. 'What if we win? You'll need to give a speech.'

His thigh tensed under her hand. 'I'm fine.'

Tara didn't agree, but it was more of an in-general disagreement than tonight-specific.

The master of ceremonies informed them there'd be a 'slight break in proceedings for coffee and dessert. Then the winner of the Business of the Year award will be announced.'

'Jonno!' Rob Barnes, the football club's president, appeared at their table. 'You and Chris Hegarty have done an incredible job with the under-eighteens. No one expected them to get into the finals, let alone win. Can I put the two of you down to coach next year?'

Tara took the opportunity to excuse herself from a dull conversation about the two religions in town—football and cricket—and headed to the bathroom. As she fished her lipstick out of her evening bag and applied it, she made the same request she'd been silently chanting all night. *Please let us win.* Although this time she wasn't sure if she meant the award or mutual orgasms.

Shannon Hegarty walked out of a stall. 'Who are you and what did you do with my best friend?'

'Still here.' Tara laughed, confused by a heavy feeling in her chest and welling tears. 'Just packaged a bit differently.'

Shannon washed her hands. 'Well, I'm a beached whale.'

'You're not. You've got that alluring pregnancy glow.'

Shannon snorted. 'That's sweat. It's so bloody hot in here. God, look at your waist. I had one of those once.'

'And you will again. Besides, I saw Chris tonight. He can't take his eyes off you.'

'He's a boob man and, I gotta say, pregnancy makes the girls shine. I might feel huge and unsexy, but Chris sees my boobs, thinks I'm a sex goddess and he's hard and ready to go. Men are so deliciously uncomplicated, aren't they?'

'They really are.' Tara forced a smile, trying to banish the image of Jon's back facing her in bed each night, irrespective of her wearing serviceable cotton, sexy silk or nothing at all.

When she arrived back at the table, Jon was deep in conversation with Vivian Leppart. The deputy mayor was always beautifully dressed and accessorised no matter the occasion, including shopping at the hardware store. Tara had tagged her the best-dressed renovator in Boolanga. Always in high heels, Vivian was a sight to behold in plumbing supplies or dodging obstacles in the timber yard—nothing fazed her. Tara assumed this was how she'd established herself as a sought-after business analyst and troubleshooter in what was too often a man's world.

Tara admired the way Vivian gave back to the community through her volunteering and the long hours she spent on shire work. Not all the women in town shared her admiration though, and often used Vivian's style and fashion choices as an excuse to voice their negative opinions. Tara put it down to tall poppy syndrome.

As Tara rested her hands on Jon's shoulders, Vivian gave her the appraising head-to-toe glance that was the specialisation of all competitive women.

'Wow! That's some dress,' she said.

'Thank you.'

'You're a lucky man, Jonathon Hooper.'

Jon nodded. 'I'd be luckier if the shire installed decent lighting in the car park behind the store.'

Vivian's face filled with sympathy. 'I tried. Unfortunately, the majority of councillors thought the money would be better spent on other projects. The consensus was Boolanga's not Melbourne.'

'Yeah, well, it's getting more like Melbourne every day,' Jon said. 'We've become a handy dumping ground for the refugees and drop kicks they don't want.'

'It's certainly creating some challenges for us all.'

'Challenges? Have you seen the graffiti in the car park and across the rubbish skips? My father ran the business for thirty years and never had a single break-in. I've copped three in the last year. It's those bloody African kids—'

'I think they're from Somalia ... or Sudan?' Tara said. 'Somewhere starting with S.'

'Oh, there's quite a few of those,' Vivian said brightly. 'Sierra Leone, Senegal—'

'This isn't a bloody trivia competition!' Jon's shoulders stiffened. 'The point is, those kids are running wild in the dark and I'm spending money cleaning up their mess. The shire—'

'Ladies and gentlemen.' The MC's voice boomed around the room. 'Please take your seats. I know you're all eagerly anticipating the announcement of which business has taken out this year's big award.'

'Tara, I've got the specs from the tiler. I'll drop in and order them next week,' Vivian said before returning to her table.

Both Tara and Jon took a big gulp of their drinks. In the late nineties, Jon's father had won this award many times, but when Ian had handed the business over to Jon it wasn't the shining star it had once been. There was more than one contributing factor, but a significant one was Ian's drinking. The fact Hoopers Hardware, Timber and Steel was a nominee again was testament to Jon's hard work.

Tara slipped her hand into his and squeezed. 'Nervous?'

'Little bit.'

'You deserve this.'

'The team deserves it. They work bloody hard, which is why I'm so angry about the light—'

'As you know, the winners of each category compete against each other,' the MC said. 'So just in case you've had too much to drink,

I'll remind you of the nominees: Skyros Café; Hair With Flair; the Bendigo Bank; Hoopers Hardware, Timber and Steel; Boolanga Country Butchery; Toscani Builders; and Bandicoot Brewery. I'm sure you'll agree all of them are worthy winners, but someone has to take out the gong. So, for best customer service, employee satisfaction, leadership, community responsibility and sustainability, the outstanding business of the year is ...' He fumbled with the envelope and withdrew the card. 'Hoopers Hardware, Timber and Steel.'

Tara squealed and threw her arms around Jon's neck. His arm crushed her to him and he laid a kiss on her lips reminiscent of their dating days. Her heart soared.

All too quickly, Jon was pulling away from her, shaking people's hands and making his way to the podium.

'Yes!' He held the trophy aloft, his face lit with joy. 'Not that I was competing with the old man or anything.'

Laughter ran around the room.

Jon cleared his throat the way he always did when he was about to say something serious. 'Jokes aside, this is a special win. I'm not telling anyone here anything when I say it's tough staying in business today. The drought, the water allocation issues, farmers and businesses facing bankruptcy, not to mention the ref—recent social changes in town. It all takes its toll. My team have done an amazing job and this win's as much theirs as it is mine. I'm proud of what we've achieved through hard work and sheer bloody-mindedness.'

Tara kept her gaze fixed on her husband standing tall and handsome in his dark suit. It was like looking at a new man. No, that wasn't strictly true. She knew this version of Jon—it was the passionate man who'd kept asking her out until she'd finally agreed to one drink, then one date, one weekend away, and then, on the eve of her return to Melbourne after three months in the district, she'd found herself saying yes to a marriage proposal.

Back then she'd been a city girl between cruise ship contracts, working in a summer job as the activities coordinator at the resort across the river. She'd had no intention of permanently living so far from the sea, but Jonathon Hooper, with his athletic ease, charm and boyish enthusiasm for life, had changed her mind.

Jon loved a project and he'd thrown all his energies into making the business the go-to store in the district for trade accounts and Mr and Mrs DIY. Boolanga was slowly growing, but that also meant the big boys were poking around. There were rumours Bunnings might build a store, which made Jon more determined than ever to make Hoopers number one for stock range, service and sustainability. Now that he'd won the award that officially endorsed all his hard work, he'd be looking for a new challenge. Perhaps she should create a husband-of-the-year award for him to strive for so his charm and boyish enthusiasm swung back to her.

'There's not one business in this town that isn't working hard and looking for creative ways to stay one step ahead of the next challenge,' Jon continued. 'None of us is looking for a handout, but every business owner on Irrigation Road's either battling graffiti or been broken into this year. It's time the shire stepped up and installed lighting in the car park.'

'Too right, Jonno!' a voice from the back yelled. It was followed by the tinkling of glassware and a roar of applause.

Tara glanced at the councillors' table. Vivian's head was almost touching the mayor's. Were the rumours true? Tara doubted it. Vivian was far too glamorous to slum it with flabby and florid Geoff Rayson. Besides, Sheree was sitting right there at the table. But whatever Vivian was saying to him, Geoff was nodding his agreement. Tara hoped it related to the lighting.

She raised her thumbs to Jon and mouthed, 'Love you.'

He grinned back. 'We won't let this award go to our heads. Come tomorrow morning, Hoopers will be offering its same friendly service backed by local know-how.'

'But with a hangover,' Chris Hegarty called out.

Not if Tara had her way. She'd accompany Jon on one quick circuit around the room to shake hands and pat backs—half an hour tops—and then she and her husband were going home. A slightly buzzed Jon was fine—good even; a few drinks relaxed him—but full-on drunk and he fell asleep fast. She shied away from acknowledging there'd recently been nights when he was asleep in the chair by nine o'clock, stone-cold sober.

She met him as he came off the stage and slid her arm through his. 'Great speech, darling.'

'Thanks.'

'Jonno!' Ben, the photographer from *The Standard*, waved his camera at them. 'Can I grab a photo of you and your team?'

'No worries.'

Jon had paid for the head of each section to attend the dinner. As they gathered around him and Tara, she heard Leanne Gordon say, 'Is she really going to be in the photo? She's hardly worked this year.'

'Too busy working on herself,' Samantha Murchison replied. 'Tough life being a Boolanga WAG.'

Tara squashed the urge to swing around and grab Samantha's orange spray-tanned arm. She wanted to say, 'Just because you don't see everything I do at home so Jon can concentrate on the business and keep you in a job doesn't mean I'm not part of the team.'

'Say sex,' Ben said from behind the camera.

Amid the mixture of mirth and groans, Jon laughed and gave her waist a squeeze. 'Sex!'

For the first time all night, Tara relaxed.

While Jon paid the babysitter, Tara checked the kids were fast asleep. When she came downstairs, the TV was on but Jon was sitting on the couch with his head back, his eyes closed and a smile on his lips. He looked tired but happy and she planned to make him happier still.

The tight fit of her dress prevented her from straddling his lap so she kneeled between his legs and put her hands on his thighs. 'Hey.'

'Mmm.' His eyes stayed closed.

She reached up and undid his tie before pulling it out from under his collar. 'It was a great night.'

'Yeah.'

One by one, she undid the buttons of his shirt and pressed a kiss on each bit of warm exposed skin. His hand lightly stroked her hair and by the time her lips reached his belt, her body throbbed with heat and anticipation. Excitement made her fingers fumble on his belt buckle and it took her two attempts before she smoothly slid the leather from around his waist. Then she undid his fly and reached into his boxers.

He wasn't completely hard so she treated him to her mouth, closing her lips around him.

His thighs jerked. 'What are you doing?'

She blinked up at him, her brain fuddled by need. Had he just asked her what she was doing? She must have misheard him. She concentrated on the pressure of her mouth on him and her own building desire.

His hands gripped either side of her head and he gently pushed her away. 'Stop.'

Startled, she released him. 'Did I hurt you?'

'No.' He zipped his pants. 'But should you really be on the floor in that dress?'

His concern for her frock was unexpected, but he had a point. It had cost a bomb and it wasn't designed for kneeling.

Pressing her hands on his thighs, she rose. 'How about you peel me out of this dress, throw me on the bed and have your wicked way with me?' *Please.*

He gave her a long look, his velvet brown eyes caressing her like they'd done so often in the past. Her recently wobbly world steadied.

He took her proffered hand and together they climbed the stairs to their bedroom. Jon shucked off his clothes and she stepped in, kissing him. His penis stirred, pressing against her belly, and Shannon's words, 'men are uncomplicated', came back, reassuring her.

Smiling to herself, Tara deepened the kiss. He returned it, but without the urgency vibrating inside her that wanted to skip foreplay and go straight to the main game. Jon's touch was almost languid, as if he had all the time in the world. Normally she loved this focused and dedicated warm-up—a delicious prelude. But she'd spent the day fantasising about this moment and been on high alert, wet and aroused since breakfast. She was about to combust.

Shut up. Be mindful. Enjoy it.

His hands played lightly in her hair, scattering pins and releasing her up-do. Then his lips trailed along her neck and his fingers tugged gently on the zipper of the dress. Cool air danced along her spine and she shivered more in delight than from cold.

Watching his face, she dropped her arms and the dress fell to her hips.

He groaned.

She smiled. 'It gets better.' She wriggled her hips and the material fell, pooling at her feet.

The light in his eyes was familiar and welcome. 'Christ, T.'

'Not bad for a mother of two, right.'

'Not bad at all.'

And then they were on the bed. He was kissing her breasts and her belly, and then his tongue was flicking and darting in and out of her. She was dancing on the edge of a cliff, pirouetting along the sheer drop, wanting to leap but still connected to earth by the tips of her toes. She heard herself moan, tormented by the promise of release and ravaged by layer upon layer of sensation. Her head thrashed, her belly clenched, and her hands, despite not wanting to hold onto anything, closed around the edge of the mattress.

And then she was crying out and free-falling, tumbling over and over into a maelstrom of bliss.

When her breathing finally slowed and the silver spots behind her eyelids faded to black, her vagina twitched, wet and ready to close around Jon and welcome him in.

She opened her eyes to the warm yellow glow of the bedside lamps. It took her a moment to realise Jon had rolled away from her and she was looking at his back. Snuggling in, she kissed his shoulder, then dropped her hand to his hip and finger-walked towards his penis.

He moved his thigh, bringing his knee up towards his chest, blocking her touch. 'It's been a huge night, T.'

Her body jolted as if shocked by electricity and her mind grappled with his words. 'But we're only halfway.'

'That's okay.'

Frustration and fury demolished her post-orgasmic glow. 'It's not okay! We haven't had sex in weeks.'

He rolled over to face her, his mouth unusually hard. 'What the hell do you call what just happened? It sounded like I just gave you a mind-blowing orgasm.'

'Yes ...' But she craved the intimacy of having Jon deep inside her, feeling him shudder against her as he came.

She wanted him to hunger for that intimacy too. She needed it to silence the critical thoughts in her head. To prove without a shadow of a doubt that the reason for his distraction over the previous months was connected to his drive to win the award. That it had nothing to do with him not finding her attractive or—

Her mind swerved away from the horror that he might be getting his sexual gratification elsewhere.

She needed concrete proof that the last few months were an aberration and now he'd won, everything would return to normal. But nothing about the tension tightening his cheeks or the shadows under his eyes reassured her.

Despite her disappointment, she remembered something she'd read about not having difficult discussions in bed and naked. *Now's not the time, Tara.*

She reluctantly heeded the warning. 'Thank you.'

His mouth tweaked into a tired smile and he dropped a perfunctory kiss on her cheek. 'You're welcome. It was a great night.' He rolled away.

She blinked away tears until she could trust her voice not to waver. 'I'm so proud of you winning best business.'

A gentle snore was his only reply.

CHAPTER

2

Helen hung up her apron now the moderately busy lunchtime rush at Boolanga's Acropolis Café was over. She was looking forward to spending the afternoon in the community garden, despite the prospect of a committee meeting.

'Helen, you want that expired pita bread?'

'Thanks, Con. That'd be great.'

This hospitable version of Con Papadakos was a far cry from the man she'd met on a warm winter's afternoon three and a half years earlier. Faint from exhaustion and with five dollars in her wallet plus the fifteen cents she'd found scouring all the crevices in her car, Helen had gone directly from Riverbend picnic ground to the community noticeboard outside the supermarket. There'd been buy, sell and swap notices, information about courses run by the Neighbourhood House, advertisements for local businesses and a note from a backpacker seeking a ride to Melbourne, but no jobs.

Light-headed and dispirited, she'd walked towards the library to lodge her JobSeeker form. Helen loved libraries. They were a source of free wifi, newspapers, magazines and books, as well as a haven from the heat, the cold and the rain. Each time she visited a library and handed over her City of Melbourne library card, the staff assumed she was travelling and enjoying early retirement. She'd never disabused them.

On her way down the main street she passed a fish and chip shop. Closing her eyes, she breathed deeply, savouring the tempting aroma of hot salty oil. She'd taken to luxuriating in the scents of foods she'd once taken for granted. Now those not-so-special treats were as out of reach as a Prada handbag.

'You okay?' a woman asked. 'You need water?'

Helen opened her eyes. An elderly woman of indeterminate age, dressed head to toe in black, stood in the doorway of the shop.

'I'm ...' But even people she'd once thought of as friends considered the truth to be inconvenient, let alone strangers. 'A glass of water would be great, thanks.'

'Come.' The woman disappeared through the PVC insect curtain.

Helen followed and noticed a handwritten sign on the window: *Help Wanted.* She didn't believe in signs—not any more—but she'd be foolish to ignore this one. Years earlier, when she'd met Theo, his parents had owned a fish and chip shop. Despite being an electrician with his own business, he'd worked in the shop on Friday nights to cover the peak period. Starry-eyed and happy to spend any time with him, Helen had allowed herself to be co-opted to the cash register. Although Theo and his father manned the fryers, she'd watched and learned, surprising the family when she stepped up to cook after George was hospitalised for heart surgery.

'Here. Sit.' The woman thrust a cold glass of water into Helen's hand.

'Thanks.' She pointed to the sign. 'You still need help?'

The woman studied her, then called out in rapid-fire Greek. A man in his forties appeared from the residence behind the shop. His Greek wasn't as good and this time Helen's out-of-practice ear caught a few words, including 'too old, *yiayia*'.

Having undertaken a graduate diploma in community services along with other compulsory retraining courses and enduring a year of job rejections, Helen honestly thought she was beyond reacting to the 'too old' label with anything other than benign resignation. But with last night's trauma still foremost in her mind, dormant frustration surged. It was fast food, for God's sake!

She stood and in faltering Greek—a language she hadn't spoken in a very long time—managed to spit out, 'You want someone who looks pretty, or someone who knows how to cook and count change?'

The man's cheeks reddened.

His grandmother laughed and opened her arms wide. 'You Greek?'

With her name, her dusky skin and dark brown eyes, and before age and grief had stripped her inky hair of its colour, Helen had easily passed for Greek. Taking Theo's name had added to the illusion. Given everything he'd stolen from her, she may as well use one of the few things he'd left behind.

'I'm Helen—Helen Demetriou—and I can cook everything on the menu.'

The elderly woman nodded thoughtfully before handing Helen an apron. 'You cook. We eat. Then we talk.'

The grandson crossed his arms but stayed silent, clearly not prepared to go against his *yiayia*.

Helen checked the temperature of the oil and hoped with every part of her that cooking fish and chips was like riding a bike. Fortunately, it was a skill that required little dusting off and she'd been permanent part-time ever since. Her frying skills had even won the Acropolis Café a Golden Chip Award.

Con had no idea she'd arrived in Boolanga homeless and Helen had never enlightened him. He thought she shared the leftover food he offered with friends—only strictly speaking, the women in the parks around the district weren't exactly friends. They were acquaintances whose shared experience was homelessness.

Helen had a sixth sense for these women. Their dignity, ringed by quiet desperation, called out to her. They didn't want charity. They didn't want anyone to know their car was their home or that all their worldly possessions fitted into a two-dollar-shop bag. It was enough just getting through each day without the added burden of crippling shame that others knew the truth. So twice a week at the end of her evening café shifts, she took food that would otherwise be thrown out, drove to a park and invited people to join her. It wasn't much but it was one meal free of cost and concern.

It was also data collection in her fight to disabuse the community that homelessness wasn't an issue for Boolanga. If she asked the residents of the town about the local homeless, she knew they'd say, 'None here. It's a city problem.' Except it was very much a country problem too. These women were the invisible homeless, overlooked by emergency housing because children weren't involved. Women like Helen herself who, at a time of their lives when they should be assured of secure housing, were unexpectedly couch surfing, being resented boarders in their adult children's homes, forced to live in transition communal housing, or, worst case scenario, sleeping rough in their cars or on the street. Homeless.

Not that Helen ever considered women like Sue, Tracey, Agape, Roxy, Josie and others as numbers, but they came and went often enough for her to know their housing was unstable.

'Drop in around seven. I might have some leftover chicken for you too,' Con said.

Helen slapped him on the shoulder. 'You're a good man, Con.'

'Don't go telling anyone or I'll have all the bleeding hearts wanting things for free.'

It was a short drive to the community garden and five minutes later, Helen was striding through the decorative gates, breathing deeply and feeling her tension draining away. It happened every time she stood beside her plot.

Ignoring an unwanted ache in her knees, she bent down and pressed her hands into the rich red-brown loam. Its warmth and power ran up her arms like vines before spreading across her chest and affirming life, just as it did with her vegetables. She silently acknowledged the traditional owners of the land past and present, and gave thanks for finding a haven in Boolanga. She considered herself a local, even though she knew to attain that status she needed a relative in the cemetery. That was never going to happen—she no longer had anyone left to bury.

Although Helen was grateful to the Papadakos family, it wasn't her part-time job at the Acropolis Café that had lifted her out of poverty; it was the community garden.

Soon after arriving in town, she'd noticed a weed-infested garden bed and had boldly taken it over, weeding and harvesting the seeds, bulbs and tubers from the previous occupant's plantings—garlic, spring onions, broccoli, potatoes, carrots, cabbages and herbs. No one had questioned the long hours she'd spent in the garden and she'd successfully hidden her homelessness in plain sight.

People had got used to seeing her in the café and they accepted her presence in the garden, happy she was tidying up the eyesore plot. Nothing got under members' skin more than a weed-infested bed. It was one of few eviction sins.

As Helen got to know the other plot holders, she'd traded broad-leafed Italian parsley seeds for tomatoes, coriander seeds for broad beans, and potato sets for rhubarb crowns. Eventually, the committee told her she needed to officially join.

Finding the thirty-five-dollar fee in her fortnightly budget had been tough and she'd bulked out her meals with vegetables for two weeks straight, but it was the hundred-dollar key deposit that had proved to be her nemesis. It was impossible to provide that sum in one go and still eat protein.

Helen had aimed to set aside ten dollars a week, although five was more realistic. She'd fudged and dodged reminders to pay the key deposit until Judith, who'd never known a day of hunger in her privileged life, had accosted her between the beans and the cabbages. Helen had handed over fifty dollars, feigning ignorance of the full fee. Unfortunately, Con had paid her the night before and Judith's beady eyes had noticed the extra cash in her wallet and promptly demanded the other fifty. Helen's fingers had cramped tightly around the note that represented petrol and her phone recharge, but Judith had plucked Dame Edith Cowan out of her hand with the precision of a magpie pulling on a worm.

It was a group of bored and drunk teenagers and their spur-of-the-moment decision to raid the garden that had changed Helen's life. If they'd acted ten minutes later, she would have already left to spend the night in the park across the river—one of seven haunts she randomly rotated to avoid detection. As it was, she'd been reading in the garden's shelter when they'd tumbled in. The upshot was the police gave the kids a verbal shellacking, the shire offered Helen the position of caretaker, and when she mentioned her graduate diploma in community services they made her the coordinator of the garden.

Her first job had been supervising the teenagers' community service. It turned out that two of them had green thumbs. Ignoring the mutterings of some of the committee, Helen had given Trent and Jax their own plot on a three-month probation. Jax was still gardening.

Her second argument with the committee was reducing the key deposit for people on Centrelink payments. The old guard had dubbed her a bleeding-heart leftie. Far from being offended, Helen wore the moniker with pride.

And the icing on the cake? The caretaker role came with an old and rundown Victorian cottage at the bottom of the orchard block. Helen didn't care that the floor sloped, that the stove was the original wood-fired Metters or that the water hammer almost deafened her whenever she turned on the hot tap. The cottage was home, and her car was thankfully only a means of transport.

Today, with half an hour before the committee meeting, Helen took advantage of the unusual quiet to dig compost into the soil in preparation for new strawberry plants. It was surprising to find the garden empty at this time of day. Normally there was at least one other person tending their bed and Helen was used to being interrupted with questions and complaints.

She was pushing some hair out of her eyes with the back of her gloved hand when she noticed a woman hovering by the gate. Although she was too far away for Helen to make out her facial features, her vivid clothing of bright greens and blues and the turban on her head made her unmissable.

Helen loved the way so many women from the African diaspora embraced colour. 'Hello!' she called.

The woman glanced around as if she assumed Helen was talking to someone else.

Helen waved a soil-covered glove and smiled encouragingly. 'Come in.'

The woman took a couple of tentative steps and, at Helen's nod, strode over. 'Is this your garden?' Her accent combined with wonder, giving the rise and fall of the words a lyrical beat.

'This bed is mine to use but—' Helen waved her arm to encompass the large lot, '—it's a community garden so it belongs to the town.'

The woman's eyes sparkled. 'I live in town. So I can grow things too?'

The committee made the answer to that complicated, but Helen didn't let complicated overly concern her. For most of her life she'd rigidly followed the rules, too scared to break a single one—until her experience of homelessness taught her that following the rules didn't protect her one iota. The realisation had generated a profound philosophical shift.

'Probably,' she said. 'I'm Helen. What's your name?'

'I am Fiza.'

'What sort of things would you like to grow, Fiza?' Helen had no idea what constituted African food, and given the continent had—what, forty countries, fifty?—she imagined the food could vary a lot from north to south.

'Maize!'

'That's like corn, isn't it?'

'It grows on a cob but it is not as sweet as corn. We use it for dura, asida ...' Her hands flew up, golden rings flashing in the sunshine. 'Many things!' Her previously cautious expression was suddenly animated. 'Do you think I can grow maize here?'

'Maybe. Is it hot enough?'

'I hope so. We moved from Melbourne for the sunshine.' She shivered. 'In the camp, they asked us, "Where do you want to live?" We didn't know Melbourne was so cold.'

Helen could relate. Up here on the Victorian–New South Wales border, they experienced more sunshine and heat than in the big southern city. 'You'll definitely be warmer here. Where are you living?'

'We are in a small flat, but I have three children. I am looking for a house in a nicer part of town. They are not easy to find and when we do ...' She shrugged, the movement loaded with resignation.

Helen filled in the gaps. Fiza's lack of success in the rental market was probably due to the combination of price with an overlay of racism. There were plenty of houses for rent in Boolanga, but increasingly more and more were geared towards tourist rentals. Even the old weatherboards, once the backbone of the rental market for locals, were being thrown up on Airbnb, leaving little in the way of affordable housing.

'May I come to the garden?' Fiza managed to combine reticence with determination.

Helen smiled, recognising some of herself in the other woman's manner. 'Sure. I have to go to a meeting soon, but can you come back at three? I'll show you around and explain everything then. Get you to fill in some forms—'

'Forms?' Wariness replaced Fiza's eager anticipation.

Helen wondered how many forms Fiza must have been required to complete to come to Australia. 'It's just your phone number and your address to prove you live in town.'

'We have been in Serenity Street for five months.'

Helen understood why Fiza wanted to move. 'Would you like to take home some carrots? Green beans?'

'Are you sure?'

'Absolutely. I've got plenty.'

Helen dug up some carrots and encouraged Fiza to pick double the amount of her initial bean harvest.

'Thank you, Helen. I will come at three o'clock.'

'Great. See you then.'

The committee members were now drifting into the garden, heading straight to the 'kitchen'. It was really just a shelter with a barbecue, wood-fired pizza oven, running cold water, a sink, power and a kettle. Someone would have brought lamingtons or a plate of Anzacs for afternoon tea and the members would be keen not to miss out.

'Afternoon, Helen.' Bob Murphy swung off his pushbike and leaned it up against the fence. His border collie sat, panting from his run. 'I've been tinkering with the mower and she's running like a dream. Thought I'd drop her back this time tomorrow?'

Helen knew that was code for 'and I'll stay for a cup of tea'. Bob was a relatively new member and as much as Helen appreciated him taking on the task of keeping the community garden's mower going, she preferred having cups of tea with people in public settings, not inside her cottage.

'Thanks. If I'm not around, just pop it in shed two.'

'Hello, Bob. Helen,' Judith, the president, called out, waving a bright red folder and tapping her watch. 'We're ready to start.'

Helen stifled a sigh. She wasn't a huge fan of the monthly committee meeting. Often it took far too long to achieve very little.

A smile creased the grey stubble on Bob's weather-worn face and he winked at her, acknowledging Judith's obsession with meeting protocol.

Helen ignored the gesture for two reasons. As the caretaker of the community garden, she couldn't be seen to side with anyone.

As a woman, she had no desire to give any man even a hint of being interested.

She joined the committee around the large wooden table and scanned the agenda. Thankfully, it looked straightforward.

'I did the equipment audit,' Bob said. 'A fair bit needs replacing, and a few things are a tetanus hazard and should be thrown out.'

Judith looked at Helen. 'Will the shire pay for replacement tools?'

'They gave us a large grant last year for the water tanks, but I'll run it past Messina and Vivian. Unlike some of the councillors, they're very supportive of the garden.'

'We could always apply for a Saturday sausage sizzle at Hoopers,' Bob said. 'That'd raise a few hundred dollars. I've made my own snags for years. Happy to make a batch using the herbs from the garden. Might be an extra selling point.'

'Thanks,' Helen said. 'That's certainly an idea worth considering. We could also sell some produce. Since we installed the watering system, almost every plot is groaning. I've been offering my lettuces, carrots and coriander to all and sundry, but everyone's in the same boat. I think it's time to formalise a plan for surplus food.'

'Good idea,' Dot said.

'What did you have in mind?' Bob asked.

Helen was torn between her two passions—helping those in need and raising necessary funds for the garden. 'Donating it to the food bank. Having a stall at the farmers' market. Or both.'

Judith pursed her lips. 'The garden's not a collective. People have different reasons for having a plot.'

Helen couldn't deny that. Initially, her plot had been all about survival. Not that anyone in Boolanga knew that. Homelessness made people uncomfortable, including herself, so it was easier to pretend it had never happened.

'That's true,' she said to Judith, 'but the garden's a community and communities work together.'

'We do work together. We have a mowing roster and working bees—'

'And rotting vegetables in some plots when people have more produce than they can use or give away to family. Isn't it better to donate it to the food bank?'

'I have a big family so I never have leftovers,' said Vin.

'Obviously, any food donations would be voluntary,' Helen said.

'Best to minute that, Sharon,' said Judith. 'We never quite know with Helen.'

Helen didn't react. She was used to this sort of slap from Judith and refused to be deterred. 'The Liparis have resigned due to ill health and are currently in Shepparton. Are there any objections to me harvesting their plot for the next farmers' market and generally tidying it up?'

There was a mumble of 'no', 'that's fine', and 'tidy is good', before Judith said, 'Any monies raised will go towards new tools.'

'Of course. And I'll put a poster on the noticeboard offering people the opportunity to donate surplus food to the stall. Anyone like to join me on the day?'

'Be happy to,' Bob said.

'Thanks.' But Helen would prefer it if someone else came along too. 'Anyone else? Any time you can offer between eight and eleven would be appreciated and very welcome.'

'Bit short notice, Helen,' Sharon said.

'Busy day, Saturdays. Got the grandkiddies and their sport,' Vin said.

Dot was staring off into the distance and didn't reply.

'Sorry, Helen. Commitments,' Judith added.

'No worries. Maybe next time?'

'Before you go planning this as an ongoing event, it's something that should be discussed with the general membership. Minute that, Sharon, for the next AGM.'

Helen clenched her jaw. The AGM was months away and this was Judith's way of sidestepping any issue she didn't agree with, hoping time would bury it.

'I'm happy to pilot it for three months and write a detailed report for the AGM,' she offered.

Judith winced, clearly torn between her love of a report and the fact it might come back to bite her. 'If you want to take it on, Helen, that's up to you, but there are no guarantees it will be ongoing.'

'It might be a good way of highlighting the existence of the garden to the community,' Bob said.

'Good idea,' Dot agreed.

'We've got a couple of empty plots that need gardeners,' Bob added.

A seed of hope sprouted in Helen's chest. Although she didn't know enough about Bob to predict how he'd react to what she was about to suggest, she needed allies if her plans for the garden had a hope of coming to fruition. Not that Dot wasn't an ally, but Helen needed practical rather than in-principle allegiance.

'And talking about community, our garden's no longer truly representative of Boolanga's community,' she said.

Vin groaned. 'What are you on about now, Helen?'

'It's a pretty white, able-bodied garden.'

'You saying we need to build some raised beds so the nursing home set can get their hands in the soil?' Enthusiasm lit up Bob's eyes. 'That's something I could get behind.'

'It's one idea,' Helen said. 'So is reaching out into different parts of the community. Like to Fiza, who wants to take over plot seventeen.'

'Who's Fiza when he's at home?' Vin asked.

'Fiza is a she and she lives in Serenity Street.'

Vin's bushy brows pulled down at the mention of the address. 'So she's one of them refugees.'

'It isn't only refugees who live in Serenity Street, Vin,' Dot said.

Helen threw her a grateful glance.

'Where's she from?' Judith asked.

'Melbourne. She's been in Boolanga five months.'

Judith tsked. 'I mean originally.'

'I'm not sure.' It was the truth, but had Helen known, it wouldn't have changed her reply. 'Not that it matters. She lives in Boolanga and is keen to have her own plot and grow vegetables, so she well and truly meets the criteria for membership.'

'Is she a towel head?' Vin asked.

Helen's hands fisted in her lap. 'I don't understand your question.'

'I think Vin's asking if she's Muslum, right, Vin,' Dot said.

'Muslim,' Helen automatically corrected. 'We talked about gardening not religion. Besides, religion isn't a membership criteria.'

During the conversation, Sharon had been riffling through papers and consulting her phone. 'Sorry, Helen. I've already offered the two spare beds to other people.'

'Really? Why wasn't there an agenda item on new members?'

Sharon met Helen's combative gaze with one of her own. 'They verbally committed yesterday. There wasn't time to process the paperwork and their membership fees before today's meeting. They'll appear on next month's agenda.'

'Good work, Sharon,' Judith said. 'It's wonderful the garden's at capacity again. Now, the date of the next meeting ...' She flipped through her diary. 'The tenth. Who's for a cuppa and a piece of passionfruit sponge? My chooks are currently laying eggs the perfect size for sponges.'

'Me!' Dot eagerly got to her feet.

While people drifted to the kettle and the food, Helen took a moment to calm her seething rage at being snookered by Sharon in an act she couldn't prove was racism, despite it being written all over it.

Bob said softly, 'Sometimes herding cats is easier.'

'You were very quiet. Do you agree with them?'

His easygoing demeanour faded. 'I'm disappointed you feel the need to ask.'

Bloody men and their fragile egos! But as Bob walked away, Helen knew that for the greater good of the garden, she'd have to offer him a cup of tea tomorrow at three after all.

CHAPTER
3

Jade Innes loved her baby in a way that filled her heart to bursting, yet riddled it with empty air pockets—a lot like that cheese rich people bought. Some days, it felt like she was the only person who adored Milo's gurgling laugh and found it hilarious the way he sucked his toes. That she was the only person who needed to blink away the prickle of tears when he gazed up at her with his huge eyes, the same vivid blue as the little wrens that jumped about in the bush near the community garden. Sometimes it felt like she was the only person who truly loved him.

Don't be a stupid cow, she reminded herself sharply. *Corey loves Milo.*

The reassuring thought made her smile and took her back to the first time Corey saw their son.

'Fuck. He's as red as a rabbit after I've ripped off its skin.'

Jade had laughed and cried with happiness and exhaustion. Labour had hurt like nothing on earth, except perhaps her mother's words. She'd touched their baby's red and scrawny head, studied his closed eyes and wondered at the spider web of blue veins across his lids.

The midwife had pursed her lips at Corey—again. It was obvious from the moment they'd checked into the hospital that the woman had a poker up her arse. Old battleaxe.

Jade didn't understand why the olds got their knickers in such a twist about her and Corey having a baby. They weren't kids. And hadn't everyone been banging on at her since she was sixteen about the responsibilities of being an adult? That and the many ways she was failing at it. Well, she'd shown them what being an adult looked like. Nothing was more responsible than being a mother.

The midwife had muttered something about kids having kids, but Jade was nineteen and Corey was twenty-two. Plus the midwife didn't know Corey like Jade knew him. He might sound tough and look it—not all his tattoos were pieces of art created by professionals—but hidden underneath the blotchy ink was a man with a soft and mushy heart. A man who loved her and their son.

It was Corey who'd named their 'skinned rabbit' Milo after his favourite drink—favourite non-alcoholic drink, Jade corrected herself. He'd wanted to call him Jack Daniels.

Jade believed the father should name his kid. If her mother had let her father name her Barbara after his own mother, perhaps he might have stuck around longer. But even so, naming their kid after whiskey didn't seem quite right.

'What was your favourite drink when you were a kid?' she'd asked Corey. She'd realised later it could have been Zooper Dooper or Nesquik. Thankfully, it wasn't. And Milo was the name of Georgia's baby in *Gossip Girl*, which was cool. Also, kids who drank Milo were sporty, weren't they?

'We could call him Milo Jack-Daniels-Noonan,' she'd said.

Corey had grinned. 'Fuckin' oath.' And when the midwife had sniffed, Corey turned his dark blue gaze on her. 'Me and Jade want some privacy, all right.'

That had been almost a year ago.

Corey ambled out of the bedroom, all rumpled and sleepy after his post-sex nap. He opened the fridge and stared into the mostly empty space.

'Jeez, Jade. I'm starving.'

'Sorry. I didn't know you were coming.'

Even if she'd known, she couldn't have shopped. She was out of money until tomorrow when her Centrelink payment arrived.

'Didn't know I had to make a booking to see you.'

'Of course you don't.'

It had been more than two weeks since she'd last seen Corey and she didn't want anything to spoil his visit. She stepped in behind him, wrapped her arms around his waist and absorbed his breadth, taking a moment to remember his weight on her an hour earlier. Loving she had someone else in her life other than Milo. Loving him.

'Guess it has to be baby food then.' He plucked a jar of pureed apples from the top shelf.

She dropped her arms, maternal protection warring with a lover's indulgence. 'That's Milo's dinner.'

'He can eat the pumpkin. You like pumpkin, don't you, mate?' He ignored Milo's protest as an open jar of apple sauce walked straight past him.

Corey checked his phone while he downed four spoonfuls of the apples, then offered Milo the fifth and final one. Jade opened the pumpkin and served it with the last dry biscuit in the packet and a bottle of milk.

'Macca says he's got work for me,' Corey told her.

'What's it this time?' Jade didn't trust Macca or his jobs. They always sounded better than the reality and Corey had lost money on the door-to-door vacuum cleaners.

'Lightbulbs.'

'I don't get it.'

He squinted at his phone. 'Government's giving away free low-energy lightbulbs. I get paid for every house I install 'em.'

The fact it was legit work made her smile. 'So, the government pays you?'

'Nah. The government pays Macca and he pays me.'

Like a flame in a draught, her hope flickered and died. Macca's payments often came in ways other than money. Not that she hadn't enjoyed Corey sharing the occasional can from a ten pack of Mercury Hard cider, but Milo needed shoes and Country Target didn't barter.

'Will he though?' she said.

'Will he what?'

'Pay you.'

His eyes flashed. 'It's not like that company that fleeced him. This time it's the government paying.'

Jade heeded the warning and didn't push it. 'Great. When do you start?'

'We're gonna grab dinner at the pub and talk.'

Since Corey's unexpected but welcome arrival, Jade had been daydreaming about snuggling up on the couch with him watching *Survivor*. He loved the show and always spent a large part of the hour telling her how he'd do it better than the contestants. And he would too—he'd been surviving since he was fourteen when his parents kicked him out. He'd done all sorts of things since then—worked in the fruit factory, done some panelbeating—but he preferred farm work and being in the bush. He was a crack shot with a gun—few foxes or rabbits were safe from his sights.

But if Corey went to the pub to meet Macca, there'd be no watching *Survivor* together and she'd be home alone with Milo. Again. It had been ages since she'd gone anywhere and if she went to the pub, Corey might shout her a parma.

'Can I come?'

He stood and pocketed his phone. 'Nah.'

'Why not?'

'You know Milo screams blue murder when there's noise. Besides, me and Macca are talking business.'

Disappointment pinched and bruised her. 'Maybe Macca could hire me too?'

'That'll stuff up ya Centrelink.'

'Not if I do a few hours a week and don't earn over the limit.'

'And who'd look after the kid?' Corey crossed his arms. 'No stranger's looking after him. There's pedos and all sorts out there. You had him, you look after him.'

For the briefest moment, she wanted to hate him. Not only for implying that she'd had a choice to have Milo, but for highlighting she was mostly alone in raising him. But the feeling fizzled as fast as it flared. There was no point letting it catch and burn, yelling at Corey and having everything go to hell. Watching him leave without a guarantee he'd return.

Right now, things were exactly as they should be—Corey was working and she was looking after Milo. That's what family did; they worked together, were a team. And the three of them were the only family the other had—it was the bond they shared. They needed to be here not only for each other, but for Milo. Her beautiful baby deserved the childhood she and Corey never came close to living.

Corey jangled his keys. 'I've gotta go.'

'Will you be back for *Survivor*?' The words tumbled out before she could stop them. She held her breath. Corey hated being asked about his plans.

'Yeah, prob'ly. I'll bring back a pizza, all right?'

'Awesome.'

'Catch ya later.'

He didn't kiss her or Milo goodbye, but then he never kissed them hello either. That sort of shit only happened on the telly.

He disappeared out the door and the broken screen crashed back with a loud metallic thump. Jade jumped. Milo cried.

The only reminder of Corey having been in the flat was his musky scent and the stinking pile of dirty washing he'd dumped in the laundry basket. But Jade preferred the mix of sweat and grime to the sharp freshness of laundry powder—it meant Corey would be back.

When Corey was away working, Jade took long walks with Milo. Somehow being outside made her feel less alone in this stinking town. Corey had insisted they move here from Finley and given what had gone down with her mother, Jade hadn't objected. But she wasn't a fan of the riverside town.

Outside of the unit, the only other place in Boolanga she felt comfortable was the library. There was something soothing about sitting and reading surrounded by books. Books were her catnip—company and an escape from her life on mostly long and lonely nights. The library also saved her money. It was a place to hang—warm in winter, cool in summer and with free wifi. People who whinged about how slow the NBN was had no freaking idea how lucky they were to afford the internet at home.

As Jade approached the red-brick building, Milo's stroller activated the automatic doors—another reason Jade loved the library—and then Fran, the librarian, was waving hello.

'Oh good! You're just in time,' she said.

'Why? Are you closing? Do I have time to borrow something?' The thought of leaving without a book sent anxiety scuttling in Jade's veins. 'I've finished *Jasper Jones* and you said I should read *To Kill a Mockingbird* next.'

Fran smiled. 'There'll be plenty of time for books after Baby Time.'

Jade's stomach cramped so fast she almost doubled over. *You dumb, stupid cow!* How had she forgotten it was Wednesday? Worse than that, why had she come to the library right on eleven fifteen? Dread dragged at her and she reluctantly glanced beyond Fran to the group of well-dressed women sitting in a circle holding their babies in their laps.

'It's music again today,' Fran said encouragingly.

The last time Jade had attended Baby Time, she'd felt stupid sitting there singing and clapping when Milo's only response was to huddle in her lap and bury his face in her chest. It hadn't helped that all the other babies had cooed and clapped and smiled and drooled. Failure had pinned her to the carpet, twisting shame and humiliation into every cell and was accompanied by the barbed message: *Why did you think you could do this? You suck as a mother like you suck at everything else.*

The side-eye glances of the other women hadn't helped. They were all much older than her—every mother in town was—and most of them were either married or lived with their partner in big houses close to the river. At the first class, a couple of them had quizzed her, then said, 'Wow! I could never have done what you're doing when I was your age,' as if Jade had a choice.

When Fran had left the room to get a hand puppet, the Queen Bee of the group had asked, 'Does Milo have a dad?'

What sort of a stupid question was that? Of course he had a dad, but she'd been so pissed off, she'd said, 'Nah, it was an immaculate conception.'

A couple of the women had laughed but not the Queen Bee. She'd given Jade the stink eye then ignored her. That suited Jade to a T.

'And after class, this time you can go to Bert & Bears with everyone,' Fran suggested softly. 'It will be nice for you to have some company.' Her face shone with enthusiasm. 'The great thing about a mother and babies group is you're all experiencing the same things. It gives you lots in common and breaks up the week. It's a perfect antidote to loneliness.'

Jade didn't agree. When she was with this group of women, her stomach churned, sweat beaded under her arms and she'd never doubted her mothering abilities more. She'd already been to the café with the other women. It was the reason she'd been dodging Baby Time for the last two weeks. Kasey—the only one who wasn't a total stuck-up bitch—had invited her.

Jade had been pleased to be part of the pram parade crossing the road, but once inside the café, everything changed. When she saw the food and drinks prices, she'd stuck to sipping the water the waitress had fancied up with bits of lemon.

The group had talked about their holidays—Noosa was divine, Byron too busy—how they only fed their babies organic vegetables, only dressed them in bamboo onesies that cost what Jade paid each month for her electricity, how tired they all were and how their partners tried but 'he doesn't fold the laundry properly' or 'he said he cleaned the toilet but honestly, I had to do it again'.

Jade had sat mute, convinced she was visiting a foreign country. Apart from the fatigue, nothing about their lives was familiar. She didn't own a car, didn't even have her driver's licence and she'd never been on a plane. Other than school camps and the scholarship she'd won to summer camp at Portsea when she was fifteen, she'd never had a holiday. She could count on one hand how many times she'd travelled to Melbourne—always by train or coach. And when Corey was in town, he never cooked or cleaned, and if she'd owned a washing machine, he wouldn't know how to turn it on, let alone peg the washing out or fold it.

These women treated motherhood as a competitive sport, but Jade couldn't afford to join their club, let alone buy the uniform. Being in their presence only made her lonelier. Which was saying something when she didn't know anyone in town and sometimes when Corey was away, the unit closed in on her like a jail cell.

'Sorry, Fran, I can't stay today,' she said. 'Milo didn't sleep much last night and he's really clingy. I only walked up here to send him to sleep.'

Disappointment dimmed Fran's smile. 'He does look like he's just nodding off. Never mind. Let's try again next week.'

No way in hell. 'Sure.'

As much as she hated lying to Fran, who'd only ever been kind to her, the refusal was self-preservation. Nothing would entice her anywhere near the library on a Wednesday ever again. She'd take being home alone every time over being judged wanting by that group of stuck-up bitches.

CHAPTER

4

Despite the outcome of the committee meeting several days ago, Helen was yet to break the news to Fiza that there wasn't a plot available for her. So confident was she of finding a way around the problem, she'd texted Fiza to reschedule the visit as soon as the meeting had ended. Fiza had replied immediately with a thumbs-up emoji and followed with a message containing her address *for the forms*. But Helen was still scratching for a solution.

Agitated and unable to settle, she took herself for a long walk along the river, confident that breathing in the eucalyptus-scented air and watching sunshine and shadow playing across the water would soothe her jangles. But a brisk four kilometres later, she was back at the top of her driveway and no closer to a state of calm than she'd been when she set out. Every time she remembered how Judith and Sharon had gazumped her, frustration and anger surged and she pictured her GP tut-tutting about her blood pressure.

Helen lovingly ran her hand along the curlicue on the old decorative woven-metal gate. The cottage with its orchard was on the edge of town, bordered by the community garden, some fallow hectares and two roads—one a gravel track to the river. It was a peaceful spot and Helen treasured the space, even if the cottage was maintained at just above habitable. According to Fran at the library, after the Great War the surrounding land had been an experimental farm, helping injured returned servicemen get back on their feet. During the Second World War it had served as an internment camp, and in the following decades been leased to a variety of farmers.

In today's climate—both weather and economic—it was no longer a large enough parcel of land to generate a farm living. The shire had divided it into three uneven parts—short-term grazing, the community garden, and the section closest to the river that was under the management and guidance of the local Landcare group along with the Indigenous community. Native grasses and tree plantings were restoring the land to what it had been before a hundred and fifty years of farming had irrevocably changed the landscape. But what really made Helen's heart sing was, unlike their New South Wales cousins across the river, the Mookarii Shire hadn't sold their soul to a resort. The land belonged to the community.

During her shifts at the Acropolis Café, Helen constantly heard rumours about plans for the land—anything from the shire selling it to a consortium to returning it to the Yorta Yorta people. Whenever she gazed at the paddocks, she saw a tiny housing village for women aged fifty-five and over. The year before, she'd started meeting quietly with individual councillors to test the waters and garner support for an affordable and sustainable housing project— tiny houses. Consultation was taking longer than she'd expected because, between their paid jobs and their shire commitments, the

six councillors were busy and hard to pin down. Of the four she'd
met with, their responses had ranged from barely lukewarm to fully
invested.

Getting a meeting with the mayor, Geoff Rayson, had proved
impossible and Helen couldn't decide if he was the problem or
his officious secretary. Each time she'd tried, he was either fully
booked, overseas, at a local government conference or sick.

She'd been ready to give up when the deputy mayor, Vivian
Leppart, had called her. 'I've got good news, Helen! I've been
working on the mayor for the last few months and he's given his
"in-principle" agreement for the tiny houses.'

'That's incredible! Thank you.'

'My pleasure.'

'What's next?'

'A formal submission.'

The opportunity to use her dusty qualifications was exhilarating and Helen had loved every minute of the process. She got a
thrill each time she pictured a cluster of tiny houses, a communal
kitchen and living space for classes and gatherings, and a large community garden. She'd researched and established strong links with
the people who'd been involved in housing projects around the
country and along the way she'd collected an arsenal of useful tips,
including applying for a small grant to pay for draft plans so there
was no ambiguity around the project. She had no intention of being
stymied at any point due to lack of information. The hardest part
so far was waiting to hear what the councillors who supported the
project—Cynthia, Messina and Vivian—thought of the recently
completed submission.

Helen walked through the orchard. It had been planted back
when the land was an experimental farm. Although not technically
part of the garden, it was on shire land and the garden members

considered it theirs and cared for it zealously, treasuring the mix of fruit and nut trees—apricot, nectarines, peach, pear and plum, almonds, hazelnuts, walnuts, macadamias and pistachios. Unlike a Melbourne community garden they'd visited, where a couple of clueless blokes had pruned fruit trees with a chainsaw, up here retired orchardists fought to be on the roster. More than once, Helen had been forced to intervene with a bottle of grappa and a sack of diplomacy. Lesson learned, she now allocated trees to members so there was little opportunity for disputes.

She checked on her bees—all busy feasting on spring blooms— then crossed the vast expanse of the cottage's 'lawn'—a dustbowl in the summer and potential silage and snake habitat in spring. Closing her hand around the wire on the cyclone fence that separated the block from the community garden, she sighed in frustration. The plots along the fence line were full-sized but only half of them were working at capacity. This was an ongoing source of aggravation. In the years Helen had been involved in the garden, she'd suggested gently, loudly, subtly, blatantly and often that the under-utilised beds be halved so new members could join. It would be a win-win for all as a smaller bed was more manageable for the plot holder, and the ensuing new bed would provide an opportunity for new members to become involved, but the idea was consistently rejected.

After the recent committee meeting, Helen had made another round of phone calls, but no one wanted to divide their plot. Should she halve her own bed so Fiza could join? But Helen had seen the zeal burning in Fiza's eyes for a patch of dirt of her own. A small plot wouldn't be enough.

Helen hated how she'd raised Fiza's hopes and was now about to dash them. It was tempting to text the bad news, but she knew that was a cop-out—it must be done in person. A surge of anger at Judith and Sharon had her kicking the red dirt like a kid whose request to play had been rejected. Her boot connected with a stray canola plant valiantly shooting in the dry ground.

She squatted, wrapped her hand around it and pulled. She stilled, staring at the fine roots as if she'd never seen a bare-rooted plant before.

This was it! This half-dead plant screamed solution.

Fifteen minutes later and panting slightly, Helen stood on Serenity Street. She'd heard some of Boolanga's locals refer to Serenity and its intersecting streets as 'The Ghetto', despite having never visited. During her university placements, she'd spent time in some dodgy parts of Melbourne and, although the lack of tended gardens in Serenity Street gave it a down-and-out feel, it lacked the rubbish and used syringes of its city counterparts.

A few kids played on the road—some riding old bikes assembled from a mishmash of pre-loved parts, while others kicked a well-worn soccer ball.

A small group of women wearing headscarves stood chatting on the concrete ramp in front of a block of flats. They fell silent as Helen approached and a few looked as if they wanted to shrink into the brick walls.

She smiled at them. 'Hello. Lovely day.'

They smiled shyly and nodded.

One of them pointed at Helen's hand. 'You want pot?'

Helen was surprised to see she was still clutching the canola. 'Oh, no, thanks. I'm not going to plant it.'

'So why you carry it?'

'I forgot I was holding it.'

The younger woman's eyes scanned her as if she was checking for signs of dementia. 'You are lost?'

Helen laughed. 'No. I'm Helen Demetriou from the community garden. I'm looking for Fiza. Do you know her?'

The woman shook her head. 'What is community garden?'

'It's a place where people without a garden can grow things.'

'Where is this?'

'Riverfarm Road. Near the caravan park and the oval.'

'Ah. I know this garden, but I think it belongs to people.'

One of the other women said something in a language Helen didn't recognise, and then the woman who'd been speaking earlier said, 'Please. Come.'

Helen followed the women into a ground-floor flat and they showed her the tiny outside space. Almost every available centimetre was filled with small black pots of neatly cut chives and chaotic coriander. Tomatoes trailed up the fence.

'Wow! I've never seen so many chives.'

'We use in our food, but this our only garden for many families.'

'What's your name?' Helen asked.

'Aima. And this is Kubra and Baseera.'

'Hello. What language do you speak?'

'Dari and Hazaragi. We are Hazara.'

'From Afghanistan?'

Aima smiled. 'You know it?'

'I know where it is on the map.'

'A long way from here,' Aima said wistfully, before adding urgently as if she may have caused offence, 'But Australia is good to us.'

'Is it?' Helen wondered out loud and immediately saw Aima's confusion. 'Tell me, what would you grow if you had a bigger garden?'

'This is easy. Chives, coriander, lettuces, cucumbers, chilli, mint,' Aima said.

'What if you had lots of space? What else would you grow?'

Aima asked the other women something and translated their replies. 'Spring onions, potatoes, beetroot, carrots, garlic and sunflowers.' She put her hand on her heart. 'And you say dream, so I say nut trees. Almonds, walnuts and pistachios. Oh! Grapevines too. Then we make all our foods.'

Helen laughed. 'That sounds wonderful.'

'It would be. We do this in your garden?'

Helen looked at the wilting canola and remembered what had propelled her to Serenity Street. 'The community garden's full, but there's land next to it where we can extend. But we'd be starting from scratch. It would be a lot of work.'

Aima's forehead wrinkled. 'We have to scratch the dirt? You mean dig?'

Helen laughed. 'Yes, dig and mulch and water. We'll have to build the garden beds. Are your friends interested?'

Aima spoke to Kubra and Baseera and there was lots of smiling and nodding. Then a gabble of voices broke out and they were talking over the top of each other.

'We say yes,' Kubra said softly.

'Thank you,' Baseera said.

'Excellent!' They exchanged phone numbers and Helen left with an arrangement to meet them at the cottage the following morning after school drop-off.

Flying high on the buzz of a new idea, not to mention a way of putting it up the garden committee, Helen returned to looking for Fiza's flat. The numbers she had on her phone didn't match those on the street. Had Fiza transposed the flat and street number?

Helen texted her and waited five minutes. When Fiza didn't reply, Helen crossed the road and retraced her steps. She stopped outside a classic pale brown brick 1970s' unit complete with arches. The wooden gate under the arch was jagged and rotting at the bottom. Faded sheets hung across the front windows and weeds grew along the concrete drive. But there was a cracked terracotta pot close to the front door containing a riot of cerise geranium flowers, which tumbled over each other despite a collection of cigarette butts in the soil. Then again, a nuclear explosion may not be enough to kill a geranium. In the face of the surrounding building decay, Helen recognised the presence of the plant said 'I care'.

The shrill cry of a baby jarred the air. Despite the passage of years Helen shuddered, remembering Nicki's screams, her own powerlessness to comfort her and the unending sense of failure. She pushed the thoughts down deep where they belonged and knocked on the door.

The baby stopped crying and a young woman cracked the door open just enough for Helen to glimpse white skin and muddy blonde hair. It was unlikely this was Fiza's house.

'Hello, I'm Helen from the community garden and—'

'You selling stuff?'

'Ah, no. I'm looking for Fiza. Does she live here or in one of the other units?'

'What's a Fiza when it's at home?'

'Fiza's a woman.' Helen hesitated then added, 'She's from somewhere in Africa.'

'I see African kids at Tranquillity.' At Helen's confusion she added, 'It's the park at the bottom of the street. I take Milo there.'

Helen didn't know if Milo was a dog or the baby and thought it probably best not to ask. 'Thanks. I'll try the park. Sorry to trouble you.'

'Wait.' The door opened a little wider and Helen noticed the young woman looked barely twenty. 'Does this garden grow organic food? I don't like giving Milo stuff full of pesticides but organic's really expensive.'

Helen remembered the cigarette butts in the pot plant and wondered if she thought eating organic food would offset the fact she was filling her lungs with smoke. 'I grow my own vegetables and try to only use garlic spray and pyrethrum.'

The girl gave her a blank look. 'So not chemicals?'

'They're natural pesticides.'

'Cool. You said community. I'm part of the community so that means I can get free food there, right?'

Helen opened her mouth to say, 'It doesn't work that way,' and immediately thought of the Liparis' bed she needed to harvest. With her hours at the café and the new garden project, she was fast running short on time.

'If you help me harvest for the farmers' market, you can keep some of the veggies.'

The girl's eyes narrowed like a cat's, instantly wary. 'You want me to work all day for you and then you'll pay me in vegetables? That's not even legal!'

Helen tried not to sigh. She knew this type of person all too well—they believed the world was against them and they deserved everything for nothing. 'That's not what I'm suggesting. It's more like you exchange one hour of your time for some vegetables.'

'Why?'

Spare me. 'Because I need some help and you want some home-grown vegetables.'

'Organic.'

Helen was fast regretting her offer. 'Yes, well, close to organic. I don't have an actual certificate because I'm not a commercial grower.'

The baby, who looked like he was close to one, lifted his head from his mother's shoulder and beamed a toothy smile.

'If I come, so does Milo.'

Helen couldn't decide if the girl was being defensive or antagonistic. Not that it mattered when the result was much the same—difficult.

'Does he sleep in the pram?' she asked.

'No! He's got a cot.'

She counted to five. 'I meant, does he fall asleep in a pram or a stroller? If he does, walk down at his nap time and park him under one of the trees. That way you'll have time to garden.'

'I'm not coming for crap like radishes or any weird stuff.'

The Liparis grew fennel and celeriac. Helen thought longingly of Fiza's and the Hazara women's enthusiasm for the garden. Did she really need the prickly angst of this belligerent teenager who, despite her claims to want organic food, probably ate white bread and drank sugar-laden soft drinks?

Tell her it's only weird stuff. 'What vegetables do you eat?'

'Potatoes, carrots and pumpkin. But only butternut pumpkin.'

Helen thought of her own plot. 'Any green veg? Cabbage, broccoli?'

The girl screwed up her mouth. 'I like peas.'

'Peas aren't quite ready yet, but I can promise you potatoes and carrots.' Her patience level drained to barely there. 'It's up to you if you come or not. The garden's on Riverfarm Road.'

'I know! I walk past it heaps. Milo likes looking at the mural and that funny-looking metal thing.'

Helen loved all the art in the garden too. She wished she'd known the artist who'd created so many delightful nooks and crannies and filled them with surprises. Sadly, the woman had died well before Helen had joined, and none of the current committee had an artistic bone in their bodies.

'Can you come tomorrow or Friday?' she asked.

'Maybe. What's your name again?'

'Helen Demetriou. And you're …?'

'Jade.'

Helen wasn't surprised Jade didn't offer her surname and she didn't push for it. She had a hunch Jade wouldn't show up at the garden. Most of her hoped the hunch proved correct.

CHAPTER
5

Tara watched Flynn and Clementine race across the Dusseldorps' garden and fling themselves onto the jumping castle. It was Ace's seventh birthday and this year Beth had gone all out with the entertainment.

'Leaving feels weird, doesn't it?' Tara said to Kelly as they walked back to their cars. For years, they'd stayed on at children's birthday parties, 'helping' the hostess by drinking wine and loosely supervising.

'Leaving feels wonderful and even better, Al's busy tinkering with his precious Valiant. I'm planning to sit in the shade and crack open the book group book. What about you?'

'I thought I might seduce my husband.'

Kelly laughed. 'Too funny. As if you'd waste a perfectly good Saturday afternoon when you know he'll throw a leg over tonight anyway.'

Tara laughed too, hoping it sounded normal and not strung tight like every muscle in her body. She'd taken a risk with the line about seducing Jon, but it had got her the information she wanted. Kelly and Al were still having regular sex, even if it sounded like Kelly thought it was a bit of a chore.

'You got me,' she joked. 'I'm reading *Anna Karenina* too. Last time Monique chose a book I didn't finish it and she told me off in front of the group, remember?'

'Oh, she's "FIGJAM" for sure. What's the bet she serves Russian food and vodka.'

'As long as it's honey cake and not pickled herring,' Tara said.

She hopped into the car, excitement skipping. With the children out of the house for two hours, this afternoon was perfect for couple time. Jon was hardly going to claim fatigue in the middle of the afternoon. Since the business awards, he'd been less distracted, although he'd gone to bed before her most nights this week to 'catch up on sleep'. But this morning he'd bounced out of bed before her to hit tennis balls to the kids, so he was all caught up and relaxed.

At lunchtime she'd asked him if he had any plans for the afternoon.

'Thought I'd mow the lawn and test that new whipper snipper on the daisies down the side of the pool,' he'd said. 'They need hacking back.'

Company reps were always giving Jon demonstration models of tools and equipment. He said it was important to test them before he recommended them to customers, and Tara teased him that his testing was really playing.

Jon still had the physique of a footballer—solid thighs, broad muscular back, giant hands. No one who met him underestimated the raw power of his body—he could heft huge bags of potting mix and concrete without breaking a sweat—but it was the unexpected delicacy of such big hands wielding pencil pliers or sketching a detailed plan that surprised people. As much as Tara loved watching him flexing muscles big and small, this afternoon she planned to entice him away from the garden and into the spa to work out some different muscles. But first she needed to sow some seeds, or as Jon used to say to her, 'get your motor running'.

Opening a text message, she selected his name, pushed away the embarrassed voice in her head and tried sexting him for the first time.

Are you all hot and sweaty after working so hard?

It's not that hot

He obviously had no idea she was flirting. And why would he? Their texts were normally *please buy milk, did you order the mulch?* or *remember to call your dad*.

Tara tried again. *I'm hot and sweaty just thinking about you* She added a kiss-blowing emoji.

She hit send, then shoved her phone deep into her handbag. Denny North was flexing his muscles with a mobile phone blitz and he'd already given her a warning about touching her phone in the car. The children had been goggle-eyed and wasted no time telling Jon, 'Mummy got into trouble from the policeman.'

She pointed the car towards home, but didn't get beyond the railway crossing before losing ten minutes waiting for a freight train to pass. It almost killed her not to peek at her phone.

A group of teenage boys ambled past and before she'd consciously thought about it, her right forefinger was pressing the door lock button. Thankful for the protection of tinted windows, she studied the boys. In typical adolescent fashion they varied in height from short to extremely tall, but most of them lacked adult male heft. They wore jeans, T-shirts and runners, although one wore shorts. Apart from their dark skin, they looked like most of the teenagers in town. Were these the boys causing Jon and the other traders so many headaches? Increasing the cost of their insurance policy? Distracting Jon from his family?

The railway bells finally stopped ringing and Tara crossed the line, driving the short distance to Tingledale. The first time she and Jon had seen the old Federation house with its distinctive steep pitched roof, ornate fretwork and wide verandas, they'd fallen in love. The massive renovation they'd undertaken had only strengthened their affection and pride in their home.

As she approached the turn-off, Jon's muffled text tune played in her handbag. She almost pulled over to read it, but decided to savour the anticipation. Everything was in place for a magical afternoon. She was wearing her bathers under her clothes, and she'd set up snacks and cold drinks in the outdoor kitchen's fridge. All she needed to do was hit the button on the spa then find Jon.

She turned into the long drive and her buoyant mood flatlined. Her father-in-law's car was parked behind Jon's.

Goddamn it, Ian! Why today?

It wasn't that she disliked Jon's father—although his drinking bothered her—but they'd seen him on Thursday for the weekly roast. He was much easier to entertain when the children were home and she couldn't fathom why he was here—he usually played bowls on Saturday afternoons.

She parked and checked her phone. *Dad's here. Sorry. Raincheck xx*

Jon wanted a raincheck! Hope soared and Tara recalibrated her plans. She'd give Ian a cup of tea and a slice of fruitcake, cut a hunk for him to take home, then shuttle him out the door. That still gave her and Jon plenty of time before she had to collect the kids.

Opening the car door, her ears were assaulted by the deep vroom of a two-stroke engine and the squeal of a saw against wood. Her heart sank—the combination of Ian and the chainsaw was the opposite of quick.

She unlatched the side gate and walked down to the bottom of their large native garden, deafened by the noise. Jon was three-quarters of the way up the big gum, wearing a safety harness, a hard hat, safety goggles and ear protection. Ian, also wearing a hard hat, was gesticulating wildly and Chris Hegarty stood by his ute in the adjacent paddock, interest keen on his face.

When Jon rested the saw, she called out, 'Hi,' trying hard to hide her annoyance.

'Hello, love.' Ian moved in for a quick kiss. 'I didn't expect to see you. Jon said you were in town for the afternoon.'

She glanced up at her husband who was still wearing earmuffs. If he read the WTF question on her face, he didn't acknowledge it. Instead he smiled and gave her a wave as if he was exactly where she'd expected to find him.

A few weeks earlier they'd discussed lopping this limb off the widow-maker. As much as she loved river red gums, they were unpredictable, often dropping branches on deathly still days. She'd never forgive herself if it fell and killed someone, but Jon hadn't mentioned taking it down today. Chagrin on Flynn's behalf needled her—their son would have loved watching this.

Jon pulled the ripcord on the chainsaw, the roar reducing hearing to impossible. Tara considered staying to watch, but the blokey atmosphere drove her inside.

Ignoring the clean washing calling to be sorted and the overdue giftware order for the store, she picked up *Anna Karenina*. Flipping past twenty pages of introductory text, she mused on the first line about happy families being all the same but unhappy families being miserable each in their own way. She reassured herself that she and Jon weren't miserable—they just needed time together to reconnect. Feeling reassured, she settled in to read about the Oblonsky family's troubles.

Eventually, it was the extended silence that roused her from the book and propelled her off the couch. She found the men gathered in the outdoor entertaining area, chatting, drinking beer and demolishing the platter of nibbles she'd prepared for her and Jon to enjoy from the sensual warmth of the spa.

Jon crossed the deck, meeting her by the door. 'Where were you?'

'Reading.'

'Nice.' His smile was warm and wide. 'Do you want a drink?'

'I have to leave in ten to pick up the kids.'

'No need.'

'What? Why?'

Chris ambled over. 'Shan's picking them up. It's the least we can do when you're giving us that beautiful wood.'

Chris crafted stunning furniture and back when it was still a hobby, Jon had commissioned him to make their bed as a surprise wedding present. Two years ago, one of Chris's loveseats had won a Vivid design award and now furniture making was his career and his pieces were sought far beyond Boolanga.

Tara thought of her heavily pregnant friend and wondered why Chris thought putting Shannon out was helping. 'But it's out of her way.'

Chris's smile faded to wary and he shot Jon a look. 'Have I just put my foot in it?'

'Nah, mate.' Jon slapped him on the shoulder. 'It's all good.'

Chris didn't look convinced, but he didn't say anything more and walked back to Ian.

Jon was grinning like a kid fighting to keep a secret. 'Shan's coming because I've invited the gang for dinner.'

Tara stared at him, unable to form a coherent sentence as her mind grappled with the state of the house. The bathrooms needed wiping, the dishwasher was full of dirty dishes and the sink groaned with the overflow.

She dropped her voice. 'Why didn't you tell me?'

'I was up a tree when you got home,' he said easily as if that explained everything.

She almost asked, 'Why, when we were supposed to be in the spa and bed all afternoon?' Except, in her desperate desire to spice things up between them she hadn't told Jon her plans. She'd wanted the element of surprise and to build the anticipation with the texts so it spilled into desire. Irritation dug in. Damn it! He'd told her he was going to mow the lawn.

'Besides,' he said reasonably, 'if I'd told you before now, you wouldn't have read and enjoyed a break from the kids.'

'But now I have to do everything in less time!'

'No, you don't. I've got it sorted. I've pulled meat out of the freezer, there's heaps of stuff in the garden to make a salad and I asked Rhianna to pick up a cheesecake. Too easy.'

Too easy, my arse. Jon was the big-picture person and she looked after the minutiae, following behind with a brush and pan. She'd be organising crockery and cutlery, glassware and serviettes for the two courses, not to mention wrangling children high on sugary party food, while he held court at the barbecue.

'And you're making the salad, right?'

Sheepishness replaced his brash confidence. 'The bloody cockies shat on me and I need to grab a shower. Sorry.'

Despite the bird poo, and the way dust stuck to his skin outlining the previous position of his goggles, his eyes sparkled at her. She saw her Jon, happy and relaxed, and her irritation faded.

'I'll make the salad.'

'Thanks, T.'

'But you owe me.'

'Always.' He brushed his lips on her cheek and his scent of freshly cut wood interspersed with sweat tickled her nostrils.

Her hands pressed against the bulk of his arms, the muscles unyielding under the grip of her fingers. She breathed deeply, wishing their soon-to-arrive guests far far away. 'Promise me it won't be a late night.'

Before Jon could answer, the toot of a horn broke the late afternoon air.

'You don't mind if Gerry comes for a drink, do you, Tar?' Ian said.

She hated the phrase 'you don't mind' because it was never asked as a question—it was always delivered as a statement. Gerry wasn't her favourite person, but she made the mistake of glancing at Jon whose expression said, *please don't rock the boat.*

Gerry was already walking through the gate, his obligatory slab of beer tucked under his arm. 'You bastards started without me?'

'G'day, Ger. You know Chris?' Jon relieved Gerry of the beer and offered him a cold one from the fridge. 'Get this into you. I'm just grabbing a shower. Tara and I will be back in a jiff.'

Gerry's grin morphed into a leer. 'You can wash my back any time you like, Tara.'

'In your dreams, old man,' Jon said, echoing Tara's thoughts and enveloping her hand inside his meaty one.

The feminist in her arced up at the macho, staking-a-claim gesture, but the part of her that craved sex sat up, lust tingling.

Gerry laughed and twisted the top off his beer. 'Don't hurry back on our account, eh, boys?'

Hoping Chris or Ian would tell Gerry to shut up, Tara hurried Jon inside and straight to their ensuite. She flicked on the shower and pulled off her T-shirt.

'What are you doing?'

She finger-walked her hand up his chest. 'Exactly what they think we're doing. A quickie in the shower.'

He batted her hand away and stepped back. 'No! Jesus. What's wrong with you?'

Tears stung her eyes. 'Nothing is wrong with *me*.'

His nostrils flared but he didn't rise to her bait. She glanced at his crotch—nothing rising there either. Despair broke her.

'Don't you find me attractive any more?'

His arms rose and fell and his expression lurched between bewilderment and anger. 'What the hell sort of question is that?'

'A valid one.'

'It's not.' He picked up her T-shirt. 'Look, I don't know what's going on with you lately, but we don't have time to talk about it now. Put this on. Make the salad. Please. The others will be here soon.'

She hated being told what to do, but what was the point of staying in the ensuite when he'd made it clear he wasn't going to touch her. But she sure as hell wasn't putting the T-shirt back on. She tossed it into the laundry hamper, then painted her lips a fire-engine red before stalking into the bedroom.

The 'gang' were their best friends—Shannon and Chris, Rhianna and Brent Stevenson, and Kelly and Al Kvant. Jon, Rhianna, Brent and Al had all grown up together in Boolanga. Although Tara got along with everyone, she was closest to Shannon.

Since the arrival of children, the gang's gatherings had moved from the club rooms and the pub to Tingledale. The large living areas, the pool and the outdoor kitchen made entertaining easy and Jon loved playing host. Tara usually enjoyed it too but tonight, despite the laughs with Shannon, everything felt like a chore.

Shannon came back into the kitchen rubbing her back. 'The kids are parked in front of a movie and the leftovers are wrapped and in the fridge. I say it's time to kick back.'

A whoop of laughter floated in from the deck.

'Good idea,' Tara said. 'Let's head out and join the others. Jon's lit a fire.'

'This baby's treating my bladder like a trampoline tonight. I'll meet you out there as soon as I've had a wee.' Shannon waddled off towards the bathroom.

Tara was carrying a wine for herself and a mineral water with a twist of lemon for Shannon when she met Kelly coming in from the deck.

'Need a hand with anything?' she asked.

By now, Kelly's timing no longer surprised Tara. 'Thanks, but it's all good.'

'Great.' Kelly smiled and sat on the couch, her gaze flicking over Tara. 'Nice top. Bit of a change from the yummy mummy activewear.'

Tara set down the glasses, trying to work out if Kelly was paying her a compliment. Sometimes she found it hard to tell. 'And a change from the Hoopers blue polo,' she said.

Kelly snorted. 'When was the last time you wore one of those?'

'You saw me wearing it on Friday when you bought the maidenhair fern,' Tara said tightly.

'Jeez, Tara, lighten up. Did you lose your sense of humour along with the weight?'

The words stung like a wasp. Lately, Tara had been wondering if Kelly wasn't married to Al, and if Clementine and Brooke weren't such good friends, would she choose to spend time with her? She gulped wine, deciding to laugh off the barb. If she defended herself or her job flexibility, it would only give Kelly an opportunity to trot out her favourite line: 'Sleeping with the boss helps. Joking!'

Kelly worked three and a half days a week at the cheese factory and Tara knew she resented her own limited hours and flexibility. More than once, Tara had tried to explain what she gained in flexibility, she lost in many other ways. The staff didn't consider her part of their team, and when she walked into the tearoom, conversations stopped. Yet she was expected to organise all the birthday morning teas, throw the farewell parties and baby showers and arrange the gifts. She was never invited to the staff's impromptu gatherings and was used to the phrase, 'Oh, we didn't think [insert any day of the week] was good for you.' The exceptions to this rule were the invitations to product parties—then she was expected to spend a minimum of one hundred dollars. She had enough scented candles to mask the stench of a sewage farm.

'What do you think of this?' Kelly continued, her eyes flashing with indignation. 'That bitch expects me to come in on my day off for training on the new accounting system.'

Tara was familiar with all the challenges involved to entice trainers to drive up from Melbourne, let alone come on a date when most of their staff were in. She also knew Kelly's dislike of her boss coloured her attitude to all requests. Kelly had never forgiven Fatima for keeping the office manager job after she'd returned from maternity leave. Initially, Dairyland had suggested the two women share the position, but Kelly, who'd worked for the company a lot longer, had refused to job-share, assuming that would trigger the promotion of her friend Rachael Dean into the position. It didn't happen. Now, Kelly never missed an opportunity to complain about her boss.

'She'll pay you though, right?' Tara said.

Kelly's mouth pursed. 'She probably thinks I'll just swap my days round that week. But hello! Childcare! She's not a mother so she has no freaking idea.'

It wasn't worth mentioning that Kelly swapped her days around whenever she received an invitation to a lunch she didn't want to miss. Or that Al's mother loved looking after Hudson and was happy to do it any day of the week.

Keen to change the topic, Tara picked up Kelly's glass. 'Want a refill before we go outside?'

'Sure. It's Al's turn to drive.'

Kelly immediately checked her phone. Tara tried not to grind her teeth at Kelly's social media addiction and walked into the kitchen. Laughter surprised her—she'd thought everyone else was outside.

Jon was standing with his back to the door, his height and breadth blocking her view of whoever he was talking to. Despite the complicated mix of anger and hurt she'd been nursing since the bathroom incident, she couldn't help smiling at the sound of his deep throaty laugh. It filled the air with his signature enthusiasm and love of life—and she realised she hadn't heard it very often recently.

It took her a moment to notice the flash of diamonds and the manicured fingers resting on his forearm. They in turn made her aware of Jon's head tilting down close to the woman's head. Jealousy sawed through her like a serrated blade.

'What's so funny?' she said, but her voice came out too loud and too high.

Jon turned so fast he swayed. At first, she thought it was a combination of his shock and surprise at being caught flirting—almost kissing!—Rhianna that made him overbalance. But then she noticed his gaze was roving wildly and taking far too long to focus on her. God, how much had he had to drink? Obviously more than enough to make him very drunk.

'I was telling Jon about Benji and the chickens,' Rhianna said. 'I can't believe he hasn't heard it.'

Everyone in town had heard that story, including Jon. When Tara had told him, his eyes hadn't crinkled at her nor had he thrown his head back and belly-laughed. Was it because he hadn't been drunk, or because she wasn't Rhianna? Tara's gut cramped, forcing dinner to the back of her throat. Why had Rhianna been holding Jon's arm? Was it because she knew he was drunk and unsteady on his feet? Or did she believe she had the right to touch him in such a familiar way?

You're being ridiculous. Tara took a long steadying breath, locking onto reason. Jon and Rhianna had grown up together and were comfortable in each other's company. Of course there was casual touching and hello and goodbye kisses. Still, the fact Jon was relaxed and laughing with Rhianna when he was so often tense with her slithered under her skin like a snake.

'We should probably go outside and make the most of the fire before the movie finishes and the kids swarm,' she said.

'Good idea.' But Rhianna didn't move. 'Coming, Jon?'

Excuse me! Seething, Tara pushed a bottle of sparkling wine into Rhianna's hand. 'Give this to Kelly.'

Rhianna's gaze flicked between Tara and Jon. 'Sure. See you out there.'

The moment she'd left the room, Tara said, 'Oh, my God! How much have you had to drink?'

'Not mush. Few beers.'

The slurred words made a mockery of his reply, bringing her worst fears into focus. Ian had a problem with alcohol. Was Jon going down the same path?

'Don't lie to me.'

'I'm not.'

'You can barely stand up!'

The chatter of young voices drifted into the kitchen. Obviously, the movie had failed its eighty-two-minute promise of holding the children's attention.

Clementine appeared, her little body drooping with fatigue. She pressed against Tara. 'Mummy, can I go to bed?'

'Of course you can, sweetheart.' Tara hugged her, thankful Clementine always flagged early. 'Everyone's going home now anyway.' She looked straight at Jon, daring him to disagree with her.

The next fifteen minutes were the usual chaos of rounding up children, wet bathers, platters and bowls, along with choruses of 'thanks for having us' and 'night', before the dark swallowed the tail-lights. During the frenzied activity, Jon had thankfully sobered up a little.

As Tara hustled a grumpy and overtired Flynn into the bathroom to supervise the cleaning of teeth, she said to Jon quietly, 'Cut off the beers so Ian and Gerry leave and we can go to bed.'

It took Tara half an hour to negotiate with Flynn on everything from toothpaste to how many pages of *Artemis Fowl* she'd read him. After closing the bedroom door she went straight to the kitchen. Usually after these gatherings Jon cleaned up, but the kitchen looked much as it had before everyone left.

A bark of laughter startled her, immediately followed by the rumble of voices. Her stomach flip-flopped, unable to settle on fury or dismay. Anger marched her outside. Ian, Gerry and Jon sat around the brazier, beers in hand.

'Ah, there she is—' Gerry raised his beer in salute, '—the most beautiful woman in Boolanga.'

'Tara, love, any chance of more cheesecake?' Ian asked.

She waited for Jon to either suggest to his father that he go to the kitchen to see for himself or offer to look for him, but her husband sat mute, staring into the fire, locked in a hypnotic spell by the licking and spitting blue and orange flames.

Tara's hands fisted by her sides. This shouldn't be happening—she'd asked Jon to send them home. Then again, not one thing that had occurred since two o'clock should have happened. Not their visitors, not Jon's rejection of her, not him getting drunk and especially not that unnamed thing she'd interrupted between him and Rhianna.

A rogue wave of hatred for Jon dumped all over her before rolling her in a blast of sand. 'I'm going to bed.'

Jade spent the morning cleaning. Some days it was enough to know she'd cleaned the unit. Other days, she fought back tears that all her hard work scrubbing at years of ingrained dirt and stained grout was barely noticeable.

She tickled Milo's toes. 'One day, mate, you and me and Daddy will live in a brand-new house where no one else has lived before. The walls will be white and we'll have real pictures on them instead of holes and stains. And we'll have a lah-de-dah couch like the one in Bennetts instead of a crap one from Vinnies.'

One day when Milo was older and she could work. One day when Corey found a job with a decent employer who didn't rip him off and paid him what he was worth. One day.

Milo's head nodded wisely as if he totally understood what she was saying. 'Ma. Ma.'

Jade's hands steepled in front of her mouth and her heart doubled in size. 'Did you just say "Mama"?'

Milo blew bubbles at her.

'Say it again. Say Mama.'

'Ma. Ma.'

'Clever boy!' Oh, how she wished Corey was here to hear him. Grabbing her phone, she turned on the camera and slid it to video. 'Milo, say Mama.'

But he'd found his plastic hammer and was banging the throw rug that covered the couch and all its suspect stains.

The volunteer bloke who'd delivered it before Milo was born had told Jade to turn the cushions over. She'd flipped them only to discover the other side was backing.

'But they're one-sided.'

He'd given a dismissive shrug. 'You're lucky to get a couch, missy. Beggars can't be choosers.'

She bet he wouldn't allow a couch like this into his house, let alone sit on it. But she was expected to curtsey and say thank you very much. Well, stuff that!

'I'm not a beggar, but you're a bastard,' she'd said.

He'd dobbed on her to Karen, the social worker at the hospital, who'd talked at Jade about anger management and how it was important to be kind to people who were 'only trying to help'. But Jade wasn't angry at the world—she just wasn't prepared to put up with pricks who thought they were better than her. Just because she needed a bit of help shouldn't mean she had to accept a couch that belonged at the tip. At least the throw rug made it look inviting, but the moment she sat on it and was jabbed by a spring, the illusion vanished.

Jade texted Corey, desperate to share the momentous news of Milo's first words: *Milo just said Mama*

She didn't expect a reply—Corey had told her he was working fifty kays out of Jerilderie—so she was surprised and thrilled to see three wriggling dots appear.

Tell me when he says dad

Her excitement balloon lost some air. She wanted to smile—after all, what father didn't want to hear their kid say 'Daddy'? But if 'dada' had been Milo's first word, she would have been just as excited. Why wasn't Corey?

She quickly blamed the communication method—there was no nuance in texts. Of course he was excited, but he was probably also disappointed that he'd missed out on hearing Milo. Well, she could fix that.

Holding up her phone again, she pressed the recording button. 'Milo, say Dada. Da. Da.'

Milo turned towards her, lost his balance and sat down abruptly, bouncing on his nappy-clad bottom. His blue eyes rounded in shocked surprise and then his face crumpled. He let out a howl.

'Oh, baby.' Jade picked him up and he rubbed his eyes. 'You ready for a nap?'

She walked into his room and was about to lay him down in his cot when she remembered that woman's suggestion about coming to the garden. Jade still couldn't work out if Helen was legit with her offer or planning to rip her off. She didn't have anyone to talk to about it either. Mind you, her mother would have said, 'If it seems too good to be true then it is,' but Charlene Innes didn't trust anyone, not even her daughter.

Not that Jade was quick to trust either, and she was especially wary with the staff at Centrelink and Human Services. The maternal and child health nurse was okay, even if she was as old as. Actually, Helen looked pretty old too. But unlike the other women her age in town who wore their white hair cut into neat and identical bobs, Helen's hair was salt and pepper and cut in a pixie style with magenta tips. The bright colour intrigued Jade. She'd only seen coloured tips on younger women.

She'd love some colour in her own hair, but she couldn't afford it. Once she'd bought colour from the supermarket, but it turned her hair green instead of the royal blue she'd hoped for. Did the colour make Helen cool or a try-hard?

Old women were hard to trust—they could look kind, caring and understanding, but sear her with a judging look that burned like a brand. A look that sneered and said *teenage mother, white trash, lazy and useless, a drain on taxes*.

Yeah, right. Jade had so got pregnant to get five hundred and sixty dollars from the government. As if! She'd got pregnant because she didn't know taking antibiotics nuked the pill and neither the doctor nor the pharmacist had bothered to tell her. By the time she'd realised she was pregnant, it had been too late to have an abortion. Now she had Milo, she was glad she'd been denied that difficult choice, but it didn't mean being a mum was easy. Most of the time she was doing it on her own.

Like today. She hadn't spoken to anyone other than Milo. Cleaning kept her busy but it also kept her inside. Some days she stayed in hoping Corey would turn up, but there was no chance of that today.

She settled Milo into the pram. 'Hey, little man. Wanna go see the picture of the big flowers and the butterflies?'

Milo fell asleep somewhere between crossing the railway line and Riverfarm Road, the rough pavement rocking him to sleep. Jade often walked this route as it took her past some of Boolanga's oldest houses and gardens. She'd always loved flowers and her earliest memories of school were sitting cross-legged on the oval making daisy chains. Back then, she'd had no idea the flowers were capeweed, she'd just loved the bright yellow petals.

Spring was still her favourite season, when blossom frothed and spring bulbs pushed up flowers that covered the colour spectrum. Since leaving Finley, she'd been teaching herself the names of flowers. When she found one she didn't know, she took a photo and asked Fran at the library. The old chook might be too eager to push her into a mothers' group but she was a walking flower encyclopedia. Jade respected her for that.

She snapped a photo of a cluster of white flowers with black centres that grew from a tall central stalk, then kept walking until she arrived at the gates of the community garden. Jade loved these gates. Hammered metal sunflowers were welded to the wire and spray-painted silver and gold. Sculptured bees on wires looked like they were buzzing about the flowers and they bounced in the breeze. At the top of the gate, the words *Boolanga Community Garden* filled an arch.

Jade hesitated, unsure if she should walk straight in. She craned her neck but couldn't see anyone working on the many garden beds, which apart from some random cheery red ranunculi and some decorative White Lion double daffodils, were sadly lacking in flowers. Scanning the area, she saw three white bee-boxes and at the very end there was a rope ladder hanging from an oak tree. Was that the tree Helen had suggested Milo could sleep under?

Halfway down the block there was an old shipping container with its doors flung open. Pushing Milo between the mostly neat beds, Jade walked to the container and looked inside. A couple of spades and forks hung off three long posts and a board was attached to the back wall. The names of the tools were written in texta, but without a shadow outline, Jade had no idea what a Dutch hoe was or what it looked like. She got the impression that the shed could hold a lot more gardening equipment. There didn't seem to be anyone about so where were the tools? Had someone robbed the garden?

She heard voices and rounded the container, but still couldn't see anyone. Then she looked beyond the cyclone fence. Ten women—some wearing headscarves—were booting spades into the ground and digging over the soil. They were talking and laughing as if working in the hot sun was the best fun ever. Not that Jade understood a word they were saying.

A familiar heavy feeling settled on her chest, pressing in on her, and she closed her fingers around the wire fence. These women belonged together, just like the mothers at Baby Time. Once again, she was on the outside, looking in. Just like at school. Just like—

'Jade!' Helen was striding towards her, wearing the same faded plaid shirt from yesterday and the same clay-encrusted, elastic-sided work boots. 'You came.'

She almost said, 'Of course,' but that wasn't close to the truth. 'Yeah.' She pointed through the fence. 'What are that lot doing?'

'Making themselves garden beds so they can plant their vegetables. Put your baby under the tree and I'll show you what to do.'

Usually older women made a fuss of Milo but Helen wasn't even looking at him. Jade parked the stroller in the shade, threw an old sarong over it to give Milo some extra protection and joined Helen at a big garden bed that was a tangle of plants and weeds.

'If you work methodically from left to right, you'll get everything. There are trowels in the shed and a wheelbarrow. When you've filled it, wheel it up to my car.' Helen glanced at Jade's hands. 'You got gardening gloves?'

As if. 'I don't need them.'

Helen's mouth pursed like she'd sucked on a lemon. 'Yes, you do.'

Jade bristled at the command. 'It's just dirt. It washes off, you know.'

'All women who can get pregnant must wear gloves.'

After Milo was born, Jade had chosen to have a contraceptive rod inserted in her arm to give her complete protection against another accidental pregnancy. But she was curious about Helen's decree. 'Why?'

'Cats poo in the garden and they can carry a virus called toxoplasmosis. I don't have a lot of rules, Jade, but this is one of them. No gloves, no gardening.'

All her life there'd been rules that everyone seemed to know about except her. Rules that came out of nowhere and bit her on the bum, like the time her mother had walked into the kitchen wearing Jade's new dress.

'Mum! I haven't even worn it yet,' Jade had said.

'So?' Charlene replied. 'I've paid for everything for years. Now you owe me.'

The memory stirred old anger that slammed into her frustration with Helen. 'You could of told me that yesterday! By the time I walk to the supermarket and back here, Milo will be awake. Thanks for wasting my time. Thanks for nothing!'

Jade wasn't hanging around for Helen to shrug her disinterest, yell back at her or give her a lecture on respecting seniors. She was about to march back to Milo when Helen pulled a pair of well-worn leather gloves from her back pocket.

'Wear these today.'

Jade's anger lessened, but it left behind a confusing sensation that was tiny part grateful and many parts annoyed. She'd felt the same the day before when Helen had suggested she come to the garden. There was something about the woman that made Jade itchy and scratchy.

'Thanks, but they're too big.'

'They'll do the job for today. I'll leave you to it.' Without looking back, Helen strode out through the gates.

Jade didn't know what she'd expected, but part of her thought Helen might work alongside her for a bit, not just abandon her to spend time with the women on the other side of the fence. Women who didn't even speak English!

Cold determination coiled the length of her spine. She'd show Helen. She'd harvest this garden bed and keep whatever the hell she wanted.

An hour later, Jade's back ached. She'd dug up something that looked like a tumour and something with feathery leaves that smelled like liquorice, along with potatoes and carrots. The best find was a huge pumpkin. She was going to keep it and make soup inside it like she'd seen on a cooking show. Corey hated cooking shows, so she only watched them when he was away. Recently she'd been watching them a lot.

The unintelligible conversation continued to drift through the fence and across to Jade, reminding her she was on her own. Mostly she hummed songs to herself to block out the sound, but a burst of rapid-fire jabber made her glance up. Using her forearm, she pushed her hair out of her eyes and felt a dusting of dirt fall and stick to her cheek, pinned there by sweat. More laughter from the women dumped over her.

What the——? Jade slashed hard with a knife and severed four heads of broccoli from their thick and sturdy stalks. Those women had no right to be laughing at her when they were just as hot and dirty as she was.

She dumped the broccoli on top of the fully loaded wheelbarrow, then puffing and panting she pushed the heavy beast to the gates and Helen's car. Opening the hatch, she found six boxes neatly positioned in two lines of three and an esky taking up the remaining space.

Jade tossed the broccoli onto the ice and sealed the esky before brushing excess dirt off the root vegetables. She was tempted to dump the lot into random boxes so Helen had to sort them. But there was something about the neatness of the arrangement and the colours of the vegetables that called to her, demanding order, so she loaded each vegetable type into its own box.

When she'd finished, she was struck by how much it looked like a painting. Vibrant green zucchinis shone, the deep purple of beet-roots looked royal, and pleasure streamed through her at the way bunches of tapered orange carrots contrasted with their fluttery fine green leaves. Jade had never considered vegetables pretty before— that was the job of flowers—except right now she could imagine a glossy wooden table with vegetables as the centrepiece.

She slammed the hatch shut and pushed the barrow down the garden, glancing through the fence as she went. The women now sat cross-legged in the orchard, eating food out of plastic containers. Helen was with them, looking like she sat on the ground like that every day of the week.

Jade's stomach rumbled and she wished she'd thought to pack herself a snack. She wouldn't mind taking smoko either except she needed to work while Milo slept. But first she needed to pee. Ten-tatively, she slid open the lock on the portaloo, bracing herself for the stench, but instead of a fetid odour, the fresh smell of antiseptic wafted out to greet her.

When she'd finished, she stepped back outside and took a moment to listen for Milo. No crying, but she looked towards the tree any-way. She couldn't see his pram, only three of the boat people. Her heart leaped, banging frantically against her chest, and then her legs were moving and she was sprinting the length of the garden.

'Hey!' The women turned and Jade saw Milo snuggled into one of them. 'What are you doing? Give him to me! Get away!'

'He crying,' the woman said, handing Milo to her.

'So? You've got no right to touch him.'

'Sorry.' Her head dipped for a moment before rising. 'You want him cry?'

'No!'

'I only hold him because you busy.' She inclined her head to the portaloo.

Jade hugged Milo tightly, not only to reassure herself he was safe but to still the adrenaline-induced jitters.

Her son's tear-stained face broke into a smile and he shot out a chubby hand, closing his fist around another woman's headscarf. She made a cooing sound and said something to him Jade didn't understand. Milo laughed.

'He is beautiful baby.' The woman who'd picked up Milo tickled him under his chin. 'You very lucky.'

Jade stared at her. Since getting pregnant and having Milo she'd been told she was stupid, crazy, a slut, a disappointment, that she was throwing her life away, being unfair to Milo and too young to ever be a good mother. Not once had anyone said she was lucky.

She tried to think of something to say, but could only manage, 'Yeah.'

'I am Aima.'

'A-mah?' Jade repeated, trying the hard A. The woman nodded, smiling shyly. 'I'm Jade. This is Milo.'

'Yummy like the drink.'

'You drink Milo?' Jade couldn't believe Aima knew it.

She shrugged. 'I like chai. My son drinks Milo.' She pointed to the orchard. 'You bring food?' Jade shook her head. 'Come. Eat ours.'

Jade hesitated. Did she really want to join them? What if their food was weird? Aima looked a bit Asian and she'd read somewhere they ate insects. But if Aima gave her kids Milo, maybe some of their food would be Aussie.

While Aima's friend played clap hands with a shrieking and laughing Milo, a tug of war played out inside Jade. Her wariness about the women's foreignness and her suspicions that they'd been talking and laughing about her pulled against their obvious delight in her son—a delight that matched her own. There were few people who shared that. Should she risk it? What was the worst thing that could happen? The food would be gross? They'd talk in their own language and she'd feel as ignored and out of place as she did pretty much everywhere in this stinking town? That Helen would tell her she needed to keep working? It wasn't like any of those scenarios were new, so whichever way it went down, she could deal.

Decision made, she picked up her backpack. 'Let's go.'

CHAPTER
7

Helen was glad yoga gave her the flexibility to sit cross-legged on the ground with the women. They'd arrived this morning directly from school drop-off and had worked like Trojans, weeding and digging. The first bed was turned over and Helen had completed the soil test. After lunch, they'd fork in the compost. Helen was donating the contents of her bin as well as the Liparis' to kickstart the project, but the women would need to start their own compost. The committee would insist on a bin rather than a bay and she wondered if they could afford to buy one. The beds also needed sleepers to bring them in line with the plots in the main garden, but again that took money.

Helen glanced at Jade who was refusing the food Aima was offering her. Why had the girl bothered to join them if she was going to be rude? Irritation jabbed at her.

'At least try a bolani,' she said. 'They're a bit like a pasty.'

'I can make up my own mind, thank you.'

'I don't doubt that,' Helen muttered under her breath. Honestly, the girl was so full of spikes and prickles it was impossible to have a conversation. 'How did you get on with the vegetables?'

'We're best friends.' But this time the sardonic tone was accompanied by a wry smile that hinted at a sense of humour.

Helen laughed. 'Did you get much done before the baby woke up?'

'It's all done except the cabbages.'

'Really?' Helen's surprise slipped out before she could stop it.

Jade scowled. 'What? Did you think I couldn't do it?'

'I think you're a lot faster than me. Thank you.'

Jade's mouth worked as if she was masticating the compliment, unsure if it tasted sweet or sour. 'I've kept two bunches of carrots, and a dozen spuds. Oh, and I found a pumpkin and I'm keeping it to make soup.' The tilt of her chin said, *just try to stop me*.

'Good for you. Would you like some fresh herbs too?'

'Do you have garlic and sage?'

'Done.'

Jade didn't thank her but reached instead for a bolani and raised it tentatively to her mouth. Her face wrinkled in trepidation while her free hand clutched her water bottle. All the women stopped talking and watched her. She nibbled the end and Aima nodded encouragingly.

'It won't poison you,' Helen said. 'Take a decent bite.'

Jade glared at her, but bit into the bolani and chewed quickly as if she was keen to get it out of her mouth as fast as possible.

'Is good, yes?' Aima asked.

Helen held her breath.

Jade nodded. 'I thought it would be too spicy but it's just potatoes and chives.'

'And lentils and a little bit chilli.'

'Can I have another one?'

Helen relaxed, the women laughed and Milo squawked at the food passing him just out of reach. Jade offered him some of the filling. He ate it and demanded more.

It was Kubra who rose first, urging the women back to work. Helen could have sat a little longer but their enthusiasm buoyed her to her feet.

She walked Aima and Baseera over to the Liparis' compost bin and left them shovelling the organic matter into a wheelbarrow and trundling it next door for the women to fork it into the bed.

'Come on, Jade, I'll get you that sage and garlic.'

Jade followed and, to Helen's surprise, immediately identified the sage from the other herbs.

'You should grow flowers too,' Jade said.

'I can't eat flowers.'

'Yeah, you can. Nasturtiums, pansies, lavender, zucchini flowers.' She counted them off on her fingers.

'You seem to know a lot about it.'

Jade shrugged and shoved the garlic and sage in her pocket. 'MasterChef.'

Helen waited for thanks, but Jade turned the pram around, said, 'See ya,' then walked away.

'Bye,' Helen said to her retreating back and relaxed. She'd been on tenterhooks since Jade had arrived. The teenager was graceless, defensive and didn't take instruction very well. And then there was the baby …

Helen gave herself a shake—it was time to weed the Liparis' bed. She reached into her back pocket. Bloody hell! Jade had walked off with her gloves.

As she was up to date with her tetanus shots, she decided not to waste more time by going to the cottage to get another pair and got busy digging, shaking, tossing and raking. Her plan was to make the bed so neat and tidy that pedant Judith would suffer from not being able to fault the handover preparation. Helen was tempted to plant an oxalis seed in the bed as an act of defiance for Fiza who'd been denied this bed, but that wasn't the fault of the new owners. Besides, the weed wouldn't confine itself to one garden bed so she'd only be hurting herself.

'Hello, Helen.'

The musical voice made her look up. 'Fiza! You made it.'

'I am so sorry. Things have been very busy for me.'

Helen stood, wiping her hands on her jeans. 'No worries. I'm just glad you're here.'

'This is my garden?'

'No.' Helen pointed through the fence. 'I'm afraid you need to start from scratch, but I'll help.'

'That is very kind, but I don't have a shovel.'

'We've got everything you need in the shed.'

'And I can use?' She clapped her hands close to her chest. 'This is wonderful. My children can help after school?'

'As long as you're here with them. Come and meet the other women and I'll show you the bed I've marked out for you.'

Helen did the introductions and the women all murmured greetings. She was surprised they didn't know each other given they lived in the same street, but then again, she kept to herself. Between the café, the garden and her work with the shire, she knew a lot of people but didn't socialise with anyone.

The women returned to their tasks and Helen and Fiza dug the perimeter of the rectangular bed. It was hard work and neither of them chatted much.

Helen was taking a water break when she heard her name being called. Judith and Sharon stood on the community garden side of the fence. Helen returned their waves. Judith beckoned. Helen's spine stiffened, but she waved again before returning to her digging. If Judith wanted to talk to her, she could walk to her.

It took Judith and Sharon less than three minutes.

'Helen, what's going on?' Judith's arm waved, encompassing all the activity.

'We're extending the garden.'

'You can't do that without consulting the committee!'

'Our lease only covers the space we have,' Sharon said.

'The orchard's ours,' Helen said.

'It's a grey area.'

'It's not. The cottage is affiliated with the garden. Don't you think it makes sense to turn this empty space into a much-needed extension?'

'We don't need an extension. Our waiting list is less than a year.'

'And I've got women here who are keen to have their own garden. We've got the space, so why wait?'

'Did you get permission from the shire?' Judith asked.

'Yes.' She'd discussed it with Messina and Vivian.

'Do you have it in writing?'

'No, but—'

'Until we have it in writing, this area's not part of the garden.'

Helen rolled with Judith's need to split hairs. 'Fine, I'll get it in writing.'

'Good. Until then, none of the equipment can be used.'

'What? You've got to be kidding?'

'I don't joke about protocol and procedure, Helen. You might be the coordinator, but you must operate within the rules.'

Helen fought for calm. 'And that's what you're doing? Operating inside the rules?'

'Absolutely.' Judith looked around at the women who'd all stopped working, sensing something was happening. 'It's what a civilised society does. As these people have chosen to come to our democratic country, they'll understand.'

'Chosen? Fleeing a warzone is hardly a choice.'

Judith sniffed. 'All I'm saying is they have to follow the rules just like the rest of us. They're welcome to fill in a form and go on the waiting list. Sharon, pass the forms out.'

'Don't waste time and paper, Sharon,' Helen said. 'These women have worked incredibly hard today creating their beds. There's no way I'm telling them they can't garden.'

'That's up to you, Helen, but they won't be gardening using the community garden's equipment.' Judith turned to face the women and clapped her hands like the retired schoolteacher she was. 'Ladies! Until this area is officially part of the community garden, you can't work here. Please return everything to the shed.'

The Hazara women looked to Aima for a translation. Helen watched their faces move from confusion to disappointment before they turned to her, their eyes full of questions.

Helen didn't want to have what would be a loud and angry argument with Judith in front of them so she said, 'After we've put the tools away, come to the cottage. I'll explain everything.'

Fiza, who was already a very tall woman, suddenly seemed to gain a couple more centimetres. She extended her hand to Sharon. 'I would like a form, please.'

Sharon jumped. 'You speak English?'

'Yes. I also speak French and Arabic.'

'I speak a bit of Greek.' Helen grinned. 'What other languages do you speak, Sharon?'

Sharon ignored her and pulled a form from her organiser, handing it to Fiza. 'You can post it to the address on the top. I'll date it when I receive it and put you on the waiting list.'

'I will fill it out now. May I borrow a pen?'

'Sorry. I don't have one.'

Helen's rage boiled over. 'What do you call that then?' She pointed to the silver pen nestled inside the folder.

'Oh. Right.' Sharon's cheeks flushed red and she reluctantly withdrew the pen and passed it to Fiza.

'Don't worry, Sharon,' Helen said. 'It's a lot safer with Fiza than Jade. She just nicked off with my gardening gloves.'

'Who's Jade?' Flustered, Sharon kept her eyes fixed on Fiza.

Someone else you wouldn't want to join the garden.

And you do?

The thought dug in under Helen's moral high ground. 'Someone who helped me clear the Lipari bed. It's ready, by the way. Ask the Bradleys to contact me so we can set up a time for orientation.'

'There.' Fiza handed back the form and the pen. 'Please date it today and put the time also.'

Sharon wrote the date and time, stowed the paper and pen away and zippered her organiser closed with a jerk. She joined Judith, who was back in the community garden having walked behind the Hazara women like a kelpie rounding up sheep.

Helen shielded her eyes and squinted. She could see the women were handing off their equipment to a man at the shed. A dog barked and she swung her gaze—a familiar border collie was tied up next to a bike. Bob. Bloody hell! Why was he relieving the women of their tools when he'd implied she'd misunderstood him? Was it payback? They'd never had that cup of tea.

Her leg muscles twitched, demanding she walk straight up to him and ask him what the hell he was doing. But there was a time and place to pick a fight and if Bob had changed sides, talking to him with Judith and Sharon flanking him would be unwise.

The women drifted back, dejection clear in their slumped shoulders. They gathered on the cottage's veranda, waiting for Helen to speak.

'Aima, can you please tell everyone that I'm truly sorry about this, but we're not going to let a few small-minded people stop us. We will keep gardening.'

Aima translated. The women murmured among themselves, but their expressions clearly stated they didn't believe Helen.

'But that woman says we not use the tools,' Aima said.

'Does anyone have any gardening tools?'

The women shook their heads.

'I've got a few I could lend you,' a male voice said.

Helen swung around to see Bob standing at the bottom of the worn bluestone steps. Frustration blew through her like a hot north wind—gritty and unsettling—and she ran with it.

'If you hadn't just locked up all the tools, we could still be using them!'

He took off his broad-brimmed hat and rubbed the back of his neck. 'Yeah, sorry about that. I arrived and found everyone returning the tools so I jumped in to help.'

'Of course you did.' *Spare me from well-intentioned duffers.*

Bob's 'niceness' got under Helen's skin. Each time they had a conversation, she became increasingly convinced he was one of those naive men who saw the world through rose-coloured glasses because an easy life had cushioned any blows.

He met her angry gaze full on, his brows rising slightly. 'I didn't realise I was aiding and abetting a counter coup.'

'I didn't stage a coup! I'm extending the garden to meet demand.'

'Which is a good idea in principle ...'

She narrowed her eyes. Did she need to reassess the 'duffer' tag? 'What's that supposed to mean?'

'Exactly that. It's a great idea, but come on, Helen. You must have known you were playing with fire when you didn't consult Judith.'

'Technically, I don't have to consult her. And I knew what she'd say. Besides, it's not up to the committee whether the garden's extended or not. That's up to the shire. Judith's being deliberately obstructive, but she'll be eating humble pie soon enough.'

'I've known Judith for years and I wouldn't bet on it,' Bob said.

Helen opened her mouth to fire back a reply but he'd already turned to face the women.

'Hello, ladies, my name's Bob. Been a farmer all my life and I only moved to town six months ago. Before you all came to Australia, where was home?'

The Hazara women explained how they'd come from refugee camps in Pakistan.

'Crikey,' Bob said. 'That's a long journey to Boolanga. I reckon the least we can do is give you a patch of dirt you can call your own. I'll bring my gardening tools down tomorrow and my wheelbarrow so you can keep going, although it will be at a slower pace.'

The women murmured their thanks.

The exchange added to Helen's disquiet that she couldn't slot Bob neatly into a box.

'Even with your equipment, we can't plant without hoses,' she said impatiently. 'And mine's not long enough to reach all the beds.'

'We use buckets,' Kubra said.

'Your best bet is to get some funding,' Bob suggested.

Helen was intimate with the grants system after exploring it for her tiny housing submission. 'The grants have all closed for this year.'

'What about talking to Hoopers about a sausage sizzle?'

Spare me. Helen shoved Bob back into the polite but clueless box. 'We can't ask these women to cook pork sausages. We'd need halal meat to make kebabs and that would dent the profit margin.'

'I believe you can buy halal beef sausages, but I'm not talking about a barbecue. I meant Hoopers has a huge garden section.'

'We don't have any money to buy anything, remember?'

Bob ignored her sarcasm. 'But you've got a nice big fence and a reasonable amount of passing traffic. Go and talk to Jon Hooper about him donating some gardening gear in exchange for signage advertising the store.'

'That's actually a good idea.'

He grimaced. 'I'll take that as a thank you. And think big, Helen. Ask for a shed. It will save everyone a long walk.'

'But that would separate the gardens and I don't want that. It defeats the point of community.' And it meant racists like Judith and Sharon would win.

'Rome wasn't built in a day,' Bob said. 'Softly, softly, catchee monkey. There's more than one way to—'

'Righto, Bob. I get it.'

Her familiar irritation with him needled holes in her appreciation of his sponsorship idea. She was already going slowly with the housing project, jumping through one hoop at a time. Why did she have to apply the same approach to a garden when it was a simple and easy thing to achieve? Before these women had arrived in Australia, they'd been through hell. Like Bob said, the least they deserved was a garden.

'It shouldn't be this hard,' she added. 'And don't even think about quoting Malcolm Fraser's "Life wasn't meant to be easy" at me.'

'Actually, Fraser was paraphrasing George Bernard Shaw. He left out the most important part.'

'Really? What was that?'

'Life is not meant to be easy, my child; but take courage: it can be delightful.'

'Pfft.'

'You don't agree?'

Helen laughed it off. No way was she debating that with Bob. It was bad enough she'd let herself be interested in the quote. She'd learned a long time ago that maintaining general disinterest in casual conversation was the best way to keep a safe distance from people. Especially men.

CHAPTER

8

'Whoa! Slow down, Tara!' Her personal trainer's chest heaved and sweat ran along his temples.

Tara flicked her ponytail out of her eyes. 'Why? Can't you take it, Zac?'

He grinned at her, all raw sex appeal and outrageous confidence—the domain of the twenty-somethings. 'You know I take whatever you give me.'

A raft of sensation skittered along her spine and her heart kicked up. It wasn't a hundred per cent due to the kickboxing. 'Is that right?'

'Yeah.' But his flirty look had faded. 'But I don't want you to hurt yourself.'

'I'm fine. Just shut up and block.'

She didn't want sympathy. She wanted teasing. Zac was both easy on the eyes and good company and she enjoyed their banter.

Unlike Jon, he made her feel powerful and in control as well as incredibly sexy and desirable.

Not that she had any plans to act on the occasional zings of attraction that sparked between them. The idea of becoming the clichéd woman having a fling with her gym instructor made her shudder. It was bad enough her marriage was channelling *Anna Karenina*. Her sympathies lay with Anna, whose husband took her for granted.

Tara slammed the boxing gloves into the pads, savouring her power. Up until three years ago, sport for her had always been tennis. Then, at her mother's suggestion, she'd added in Pilates. Early this year, she'd responded to a 'free session' offer from Zac who was new to town and promoting his business. Although she still enjoyed tennis and Pilates, neither matched the exhilarating buzz she got from her twice-weekly personal training sessions.

Tara wished her mother was still alive. Jane would have understood her addiction to the endorphin rush and the sense of well-being that always followed pushing herself to her limits. Jon didn't get it. Since Clementine had started school, he'd been saying, 'If you're bored, increase your hours at the store.' Recently, he'd added snippy comments about 'ladies who lunch'. But Tara had no intention of dropping any of her exercise. Currently, it was one of a few things that gave her joy and took her away from the niggling and unsettling feelings about her life.

Today, she planned to exhaust herself so her brain would still and she'd be free of the taunting and circuitous thoughts that Jon was looking outside their marriage. Visualising Rhianna, she raised her legs, kicking high and hard into the pads.

Zac took whatever she threw at him with an appreciative smile that carved its way across his model good looks and designer stubble before settling in his dark and fathomless eyes. Eyes that had appeared two nights ago in Tara's erotic dream.

Zac hadn't questioned her request for extra sessions this week, but why would he when it meant more money. He didn't need to know she suspected her husband and his lifelong friend of having an affair.

You don't know that until you talk to Jon. But the idea of that conversation made her gag. It was easier concentrating on the burn in her muscles and pushing herself beyond sensible limits than tormenting herself as to why her husband no longer found her attractive.

Only when the soreness in her limbs transformed to a screaming agony that consumed her mind and stole her breath did she allow herself to give in. She sank to the floor and lay on her back, panting.

'Drink this.' Zac passed her an electrolyte drink.

'Thanks.' But she lacked the energy to lift her head.

'Come on.'

'Can't.'

'I'm serious, Tara.' His hand slid under her head and lifted it as if she was an invalid. 'Drink.'

'God, you're bossy.' She sat up and his hand fell away—she hated that she missed it. But the reality was, if she excluded the hugs of the children and Jon's perfunctory kisses, Zac's occasional guiding touches during a session were her only intimate contact.

Talk. To. Jon.

'If these extra sessions are ongoing, I'll plan some different workouts for you.' Zac's gaze was fixed on her—intense and full of swirling sexuality. 'You up for that?'

Despite her exhaustion, her body fluttered. 'Up for what?'

'Mixing things up a little. Keeping it fresh so you're not bored. A woman like you deserves to be challenged.'

'A woman like me?' Given what was going on at home, she didn't know if she should be flattered or offended. 'What does that mean?'

He shrugged, the action bringing his tribal tattoo to life. 'Most of my clients hate exercising. They do it to control their weight or to keep themselves moving. But you're different—more like me. You get off on the rush.'

She always had. Jon had been amazed at how high she'd been after each birth. He'd teased her that he was more wrung out than her.

'Gotta love those endorphins,' she said.

'Yeah, the happy hormones, right?'

And right now, she was taking happy wherever she could find it. 'So how are you going to challenge me, Zac?'

'I think you should train for something specific.'

'Like what?'

'A marathon.'

She laughed but Zac didn't. 'You're serious? But a marathon ... that's huge. And the time commitment ...'

'It's very doable if you start early, break it down into achievable goals and have a training partner.'

She thought about her friends and acquaintances. None of them would want to run a marathon. In fact most of them seemed confused and offended by her need to exercise.

'Finding a partner might be difficult,' she said.

'We could train together.'

'I pay you to train me and you get to train at the same time? I always knew you were a clever businessman.'

A flicker of emotion passed across his face so quickly she couldn't tell if he was embarrassed she'd called him on his blatant hawking or if he was affronted.

'I meant outside of our current arrangement. No charge.'

She stared at him. 'You'd do that?'

'Sure. You'll push me as hard as I push you.' He nudged her shoulder with his. 'Besides, your testimonials and having my flyers at the store have brought me eight new clients.'

'You really think I can run a marathon?'

'I really do. So are you in?'

Yes! Yes! So in. 'I want to say yes ...'

'So just say it. Do something for yourself.'

But that was the problem. She wasn't just Tara, possible marathon runner with the freedom to dedicate herself to training. She was Jon's wife and Flynn and Clementine's mother, not to mention the store's giftware buyer, classroom helper, domestic controller and a gazillion other things.

'Can you send me the training program so I know exactly what I'm in for?'

The light in his eyes dimmed. 'You can just say no.'

She touched his arm lightly, needing him to understand. 'Zac, this is me trying to say yes.'

His smile radiated sunshine, warming her from the inside out. The feeling stayed with her while she showered and floated out to her car.

On the drive home, Zac's compliments and the very tempting idea of spending months training with him dominated her thoughts. Not wanting any of her happiness to drain away, she deliberately avoided looking at the property next door to Tingledale when she slowed to turn into her driveway.

Tara considered the proximity of the 'orange eyesore' to the gracious elegance of Tingledale a travesty. But apparently its orange bricks, diamond-patterned veranda rail, the name *Shangrila* written in white wrought iron beside the front door and its large airy rooms made it the pinnacle of 1960s' modern design. According to Fran at the library, Doctor Tingle's grandson had sold off forty-five acres to create a small housing estate and had built the orange eyesore for his son, positioning it close to the boundary so the grandchildren could run back and forth between the two houses.

Those familial days were long gone and the once-coveted modern home was shabby after more than a decade of being rented. It was a thorn in Tara's side. Some tenants were better than others, but as the house aged and the current owners refused to spend any money on it, the calibre of the tenants dropped. The garden, if you could call it that, was now a rambling and weed-infested mess that dispatched thriving runners of the thick, green and tenacious spiderwort and threw out oxalis seeds that dug in deep, producing green clusters that taunted her with their cheery yellow flowers.

When the grass grew too long and became a fire and snake hazard, Tara rang the managing real estate agent. Although they responded to the requests to mow, they never did more than the bare minimum of maintenance on the property. Tara had started buying Powerball tickets in the vain hope of winning and making the absent and uncaring owners an offer they couldn't refuse.

Jon's car was in the garage and she wondered if he'd come home for lunch to extend some warmth into the frosty détente that had hardened to ice since the weekend. On Sunday morning, she'd expected him to apologise for the disaster that had been Saturday night, but almost a week had passed and he hadn't said a word.

To head off any questions about why she'd been at an unscheduled gym session, Tara hid her bag inside the washing machine before walking into the kitchen. Jon was standing at the bench, which was covered by so many different sandwich fixings it gave Subway a run for its money.

'Hi,' she said.

He glanced up from the roll he was buttering and smiled, his eyes crinkling at the edges. 'Hi.'

'Did I forget you were coming home for lunch?'

'No. I'd planned to take you to Bert & Bears, but when you didn't come into work I thought I'd bring lunch to you.'

She checked his expression—no sign of criticism that she hadn't been at the store. Her heart rolled at his thoughtfulness and she almost moved in to kiss him when the memory of Saturday's rebuff slammed into her, staying her feet.

'No onion, please.'

'I know.' He squirted Dijon mustard onto the bread. 'Did you see the car in the drive of the orange eyesore?'

'No.' She poured herself a glass of water. 'Do we have new neighbours?'

'Not sure. But if we do, the good news is the car's not a paddock bomb. In fact, it's less than ten years old and recently detailed.'

'Fingers crossed then. Sorry about not making it into work. How are things?'

'Yeah, good.' He layered slices of roast beef on top of the mustard. 'I've got a job for you this afternoon if you can manage it.'

Disappointment oozed through her, thick and black like an oil slick. Lunch wasn't an olive branch after all, but a schmooze. 'What is it?'

'The community garden wants us to donate some equipment in exchange for advertising space.'

'Boolanga has a community garden?'

'Apparently. Might be good to be linked in with them if the big boys arrive in town. Bit of good will.'

She scanned the piles of neatly sliced tomatoes, capsicum, grated carrot and spied a packet of her favourite cheese—Mersey Valley Original. She opened the pantry and pulled out a new jar of pickles.

'Oh good. I thought we were out.' Jon picked up the jar and clamped his big hand around the black lid.

She opened her mouth to say, 'Can I help with lunch?' but heard instead, 'I want to talk about Saturday.'

'The end-of-season footy thing?' He grunted, unable to break the seal on the lid. 'I didn't think you wanted to go. Bloody hell, did they glue this lid on?'

Jon usually popped a lid in two seconds. Tara was the one who needed to use a rubber glove or lever a knife to break the seal.

She handed him a glove and stayed on track. 'Not this Saturday, last Saturday.'

He was gripping the jar so tightly his knuckles gleamed white and a tremor rode up his arm. 'What about last Saturday?'

Seriously? He was making her do all the work and her heart kicked up.

'Are you having an affair with Rhianna?'

The jar tumbled from his fingers. He jumped back as glass, vinegar and cucumber pickles smashed against the black and white tiles, spraying glass and liquid across the kitchen. He stared at her, his body trembling and his eyes wide and frantic like a rabbit caught in the crosshairs of a gun.

'Christ, T.'

The shaking started in her toes, racing quickly up and across her body. 'Is dropping the jar a yes or a no?'

'What the hell sort of question is that?'

'Given the circumstances, a perfectly reasonable one.'

He bent down and, with trembling hands, picked up shards of glass. 'What circumstances?'

'You and Rhianna looked pretty cosy in the kitchen. She had her hand on your arm.'

'And when I was four she used to watch me pee. It doesn't mean I'm having an affair with her!'

'Is it someone else?'

His jaw clenched. 'No.'

'Then why aren't we having sex?'

'Not this again!' He dropped the glass he was holding and stood up, pressing his palms flat on the bench. 'We're not twenty-five any more.'

'What's that got to do with it?'

'We have the same amount of sex as any other couple married with two kids, a business and a mortgage.'

'Come on, Jon. You know things have changed. You've changed.'

He shook his head. 'No, Tara. I'm an average almost forty-year-old bloke who falls into bed most nights already half asleep. You're the one who's changed. Ever since you started this insane exercise routine, you've become sex obsessed.'

'I'm not obsessed!'

'You are. You're wearing all that scratchy lace in bed instead of your soft cotton PJs. After the awards dinner you did a *Pretty Woman* impersonation, and on Saturday you wanted to have sex when we had guests on the other side of the wall!'

'I only did those things because you've been turning your back on me for months. I thought you'd like them!'

His face tightened. 'Well, I don't. I want a partner, not a porn star.'

Hurt slammed her so hard tears stung the backs of her eyes. 'So what are you saying? That me making the first move is a turn-off? I'm the reason you can't get hard?'

'Not always ...'

It hurt to form words. 'But?'

'But lately ...' His gaze slid away. 'It's a lot of pressure, T.'

Shame, anger and confusion swirled, clouding her thoughts. She craved intimacy and Jon saw her need as pressure? Fear punched her. How had this happened? For years they'd tumbled together without a second thought and now ... Was this why he'd lost his erection the last few times they'd tried to have sex?

'I didn't mean to pressure you,' she said. 'I just miss us.'

'We're still us.'

Are we? It wasn't just the lack of sex. He'd stopped cuddling her in bed, stopped sneaking up behind her and copping a cheeky feel of her breasts, and his kisses were mostly perfunctory pecks on the cheek. But if she mentioned any of that, he'd accuse her of being sex obsessed. Was she? If she was honest, she'd spent a lot of time thinking about sex. Dreaming and fantasising about it. Flirting with Zac.

'Are we still us?' she said.

'Yes.'

He walked around the bench and wrapped his arms around her. It was the first time he'd really touched her in a long time. Despite the confusing spin of emotions, she gave in to temptation and laid her head on his chest, loving the reassuring lub-dub beat of his heart.

He kissed her and she felt his love in the tremble of his body. Then his erection stirred, pressing against her. Hope soared.

She returned his kiss—deep and hard—then remembered 'too much pressure'. As difficult as it was not to grab his hand and hustle him down the hall, she held back, waiting for him to walk her backwards to their bedroom, lower her onto the bed, pop the buttons on her blouse and bring his hot wet mouth down onto her aching breasts—

He pulled his mouth from hers and stroked her hair. 'You know what I think?'

It took a moment for her lust-soaked brain to catch up and for her eyes to focus. All she could manage was a shake of her head.

'With both the kids at school, you've been struggling all year to work out who you are and what you want to do. You need a real challenge, T, and it's not losing weight you didn't need to drop or a PB at the gym. And it's definitely not our sex life.'

Annoyance added more waves to her already choppy sea of emotions. Something about the glint in his eyes made her tense. 'Let me guess. You've got a solution?'

His smile was pure indulgence. 'There are plenty of things to challenge your big brain at the store and make you feel good about yourself again. I'd love it if you took your great eye for design and expanded the paint section into an interior design service.'

'I'm not a qualified interior designer.'

'Pfft! Look around. You've got an eye most designers would kill for. Why not formalise what you did for Shan and Chris and what you're currently doing for Vivian Leppart? It will be good for you.' He radiated excitement. 'Let's set up an appointment system and get Hoopers Interior Design off the ground. We'll offer ten per cent off any decorating stock clients buy. It gives us another niche over the big boys. The personal touch.'

I want a partner. His words hammered her. Not a wife or a lover, but a partner. A business partner. Jon wanted her at work but not in bed. Her already grazed heart lost another layer and blood bubbled freely.

'That's quite a challenge.'

But Jon missed the tartness in her voice and smiled at her. 'You'll ace it.'

Once she would have floated on the compliment, but not now. Not when it put her firmly in the role of an employee.

'The first challenge is the community garden,' she said. 'Interior design will have to be the second.'

But it was a lie. She knew exactly what her next challenge would be and it didn't involve Jon or interior design.

She walked into the bathroom, closed the door and texted Zac.

Hey partner! I'm all in for Project M. Tx

She stared at the x, surprised to see it there—all her previous texts to Zac she'd signed *TH*.

What are you doing?

Justifying to herself that as marathon training wasn't part of their client–trainer relationship and no money would be changing hands, she was just signing off like she did with any friend, she pressed send.

A second later her phone pinged. *Awesome! Planning meeting this afternoon?*

Great!

Delight lifted the heaviness that had settled over her during her conversation with Jon. For the first time in a long time she felt like a woman and she hugged the sensation close, never wanting it to fade.

Exhilaration tangoed with resignation as Tara parked outside the community garden. Her mind was full of her upcoming meeting with Zac and she really didn't want to be here. She was still pinching herself that he believed she could run a marathon, and now she'd committed she didn't want to waste any time—she wanted to start now! But she'd promised Jon she'd come to the garden and Zac wasn't free until three so …

She sighed and picked up the post-it note Jon had given her with the name of the woman she was to meet. His handwriting had never been good, but even by his standards this was more chicken scratchings than words. She couldn't decipher it. 'Great going, Jon.'

Forcing herself out of the car, she was walking towards the ornamental gates when she heard a female voice calling out, 'Hello.'

She turned. 'Helen?' She didn't really know Helen beyond exchanging pleasantries on the few occasions she caved in to the kids' pester power and bought fish and chips. She glanced at the post-it and realised the scrawled I I e I e I could be Helen if Jon had connected the letters. 'Am I supposed to be meeting you?'

The older woman smiled. 'If you're Mrs Hooper as well as Clemmie and Flynn's mum.'

She shot out her hand. 'Call me Tara.'

'Thanks for coming, Tara. I really appreciate your time. Can I give you a tour and introduce you to the women?'

'That sounds lovely, but I'm a bit pressed for time. How about you tell me what you need and show me where we can hang some signs.'

Helen frowned. 'We could reschedule to a more convenient time.'

Tara didn't want to be here now, let alone returning another day. 'That would only slow things down and I'm sure you want the stock sooner rather than later.'

'If you're sure … We've got a needs list and a wish list.'

'Give me your entire list in order of priority.'

'Gardening gloves, soaker hoses and connectors, shovels, spades, trowels, rakes, hoes, weeders, two wheelbarrows, timber or recycled plastic for bed borders, compost bins, blood and bone, soil conditioner, seaweed liquid fertiliser, secateurs, seedlings, a shed, a propagating greenhouse, water tanks, an irrigation system …' As Helen talked and Tara typed on her phone, they walked away from the ornamental gates. 'We were thinking here for the sign.'

Tara looked up. They were standing in front of a fence that was below the sight line from a car. Tara cast a practised eye around the area. It had been years since she'd been here—not since she and Jon had installed the pool and removed any reason to swim in the river.

It didn't look like a lot had changed. Cattle and horses still grazed on the old experimental farm and the road remained unsealed. Whenever there was a work experience student at *The Standard*, the editor always sent them to interview the councillors about plans for the land. Inevitably, an article was written with the headline *What's Next For Riverfarm?* Then a flurry of letters followed before the topic fell silent again.

Tara pointed to the intersection. 'Could we erect a sign on that corner? I'm thinking two metres by one and a half resting on one-point-seven poles. It would catch the eye of passing traffic.'

'As well as on the fence?'

'Instead of on the fence.'

'That's bigger than I thought.'

Tara squashed the urge to say, do you want our help or not? 'I promise the sign will be tasteful. It will have our logo and say *Hoopers Hardware, Timber and Steel is proud to sponsor the Boolanga Community Garden*. The garden logo can be there too. If that's something you can live with, we'll happily fill your basic needs list and give you a shed.'

Helen stared at her, silently blinking behind her glasses.

'If you want, I'll send you the artwork so you can discuss it with your members?' Tara added.

'No. I mean, not no ... I don't need to discuss it. I ... I never imagined ... We're just so grateful!' Helen threw her arms around Tara.

For a moment Tara stiffened, uncomfortable by the unexpected display of emotion, and then grief rushed in so unexpectedly, her knees sagged. It was exactly the sort of hug her mother would have given her and she found herself returning it just so she could remember.

'It's our pleasure,' she said. 'But just so you know, we get samples that our staff use in the garden section so most of the stock will be pre-loved but still in good condition.'

'We'll happily accept whatever you can spare.'

'What's your email and phone number?' Tara typed in the details. 'I'll pull the order together then give you a call to set up a delivery time.'

'And then I'll call you to arrange a time when you can come to the garden so we can thank you properly.'

The thought of losing half a morning standing around making polite conversation with a group of old women she didn't know when she could be training didn't appeal in the slightest. 'That's really not necessary.'

'Oh, but it is. Please allow us the opportunity to show our appreciation.'

There was a hint of rebuke in Helen's tone and Tara got another flash of her mother. *It's not always about how you feel, Tara.*

'I'll look forward to it,' she said.

Except the only thing she was looking forward to was meeting with Zac and planning her marathon preparation. She sent out a wish that the community garden members would be so excited about their new equipment they'd forget all about hosting a morning tea.

CHAPTER
9

The gardening gloves had been taunting Jade for days. It didn't matter where she put them in the unit, they reappeared, their dirty leather, clumped wool and tatty red edging accusing her of theft. She hadn't stolen them—not deliberately anyway. She'd forgotten she'd dumped them on top of the pram and when she'd pushed back the cover they'd become hidden in the folds.

When she'd found them the next morning, her guts had gone all wobbly. She'd pushed Milo to the farmers' market just so she could return the gloves to Helen, but when she'd got there, the only person at the community garden stall was an old bloke in a hat who actually looked like a farmer. As she couldn't afford to buy anything, she'd walked home.

That afternoon, Milo had spiked a temperature and Jade had been stuck inside for four days holding a screaming baby. Corey must be out of mobile range because he hadn't replied to any of her texts. She'd almost lost her mind. She'd definitely cried.

Thankfully, Milo had woken up happy this morning and without a fever, so she'd bundled him into the pram and escaped. Now, she and Milo were peering through the decorative gates of the community garden looking for Helen.

An old biddy stared back, her mouth doing that thin-line thing Jade was used to from the receptionist at the medical centre and the bitch at the supermarket checkout. The look that said *useless bludger teenage single mother.*

'Yes? Can I help you?' the woman finally said.

'Is Helen here?'

The woman's mouth puckered so tightly it almost disappeared. 'No.'

'Do you know when she's coming?'

'I do not.'

The bloody gardening gloves were harder to return than a boomerang. Jade wondered how many more times she'd have to walk the one-and-a-half kilometres to the garden on the off-chance Helen was here. She was tempted to just give the gloves to the woman so she was free of them, but that lemon-sucking mouth did nothing to reassure her. The witch would probably throw the gloves in the bin instead of giving them to Helen and she'd be blamed for stealing.

Jade wasn't a thief—when she stole, it was only necessities like tampons and baby food and *only* when she had no other choice. She shouldn't care, but for some reason she didn't want Helen thinking she'd nicked these half-dead gloves.

'Try the cottage,' the woman said before turning and walking down the garden.

'What cottage?'

The woman's arm extended in the general direction of the river.

'Useful,' Jade muttered.

She passed the orchard where she'd eaten lunch with the refugee women and kept walking until she reached a rusty gate. It had beautiful metal swirls and curls at the top and Jade pictured how elegant and lah-de-dah it would have been back in the day.

'Jade!'

She turned and saw Aima, Kubra and Baseera walking towards her carrying boxes and enviro bags. They smiled at her as if they were genuinely pleased to see her. 'Hi,' she said.

They clucked and cooed at Milo who squealed in delight.

'Nice day to garden,' Kubra said shyly.

'I didn't come to garden. I have to give Helen back her gloves.'

'She is at meeting but comes later.'

Jade knew instinctively that if she left the gloves with these women, they'd return them to Helen and she'd be free to get on with her day. She needed to do a load of laundry at the laundromat and after days stuck on the couch holding Milo, the unit cried out for a clean. But still she hesitated, not quite able to part with the gloves.

Kubra was trying to balance her box of plants on the gate post and deal with the chain. Jade caught the box just as it slid off the post.

'Do you need some help planting these?'

After planting two square metres of chives in rows—it turned out the women were neat freaks so she'd really needed to concentrate to keep the plants straight—Jade enjoyed her first cup of chai and something they called naan. It was sort of like bread but flatter and tastier.

Helen still hadn't turned up and Milo, who'd been happily playing in the dirt, was now filthy and fractious.

'Thanks for this.' Jade handed Aima the glass. 'But I should go.'

'You want me to give Helen the gloves?'

Jade knew she should hand them over and be done with it, but if she did that, she wouldn't have a reason to return to the garden. The thought made her fingers close tightly around them. 'Thanks, but I'll catch her later.'

Aima's forehead creased under her headscarf and a hot brick of angry disappointment lodged in Jade's chest. 'I'm going to give them back to her!'

Aima's eyes widened at Jade's raised voice but she kept her gaze fixed on her. 'Yes, but how do you catch Helen? She is not a ball.'

Jade laughed and the brick in her chest dissolved. '"Catch her later" means I'll see her later. Meet her later. At another time.'

'Ah! English is hard and confusing.'

'Is it?' Jade had never given it any thought. 'Anyway, maybe I'll catch you later too?'

Aima smiled. 'That would be nice.'

Jade strapped Milo in the pram and walked home. When she turned into Serenity Street, she saw Corey's ute and delight danced and spun in her belly. She ran the last hundred metres to the front door and excitement made her fumble the key. It took two attempts to slide it into the lock and in the juggle of bumping the pram past the wire door and through the front door, Milo woke up crying.

'Shh, buddy. Daddy's home!' She lifted Milo out of the pram and called out, 'Hi. We missed you!'

Corey sat at the kitchen table nursing a beer. His blue gaze flicked over her. 'You've got forty-seven hours of Corey greatness to enjoy. You could have had forty-eight but you've missed an hour. Where've you been?'

'Out for the first time in days.' She leaned down and kissed him and he squeezed her arse. 'Did you get my texts about Milo being sick?'

He shrugged, leaving her uncertain if he'd received them or not. 'He can't be too sick if he's been playing in the dirt.'

'He's better today so we went to the community garden.'

'What's that?'

'It's a place where people grow stuff. I think they should grow flowers but mostly it's vegetables. I got some organic ones for Milo.'

'Organic's bullshit.'

Jade disagreed but it wasn't worth mentioning. 'You hungry?'

'Yeah.'

'You hold Milo and I'll make you a sandwich.'

'No way. He's filthy.'

Corey was wearing a stained blue singlet, grimy work pants and he smelled of sweat, dust and smoke.

Jade saw a chance for some father–son bonding. 'Why don't you have a bath together?'

He shuddered. 'Nup. Last time I did that, he shat on me.'

'You make the sandwich then and I'll clean him up.'

'I can wait.' He sucked on the beer, then pulled out his phone and checked Snapchat.

Jade stood holding their son while duelling emotions strove for supremacy. Corey hadn't seen Milo in three weeks, but he didn't want to cuddle or bath him or give her a ten-minute break from him? Then a breeze of understanding cooled her resentment. Men didn't get involved with their kids until they could walk, talk or throw a ball. *If at all.*

Unwanted thoughts of her own father wriggled in. She pushed them away—Corey was nothing like her father.

Jade kissed Milo's sweaty and dusty curls. 'Let's get you washed and into bed, mate.'

When she returned to the kitchen, Corey was sitting in the same chair but a second beer bottle had joined the first. She opened the fridge and pulled out some bread, marg, dev and tomato sauce—Corey's favourite. As she sliced the crusts off the soft white bread and slid the sandwich onto a plate, she thought about the flavours of the naan and the bolani.

'Do you want lettuce on this?'

Corey snorted and she wondered why she'd asked when he only ate white vegetables. She joined him at the table and he bit into the sandwich without asking her why she wasn't eating.

'I thought the garden would be full of stuck-up women like at Baby Time,' she said.

'None of that lot would garden. Might damage their nails.'

She laughed, happy to find a topic they both agreed on. 'All women who can get pregnant have to wear gloves.' Corey didn't ask why or how she knew this, so she kept chatting. 'But apart from the bossy woman in charge, everyone I met was friendly.'

Corey washed down the first half of his sandwich with beer then tackled the second.

'I helped them plant chives.'

'Woof are 'ey?' he asked around a mouthful of food.

'A herb. Kinda like thick blades of grass, but hollow. They taste a bit like onion and they use them heaps in cooking. They even put them in naan.'

'In what?'

'Naan. It's bread.'

'Nah.' Corey shook his head. 'Bread is bread and it doesn't have bloody herbs in it.'

'It does if it comes from India, Pakistan, Iran—'

She quickly stopped before adding *Afghanistan and parts of China*, so Corey didn't say, 'Fuck, Jade. No one likes a smart-arse.' She didn't mean to be one—she just loved to read and watch documentaries, and she had a good memory. But as Corey pointed out, it wasn't that she was smarter than him, it was because she didn't work and could watch TV all day and fill her mind with useless information. Except she never read or watched TV when Milo was awake.

Corey was leaning forward now, showing more interest in her conversation than he usually did. 'Who are these women?'

'They're from Afghanistan.'

'You've been gardening with terrorists?'

Guilt jabbed her, the sensation uncomfortable. The first time she'd seen the women in the garden she'd silently called them the same thing.

'They're just mums like me. You should see them with Milo—'

'Have you lost your fuckin' mind?' Corey's chair shot back, scraping against the lino. He was on his feet, pressing his hands down on the table, biceps bulging and the veins on his forearms throbbing. 'You've let them touch *my* son?'

'I …' Jade's mind spun and slowed at the same time, trying to choose words that wouldn't detonate a fast-ticking bomb. 'No. Of course not.'

'Good. You and me are the ones who look after him. Don't ever forget that.'

Except you're hardly here and when you are you ignore him.

The resentful thought shocked her. It wasn't Corey's fault there wasn't much work for him in Boolanga. Of course he had to follow the jobs, just like she had to take care of Milo.

'I know,' she said. 'It's up to us to keep him safe.'

'Yeah. So don't go to that garden again.'

The pronouncement prickled like a burr and her forefinger rubbed a rough cuticle on her thumb until it stung. She valued Corey's opinion and she understood where he was coming from. Hell, she felt uncomfortable—edgy—when the women talked in their own language. She hated not understanding what they were saying, wondering if they were talking about her.

Mind you, the bitches from Baby Time had never verbally trashed her to her face, but she'd caught some of them exchanging looks that spoke as loud as words. These strange women at the garden, who covered everything except their face and hands, had never sneered at her—not even when she hadn't wanted to try their food. And when she'd eaten the bolanis, they'd been excited and happy. Wasn't that being kind? And they genuinely loved Milo. Today, they'd passed him between themselves, entertaining him and giving her a break so she could do some planting. Just be Jade. For the first time in this stinking hole of a town she hadn't felt judged. She'd felt welcomed.

Welcomed by refugees—the people she was supposed to hate. It was confusing. How did she even start to try to explain it to Corey when she didn't understand it herself? If Corey didn't want her to go to the garden, she shouldn't go. But loneliness already filled so many hours in her week that just the thought of not returning cramped her stomach as bad as period pain.

Wanting to banish the ache, she grabbed his hands. 'Let's do something.'

'Good idea. We can screw while the kid's asleep.'

This was what Corey did every time he came home. He ate, they had sex and then if he didn't go to the pub to meet Macca, they watched TV. It wasn't like she was unfamiliar with the routine—it had been happening for a couple of years. But for reasons not entirely clear to her, today she wanted more. She wanted to feel like they were a family—like the people she saw when she walked to the park or along the river.

'Okay, but when Milo wakes up, let's go to Warrabeen Lagoon. You can light a fire and we can cook some snags and—'

'I'm meeting Macca.'

'Why?' It came out on a whine.

His blue eyes darkened. 'I need more lightbulbs so I can finish Cobram.'

Disappointment choked her. 'Lightbulbs? I thought you were lamb-marking at Conargo?'

'Doing this job for Macca first.'

Which meant he hadn't been out of mobile range in the back-blocks of New South Wales. He would have got her texts. Known Milo was sick.

He was busy with work.

Corey put a bottle on the table. 'I had a win on the pokies so I bought you some Jack.'

She'd have preferred cash, but soon after Milo was born she'd learned that asking for money meant she got squat. It was better to wait and receive random gifts. At least there was a black market at Tranquillity Park. 'Thanks.'

'Anything for you.' He tweaked her boob and gave her a gentle push towards the bedroom. 'Things are going great, Jade. This job's clean and easy. I'm done by four most days.'

A whoosh of anger flared as high and fast as a lit match hitting lighter fluid, scorching her from head to toe. 'Done by four' meant Corey could have driven back to Boolanga one night and helped her. He could have given her a break from a constantly crying baby.

Her feet stalled just inside the bedroom door. 'Do you love me and Milo?'

'What sort of a dumb shit stupid question is that?' He pulled off his shirt and shucked his pants, dropping them next to the laundry basket. 'Would I be here if I didn't?'

For the first time, Jade had no idea how to answer that question.

CHAPTER

10

The rain hit at five o'clock and it hadn't let up, making it an unusually slow night at the café. That was the big difference between Melbourne and living in Sun Country—up here the locals weren't used to heavy rain. At the first sign of precipitation, people stayed in rather than venturing out.

'You want to take some lamb, Helen?' Con had switched off the rotisserie and was carving the meat. 'You could freeze it or have a party with your garden mates.'

'Is it okay if I take the tzatziki too?'

'Have at it. It'll just end up in the bin. And take those six bottles of iced tea too.'

'Thanks, Con.'

Having a hunch about the weather, Helen had harvested some lettuces and tomatoes before her shift just in case. If there was anyone at the park tonight—and it was likely, given homelessness didn't offer the luxury of staying in on a wet night—she'd be able to provide them with a warm and healthy meal.

When she arrived at Riverbend, the rain had thankfully eased to an annoying drizzle and there were three cars in the car park. She recognised one of them and swore. It looked like things between Roxy and her adult daughter had broken down yet again.

Helen made three trips from the car before lighting the gas barbecue for both heat and to warm the pita bread. Thankful for the undercover picnic area, she spread a cloth, set the table and arranged the containers of meat and salad. Then she opened the drinks box that contained mugs, tea and coffee, hot chocolate, sugar and UHT milk.

There was also a specimen vase in the box and she added a couple of daisies for the centre of the table. Checking she had everything, she warmed herself some bread and made herself a souvlaki. Then she sat, knowing it would encourage Roxy to leave her car and join her.

As she ate, she flipped through the *Good Weekend*. She had a stack of them in the car—a habit left over from when it had been her home. The magazine could be read, sat on as protection from a damp seat, used to start a fire, and spread out as an extra layer of insulation on cold nights. These days Helen thankfully only read it, although last week she'd scrunched a few pages around her soup pot to keep the contents warm on the way to the park.

She was fully absorbed in an article when she heard footsteps. She glanced up with a smile, expecting Roxy. Her face fell. 'Bob? What are you doing here?'

Even to her own ears, it sounded rude and she wished he hadn't caught her by surprise. Wished she could have been quicker to hide her disappointment that he wasn't Roxy. Then again, social niceties had never been her strength.

Bob shrugged and tousled his dog's ears. 'Thought in this get-up it was pretty obvious.'

That's when she noticed he was wearing a handknitted woollen beanie, rain jacket, fishing overalls and rubber boots. An old cane fishing basket hung from his shoulder and he was carrying a rod and a small esky.

'Why are you fishing in this weather?'

'The yellowbelly go crazy in the rain. Plus, I pretty much get the river to myself so it's win-win as they say.' He glanced at the table groaning with food. 'Did the weather put off your friends?'

She ran with his assumption—it was less complicated. 'They're always a bit free and easy with time.'

'Do you mind if I cook my fish on the barbie?'

It was a public barbecue so even though he'd asked, saying no wasn't an option. But if Bob stayed and cooked, would Roxy remain in her car?

'I'm happy to share,' he added, obviously sensing her reticence.

'It's not so much that ...' How did Helen even start to explain without giving away Roxy's situation and breaking her confidence? She couldn't so she swallowed a sigh. 'Fresh fish sounds delicious.'

'Let's hope. Some cooks say it's better to put yellowbelly on ice for twenty-four hours, but back in the day people fished and ate the catch straight away. I reckon the key is filleting out the fat, using a splash of olive oil, some fresh black pepper and a lemon.' Bob whipped out a parcel wrapped in aluminium foil.

Helen laughed. 'Something you prepared earlier?'

'The rangers get shirty if you fillet up here so I did it down at the river.' He carefully placed the foil packet on the silver hotplate and checked his watch.

The border collie ambled over, gave Helen a smile and settled at her feet, his weight pressing against her shins. Helen felt her resistance to the animal weaken. 'What's his name?'

'Daisy. You okay with her there? She's getting on and always goes for the warmth.'

'It's a good trade of heat.'

'Until she gets too heavy.' He smiled. 'Do you want me to do the farmers' market again this week?'

After the debacle at the garden, Bob had ended up running the market stall on his own while she'd been putting out spot fires. 'It's not rocket science,' he'd said. 'I've got it sorted. You go and do your politicking.' So she had, spending hours on the phone. She'd called as many of the community garden plot holders as she could, extolling the benefits of both the farmers' market and the garden extension. But Judith had also been calling the members and about half of them sided with the president. The only bright spot was Tara Hooper's offer of sponsorship.

Helen's stomach suddenly lurched. In the busyness of the previous fortnight, had she actually thanked Bob for stepping in?

'Thanks for helping out. I appreciate it.'

'Too easy,' he said. 'Happy to do it again. I've got a bumper crop of spring onions and silverbeet I can add to the mix.'

'That's kind, but I haven't had many offers from the members. Dot's support didn't transfer from in-principle to practical, although Terri Morton promised rhubarb. I suppose I could bundle up some asparagus and zucchini, but is it really worth the time?'

'Big things have small beginnings. A man who moves a mountain begins by carrying away small stones.'

Helen tried not to roll her eyes at the quotes, thankful this time he'd stopped at two.

Bob's mouth curved into a self-deprecating smile. 'More to the point, I enjoyed myself.'

'Well, if it's something you want to do ...'

'I thought it was something you wanted to do.'

'It was.'

'But?'

Things had changed since she'd first mooted the idea of the stall. Now she was helping the Hazara women establish their garden as well as waiting for the shire's response to her tiny houses submission. The moment the project got the green light, her time would be consumed by the steering committee.

Bob's eyes—still bright and vivid for a man his age—were fixed on her, waiting for an answer. She didn't like depending on anyone—people invariably let her down—but at the same time she didn't want to be perceived as flaky. It was unusual for her to say she'd do something then not follow through.

'I'm sorry I can't be more specific, but there's an important project on the horizon. It's still under wraps, but when it happens it will be big. It means my time will be spread very thin.'

'Fair enough.' Bob flipped the fish parcel over. 'What if you and I do the stall together until you get too busy? That way you can teach me the ropes. You know, stuff like who's who on the market committee and all the protocols. Then you can leave knowing the stall's in capable hands.'

She reminded herself that Bob had only ever been helpful and this was a reasonable and sensible suggestion—one she should accept. But knowing that didn't make it easy to change years of protective behaviour.

'Only if it's something you really want to commit to.'

Bob laughed. 'There's no hardship in spending a Saturday morning chatting to people. Besides, it would be good to show Judith and the committee that it's a viable extension of the garden during times of surplus.' He slid the fish parcel onto a plate and sat down opposite Helen. 'I want your opinion on the fish.'

'It smells good.'

'That's a start.'

Another car arrived and parked a few spaces away from Helen's. When the occupant got out, Roxy joined her and together they walked to the pavilion. Helen didn't know the other woman but she waved.

'Hi, Roxy. Glad you could make it. Fancy some lamb?'

'Or fish.' Bob, all old-fashioned manners, rose and disentangled himself from the picnic seat.

'Roxy, this is Bob Murphy,' Helen said.

'Pleased to meet you.' Bob extended his hand. 'Hope it's okay that I've gatecrashed your picnic.'

'You and me both, Bob.' The unknown woman seated herself next to him. 'I'm Cinta.'

'The more the merrier, I always say. Right, Helen?' Roxy slid in next to her with all the aplomb of an invited guest.

'Absolutely.' Helen played along, honouring Roxy's dignity. 'Any idea if the others are coming? I've overcatered.'

'Give it ten. I sent out some reminder texts.'

Helen relaxed. Roxy hadn't stayed in the car because of Bob's presence, but because she was spreading the word of the unexpected feast on a wet night.

The women made a fuss of Daisy while Helen heated up the pita. Bob urged the women to eat the fish and the conversation turned to the many benefits of omega-3 oils including how they slowed the decline of brain function.

'So that's why I struggle with the cryptic crossword,' Cinta said. 'Not enough fish.'

Bob laughed. 'I've eaten fish all my life and the cryptic still stumps me.'

Tracey arrived with Agape, whose eyes lit up at the food. 'Halal snackpack!'

'Almost. No hot chips, sorry.'

'Don't be sorry, Helen. This looks amazing.'

Tracey sat down, pumped some hand sanitiser, spread a paper serviette across her lap and then loaded her plate with meat and salad.

As they ate, they talked and the topics ranged far and wide, from the weather to the federal government's latest out-of-touch-with-the-people stuff-up to conspiracy theories and the hike in the cost of petrol.

'Can I get anyone a cuppa?' Bob asked.

'If there's no Bundy, I guess tea will have to do,' Tracey said.

'Actually …' Bob pulled an old and battered pewter hip flask out of his fishing basket. 'There's enough whiskey in here to make everyone an Irish coffee.'

Tracey lifted an enamel mug out of the drinks box. 'I like the way you think, Bob.'

While Bob made the drinks, Roxy stared out into the dark. 'I love this place at night,' she said. 'The frogs are serenading their lovers, the possums are thumping and grunting, and the river rushes or glides, depending on the rain.'

'Enjoy it while you can,' Cinta said. 'Once the Chinese arrive, we'll be sitting under floodlights, dodging bullets as they shoot deer or ducking golf balls from night golf.'

Bob laughed. 'I don't have a problem with anyone shooting feral deer, but night golf in Boolanga? That sounds a bit far-fetched.'

Helen, who'd worked hard all evening to keep her mouth closed during most of Cinta's conspiracy theories and unsubstantiated conjectures, lost her battle to stay silent. 'The resort rumours come out to play every year. Even if there's a proposal kicking around somewhere, the shire's been rejecting them for decades. They're not going to sell to the Chinese or anyone else.'

'What makes you so certain?' Cinta asked belligerently.

'It's always been community land. Your frogs are safe, Roxy.'

'That's good to know.'

The other women were savouring their almost-Irish-coffee treat and didn't comment.

'What proposal?' Bob asked.

Damn it. The man didn't miss a trick. 'Nothing specific. I was speaking in general terms.'

His head tilted as if he didn't believe her. 'This place is special to me and my family and to a lot of folk in the district. After the Great War, my grandfather worked on the experimental farm. He proposed to my grandmother under that tree over there.' He lifted his arm to indicate the largest river red gum. 'My father got caught up in the next nightmare and was starved by the Japs. He brought home malaria as a keepsake and met my mother.

'Growing up, all I wanted was a dad who'd kick the footy with me, but he'd have bouts of fever that put him in bed for days. But the moment he was up and about, the first thing he'd do was bring me here. In Changi, it was memories of the river that kept him going. The way the morning mist hovers just above the surface and how the pelicans glide regally out of the fog, barely stirring the water.' Bob tapped the hip flask. 'This was his, and this park is his part of the river. I scattered his ashes here. Wouldn't mind if I ended up here either.'

'You'd better tell your kids that's what you want,' Helen said briskly, embarrassed she'd been so entranced by the story she'd leaned in.

'Pen and I were never blessed that way.'

Bob's general easygoing persona faded and for the first time Helen glimpsed sadness circling him—old and worn but still with the capacity to bite. A familiar tug pulled on her own grief and she quickly glanced down at her coffee, trying to halt the rising melancholy.

'Lucky for me I've got a much younger sister and a terrific nephew,' Bob said, sounding brighter. 'Still, I'm hoping Debbie and Lachie won't have to do the job for a long time yet.'

'Amen to that.' Tracey raised her mug. 'Any chance of seconds?'

After the women had drifted to the river to smoke, Bob said, 'Your friends are an eclectic bunch.'

'They are.' It was the easiest answer to avoid further comments.

'Cinta's conspiracy theories must test you though.'

'Everyone's got their idiosyncrasies.'

'Hah! True, but in Cinta's case, I think there's some mental health issues at play as well.'

Helen opened her mouth to object, but Bob hooked her gaze and said firmly, 'I fish here a lot, Helen. Tonight's not the first time I've shared a hot drink with Tracey.'

'So you know?'

'That they're likely homeless? I had a fair idea. It's bloody sad.'

Helen wasn't often lost for words but she was fighting to find any in a roiling sea of emotion. Bob had sat down and eaten with these women, treating them with respect and dignity without once giving away that he knew their circumstances.

'Thanks for being kind,' she managed.

'Kindness doesn't cost a thing.' But he squirmed, clearly uncomfortable. 'But it isn't practical, like you throwing a dinner party. To be honest, I've wanted to do more, but had no idea where to start. Giving Tracey booze probably isn't helpful.'

'Oh, I don't know. On a cold wet night, whiskey's a warming balm. Don't let your WASP morals get tangled up with practical help.'

He laughed—a joyful rumbling sound that echoed around the park. 'With a name like Murphy, I'm no more Protestant than the Pope. Mind you, I'm far more lapsed than he is. Give me the great outdoors over a church every time.' He lifted Helen's esky and placed it on the table. 'I'm guessing there's no point offering them any leftover food when they can't refrigerate it.'

'Got it in one.'

'So how long have you been sharing your food?'

'It's not actually my food, but twice a week for the last year I've brought leftovers from the café.'

His forehead creased. 'That long? How come this is the first time I've seen you?'

'I rotate through the parks on both sides of the river. Although as you can see, word gets around. If they can afford the petrol, they come and find me.'

'Only women?'

'Yes.'

'Isn't that a bit sexist?'

Her jaw tightened and she counted to five. 'I'm not defending my decision. It is what it is. I won't turn a man away, but given how it's usually men who've played varying roles in putting most of these women in their current situation, they prefer dinner to be a testosterone-free zone.'

'What do you mean by varying roles?'

'When a relationship breaks down, especially if violence is involved, then it's the women who are forced to flee and leave everything behind.'

'Sounds like it was an honour for them to include me tonight,' he said.

He kept surprising her. 'When you turned up I was worried Roxy would send out the word to the others to stay away.'

'Ah! So that's the reason you didn't greet me with open arms.'

'Yeah, right. Tell yourself that.'

Bob's eyes crinkled up as a grin wrote itself across his face and then he winked at her.

With a stomach-dropping thud, Helen realised he'd misconstrued her reply as flirting. God! Had she flirted? No. She hadn't flirted in a thousand years and even then she hadn't been any good at it. Besides, she was close to sixty. Did people their age even flirt? Of course they didn't. Anyway, she was too busy surviving and helping others to do the same.

Studiously ignoring the wink, she focused on rinsing out the cups before stacking them inside the plastic box and snapping down the lid.

'So how many homeless people do you reckon we have in Boolanga?' Bob asked, eventually breaking the silence.

'It's a transient population so it's hard to say. But certainly more than the town's limited emergency housing can accommodate.'

'So it would be good to offer food on more nights?'

'There's a need.'

'I'd like to help if I could. I don't reckon I'm too old to dumpster dive.'

'You've heard about dumpster diving?' She couldn't hide her incredulity.

'I read *The Age* and listen to ABC Radio, Helen,' he said mildly. 'I've heard about the food waste and, as the young ones say, "I know stuff".'

Helen smiled despite herself. 'They say that, do they?'

'My nephew Lachie does.' He grinned again. 'Anyway, my point is, do we source more food so we can offer it on more nights?'

We? 'The food's appreciated but it's a stop-gap measure,' she said. 'The important thing is stable and affordable housing. When we get that right, everything else falls into place.'

'Crikey.' He ran his hand through his hair, which was remarkably thick for a bloke his age. 'Where do you even start with something like that? The local MP? State or federal?'

'It's a combination of local council and state government.'

'Sounds like you know a thing or two about it.'

'I do.' She wasn't prepared to confess knowing homelessness herself, but after all the months working on the submission, she had an overwhelming need to share her vision. And Bob ticked all the boxes of being understanding, non-judgemental and wanting to make a difference. 'You know that important project I said was under wraps?'

'The one that will spread your time thin?'

She nodded. 'It's a sustainable tiny housing project for women over fifty-five.' And before he could query the gender, she said, 'For a heap of reasons, they're the fastest-growing homeless demographic.'

'And this is the plan you mentioned the shire has for the old experimental farm?'

Helen had never met a bloke who listened like Bob. 'I'm hoping so. I'm still waiting to hear officially but Vivian Leppart's confident. The land around the cottage is included in the plan and it will connect the village to the existing community garden. Each resident who wants a plot will have one.'

'Something this big usually gets run up the local rag's flagpole in the planning stages. Why haven't I read anything about it before now?'

'Softly, softly, catchee monkey,' she quoted back at him. 'There's a lot of behind-the-scenes politicking. I've been working with the female councillors and they're working on the men. Once we have the votes and the land's officially ours, we'll run a community awareness program outlining the benefits to Boolanga.'

'Hmm …' He rubbed his jaw. 'You might find yourself up against some opposition.'

'We live in a democracy and people are free to object, but at the end of the day, the shire doesn't need the community's permission to use the land. We're not building close to any existing structures or affecting traffic flow and we're not a greedy corporation. We're building a small and tasteful housing project to alleviate a social problem. It ties in perfectly with the historical use of the land.'

The women's voices were now audible as they approached the pavilion and anxiety stirred Helen's gut. She'd gone out on a limb trusting Bob and although most of her didn't regret it, old habits die hard.

'Don't discuss the project with anyone until after it's announced, okay?'

'Not even with you?'

'Not around flapping ears.'

'Fair enough.' He tapped his nose. 'Your project's as safe as houses.'

'It'd better be.' She turned and greeted the women. 'I've got some strawberries. Anyone want to take some with them?'

CHAPTER

11

Tara checked the time, feeling her frustration escalating until she was tapping her fingers on the store's information desk.

Leanne Gordon, pushing a trolley loaded with boxes of nails, paused on her way past. 'What's giving you frown lines now? I thought the police had been and said it was kids?'

'They have and they did.' The shop had been broken into again and this time the target was spray cans. Denny North had told them to expect another spate of street graffiti as if that hadn't occurred to them. 'Jon set up an appointment for me with Vivian Leppart, but she's late and I've got another meeting.'

Leanne snorted. 'You mean lunch?'

Leanne had worked for Hoopers for twenty-five years and what she didn't know about the stock wasn't worth knowing. But the usefulness of her vast knowledge was offset by an abrasive personality.

Tara forced herself to laugh, allowing Leanne to think she was going to lunch with the girls instead of a training session with

Zac. Jon would have a pink fit if she rescheduled Vivian for a gym session, but if the deputy mayor didn't arrive in two minutes, she'd risk his wrath.

'Tara!' Vivian's high heels clacked on the concrete floor as she strode towards her. 'How are things?'

'Could be better. We got broken into again last night.'

'I'm sorry to hear that. Surely the police have got some leads by now?'

'Theories but no leads. And to add insult to injury, our insurance company's insisting we install CCTV.' She almost added, 'The shire needs to light the car park,' but stopped. There was a time and a place, and today Vivian was a valued customer, not a councillor.

Vivian handed her phone to Tara. 'I need you to order these.'

Tara studied the photo. It wasn't often she coveted things but these intricate sea green, glass Italian tiles put her own bathroom in the shade. 'These are incredible.'

Vivian beamed. 'Aren't they? I saw them years ago in a gorgeous little hotel on the Amalfi Coast and I've been determined to have them ever since. Mind you, they're not cheap. I've had to delay the renovation to save up for them.'

'It will be so worth it.'

'I can't wait!'

'You might have to,' Leanne said drily. 'Unless our Melbourne supplier has any in the back of his warehouse, they'll be coming from Italy by ship.'

'That would be worst case scenario,' Tara said quickly, wishing Leanne had a clue about customer service. 'Don't worry, Vivian. We'll contact every supplier in all the capitals before we order overseas.'

'Thanks, Tara. I've spent the last five years scrimping and saving and putting up with that god-awful 1970s' mission brown décor so

I can do this extension properly. I'd hate for bathroom tiles to hold things up.'

Tara calculated the nice profit Hoopers Hardware, Timber and Steel had already made from Vivian's determination to 'do it properly' and continued to stroke her ego. 'You've worked hard. You deserve this.'

'I do. Unlike the mayoress.'

It was no secret Vivian detested Sheree Rayson. Even if she hadn't, the entire town was jealously agog at the mayor's purchase of Ainslea Park, a stunning agistment property and riding school that came with a luxury home. The purchase had surprised everyone and Tara struggled to imagine the mayor, an overweight accountant, on a horse. But perhaps Ainslea Park was Sheree's passion. Tara didn't know either of the Raysons well enough to comment. But she did know the key to staying in business in a small town was to never badmouth one customer to another.

She smiled at Vivian. 'With these tiles, not to mention the incredible view from your new balcony, *Country Living* will want to feature the house for sure.'

After a day of dealing with police and difficult customers, a fraught dinner with her tired and grumpy children and an argument with Jon, Tara was thankful it was book club night. She'd been glad of the excuse to escape Tingledale, even if it was for Monique's overstuffed McMansion inside a gated golf community on the other side of the river.

Monique passed around glasses of Russian vodka mixed with cranberry and pineapple juice. When everyone had a glass, she held up her own. '*Nostrovia*. Good health.'

'I'm pretty sure that means "let's get drunk", which is fine by me.' Kelly took a large mouthful of her cocktail.

'You can't get drunk until we've discussed the book,' Monique said firmly. 'Here, eat a cherry *pirozhki*.'

'You've really excelled yourself this time, Mon,' Rhianna said. 'Where's the Fabergé egg?'

The women laughed and Tara joined in despite her complicated mix of emotions. But the silky slip of vodka was helping as it unfurled its fire inside her, stripping away the tension that was as much a part of her as her skin. She adjusted herself on the couch, fighting for space among the cushions. Who needed this many? Tara didn't do cushions, and just as well, because this week they all would have been thrown at Jon's head.

At least Rhianna was here and not using book group as an excuse to meet Jon. Then again, Jon had vehemently denied having an affair with her. It had occurred to Tara since then that 'Are you having an affair with Rhianna?' was a closed question. A question Jon could answer truthfully. It didn't mean he wasn't seeing someone else and blaming all their problems on Tara to hide the affair.

She pushed away the agonising thoughts. Tonight was supposed to be a break from the mess that was her marriage. When Jon had asked her why she hadn't tackled the painting and decoration revamp at the store yet, she'd told him her new challenge was training for the marathon, hoping it would spark an argument that would end in make-up sex. She wasn't proud of her motivation—it felt like a tawdry last-ditch attempt to shock him into action—but she was desperate.

During the early years of their marriage when they were both working full-time, renovating a heritage-listed house and learning how to live together, they'd had some rip-roaring fights. Exhilarating sex always followed. More than anything, she'd wanted him to yell and pace and gesticulate wildly. Only he hadn't done any of those things. He'd just stared at her, his face a blank mask. It was like he'd lashed down all his emotions under a thick tarpaulin and reinforced it with a cargo net so none could escape. But the emotions were all there, quivering under the surface of the rigid stiffness of his body.

When he'd finally spoken, the words came out slowly, as if he was doing a controlled release of two at a time to prevent them spilling in a rush.

'You think ... that will ... make you ... happy?'

You coming back to me would make me happy. But what was the point of saying that? He'd decided their problems rested one hundred per cent with her and nothing she tried had changed his mind. Training with Zac was the only break she got from the suffocating weight of their marriage crisis.

Before she'd replied he'd added, 'I don't ... think so.'

'It will make me happy!' she'd screamed at his retreating back, furiously clutching onto her own anger so she wouldn't care she'd upset him. Hell, they couldn't even argue with passion any more. That gutted her as much as anything. If he couldn't be bothered to argue with her, did he even care?

She heard someone say her name and realised she'd completely tuned out of the conversation. 'Sorry?'

'Pay attention, Tara. We're talking about Anna,' Monique said brusquely. 'How she was her own worst enemy.'

'That's a bit harsh, isn't it?'

'No,' Kelly said. 'She was married with a kid. She shouldn't have even noticed Vronsky.'

Beth giggled. 'Well, I'm married but I'm not dead. When I pick up Duncan from footy training, I've been known to linger longer than strictly necessary.'

Tara ignored Beth. She was too busy focusing on Kelly's comment and feeling incensed on Anna's behalf. 'Of course Anna noticed Vronsky. Alexei was emotionally cold, preoccupied with his job and barely aware of her except when he collected her for bed. Even then he just fell asleep.'

'Sometimes I wish Jesse would just go to sleep.' Dana's eyes widened and her hand flew to her mouth. 'Oh, God. Forget I said that.'

'No chance.' Kelly's eyes sparkled, bright and eager.

Tara knew it wasn't entirely due to the vodka. Kelly's first love might be her phone, but her second was gossip.

'Please, can we focus on the book,' Monique said.

'You were the one who gave us vodka,' Rhianna said mildly.

'Vronsky made Anna feel alive. Don't we all deserve that?' Tara asked.

Kelly snorted. 'Oh, please! She was a selfish bitch and she deserved everything she got.'

'Nothing in life's that simple,' Tara said.

'It is if you've got self-control.'

'Her mistake was she didn't try very hard to hide the affair,' Erin said. 'If she had, she could have kept her son. And as long as she had sex occasionally with Alexei, he would have thought the baby was his.'

Every head in the room swivelled towards the woman whose opinions usually had to be wrung out of her. Had mousey Erin just admitted to an affair? The thought exploded in Tara's head—if Erin could hide an affair and Jon was hiding one too, then surely she could.

'That sounds like you're speaking from experience,' Rhianna said.

A pink flush raced up Erin's neck, spreading to her hairline, and her hands fluttered in her lap. 'No! Not me. God, the guilt would kill me. I'm talking about my great-aunt. On her death bed, she confessed to a twenty-year affair. We were gobsmacked. I mean, she'd worked alongside Uncle Phil on the farm for forty years, raised six kids and been both CWA and school council president.'

'Twenty years?' Monique said softly, momentarily distracted from keeping control of the group.

Erin nodded. 'She said her lover gave her things Uncle Phil couldn't.'

Tara understood. 'Like with Anna. The affair was about sex and feeling alive again.'

'Not exactly. Apparently Uncle Phil was great in bed, but he was a typical farmer and a man of few words. She said her lover gave her the intellectual stimulation she craved.'

Dana poured another cocktail. 'Has anyone had an affair?'

Tara made a note never to serve spirits when she hosted book group. But despite herself, she couldn't help glancing at Rhianna. The woman sat as serene and unruffled as ever, giving nothing away.

'Let's get back to the book,' Monique said firmly. 'Kitty and Levin—'

'Talking about affairs *is* related to the book,' Kelly said. 'Methinks you've got something to hide, Monique.'

'Oh, for heaven's sake! Do I look like I have time for an affair? I work full-time and I've got four kids if you include Hamish. Why are you giving me a hard time? It was Dana who asked the question and Beth who admitted to ogling the Boolanga Brolgas.'

Beth laughed. 'I'm just window shopping. It never hurts to take home a bit of fantasy to spice things up with Grant.'

'And Dana's already admitted she'd prefer less sex not more,' Kelly said with just a little too much enthusiasm.

'And Tara's on too much of a good thing with Jon to ever throw that away,' Rhianna said.

Tara's hand tightened around her glass. 'What's that supposed to mean?'

'Exactly that.' Rhianna's green eyes narrowed like a snake ready to strike. 'You have a husband who adores you and indulges your every whim.'

The cocktail sloshed in Tara's stomach, turning rancid. 'I don't.'

'The perks of sleeping with the boss,' Kelly muttered. She didn't add the usual 'joking!'

'Oh, come on, Tara. There's no shame in admitting your good fortune.' Rhianna's one-and-a-half-carat diamond flashed as she indicated the group. 'You're among friends.'

Was she though? She really only saw Monique, Dana and Beth at book group—she'd class them more as acquaintances than friends. And her friends in the room should be accepting of her, not demanding she justify the way she lived her life. Nothing about this scenario came close to being in a safe, non-judgemental space—it was an emotional warzone.

Fighting adrenaline, Tara tried to keep her voice steady. 'I'm as equally fortunate as you, Rhianna. Our husbands' businesses give us flexibility to work around the children. I see you at tennis on Tuesdays, at coffee on Wednesdays and at our bi-monthly lunches. How am I more indulged than you? Our lives are the same.'

Rhianna's brows rose. 'I'm not spending twenty hours a week exercising.'

'Neither am I.' Tara fisted her hand in her lap so she didn't reach out and slap Rhianna's sardonic cheek. *But at least I am exercising.*

Perhaps Rhianna read the thought on Tara's face, because her slightly overweight body flinched. 'Brent appreciates my love and support of him both at home and with the business. He doesn't want a trophy wife, and I know for a fact that neither does Jon. Just sayin' …'

The venomous words poured through Tara, locking her jaw. *I know for a fact.* How did Rhianna know? That night in their kitchen when she'd found Rhianna with her hand on Jon's arm, had he been complaining to her about Tara? Or had he confided in Brent who'd told Rhianna? And what had he confided? All scenarios horrified her and words crowded her mouth like arrows waiting to be fired. More than anything, she wanted to scream, 'If Jon thought I was a trophy wife, he'd be screwing me!' But there was no empathy or trust in this room. The truth would alienate her even more.

Erin broke the taut silence. 'These days, Anna would just get a divorce, right? Thank God for no-fault divorce.'

Monique threw Erin a grateful look. 'Divorce might not be the social scandal it was in Tolstoy's day, but women still lose more than men. Emotionally and financially.'

'My father buggered off, leaving Mum with me and my sister,' Dana said. 'He never paid her any maintenance and Mum's super is forty per cent of what the average bloke's is. She's worked hard all her life but, unlike him, she can't afford to take early retirement. Meanwhile, my bastard father's living in a million-dollar house on the Sunshine Coast.'

'Well, I've got no sympathy for pampered women who screw around on their husbands just because they're bored,' Kelly said. 'So Alexei wasn't romantic or demonstrative—whose husband is? She got what she deserved. End of story.' Kelly refilled her glass. 'So what's our next book?'

Tara almost said *Frenemies*.

CHAPTER 12

'So that's where things are at with the community garden.' Helen finished her report with a wry smile.

Vivian matched it. 'Wow! Poor you. That Judith's something else.'

'Thank goodness for Hoopers.' But Helen wasn't cadging for sympathy. 'The extension is all part of the tiny houses plan anyway, but I don't want people thinking of it as the "refugee garden" or the "housing garden". It's one big garden, serving the needs of our diverse community.'

Vivian nodded. 'Absolutely. It's a vital tool in building a cohesive community.'

'Any chance you could come and say those words to the committee?' Helen asked. 'Mention the model rules? Remind them that the garden's on shire land and it exists to reach the broader community regardless of age, gender or country of origin.'

'I can do better than that. I'll run a conflict resolution workshop for all the garden members and I'll give Parks a hurry-up on sending that letter to satisfy judgey Judith.'

'Thanks, Vivian. Sometimes I feel like I'm banging my head against a brick wall.'

'You're not. You're doing an amazing job with the garden and the park food. We're lucky to have you.' Vivian tapped her French nails on the folder Helen had delivered to her a few weeks earlier. 'I've read your submission.'

Helen's heart picked up. 'And?'

'Congratulations! It's a well thought out and beautifully executed document. It's got the perfect combination of heartfelt personal stories, stats and dollar amounts to soften the hardest bean-counter's heart.'

Relief and joy swept through her. 'So you think it's ready?'

'I do. Unfortunately, council isn't.'

Helen's euphoria evaporated, leaving a heavy weight pinned against her chest. 'But we've got four votes. You, Cynthia, Messina and the mayor.'

Vivian sighed. 'I won't lie to you. Geoff's withdrawn his support. I think he's pushing for another tilt at mayor and he's leery of aligning himself with anything that hints of controversy.'

'But this isn't controversial. We're not pulling anything down, and there's no existing housing so no neighbours to upset.'

'I know it and you know it, but we have to deal with the fact that men have a different approach to most things.'

Helen was familiar with the concept—marriage to Theo had taught her that much. 'I want to meet with the mayor but that secretary of his won't let me near him. Can you set it up?'

'I'll do my best, but pushing Geoff isn't the best way to make him change his mind.'

'You think I'd do more harm than good?'

'Please don't take this the wrong way ...' Vivian tucked some stray strands of her sleek ebony hair behind her ear. 'I find your enthusiasm refreshing, but I know these men. They like it best when they think something's their idea. We only need one more vote so we'll keep working on Don, Craig and Aki. Meanwhile, continue recording the numbers turning up to the park food nights. And why not talk to the bakery and the pub about their leftover food? You can apply for a community grant and formalise it. I'll happily support the application. All these things help sway opinion.'

Helen sank back in her chair. It wasn't the first time she'd been told she was like a dog with a bone. But if those men spent one night sleeping rough they'd understand. Perhaps she should suggest Boolanga had its own version of Sleep At The 'G.

'Chin up, Helen.' Vivian smiled encouragingly. 'We'll get there. Meanwhile, as we're still chasing votes, the important thing is to keep the submission under wraps. The last thing we need is *The Standard* getting hold of it and using it to light outraged fires in the community.'

Helen's stomach sank as she remembered telling Bob about the submission. She quickly reassured herself, recalling his promise to keep the information 'safe as houses'. The local press was far more of a risk than Bob.

She grimaced. 'You mean something like that article on the need for overhead lighting in the car park because of Boolanga's so-called African gang? I told Peter Granski he can't pass off rumour-mongering under the guise of investigative journalism.'

'And there's the problem,' Vivian said. 'The traders on Irrigation Road are a powerful lobby group who spend a lot of money advertising with *The Standard*. Of course Peter supports their nonsense.'

Helen's nails dug into her palms. 'But it's not like we're building a jail or a toxic waste dump. No one has any reason to be upset by the project.'

Vivian sighed. 'Never underestimate the public, Helen. We don't want our progressive housing project to be burned to ash before we've even started.'

The thought sent horror scudding through her. 'Mum's the word.'

Jade had done what Corey had asked—she hadn't gone near the garden. If she didn't count the checkout chick at Foodworks or the bloke on the end of the phone at Centrelink, the only person she'd had a real conversation with in days was Fran at the library.

When Jade saw seven shiny copies of a book called *Anna Karenina* on the returns shelf, she'd asked, 'Is this a new release?'

'No, it's a classic.'

Jade was whipped back to her senior school years and Mrs Kastrati. The English teacher often banged on about the classics and life's lessons. More than once she'd said, 'Jade, if you'd bother to apply yourself, you're very capable of going to university,' as if that softened the blow of the returned essay covered in red ink.

Fran picked up the book and hugged it like a teddy. 'The first time I read *Anna*, I was at university and I fell in love. I've read it about ten times since.'

Jade stared at the thick hardback. 'How many pages?'

'Eight hundred.'

'Eight. *Hundred?*' She'd never read anything that length.

Fran smiled. 'I promise it's such a great story, it doesn't seem that long. It was originally published in instalments in a magazine.'

'Like *The Middletons?*' Her mother had always gone straight to the serial story in *Yours* magazine.

'Pretty much. Tolstoy wrote about the lives of rich Russian families. Even though it was written over a hundred years ago, not a lot's changed. We still experience the agonies of falling in and out of love. We still have money problems. We try to do our best but make lots of mistakes, and we spend our lives trying to work out who we are and how we fit in the world. Sadly, just like in Tolstoy's time, too many people are still living with the threat of war and poverty.' Fran tapped the book. 'It's still very relevant. You should read it.'

Jade was sceptical. 'I don't think I could finish it in three weeks.'

'I'll just keep renewing it for you until you've finished. The Russian names can be a bit confusing at the start, especially as everyone has a formal name and an informal one, but I'll photocopy the family tree for you. That way you won't need to keep flipping to the front of the book to check who's who.'

Jade had regretted asking about the novel, but with Fran pushing the book and the photocopy at her, it felt rude not to accept. As she walked home, she'd felt the weight of an unwanted obligation in the pram basket. She probably wouldn't have started reading it except the power went out. Without the TV for company, she'd opened the book, surprised at how easy it was to read even with the Russian names. When her head-torch batteries had died, she'd yelled into her pillow.

Now, it was killing her not to read ahead—twice she'd had to claw her fingers back a hundred pages. She loved the excitement that pulsed between Anna and Vronsky but sensed things wouldn't end well. And Kitty frustrated her so much! Why couldn't she see how much Levin adored her? But even with the companionship of the big book, Jade was going stir-crazy without adult conversation.

Sunshine poured into the living room, calling her to the community garden, but she had a gnawing suspicion deep in her gut that if she gave in and went, Corey would turn up. He hated it when she wasn't home to greet him and she didn't want to lie to him.

Corey had been gone four days. Over the previous eighteen months, she'd learned by a process of deduction that if he was working on a farm he was absent around twelve days before returning for two. But this lightbulb installation job was different so there was a chance he'd be home today or tomorrow. Or not. Experience had taught her if she asked when he was coming home he was always vague on details. If she texted him the question, he ignored it. A few months earlier she'd concluded that asking delayed his return so she'd stopped.

She rubbed the broken skin on her cuticle, welcoming the smart. 'Stuff it!'

She brought up a new message for Corey and typed *I'm lonely.* Well, it was the truth. *When are you coming home? Miss you so much!* Then she added a string of kiss and heart emojis. Corey hated emojis.

'There's no way Daddy's coming home today, kiddo. Let's go.'

Anticipation sliced three minutes off her usual walk time, but Jade's bubbling excitement flattened like stale lemonade when she arrived and found the garden empty. Tears prickled and she blinked fast. What the hell was wrong with her? She didn't cry over shit like this.

She cuddled Milo, kissing his chubby cheeks, then said brightly as much for herself as for him, 'Look what Mummy planted.'

She squatted down. The chives were clumping and thickening nicely and the soil was damp. The women must have been here recently, but even so there were snails snuggling up to the tender new leaves on the tomato seedlings. She tossed the marauders out of the bed, planning to stomp on them. After that, she probably should go to the cottage and return Helen's gloves.

'G'day.' It was the bloke from the farmers' market and an old dog with a friendly face.

She stood up. 'I'm allowed to be here.'

'I'm sure you are.' He extended his hand. 'I'm Bob.'

Old codgers didn't usually offer to shake her hand. She couldn't remember shaking anyone's hand since she'd won the reading prize at school in year nine. She hesitated for a second then slid her hand into his for a quick shake, pulling it away fast. 'Jade.'

'And who's this little fella?'

'Milo.' She looked at her feet then, unsure of what to do or say next.

'Which bed is yours?'

'I don't have one.' In case he questioned her on why she was here she added, 'But I helped plant this one.'

'Good for you.'

She checked his craggy silver-stubbled face for signs he was taking the piss. But he was smiling at her as if he was pleased for her. Or pleased she'd helped.

'Are you thinking of getting your own bed?' he asked.

'Not if you can't grow flowers.'

'Who said you can't grow flowers?'

'Helen.'

He frowned. 'Are you sure she said the words "you can't grow flowers"?'

Something about the way he asked the question made her reluctantly revisit her conversation with Helen. 'She said, "I can't eat flowers." And I said, "You can." Some anyway.'

His frown lifted. 'I think she was talking about herself rather than a decree on what you can and can't plant. If you want to grow flowers, you can grow flowers. The only rules are that you look after the plot and keep it neat and tidy. Don't let the weeds take over.'

Eagerness fizzed in Jade at the thought of growing dahlias, gerberas and sunflowers. 'Can I have my own patch?'

'I don't see why not. We just have to run it past Helen first.'

Dejection swooped in. 'I don't think she likes me.'

He gave her a conspiratorial wink. 'Sometimes I feel the same way.'

Jade laughed. 'Does she boss you around too?'

'Little bit. I know she can be a bit spiky, but she's fair. If you really want a bed, I'm sure she'll allocate you a space.' He started walking and when she didn't follow he turned back. 'Come on.'

'Where?'

'To find Helen.'

Her heart beat faster. She didn't share Bob's confidence that Helen would welcome her into the garden. 'Um ... maybe another day.'

'Nothing ventured, nothing gained, Jade. There's no time like the present. *Carpe diem.*'

What did fish have to do with it? 'Carpe what?'

'Seize the day. It's Latin. Horace was a Roman poet and he said something like "Time is fleeing, seize the day and put no trust in the future".'

Jade had never really trusted the present let alone the future. 'So it's an old dude's way of saying "Just do it"?'

'Smart girl. Exactly that.'

And although she knew she should be wary of strangers who gave her compliments, especially men—young, old or otherwise—she followed him and his dog.

Helen had just arrived home from her meeting with Vivian when she heard a knock on the front door. No one ever used the front door. Then again, few people visited and she didn't have a problem with that. It was easier to stay private and keep the past where it belonged if she met people out in the world rather than inviting them into the cottage.

She tugged on the stiff front door and finally got it open to reveal Bob and Jade standing on the veranda. Astonishment made her blurt, 'You went home with my gloves.'

Jade's chin shot up. 'It was an accident. I tried to give them back to you at the farmers' market but you weren't there.'

'I doubt that's my fault, but thanks for returning them.' Helen held out her hand.

'About that ...' Bob's fingers kneaded the brim of his hat. 'If it's okay with you, can Jade hold onto the gloves for a bit? We've been having a bit of a yarn and she'd like her own plot. Wouldn't you, Jade?'

The girl's gaze fell to her feet before rising to Helen's face. 'Yeah. I wanna grow flowers.'

'Flowers are a one-day wonder,' Helen said stiffly. 'You'd be better off growing vegetables so your pension goes further.'

'True. Growing flowers from seeds and cuttings and enjoying the results is shockingly frivolous,' Bob said, his eyes twinkling.

Jade smirked and Helen got the message loud and clear—she was being too harsh. Again.

'If you have a garden plot, you do realise you'll have to come every couple of days to water and weed?'

'Well, duh.'

'If you lose interest, you lose the plot.'

'If I lose interest, I'll tell you I'm leaving.'

The comment surprised Helen and she had to concede it was far more honest than what she was used to from other garden members. In the last year, three members just stopped turning up, allowing weeds to overrun their beds. Protracted phone tag and uncomfortable phone calls followed, always with promises of 'I'm onto it. We'll do it this weekend'. Nine times out of ten they never showed up and Helen wasted her time issuing the three warnings required by the model rules before the plot could be assigned to the next person on the waiting list.

'Thank you, Jade. Being told upfront you no longer want the plot would be much appreciated.'

Jade's kohl-ringed eyes blinked at her, clearly startled. Helen's permanent irritation with the girl ran into uneasy and prickling guilt.

'We've had a donation of new gloves, so give me back mine and you can choose a pair that fits you better,' she said.

'You serious?'

'No, I just want my gloves back.' But the joke fell flat. 'Yes, I'm serious. I've just opened the box so you can have the first pair.'

She directed Jade to the box in the hall. When the girl had disappeared into the gloom, Helen stepped out onto the veranda so Bob didn't ask to come in.

'Thanks for this,' Bob said.

Helen still thought flowers were a waste of water and was annoyed that Bob was indulging a teenage fancy. 'Let's see if her enthusiasm survives a long hot summer.'

'She might surprise you.'

And pigs might fly.

Jade reappeared waving a pair of white and mauve gardening gloves. 'These are so cool!'

Helen was struck by how a pair of three-dollar gloves had lifted the semi-permanent scowl on Jade's face, revealing a pretty young woman. A very young woman.

Tendrils of care tried to cling but Helen sloughed them away. She had more than enough on her plate and, thankfully, Jade struck her as someone who could take care of herself.

CHAPTER

13

When Tara arrived home from the PFA meeting at the primary school, she was surprised to find Jon still up. For weeks he'd been going to bed early. Once she would have breezed in, kissed him on the cheek and cuddled up on the couch to regale him with tales of powerplays on the committee and how she and Shannon spent most of the meeting rolling their eyes. But that sort of relaxed intimacy was a casualty of the war that was their lack of a sex life.

'Hi,' she said to his back.

Jon didn't turn from staring out the large bay window into the dark. Nor did he comment on the fact she was home earlier than usual.

'Were there enough icy pole sticks to finish Flynn's homework project?' she asked.

Jon loved helping the kids with projects but she usually had to rein in his enthusiasm and remind him he was helping Flynn, not the other way around.

'Yeah. Done.'

His words came out on a staccato beat. She pictured a frustrated Flynn trying to get his hands on his own project.

'Are the kids okay?'

'The kids are fine.' He turned to look at her, his face lined with fatigue. 'We've got new neighbours.'

She crossed her fingers. 'The detailed Subaru?'

'That's the one.' He didn't sound as pleased as he had the first time he'd mentioned the car.

'You've met them?' she asked. 'Do they look more like our type of people than the last three?'

'I haven't met them but I've seen them. They're definitely not our type.'

Tara's stomach dropped. 'They can't be any worse than the flannel-shirted, dental disaster, pit-bull-owning, five-car-wrecks-in-the-yard neighbour.'

'They are.'

'How's that even possible? Lyle did time at Dhurringile.'

'They're African.'

Her mouth dried. 'It might not be so bad.'

'Hah! So far I've counted three kids and one of them's a teenage boy.' His throat worked. 'Jesus! Those bloody kids are giving me enough grief at work. I don't need them living next door. I'm moving the trampoline to the other side of the garden.'

Tara nodded her agreement, thinking about the group of black teenage boys she often saw around the railway crossing. Was the teen next door part of that gang? Would they hang out next door? Her ripple of anxiety peaked into a wave.

'Should we install a security system here as well as at the store?' she said.

'Already one step ahead of you. Darren's coming tomorrow.'

'Thank you.'

But her relief at the safety and peace of mind a security system offered didn't compensate for the fact Tingledale was losing its innocence. Still, hope zipped in under the crust of her resentment that had been thickening over the weeks. Jon was protecting her and the children, putting them first.

She laid her hand on his arm. 'I'm exhausted. You coming to bed?'

'Soon.' But he picked up the remote and turned on the television.

'Soon' meant at least an hour, which guaranteed she'd be asleep. The crust around her heart cured into a hard shell.

Two days later, Tara was with Zac at the five-station fitness park that was strung along the walking track by the river. They were doing a strength session as part of her marathon training. Tara understood the importance of leg presses and curls, walking lunges and calf raises to strengthen her legs. But chin-ups?

She stared at the bar above her. 'Why?'

'They're good for your core. They stabilise the spine so help reduce back injuries. Plus they're great for your grip.' Zac grinned. 'You won't need to ask your husband to open any jars for you.'

'Well, there is that.'

'Let's start on the lower bar so I can show you the correct position. The important thing is to hold your hands shoulder-width apart.'

Tara closed her hands tightly around the bar but all she could feel was Zac's body heat invading hers. It whipped through her, dominating every thought and igniting weeks of unsatiated need. Her pelvic floor clenched.

'Before you pull up, make sure you've pressed your legs together to maintain a strong midline.'

No problem there—her thighs were already pressed tight, enjoying the delicious tingles. With Zac's bulk behind her and his breath on her ear, longing raced across her skin, raising a shiver of goosebumps.

'You mean like this?' She leaned back and her body spooned against his as if they'd been designed to fit together. It felt amazing. He felt amazing. She wanted to stay there forever. The one tiny part of her brain not drenched in serotonin instructed *Move now!* But her body knew what it wanted and it didn't move a millimetre.

'That's the way,' Zac said. 'Now you lift.'

He stepped back, giving her room to position herself on the higher bar. A moan rose on a sea of disappointment, the sound shocking her.

'You've got this, Tara.' Zac misinterpreted her strangled sound as anxiety. 'Remember your hands and start with a dead hang.'

Focus. She hoisted her body's weight upwards. Her chin rose above the bar once, twice, thrice. Her arms screamed. Searing pain branded every cell, stealing oxygen and depositing burning lactic acid. 'Can't ... do ... Argh!'

Her fingers unfurled and she dropped, bending her knees to more easily take the fall. 'I hate chin-ups!'

'I never said they were easy.' Zac promptly did ten.

She watched his biceps bulge and the rise of blue veins as thick as rivers on his smooth olive skin and allowed herself to wonder what it would feel like to run her fingers along those strong toned arms. Then she imagined it.

He dropped to his feet and grinned. Her head spun.

'Show-off Gen Z brat,' she managed.

'Nah. Motivation.'

Tara struggled to cobble together a semblance of concentration. 'I think you're confusing your terms. How is me watching you do something I can't possibly do be motivation?'

'Inspiration then.'

She snorted. 'I don't think so. You know you're young, fit and buff and you enjoy flaunting it.'

'And you like watching me.'

The words hung there between them, like a line waiting to be crossed.

She wanted to hurdle it—say the words that would propel her onto the other side—but her mouth dried, sticking the sounds to her tongue.

'When I started chin-ups I couldn't even get my chin over the bar,' he said, the teasing glint in his eyes fading.

An ache throbbed under her ribs. 'That sounds like more schtick from the personal trainer's handbook.'

'Truth. I sucked at them, but your first time you did three.' He looked straight at her. 'You inspire me to inspire you.'

Her cheeks were suddenly wet, tears coming out of nowhere. She didn't know who was more shocked—her or Zac.

'Shit, Tara. Sorry. I didn't mean to upset you.'

She shook her head and, without a tissue, breathed in a rattly sniff. 'You didn't upset me. I don't know what's wrong with me.'

But she did know. The lukewarm distance that had entered her and Jon's marriage bed months ago was now cold and unambiguous. Jon didn't want to have sex with her and the pain of it threatened to swamp her.

Zac gave her a sideways look. 'I've got sisters …'

Wiping the tears away with the back of her hand, she laughed. 'Is that code for "Are you premenstrual?" And if it is, I can't decide if you're brave or foolish.' She sighed. 'I'm just tired.'

And sad. And angry. And frustrated. And I can't stop thinking about jumping you.

'Did you go see the dietitian I suggested?'

'Not yet.'

'Tara!'

'It's on my list.'

'Well, bump it up. It's serious. You have to eat the right amount of calories for all the running, and the right food to help your post-exercise recovery.'

For a moment she envied his life. How simple it must be to focus solely on himself.

Her watch beeped. 'I have to go or I'll be late.'

'No worries. I'm teaching a class in fifteen. See you tomorrow.'

Tara whipped home to shower before heading to school. Each week she spent an hour as a classroom helper listening to children read. She was halfway down the hall when the piercing siren of the security system slammed her heart against her chest.

'Bugger!'

She raced back to the controls and plugged in the numbers, silencing the alarm. Slumping against the wall, she tried to slow her racing heart, but when her phone rang it added to her jangles. It was the security company.

'Sorry! It was my fault,' she said. 'I totally forgot we had one.'

'No worries, Mrs Hooper. Everyone forgets at least once in the early days.'

'I won't forget again. It gave me a hell of a fright.'

Delaying her shower to make herself a steadying cup of tea, she was sipping it when she saw a black woman in the garden. Still under the control of adrenaline, she whipped open the door and marched out onto the deck.

'*What* are you doing?'

The woman glanced around, clearly startled. 'I heard the siren.'

'The alarm's supposed to keep people away not invite them in.'

The woman's hand rose to touch the colourful turban on her head before falling back to her side, but she kept her gaze on Tara. 'I am Fiza. Your new neighbour.'

Tara couldn't decide if the woman's lilting accent was French or something else, but it really didn't matter. What mattered was the fact she was standing uninvited in the garden.

'What were you planning on doing if the house was being burgled?' she said. 'Blind the thieves with your hot pink headscarf?'

Fiza's chin lifted. 'I would telephone the police.'

Tara scoffed. 'That's the point of the security system. Thank you, but we don't need your help.'

Fiza hesitated a moment, clearly debating whether to say something else. Tara was about to ask her to leave when she turned and crossed the garden to the old stile the Tingle children had used fifty years earlier.

Heritage listing be damned. Tara would ask Jon to dismantle the stile tonight.

CHAPTER
14

Jade carefully placed a box under Milo's pram, trying not to spill the contents. Bob had suggested she 'strike' some plants by shoving cuttings into jars of water and he'd even lent her his secateurs. She'd hidden them in case Corey came home and used them for cutting duct tape or prising open lids. She needn't have bothered—Corey hadn't been home in over two weeks.

Just as she was leaving for the garden, Macca arrived, marching into the unit as if he owned it. She'd never liked him. Once, he'd cornered her at the pub in Finley when Corey was in the men's, dropping his head in close and telling her what a slut like her deserved. Fear and fury had moved her, ducking her under his arms and away.

'Say stuff like that again and I'll tell Corey,' she'd hissed. 'He'll pistol-whip your skinny arse.'

Whether it was because she'd got pregnant soon after or Macca knew Corey was a crack shot, he'd never tried it on again. But he always treated her like she was a problem or she existed to pour him drinks and refill the chip bowl. Either way, she found it impossible to relax around him.

'That's not yours to take,' she objected as Macca unplugged Corey's PlayStation.

'It's not yours to keep.'

'Where is he?'

'Secret men's business.' He tapped his nose and leered, clearly getting off on the power trip.

She changed tack as he pushed past her to the door. 'You better bring it back before Milo's birthday. Corey wouldn't miss that.'

'You keep telling yourself that, sunshine.'

He slammed the door behind him and she jumped. Milo cried.

'Shh, buddy, it's okay. That horrible man's gone now and Daddy will be home for your birthday. He misses us. We miss him.'

You keep telling yourself that.

An unfamiliar sensation knotted her stomach, heavy and mocking. She did miss Corey. He missed them too. He loved them—she knew that. And the only reason he didn't text much or call was because he was busy.

On the walk to the garden, the knot loosened a little, but it didn't completely untie until she was standing in front of her garden bed. She still pinched herself it was hers. Lifting the cuttings carefully from under the pram, she checked the tiny white roots on a hydrangea, a geranium, a coleus and some Federation daisies. The day before, the supermarket had discounted a half-dead punnet of petunias and she'd haggled them down even further to a dollar, pointing out it was more than they'd get when they dumped them. Her plan was to lavish the annuals with TLC, liquid fertiliser and surround them with snail bait so they created a colourful border.

She moved a sleeping Milo into the shade, then pulled on the new gloves. Delight buzzed her as she flicked her wrist, admiring the way the gloves fitted her small hands.

Using the key Helen had given her, she opened the glossy black lock on the shiny silver shed. As she surveyed all the equipment and picked up a trowel and a watering can, she gave a whoop of joy. It echoed back to her. She was a member of the garden and allowed to use all this lovely gear.

Later, when she was lugging the watering can back from the tap, she saw a flash of fuchsia pink, royal blue and emerald green. A tall and slender woman was walking towards her, her face wreathed in a smile and her hand up in a wave. Jade's body involuntarily flinched, wary and curious at the same time. She'd never been this close to anyone so black.

'Hello.' The woman's teeth were brilliant white against her full dark lips. 'I am Fiza.'

Jade had expected a heavy and unintelligible accent, but Fiza was a lot easier to understand than the Hazara women. Just like them, she covered her head, but that's where the similarities stopped. The Hazaras' scarves were plain material, mostly black or white, that fell around their faces and covered their shoulders like the habits old nuns wore. But there was nothing plain about Fiza's scarf or the intricate way it was tied. Three shades of colour—hot fuchsia to barely pink—were braided together across the top of her head and wound in a knot that sat high like a crown. Fiza was tall, like the models in the *Vogue* magazine Jade had read at the doctor's, and the topknot was a flash of colour that made her stand out even more. How did she get it to stay on her head?

Fiza was staring back at Jade, her eyes full of questions. 'Do I have dirt on my face?'

Jade's cheeks heated and a spurt of anger got tangled with her embarrassment at being caught staring. 'Could I tell if you did?'

'Not as easily as I can see it on your face.' She pointed to Jade's left cheek. 'You have a smudge.'

'Oh, right. Thanks.' Jade wiped her cheek on her sleeve, prickling with surprise that the stranger had bothered to tell her. People a lot closer to her had allowed her to walk down the street with her dress tucked into her undies or, worse, with period blood staining her pants. She got a sudden urge to explain herself, which was weird, because she hardly ever did that unless it was demanded of her. 'I wasn't staring at you. I was trying to work out how you made that cool knot on your turban thingie.'

'It's not hard. You could do it.'

'Yeah, but I don't have to hide my hair.'

Fiza laughed. 'Not even on a bad hair day? It's a handy trick to know. My mother taught me, but you can learn from YouTube.'

'You're shitting me?'

'Lots of Muslim girls have their own Instagram accounts and YouTube channels for hair, make-up and fashion tips.'

Jade was still digesting this unexpected piece of information when Fiza said, 'I hope your new plants grow better than my maize.'

'What's maize?'

'It's like corn.'

Jade was on a fast learning curve about gardening with information from Bob and books Fran from the library had recommended. 'Did you test the soil before you planted?'

'I did everything the way my father taught me, but ...' Fiza's straight shoulders sagged. 'Perhaps I have been away too long. My maize is struggling and I don't know why.'

A wail came from the pram and Jade hurried over to unstrap Milo. 'Hey, buddy, did you have a nice sleep?'

'G'day, Jade.' Bob crossed the garden and ruffled Milo's sleep-damp hair. 'Hello, sport. You just wake up?'

Milo extended his pudgy arms towards Bob and his glasses. The man laughed, ducked and weaved. Squealing, Milo flung himself sideways and Jade had to tighten her grip.

Bob grinned. 'Want to come to Uncle Bob?'

The nice ones are always the pedos. Corey's warning sounded loud in her head and she hesitated, even though she didn't want to.

Bob was kind. He'd suggested she get her own garden bed and stuck up for her when Helen said she should grow vegetables. He'd even done most of the digging and given her advice whenever she asked. Unlike Helen, he didn't lecture her and he could take a joke. Not once had he asked her for anything. That niggled. Why hadn't he asked her for stuff? So she'd trust him with Milo? So he could hurt him?

Yes. No. Maybe …

Bob's smile had faded and he dropped his arms to his sides. 'Sorry, Jade. Didn't mean to make you feel uncomfortable.'

The same confusing feelings of anger and embarrassment that she'd got with Fiza shot back into place, only this time she didn't know if she was cross with Bob, Corey or herself.

'He might break your glasses and I can't pay for new ones.'

'No worries, love. I understand.' But the twinkle in his eyes had dimmed. He looked away, his gaze landing on Fiza. 'I'm sorry, I didn't see you there.'

Jade snorted. Fiza was almost six feet tall, black, dressed like a rainbow and impossible to miss. 'Jeez, Bob. Get your eyes tested.'

'I was being polite, Jade,' Bob said calmly. 'How about you introduce us.'

Jade was whipped back to school and Mrs Kastrati's useless lesson on how to introduce someone and give a thank you speech. Who did that?

She rolled her eyes and chanted, 'Bob, I'd like you to meet Fiza. Fiza, this is Bob.' An idea hit her. 'Hey, Fiza! Tell Bob about your sick maize. He's a farmer so he might know.'

Fiza shook Bob's hand. 'I am very pleased to meet you, Bob. Could you look at my maize? I am in need of advice.'

'Point me at it.'

They all walked up the hill to Fiza's plot. Purple and green plants Jade didn't recognise were growing well, but the bigger bed contained limp-looking seedlings with yellow-tinged leaves.

Bob squatted down and crumbled some soil in his hand. 'This looks like a good mix of dirt and compost and your kale and mustard leaves are certainly loving it. Do you know anyone who's grown maize here before?'

Fiza shook her head, the tiny crystals on her turban flashing silver in the sunshine. Milo clapped, delighted at the light show. 'I thought because it is hot here too, growing maize would be easy.'

Bob stood and dusted his hands on his work pants. 'Reckon it might get colder here at night than—where exactly?'

'Sudan.'

'Right. Don't know much about Sudan, I'm afraid. I milked cows for forty years and I grew a few crops to feed them but never maize. But my nephew, Lachie, works with crops. I'll get him to pop in. He might know where to start.'

'It is not too much trouble?' Fiza said.

'No trouble at all, love. Meanwhile, I've got one of those greenhouse tents in my shed. Let's erect it over these little battlers and see if they do better with a blankie, eh?'

Jade handed Bob back his secateurs, wishing she could see everything he had in his shed. 'What don't you have?'

His eyes dimmed again and Jade almost said, 'Sorry'. She stopped herself in time. It was dumb to apologise when she hadn't said or done anything to upset him.

Helen returned from her early morning riverside yoga, pulled the paper out of the letterbox and was walking down the drive when she heard the gurgles and squeals of a happy child. Her heart cramped like it did every time she heard the joyful sound.

Expecting to see one of the Hazara women, she walked through the trees and stopped short. 'You're here early.' It came out far more accusatory than she'd intended.

Jade looked up from her kneeling position, her mouth setting into a defiant line. 'It's not like I get to sleep in. Milo woke me up at five. And it's gonna be hot. Bob says there's no point watering in the middle of the day 'cos the plants wilt.'

'He's right.' Helen surveyed Jade's rag-tag plantings and swallowed a groan at the petunias and hydrangeas—such water-hogging plants. 'Peas have pretty flowers too, you know, *and* you can eat them.'

'Yeah, but they need to climb. I don't have anything for that.'

Helen thought about the decades of accumulated junk at the cottage. 'There's a broken bedhead you can have if you want.'

Jade studied her plot as if it was a painting. 'That might look kinda cool. You know, like a piece of sculpture.'

Helen thought that calling a rusty bit of metal 'art' was a stretch. 'Come and get it now if you like and I'll give you some pea seeds too. They germinate pretty quickly.'

Jade picked up Milo, who protested, and strapped him into the pram. She produced a rusk from a bag and he instantly quietened.

'Is he teething?' Helen asked, surprising herself.

'Yeah. Teething sucks.'

'For you or for him?'

'Both.'

They walked back to the cottage in silence.

Helen pointed under the veranda. 'It's under there.'

Incredulity splashed across Jade's face. 'It can stay there.'

'I thought you wanted it.'

'Not if I have to go in there I don't.'

Helen sighed. 'I'll give you a torch.'

'A torch isn't gonna keep me safe from spiders and snakes.'

'Believe me, Jade, you'll face worse things in life.'

The girl's eyes narrowed. Helen couldn't decide if she'd already faced confronting moments or if she thought Helen was pulling her leg.

'If you've faced worse, then you go in and get it,' Jade said.

Helen thought about the confined space under the house and shuddered. Since her experience of living in her car she avoided small dark places as much as possible.

'Perhaps we could ask Bob.' The words were out of her mouth before she could stop them.

Jade grinned. 'He'd do it too.'

That was what Helen was afraid of. 'But as independent women, we should do it ourselves.'

'Why? Neither of us wants to. Anyway, blokes get off on that commando shi—stuff. Makes them feel useful.'

It would make Helen feel beholden. 'I've got a long pole. Maybe I could hook the bedhead and pull it out?'

A dog barked and Jade pointed to the top of the garden. 'Or you could just ask Bob. He's up there, fiddling with Fiza's tent.'

'No, we can sort—'

'Hey, Bob!' Jade yelled. 'Can you give us a hand?'

Bob's arm shot up and Helen groaned. She didn't know which was worse—suffering a panic attack under the house or looking needy in front of Bob Murphy. A young man emerged from the greenhouse tent, joining Bob.

'Who's that with him?' she asked Jade.

'Dunno.' Jade jiggled Milo's pram to stop him grizzling.

'Morning, ladies,' Bob said. 'I'd like you to meet my nephew, Lachlan McKenzie. Lachie, this is Helen and Jade. The cute little bloke is Milo.'

Lachlan, who was wearing a shirt with an embroidered company logo, took off his Akubra hat and shook both their hands before squatting down to Milo's level. 'G'day, squirt. Enjoying that, are you?' Rusk was smeared all over Milo's pudgy cheeks.

'What can we do for you?' Bob asked.

'Nothing,' Helen said. 'Jade jumped the gun.'

The girl rolled her eyes. 'There's an old bedhead under the house we need.'

Bob shuddered. 'Maybe we can fish it out with a pole?'

'That was my suggestion,' Helen said.

Bob threw her a grateful look. 'I've got an old pool pole at home. I'll duct tape an awning hook onto it and see how we go.'

'Ever since a redback put Uncle Bob in hospital, he's had a thing about spiders,' Lachlan said. 'But if you've got a torch, I'll shimmy in and get it.'

Jade's 'Cool!' rode over Helen's 'You'll get filthy'.

'No farmer ever expects me to turn up clean.'

Helen glimpsed a younger Bob in the man's grin. 'Well ... only if we're not holding you up.'

'If you want me to grow vegetables this badly, Helen, go get the torch,' Jade instructed.

'What did your last slave die of?' she muttered as she took the steps two at a time.

'Talking back.'

Helen spluttered, losing the fight not to laugh.

After Lachlan emerged coughing and covered in a hundred years worth of cobwebs, he carried the metal bedhead up to Jade's plot. Their voices drifted down the hill, Lachlan's rumbling baritone saying 'What about here?' followed by Jade's husky, 'A bit to the left'.

'That one knows exactly how to put people into service,' Helen said crisply. 'Your nephew's too kind for his own good.'

'You know we could have got it out with a hook and pole, right?' Bob said ruefully.

She smiled, enjoying a rare moment of simpatico. 'Of course we could have. And stayed much cleaner.'

'Mind you, then Lachie couldn't have shown off to impress Jade.'

Helen snorted. 'I thought he was protecting you from your arachnophobia.'

'It's just a healthy respect for redbacks, thanks very much. But I reckon he would have elbowed me out of the way regardless.' Bob winked. 'It's what I would have done when I was his age.'

'But Jade's got a child. Ergo, there's likely a father somewhere in the picture.'

'I think you're moving way beyond the thought processes of a young buck struck by a pair of sea green eyes.'

'Cat's eyes. If you corner her, she'll bite and scratch.'

'We're all capable of that, Helen.' Bob's stomach gurgled loudly. 'Excuse me. Lachie arrived before breakfast. Any chance of a cuppa?'

'I suppose I could manage that. Has Lachie had breakfast?'

'Doubt it.'

'I'll rustle something up then.'

'I can help.'

'No.' Her heart thumped so fast she heard it in her ears. Bob was looking at her as if he was about to object, so she grabbed the still wrapped paper she'd abandoned on the table. 'Here. Read this. I'll be back in a bit.'

She marched into the kitchen, her mind racing. What could she make? She didn't have any bacon and she was out of cereal and bread. The kettle on the old wood stove was always close to the boil so tea was easy, but she'd promised more than that.

Her gaze strayed to the oven and she winced before pulling herself together. Opening the oven door, she checked the temperature, topped up the fire box and fiddled with the dampers.

'Come on, you old bugger. Don't let me down today.'

Grabbing flour, sugar and milk along with some of her own raspberries, she got mixing. Although the ancient cast-iron gem scone mould had come with the old stove, she'd never used it. Gem scones were inextricably tied up with love, grief and hate, but today, needs must.

Holding herself together, she whipped the butter and sugar and poured the mixture into the hot greased moulds. She sucked in deep breaths as she laid the tea tray with mugs, plates, knives, milk, sugar and jam. But when she pulled the golden brown treats from the oven, she lost the battle and tears fell, wetting the oven mitt.

Memories rushed over her like racing flood waters. Nicki's smile whenever Helen pulled gem scones out of the oven. Theo's grin as he scarfed half the batch. His later derision of the treats as 'Aussie pap' and his demands for baklava.

Her chest cramped with regret. This was why she fought the temptation of being lulled into happy recollections of the past. Memories were wolves in sheep's clothing. They inevitably sank their jagged yellow teeth into her, shocking her with pain.

Enough!

She dumped the hot gem scones onto a plate, wiped away the evidence of her tears and marched the tray out to the veranda. Daisy stood up, hopeful of a treat.

Milo was snuggled on Jade's hip and she and Lachie were peering over Bob's shoulder looking at the paper.

'It's called alliteration,' Bob said.

'Tea's up,' Helen said.

Bob hurriedly folded the paper, pushing it to the edge of the table. As Helen moved to set down the tray, she asked, 'What ridiculous headline has Peter Granski come up with today?'

'*Slum Sullies Scenic Spot*,' Jade said. 'Mrs Kastrati would have slashed it with her red pen. It doesn't even make any sense. The houses aren't built yet.'

A wave of nausea rolled Helen's stomach and her fingers loosened on the tray. It tilted wildly, sending tea sloshing and scones tumbling.

Bob grabbed it, sliding it onto the table as Lachlan dived for the scones. He caught the plate on the tips of his fingers like a cricketer sliding in for a low ball.

'You okay, Helen?' Jade asked. 'You've gone sorta grey.'

Bob pulled out a chair. 'Sit down before you fall down.'

She sat, but only because her legs threatened to fold underneath her. 'Show me the paper.'

'How about a nice cup of tea first?' Bob reached for the sugar.

'Show. Me. The. Paper!'

Lachlan exchanged a mystified look with Jade before picking up *The Standard*. 'Here you go.'

The print was blurred and she leaned back, trying to focus, but it was no use. She held out her hand to Bob. 'I need your reading glasses.'

He reluctantly pulled them out of his pocket and she slid them onto her nose—they were still warm from his face. The words came into focus, sharp and black against the white.

A reliable source informs us that a social housing project—insert low rent, low standards and a mess of social problems—is going to be built on some of the most valuable land in the shire. It's an outrageous proposal. Think about it. Which would you prefer? A beautifully landscaped country club with world-class facilities? Or burned-out cars, used syringes and a ghetto of addicts? Complete the online survey and have your say.

Helen's hands shook so hard the paper rustled, but she didn't know if the trembling consuming her body was shock, anger or both. How had *The Standard* learned of the submission?

Safe as houses. Her pre-yoga green tea rose on a sea of acid, the bitterness filling her mouth. This was her fault. Why had she confided in someone she barely knew?

Tugging the glasses off her face, she tossed them across the table at Bob. 'You bastard! Of all the people in this town you could blab to, you had to tell Peter freakin' Granski?'

Bob rocked back in his chair as if propelled by a slap. 'I've kept your secret. Hell, I'd sooner cross the street than confide in Peter bloody Granski.'

'I don't believe you!'

'Steady on, Helen,' Lachlan said equably. 'Uncle Bob might be a wimp around redbacks, but he's a man of his word. If he said he kept your secret, then he did.'

Helen ignored him. She only had eyes for Bob, scrutinising his face for signs he was lying—a twitch in his cheek, a lowering of his gaze. But he was looking straight at her, his gaze steady.

'Well, if it wasn't you, who was it?' she demanded.

'Why are you being such a bitch to Bob?' Jade asked.

'There are four councillors who are yet to give you their support, Helen,' Bob said.

'Bloody men in suits!'

'I have to get to work.' Lachlan backed away as if Helen was aiming a loaded gun at his head.

'Don't worry about her,' Jade said. 'She's old and she gets weird sometimes. Here.' She shoved jam-covered gem scones at him. 'Thanks for helping with the bedhead. It looks awesome.'

'No worries.' He ruffled Milo's hair. 'See you, squirt. Uncle Bob, I'll call you about the maize later?'

'Yeah. Good. Thanks, Lach,' Bob said distractedly.

Helen didn't say goodbye—she was already on the phone to Vivian.

CHAPTER
15

The deputy mayor pushed a frothy cappuccino towards Helen. 'Drink this. You look like you need it.'

'It's a disaster!'

'It's not great.'

Helen's gut burned and had been since eight this morning. 'Who would do something like this?'

'Who knows. Maybe someone who hates affordable housing?'

'Or hates women.'

'Well, there is that.' Vivian stirred her latte. 'I think we can safely rule out Messina and Cynthia. Craig and Aki are fence-sitters, so I can't imagine them doing anything, but dodgy Don's a different matter entirely. He could be our leak.'

'What about the mayor? You said he didn't want any controversy?'

'True and Granski just made it controversial. Mind you, so are two all-black SUVs coming out of Ainslea Park. It looked like a presidential cavalcade.'

'I don't understand.'

'Wealthy international horse-racing people who don't want to be recognised.'

'You mean sheiks?' It sounded utterly crazy for Boolanga. Almost as crazy as Cinta's conspiracy theories. 'I heard a rumour that a Chinese consortium wanted to buy the land to host parties to hunt deer and kangaroos.'

Vivian laughed. 'Don't go drinking the Kool Aid, Helen. The shire would no more sell to the Chinese than fly to the moon.'

'So you don't think there's any truth to Granski's suggestion of a country club?'

'Half the town belongs to the country club on the other side of the river. Building another one won't give investors good ROI.' Vivian caught Helen's blank look. 'Return on investment.'

'If there isn't a country club or resort being considered, why would someone leak the submission?'

'Good question. And this is the third "reliable source" article Peter Granski's printed in the last couple of months. After Jon Hooper's call to arms at the Chamber of Commerce awards, I'm starting to wonder if the Irrigation Road lobby group are bribing a staffer.'

'But this hasn't got anything to do with car park lighting.'

'It has *everything* to do with it.'

'How?'

Vivian read aloud from the editorial. '*Boolanga's rising crime rate is of grave concern. Surely, we need to fix this problem before we invite the homeless and unemployed into our town and add to our current social problems.*'

'That's outrageous!'

Vivian's mouth pulled into a sympathetic smile. 'Welcome to the rough and tumble of politics. Unfortunately, the Right currently control the mouthpiece.'

Fury and frustration spun inside Helen like a tornado. 'How can we hose down these unsubstantiated claims?'

'I'd suggest a public meeting, but you only need a couple of loonies to come along and it will do more harm than good. We want to bring councillors on board, not put the wind up them. We need them focusing on the community's needs, not worrying about re-election.'

'I want to know which misogynist leaked it!'

'You and me both. Let's meet with Cynthia and Messina and see if they've heard any gossip from the other councillors, because I know dodgy Don will just lie to my face.'

Helen thought of the months of work, not to mention the love that had gone into the submission. The idea that the tiny housing village might not be built gutted her. 'I can't sit back and do nothing.'

'I'm not suggesting you do. Write a letter to the editor.'

'Huh! As if Granski would print it.'

'Ah, but he will.' Vivian's eyes glinted with the anticipation of a battle. 'He has to at least appear to show both sides of an argument. Even if your letter's the only one that's pro tiny housing, it's a start.'

Ideas started popping. She'd ask Roxy and the other women if they'd be prepared to write a letter to the paper. *Ask Bob.*

'From little things big things grow, right?'

Vivian rolled her eyes. 'Personally, I'm not a fan of aphorisms.'

Neither was Helen but somehow this one felt right.

Thursday was the day in the week Jade looked forward to and enjoyed the most. The Hazara women worked in the garden and before they left for their English class they always insisted

Jade share their lunch. They never accepted her offer of a
vegemite or a peanut butter sandwich and at first their refusal
didn't bother her, because the food she packed was for Milo. One
of her strategies to make her money last two weeks was eating a
big breakfast and skipping lunch. But as the women kept insisting
she eat their food, it was making her uncomfortable. Last week,
she'd deliberately gone home before lunch to avoid spending
half an hour feeling bad about sponging food or upsetting them.
Except instead of feeling better, she'd felt irritable and cranky all
afternoon. And tired. So very tired.

Milo hadn't slept through the night in over a week and he was
fractious and chewing everything in sight. He cried when he
was held and he cried when he was put down. Why did cutting
teeth burn the skin on his bum red as well as his gums?

When he'd refused to have an afternoon nap, she'd stood at the
door of his room and yelled, 'Just shut up! Go to sleep!'

He'd gone silent for a second, his face startled at the unfamiliar
screeching sounds coming from her mouth. Then his big blue eyes
had filled with tears and he'd sobbed, his little body shaking as hard
as if she'd struck him.

Jade's heart had spasmed, twisting in her chest and pumping out
a cocktail of guilt, anger at herself and utter despair. But the taunting chaser was worse—*You're just like Charlene.*

'I'm bloody not!' She'd scooped up Milo and hugged him close,
her tears dampening his curls. 'I'm sorry. I'm sorry. I'm so sorry.'

She was desperate to talk to someone and receive confirmation that she was nothing like her mother. But she didn't have any
friends in this hole of a town and no one knew her mother, except
Corey. He hated Charlene more than Jade did—although that was
hard to imagine. When Milo was born, he'd said, 'You better treat
this kid better than our mothers treated us.' Jade hadn't needed to

be told—she'd spent the previous six months promising her unborn baby the same thing. And Corey knew she was a better mother—he'd seen how much love and care she gave Milo. He'd tell her she was nothing like Charlene.

She opened a text and typed out what had just happened, but with each word, doubt crept in. Would Corey really understand how hard it was being at home with a baby all day, every day? It wasn't like he ever spent any time alone with Milo. He wasn't so tired that he nodded off in the laundromat and woke up terrified someone had stolen Milo. He wasn't holding a crying baby for hours on end and finding it hard to pee on his own, let alone take a shower.

A hot rod of indignation slid in, straightening her spine. If Corey was here helping her, she wouldn't be yelling at their baby! If the Hazara women had eaten her sandwiches, she'd have stayed for lunch and they'd be cuddling Milo and she wouldn't have yelled at him. None of this was her fault!

You don't like vegemite sandwiches so why should they?

The thought burned as she stabbed the backspace key, deleting the text. She shoved the phone in her shorts' pocket, bundled Milo into the pram and walked to the library.

'Hey, Fran, what's something easy to cook but tastes good and I can take to a picnic?'

'Why don't you look at taste-dot-com? Ignore the over-the-top fiddly stuff and go for something simple like marinated chicken or club sandwiches.'

Jade didn't know what a club sandwich was. As sandwiches were the problem, she checked out the chicken. Instead of buying her weekly treat—a Vodka Cruiser—she bought chicken drumettes and marinated them in soy sauce, honey, garlic and ginger. Bob gave her the garlic and Helen donated coriander, then suggested sprinkling sesame seeds over the chicken. She also gave her some ginger. Jade couldn't believe that an ugly root had such a beautiful and perfumed flower.

Now was the moment of truth and Jade held her breath, keeping her eyes on the women.

Kubra licked her fingers. 'This is very good.'

'Really? You like it?' Jade struggled to believe the compliment.

'Yes. You very good cook.'

'Not really. I just followed the recipe.'

'That's how we all start,' Helen said. 'The only difference between a good cook and an average one is interest and learning from disasters.'

And money. Jade couldn't afford any disasters if it meant throwing out food.

'Kubra, do you have a recipe for your bolanis?' she asked. 'I'd like to try and make them.'

'My mother teach me. Come to my flat and I show you.'

'Yeah?'

Corey will have a fit.

Corey doesn't need to know.

'That would be awesome.'

As the conversation ebbed and flowed, Jade glanced at Helen, who was quiet today—even her magenta tips drooped. Helen didn't boss the women around like she bossed Jade and usually she asked them all sorts of questions as if she was really interested. But ever since she'd got all bent out of shape over that newspaper article and yelled at Bob—Jade still hadn't forgiven her for that—she seemed different.

Jade had asked Bob what her problem was and he'd said, 'It's Helen's story to tell.' But Jade wasn't asking Helen. If she did, Helen would yell at her too and tell her it was none of her business. Just like Charlene, only with less swearing.

But today Helen hadn't bossed Jade all morning and she'd hardly said anything over lunch. Something was off. Jade didn't know why she cared, but part of her wanted grumpy Helen back.

'Hey, Helen, you know how you're obsessed with vegetables?'

Helen's brows rose above her glasses, lightening the frown lines. 'I'd hardly say I'm obsessed, but go on.'

'I planted some of that ginger root you gave me.'

'I hope you soaked it in water first.'

There was no 'Good idea, Jade', like Fran at the library would have said, but Jade got a zip of delight at hearing familiar Helen.

'Well, duh, I YouTubed it.'

Aima said something that was probably 'Come on, you lot, it's time to go to English class,' and the women rose and said goodbye. Helen left too, muttering something about a meeting.

Milo was asleep and as Jade didn't need to be anywhere, she pulled out *Anna Karenina*. It was getting interesting. Anna had just discovered she was pregnant with Vronsky's baby and Vronsky wasn't exactly happy about it. Jade could relate. Corey had disappeared for two months after she'd told him she was pregnant.

But he came back, she quickly reminded herself.

'Hello, Jade. What are you reading?'

She glanced up at Fiza's lyrical voice and held out the book. 'A crazy Russian love story.'

'So many words!' Fiza laughed. 'I cheated and watched the movie.'

'How's your maize?'

'I'm scared to look.'

Jade really wanted to get back to her book. 'They're just plants.'

Fiza's sunny smile faded.

Jade didn't understand why the seedlings' survival was so important to the other woman, but something made her say, 'I could come and look with you.'

'Thank you, but you are reading. I will tell you what Lachlan suggests.'

Jade had closed her book and was standing before she realised what she'd done. 'Nah, all good. Let's go and check them out.'

Lachlan was waiting at the tent with a massive white bag filled with brown pellets. He pulled off his hat just like Bob did. Jade wondered why they did that when the point of a hat was to keep the sun off their faces. He pushed his sunglasses up too and just like the first time she'd met him, she noticed his eyes were ringed by thick chocolate lashes. Had Bob looked like this when he was younger?

'G'day, Jade. Hi, Fiza, I reckon I might have a solution.'

Fiza's smile returned. 'That's wonderful.'

'Is that chook poo?' Jade peered into the bag. She'd read it was loaded with nitrogen so it was good for the garden.

'Better! Worm castings. They're full of bacteria and fungi, protozoa and nematodes.'

Fiza's brow furrowed. 'I am a nurse. This is good bacteria like inside us?'

'Yeah, pretty much.' Lachlan's face lit up with enthusiasm and his hands moved as he talked. 'It converts the inorganic forms of nutrients in the soil to organic ones so the plants can use them. It means stronger plants, so they're more resistant to disease. We're getting good results with all sorts of crops so it's worth a shot with your maize.'

'So I just dig it into the soil?'

'Yep. And I'd keep the tent over them until the seedlings have doubled in size and they've lost their yellow tinge.'

Jade thought he was expecting a lot from worm poo. 'You sound confident.'

'It's good stuff.'

'What if it doesn't work?'

'Steady. No negativity around the plants.' But his face crinkled in a smile.

Jade snorted. 'Fiza, you better sing some African songs to your maize. You know, trick them into thinking they're in Sudan.'

'A wimohweh, a wimohweh ...' Lachlan broke into 'The Lion Sleeps Tonight'.

Embarrassment for him filled Jade. 'I thought you didn't want to traumatise the plants.'

He laughed, but didn't look embarrassed or pissed off. 'It's that or "Circle of Life". I could ask the choir to come down. We sang "Ipharadisi" last year, although I think it's a South African freedom song.'

'Ipharadisi is Paradise in Zulu,' Fiza said.

'A long way from Sudan, right?'

Jade was gaping at Lachlan. 'You're in a choir?'

'Yeah. The Boolanga Blokes. It's a bit of fun and we raise some money for local charities.' He swung his attention back to Fiza. 'Do you need a hand spreading the pellets?'

'You are very kind, but I would like to do this myself.'

Jade would have let Lachlan help. 'Why?'

'For my father,' Fiza said quietly.

Jade's gut squirmed. She had learned by sixteen that trying to impress her father wasn't worth it. When she was thirteen, she'd won the essay prize at school and had wanted her father to know. Wanted him to be proud of her. She'd sent an email to the address Charlene had on her phone, but he'd never replied. For three years she sent him her high school reports, and then one Christmas he sent her ten bucks and a card saying *You got your brains from me.*

In year ten, Charlene had hassled her to work as many hours as she could, which meant less time for school. Jade's marks had dropped and then her teachers—especially Mrs Kastrati—hassled her to work harder, but they were easier to ignore than Charlene. That report was the first one she didn't send to her father. And he hadn't asked about it, which had hurt more than the teachers' comments of *a disappointing year* and *needs to apply herself to reach her full potential.*

The last time she sent her father anything was when Milo was born. The email had bounced and the text message said undeliverable. At least having no way of contacting him saved her from more disappointment when he turned out to be as useless a grandfather as a father.

'Fair enough, Fiza,' Lachlan was saying. 'I get it—it's your project. But if you don't mind, I'll keep an eye on them. I reckon by this time next week we'll have much happier plants.'

'I hope so,' Fiza said.

'Catch you later,' Jade told her, and turned the pram down the hill. Lachlan fell into step beside her.

'Your peas sprouted?' he asked.

'Not yet.'

'Should be soon, eh?'

'Yeah.'

Say something else. But all her words seemed to have fallen out of her head. All she could think about was the fact her T-shirt was smeared in dirt and she hadn't washed her hair.

So? You're not trying to impress him. The thought unsettled her and she suddenly wanted to leave.

'I have to go.'

'To Helen's meeting?'

'Yes,' she said distractedly, not aware they'd reached the cottage. 'What?'

'Hello, you two.' Bob handed them some papers. 'Thanks for coming. Helen's got some examples but feel free to do it in your own words.'

'What's this?' Jade scanned the paper. 'You want me to write a letter about houses for old women?'

'One day, God willing, you'll be older, Jade.'

'Yeah, but ...' She thought about how she struggled to pay her own rent. 'What about affordable housing for single mothers?'

'You're right, that's important too.' Helen walked out of the cottage and set down a jug of water and some glasses. 'But your Centrelink payment's been indexed. The dole is the same as it was twenty-five years ago. It's impossible for an unemployed single woman to afford the rent to live on her own, and when you're over fifty-five it's almost impossible to get a job.'

Jade put down the paper. 'Yeah, well, I don't get how a letter's going to work.'

'Unlike that filthy rag of a paper, we'll tell the real story.' Helen handed her a pen and paper. 'You write it and I'll post it.'

Jade laughed. 'Snail mail? Who even does that? Email's old school now. You should start a Facebook page.'

Bob nodded. 'She's got a point, Helen. All the pollies are on Twitter.'

'What about an online petition?' Lachlan said.

'There's nothing to petition yet. What I want is to correct the misinformation being peddled by Granski.'

'Might be worth doing it both ways,' Lachlan suggested. 'If you start a Facebook page, I'm happy to invite the blokes at choir and the tennis club. Well, the ones with a social conscience anyway.'

Jade snuck a sideways glance at Lachlan. He was what, twenty-five? Definitely less than thirty anyway, a bloke and working in what Jade assumed was a good job. Why did he care about homeless women? He probably didn't even know any. But he was offering to help Helen, who'd yelled at him and Bob the other day. Jade didn't get it, but that didn't stop a twist of envy that he had friends he could ask to help. The only person she knew who might be interested was Fran at the library and she wasn't a friend.

'I don't even have Facebook,' Helen was saying. 'Or a smartphone.'

'You don't need a smartphone. I'll set it up on your computer,' Jade heard herself saying before fully thinking it through.

'Good on you, Jade.' Bob smiled encouragingly.

'My laptop's a dinosaur and I don't have the internet,' Helen said.

'I'll do it at the library.'

'Just setting it up won't be enough. You'll need to show me how to work it too.'

'I s'pose I can do that.'

'Don't put yourself out on my account.'

'I won't.'

Even though teaching a super-grumpy Helen would be a pain in the arse, it wasn't enough to dent the rush of exhilaration spinning through her. For the first time, Jade knew more about something than Helen. It felt fantastic.

CHAPTER

16

'Thanks for your help, but what if I've got it wrong?' The young bloke's hand rested on the box. 'She's fussy.'

Tara had just sold him a state-of-the-art mixer with ten attachments that made it everything from a food processer to an ice cream maker and a meat grinder.

'Unless she wants a different colour, I think you're safe. But keep the receipt. If she doesn't like it, send her in and I'll personally help her find exactly what she wants.'

When he'd walked away from the counter Tara eagerly checked her phone for a message from Zac about a possible afternoon run. Nothing. Her butterflies flatlined. She was staring at the screen, willing a text to appear, when the device vibrated in her hand, making her jump.

'Tara Hooper.'

'Tara, it's Sam. Jon needs you at the store. Now!'

Tara bristled at the bookkeeper's critical tone. 'I'm here. I've been serving customers for the last hour.'

'Come to the timber yard office immediately.'

Before Tara could ask why Jon had asked Samantha Murchison to call her instead of finding her himself, the line went dead. Was this a new low in their relationship?

Irritated, she exited through the garden section, marched to the portable office in the timber yard and tugged open the heavy door. A white-faced Jon sat on a chair with his head tipped back. Samantha's face was almost as pale as his and her gloved fingertips pressed a wad of bloodied gauze against his forehead.

'Oh, God!' Love for Jon surged to the surface, trouncing Tara's frustrations.

'Here.' Samantha stepped away smartly. 'I don't do blood.'

As soon as she moved her hand, blood gushed down Jon's forehead, dripping off his eyebrow and onto his thigh. The sight pierced Tara's shock and she darted forward, snapping on a pair of gloves from the open first-aid kit. Jon flinched at the pressure of her fingers on the gauze.

'What happened?' she asked.

'Some moron didn't stack the F-seventeen properly. I came around the corner and slammed straight into it.'

'Did you black out?'

'Don't think so.'

Tara eased the gauze away, trying to estimate the depth of the wound before the blood squirted like a geyser, obscuring everything. She just had enough time to glimpse jagged skin edges and a flash of white before blood pooled again.

'You need stitches.'

The fact Jon didn't argue worried her.

He was unsteady on his feet and needed her help walking to the car. Although she was strong, she was slight and his height and weight threatened to knock her off balance.

During the short drive he was unusually quiet and each time his eyes fluttered closed she panicked he'd blacked out. She kept up a line of patter trying to keep him awake.

'At least your timing was perfect. Any earlier and I might not have sold the eight-hundred-dollar mixer.'

He didn't even manage a smile.

Their doctor was on holidays and the locum, like so many doctors in the country, had a heavy accent that was challenging to understand. But he asked all the important questions and sewed like a tailor so Tara relaxed.

Despite the chasm of coolness stretching between them, here in the treatment room it seemed the most natural thing in the world to slip her hand into Jon's. He didn't object. In fact his thumb moved jerkily back and forth, caressing her skin while the doctor stitched his scalp. It was as close as they'd been in months and she blinked fast to stop tears from falling.

When the doctor left to get the tetanus injection, Jon squeezed her hand. 'Sorry.'

'This isn't your fault.'

'No.' A long breath shuddered out of him. 'I love you, T.'

'I love you too.' She did, but recently he was hard to like.

His troubled gaze sought hers. 'We're okay, aren't we?'

His need for reassurance dug in under the wobbly foundations of their current relationship. The problem was, she couldn't tell if it was shoring them up or destabilising them.

Her phone buzzed in her bag. Zac. Familiar tingles swirled across her skin. Guilt chased them.

'I want us to be okay, Jon. I really do.'

'So do I.'

Did this mean he was prepared to do something about their sex life? 'I want things to be like they used to be, don't you?'

His expression smoothed into an unreadable mask. Her heart sank. *Keep going. It's too important to let this slide.*

'Ask the doctor about the drop in your sex drive.'

Horror streaked across his face. 'No way!'

How could he ask her to confirm they were okay as a couple when clearly they hadn't been for months, yet not want to do something about fixing their biggest problem? She knew he wouldn't make an appointment off his own bat to discuss his erectile dysfunction and they'd just end up having another argument. Everything would be her fault. Again.

'But you're right here. Please.'

The doctor returned holding a syringe. After jabbing Jon in the arm and thrusting a page of printed instructions at Tara, he said, 'Anything else today?'

'All good,' Jon said as Tara said, 'Actually, yes.'

The doctor glanced between them, clearly confused. Jon's previously impassive expression twisted into anger.

Tara looked away, holding her nerve as guilt bounced off frustration, neatly dodging anything connected to betrayal. If Jon truly loved her and wanted things to improve, this was the solution. If he couldn't see that, she'd step up for them both and to hell with embarrassment. And, God! Why was he even embarrassed? Women had to expose their private parts for breast checks, pap tests and childbirth. Jon's problem didn't even need an examination.

She cleared her throat. 'Recently, my husband's had some trouble with …' Sweat beaded on her forehead. This was harder than she thought. 'Things in bed have been … We need a prescription for Viagra,' she finished quickly.

Jon was breathing hard and he'd knotted his hands in his lap. The doctor stared at his shoes and Tara's heart raced as hard as if she'd just sprinted a hundred metres. For a moment, taut silence stretched between the three of them, then the doctor tapped on his iPad. A printer across the room whirred into action.

Relief surged through Tara, justifying the excruciating encounter.

Jon heaved, the sound violent, and vomited onto the floor.

Tara bypassed the silk lingerie and pulled out an old pair of shortie cotton pyjamas that predated Flynn's arrival. She thought she'd turned them into rags a long time ago but apparently they'd been missed in a regular clear-out. There was nothing sexy about them. She'd bought them specifically for a camping trip so she could walk to the toilet block without being arrested for indecent exposure. But they were cotton and soft—two things Jon had told her he missed.

Jon's head had healed fast and his stitches were out. Neither of them had mentioned the Viagra. The prescription had sat for a week with the wound care instructions and the repeat prescription for antibiotics. Tara had crossed her fingers that Jon would take responsibility for it and get it filled, but as each day passed, hope shrivelled. Today she'd caved in, driven to Cobram and got it filled there.

She'd read the instructions—take the tablet between thirty minutes and four hours before intercourse. She'd been tempted to crush one into his dinner but the subterfuge went against the spirit of the endeavour to bring them closer together. So she'd left the packet and the instructions on the ensuite vanity so he'd see them when he took his after-work shower. It had almost killed her not asking him if he'd taken a pill, but his earlier words of 'too much pressure' silenced her. He'd shaved, which bolstered her hopes. So did the fact he was now cleaning his teeth instead of being downstairs watching TV or in bed asleep.

She heard the flush of the toilet and his call, 'Bathroom's yours.'

By the time she'd pulled on the pyjamas and finished brushing her hair, he was already in bed and reaching for his bedside lamp.

Panic skittered through her. 'I won't be long.'

She lifted the toilet lid and was turning to sit when something in the bottom of the bowl caught her eye. Leaning down, she noticed flecks of blue, except the blue toilet cleaner had run out and she was yet to replace it. Suspicion stung like a dart. Her foot hit the pedal on the bathroom bin; nestled under a discarded toothpaste tube and her make-up remover wipes were two empty silver pill foils.

Fury blew through her like a hot northerly, scorching everything in its path.

She stomped out of the bathroom and turned on the overhead lights. 'You flushed them down the toilet?!'

Jon's arm rose to shield his eyes. 'I don't need them.'

'You do need them! We need them.'

He grunted and pulled the sheet over his head before rolling away from the light.

She sprinted across the room and hauled back the sheet. 'No! You don't get to do this. You told me you wanted us to be okay. Well, you caring about our sex life is part of us being okay.'

He sat up jerkily, his face thunderous. 'And you caring about me is part of us being okay too. I told you I didn't want those fucking pills but you ignored me. Do you have any idea what will happen if the club finds out about this?'

'I'm not stupid! I went to Cobram.'

'Oh, right. Like those fifty kays will protect our privacy. And great going, Tara. You chose the pharmacy where Kelly's sister works.'

'No. I deliberately went to the other one.'

'Yeah, well, if you still went to lunch with the girls instead of bloody marathon training, Kelly would have told you that Belinda changed jobs last week.'

Tara's heart pounded in a different way. 'She wasn't there.'

'Doesn't mean she won't find out. I'll *never* forgive you if this gets out.'

'You'll never forgive me?' Her voice spiked on a shriek, all concerns of their privacy vanishing. 'I'm the one trying to save our marriage. You're the one making it all about you! I'm so angry right now, I can't even look at you.' She grabbed her pillow.

'Where are you going?'

'To sleep in the spare room.'

'Oh, right. And that makes it so easy for us to have sex.'

'You never want to have sex!'

'That's a gross exaggeration.'

'Fine. Prove me wrong.' She waved the foil packet at him. 'You missed one. Take it now.'

'I'm not having angry sex with you, Tara.'

'You've got half an hour to calm down.'

He grabbed the packet. With shaking hands, he pressed the pill into his palm and swallowed it. 'Happy?'

A desperate wave of sadness hit her, loosening her knees and depositing deep fatigue and resignation. She hadn't been happy all year and one small blue pill wasn't enough to fix her.

They went to bed but they didn't have sex. Of course they didn't. They lay side by side, their bodies rigid with bitterness and resentment. Although Tara searched, she couldn't find a single pond of calm anywhere inside herself to float on. Instead, her feelings of betrayal fermented.

Jon didn't say another word and at the twenty-minute mark he was snoring gently, air whistling between his teeth. The sound brought her simmering outrage to boiling point and it spilled over, energising her fatigue. How could he possibly sleep?

Except it wasn't a peaceful sleep. His legs constantly thrashed, tangling in the sheets as if he was fighting something or someone. Was it her? When his foot landed a blow on her shin, she flinched and reached out to shake him awake. Only what was the point? He'd accuse her of self-interest.

She got out of bed and collected her phone from the kitchen before going to the guest room and closing the door.

She texted Zac. He replied instantly, the ping loud in the silent house. She hurriedly turned her phone to silent before typing *I wish we could run right now*

It's a full moon. I'm up for it
You serious?

A line of repeating running emojis appeared on her screen—a blonde-haired woman followed by a black-haired man. Her and Zac. Him chasing her. A tingle spun between her legs.

Another text came in. *Meet me at Riverbend in fifteen?*

She thought about the kids. They didn't have coughs or colds. Neither had woken with a nightmare in months and these days once they were asleep they were out cold until daybreak.

And Jon? Would he wake up and notice her gone? Would he care?

Did she?

Breakfast was a shambles. Operating on four hours' sleep, Tara made coffee and lunches on autopilot.

Jon appeared before the children with black shadows under his eyes and three bits of toilet paper stuck to his face. She steeled herself against the few strands of sympathy that wanted to weave themselves around her heart.

Instead of asking how he'd slept, she said, 'Got into a fight with the razor as well as your wife?'

He grunted and poured coffee. She waited for him to comment on the fact she'd spent more hours out of their bed last night than in it.

'You coming in today?' he asked.

Disappointment sat heavily in her gut, but she couldn't tell if it was because Jon hadn't noticed she'd been missing or because it denied her the opportunity to tell him she'd gone running.

'I've got that thank you morning tea at the community garden,' she said. 'And then I'm catching up with Shannon. Two things you approve of so that should make you happy.'

'I want you to be happy.' Something akin to sadness momentarily softened the discontent in his eyes, then vanished. 'There's a staff meeting at two.'

'Two?'

'Yeah. I changed the time so you could make it.'

She met his combative look with one of her own. 'I've got training at two.'

He didn't say anything but his face morphed into the expressionless mask she was coming to expect whenever he got angry. He slammed the lid on his keep cup. The cup tipped and coffee swam over the bench. Swearing, he picked up his keys and, without a backwards glance, walked out the door.

'I'll clean it up then, shall I?' Tara yelled at the slamming door. She threw a cloth over the liquid, catching it just before it dripped down and filled the drawers.

Clemmie ran in wearing her school uniform and sat to eat her cereal. 'Mummy, can Leila and Sammy come over and play after school today?'

Tara ran through the girls in Clemmie's class and drew a blank. 'Who are Leila and Sammy?'

'You know, the twins.'

Flynn picked up the juice box and Tara watched him pouring it into his glass as if that was all it took to prevent him from spilling it everywhere like his father.

'Can they, Mummy?'

'Can who what?'

'Can the twins come over and play!'

Tara's thoughts drifted to the kids in Clemmie's dance class and at Pee-Wee tennis and still came up short. 'But we don't know any twins.'

Clemmie rolled her eyes. 'Yes, we do.'

'We played with them yesterday.' Flynn put the juice back in the fridge and carried his very full glass to the table.

Tara's head pounded from a combination of lack of sleep, a prolonged adrenaline rush from running with Zac on a still cool night drenched in moonlight, and sustained anger at Jon. She knew she'd been distracted the previous afternoon, busy building Viagra castles in the air and believing the little blue pill would magically heal her marriage. Huh!

They'd arrived home after swimming lessons and Flynn and Clemmie had been tired and hungry. When they'd bickered over the iPad, she'd sent them outside with snacks. She'd been surprised, but pleased, when they didn't try to come back inside within five minutes. It had reinforced her belief that the more time kids spent outside, the better it was for their imaginations. They'd entertained themselves so well she'd had to ring the dinner bell to summon them inside. There hadn't been any time to play with anyone—

Her coffee cup stalled halfway to her mouth. 'Where did you play with these twins?'

'On the trampoline,' Clemmie said.

'Sammy's awesome! He can do double somersaults.' Flynn's eyes shone with admiration. 'His big brother, Amal, is going to teach me.'

The neighbours. 'No!'

Flynn's knife clattered onto his plate. 'Why not?'

'Because they're dangerous.'

'Somersaults aren't dangerous,' Flynn said belligerently.

But African teenage boys are. 'The twins shouldn't have been here uninvited.'

'They weren't. I asked them,' Clemmie said.

'You should have asked me first.'

'But you told us to stay outside.'

Her daughter's logic snapped her already stretched restraint. 'You know the rules, Clementine Rose Hooper!'

Clemmie's blue eyes swam with confusion. 'What rules?'

'Not talking to strangers.'

'But they're not strangers. They're neighbours.'

'Exactly. And when Lyle lived there we told you not to go anywhere near him.'

'Yeah, but he was scary,' Flynn said. 'The twins are cool.'

'I don't care. You both did the wrong thing so they're not coming over.'

'That's so unfair!' they chorused.

Something about their united complaint made her compensate. 'Brooke and Benji can come instead. Now go and get ready for school.'

As Tara reached for the paracetamol, her phone vibrated with a message. She turned it over.

Training by moonlight's my new favourite thing. Zac had placed a moon between the two running emojis that represented each of them.

Her headache eased. *Mine too. Tx*

CHAPTER
17

At school drop-off, Tara suggested to Kelly that Brooke come for a play date that afternoon. 'I'm hoping Benji can come as company for Flynn but I'm happy to have Hudson as well. It will give you an hour or so to yourself after work.'

'I've got a better idea,' Kelly said. 'Seeing it's Friday, why don't Rhianna and I bring something and then the guys come too? It's been ages since we did that. We haven't seen you since book group.' An accusatory tone clung to the words.

Tara didn't want to invite the woman who'd accused her of not appreciating her husband. 'I'm not sure Rhianna's—'

'What about me?' Rhianna arrived just as the bell sounded.

'Gang night at Tara's,' Kelly said.

Rhianna's brows rose. 'Really?'

'Why really?' Tara said coolly.

'I'm just surprised you've got the time. Jon said you're flat out with this crazy marathon plan.'

Tara's fingers curved into her palms and she focused on the discomfort instead of saying something she'd regret. 'I thought it might be nice for us to all get together before Shannon gets busy with the baby.'

'You make it sound like she's leaving town.'

Kelly laughed. 'Shan's never let a kid stop her from socialising before.'

Just like at the last barbecue and book group, Tara was left feeling criticised. Had she really changed or had Kelly and Rhianna?

On the drive to the community garden for the dreaded morning tea—Helen had refused to take no for an answer—she called Shannon and mentioned the barbecue.

'That's a perfect plan if it can be tomorrow night instead?' Shannon said.

'Too easy.' Tara got a zip of pleasure at the thought of telling Kelly that the play date for the kids was still on, but not the barbecue the woman had invited herself to. And if Kelly and Rhianna were busy tomorrow night and couldn't make it, tough.

'Sensational. Chris and the kids and I will be there with bells on.'

'Great. But this doesn't change today's plans.'

Tara was really looking forward to lunch, because now she no longer had a kid at preschool, she and Shannon were on different weekday schedules. She didn't see as much of her friend as she used to or wished to and she desperately needed some one-on-one time with her. Perhaps over lunch Tara could broach the topic of Rhianna and Kelly ganging up on her. Or not ... Shannon was so easygoing she'd probably tell her she was imagining things.

Tell her about Jon. But that was impossible. Shannon would tell Chris.

'Actually, Tara, if it's okay with you,' Shannon was saying, 'I've got a million things I have to do before we—before the baby comes.'

'Oh. Right. Sure. I get it.' The weight of her disappointment almost flattened her.

'Thanks! You're the best. See you tomorrow.'

Tara pulled in beside the new sponsorship sign and snapped a photo for the Hoopers' Facebook page. At the end of morning tea she'd take photos of the gardeners holding some of the donated tools. It would make a change from pictures of the junior football and cricket teams, who Jon sponsored by providing the uniforms.

Before she slid her phone into her handbag, she checked for texts. There could be something important from the school. *You tell yourself that …*

She created a new text. *Hey Zac, I'm still buzzing.* Shivers ran up and down her spine as she willed him to reply.

Excellent!

I've got an unexpected opening at noon, she typed.

Cool! You want to shift 2pm to 12?

Did she? Of course she did. It meant she'd see Zac two hours earlier. It also meant she could attend the staff meeting at two, but did she want to? Not really. She didn't want to do anything to oblige Jon, but if she turned up it would appear like a gesture of goodwill. And right now, appearances were the only thing holding their relationship together.

She pressed the thumbs-up emoji.

Eat now! A string of running emojis followed.

Delight twirled and danced inside her as she drove the short distance to the garden car park. The ornamental gates were open, but Helen had told her the morning tea was on the veranda of the cottage so she didn't enter.

'Yoo-hoo! Tara!'

She tried not to sigh. She'd met Judith Sainsbury at Ian's seventieth birthday party and had been stunned when the woman told the catering staff to serve the cake despite the fact the event was at Tingledale.

'Hello, Judith.'

The woman reached her, puffing slightly. 'I'm glad I caught you.'

'Oh?'

'I want to know who gave you permission to erect that rather large advertising sign?'

'The sponsorship sign?'

'Is that what it is?'

Tara was proud of the design and aesthetics of the sign. It didn't look anything like blatant advertising for the store.

'The community garden's logo's there too,' she pointed out.

'You do realise you haven't donated to the community garden.'

Tara gestured towards the new shed on the adjacent block that was surrounded by burgeoning garden beds. 'That looks like a community garden to me.'

'Well, it's not. Helen's gone rogue. You've given tools to illegal immigrants.'

Tara's temples throbbed. 'Illegal immigrants? I thought all of those were in detention centres in other countries.'

Judith huffed. 'They should be. Instead they're here in Boolanga, breaking the law. But I don't have to tell you and Jon about that, do I? Ian said you've had to install security cameras at the store. Boolanga's always been such a safe place, but now! Well, it's an insult to our values. Our way of life is under threat! To be perfectly honest, Tara, I'm surprised you and Jon were prepared to give those people anything.'

'Helen said it was for the community garden extension.'

'Yes, well.' Judith's lips pursed. 'You're not the first person she's deceived.'

'I didn't know.' Anger stirred, gaining momentum fast. How dare Helen lead her to believe the refugee garden was part of the community garden.

'If you want to withdraw your donation, the community garden will happily take over the equipment.'

Something about the glee in Judith's voice snagged, but Tara couldn't think why. Then the memory of Helen's words rushed back: *Can I give you a tour and introduce you to the women?* Tara's building indignation ran slap-bang into Helen's invitation—the one she'd refused. Nausea churned her stomach. Judith *wanted* her to feel aggrieved and deceived. As much as Tara wanted to embrace that easy out, she couldn't ignore the fact that she'd rejected the opportunity to get all the information. She'd been furious with Jon and more interested in meeting Zac. Not only had she donated to a refugee garden, she appeared to be in the middle of a dispute between Judith and Helen. What a mess!

'I'll think about it, Judith.'

With her thoughts bouncing as wildly as one of Flynn's superballs, she walked to the cottage. Clusters of balloons in Hoopers' signature colours were tied to the veranda posts and a bright and beautifully embroidered tablecloth covered a trestle table groaning with food. Dishes of dates and figs, yoghurt, dips and flatbread, along with scones, jam and cream battled for space around a samovar.

A group of women wearing red headscarves decorated with intricate beadwork stood chatting together, but three women stood out. Helen, with her spiky magenta-tipped hair; a young woman with a muddy blonde ponytail holding a baby on her hip; and a statuesque black woman wearing a turban the colour of sunshine on a ripened wheatfield.

Tara's feet stalled. Dear God, what had she done?

'Tara! Welcome!' Helen beckoned her onto the veranda and the chatter behind her died away. 'Ladies, I'm thrilled to introduce you to Tara Hooper. Without her and her husband, Jonathon's generosity, our garden wouldn't be thriving like it is.'

Applause rippled around her, but Tara's gaze stayed fixed on Fiza, who in turn was looking straight at her, her expression unreadable. Tara couldn't decide if it was a triumphant 'gotcha' gaze or one of utter disinterest.

The woman with the baby moved between them, breaking the contact. She shoved a plate of food at Tara. 'Eat these.'

'I, um—'

'No, seriously. Eat them. They're so good.'

Then hot tea was being pressed on her by a woman with a shy smile, and Helen was introducing her to everyone individually. Tara's tongue struggled to wrap itself around some of their names and her brain flailed trying to remember them. They shook her hand gently, their eyes cast downwards, before thanking her in quiet tones. Fortunately, Fiza seemed to have disappeared.

A woman called Aima invited her to come and view their garden. 'We are so happy we grow our food here.'

'They're obsessed with chives,' Jade told Tara.

'Obsessed?' Aima asked.

'It means you think about them all the time,' Jade said.

'Ah! So you are ob-sessed with flowers.'

Jade laughed. 'Good one, Aima.'

'What's inside the greenhouse?' Tara asked.

'Fiza's obsession,' Jade said.

Tara wished she hadn't asked.

'Where is Fiza?' Helen glanced around. 'She was keen to show off her maize.'

'She said she had to go,' Jade said.

'Go? Why? She—I hope everything's okay. It wasn't one of her children, was it?'

Jade shrugged. 'I dunno. She said to leave her bowl on the veranda and she'll pick it up tomorrow. I wouldn't want to eat lentils every day, but this dip isn't too gross. Milo's loving it.' She swept bread through a red dip and offered it to the baby, who licked it off the crust.

'Helen, is there somewhere quiet we can have a word?' Tara's voice caught on the enormity of what she'd done.

'Sure. Come inside.'

Tara followed Helen into the cottage's kitchen and down a dark hall into the living room. Her renovator muscles flexed and memories of restoring Tingledale crowded her. High on love and the excitement of being newly married, she and Jon had spent nights and weekends knocking out lath and plaster walls. They'd found hidden mantlepieces that had been covered up years earlier and, under layers of wallpaper, the remnants of the original paint. Then they'd built the house up again—a commitment to their future as a couple and hopefully a family—installing hydronic heating, insulation, new bathrooms, a cook's kitchen, and lovingly restoring the Australian fauna and flora motifs in the plaster cornices.

This cottage lacked the grandeur of Tingledale but its bones were solid.

'Is this the original wallpaper and fireplace?' she asked.

Helen looked at the faded pattern as if she'd never noticed it before. 'I guess so. The house belongs to the shire and they do the bare minimum to keep it habitable.'

Could this be a project for Hoopers to showcase their products? Tara's mind recoiled from the idea so fast it gave her whiplash. Suggesting something like that to Jon would only reinforce her status as a business partner not a lover.

Who was she kidding? That was already a done deal.

'If the shire's not interested in doing it up, they should sell it to someone who is,' she said. 'They could jack it up and move it.'

'I'd rather they didn't.'

'But it's a piece of Boolanga's history that's fading away.'

'And if they sold it, I'd have nowhere to live and I quite like it here.' Helen smiled, softening her dry tone. 'Don't the garden beds look fantastic? I hope you can see how much your donations have helped. I thought it might be nice to take some photos with you and the women for our new Facebook page.'

Tara took a steadying breath. 'About that. We've got a bit of a problem.'

Helen frowned. 'We do?'

'Yes. When you came to us and asked for donations, we didn't know this was a refugee garden.'

'It's not.'

'It clearly is. Every one of those women out there is a refugee.'

'That's a pretty big statement. Jade's not. How do you know these women aren't here on skilled migrant visas?'

'If they were, they'd be working not gardening.'

'Fiza works. You can't tell someone is a refugee just by looking at them. Believe me, you can get a very warped view of anyone with one quick glance.'

You never get a second chance to make a first impression. The words rippled the pool of Tara's beliefs instilled in her by her mother.

'And Jade isn't a single teenage mother?' she asked.

'She is a teenage mother, but not for long. Her birthday's coming up. As for single, she may well have a partner. I don't know because I haven't asked her. It's really none of our business.'

The words were a rebuke, adding to Tara's discomfort. But before she'd worked out how to respond, Helen was talking again.

'Yes, these women arrived here with refugee status, but on their fourth anniversary they'll be conferred with Australian citizenship. This garden is an extension of the community garden and everyone here is a member of our community.'

'Judith says it's nothing to do with the community garden. That it shouldn't exist.'

Helen's shoulders squared. 'Judith doesn't want it to exist, but that's irrelevant. We have written permission from the shire and Judith has the letter.'

'Either way, you've put me in a very difficult position.'

'I don't see how. It's not my fault Judith's been in your ear.'

'I'm not talking about the feud you and Judith have going on. I'm talking about the fact you have Africans gardening here.'

'We currently have one delightful Sudanese family gardening here. And you would have known that if you'd accepted my invitation for a tour the first time we met. Are you saying if you'd known about Fiza, you wouldn't have helped?'

Agitation skittered, bumping into Tara's discomfort at her own mistake. 'I'm saying that African kids are breaking into our store and stealing. Imagine how I feel knowing our generosity's helping the people causing us constant stress!'

'Surely if you know who's breaking into the store, they've been arrested by the police.'

Tara's arms crossed automatically as if warding off an attack. 'They haven't been caught yet. But they will be soon. We've installed CCTV. If my husband finds out about this, he'll have a fit.'

'Will he hurt you?' Helen asked gently.

'What? No! Of course not.'

'So to avoid an argument about *one* Sudanese family who are gardening here and are probably not stealing from your store, you're prepared to disadvantage twenty women who have just generously thanked you.'

The words sprayed like shot, stinging and accusing. 'I don't have to listen to this.'

'True, but this is your mistake, Tara. If you'd refused to help from the start, I would have been disappointed but I'd have accepted it. But you didn't. Hoopers' sponsorship is very much appreciated and will continue to be unless you withdraw it. I'm hoping you'll take responsibility for your actions in a way that doesn't prejudice innocent people ...'

It was as if her mother was using Helen to channel her beliefs from the grave. *Own your mistakes, Tara. Learn from them.*

'... people who've already suffered more upheaval in their lives than you're ever likely to experience.'

Tara was fast getting sick of the privilege insult. 'You have no idea what I've experienced.'

'That's quite true,' Helen said evenly. 'Just like you don't know what I've experienced. But I'll tell you one thing we have in common. Neither of us have been forced to flee the country we love and call home to save our lives or those of our children.'

'I'm not racist. I'm not objecting to refugees per se. Just the ones who are breaking the law!'

'No one should be breaking the law. How about this for an idea? Leave the sponsorship in place until you know *exactly* who is behind the store break-ins.'

Tara wanted to argue with the logic, but it ran up against the way her mother had raised her and the lesson she was constantly teaching Flynn and Clemmie—be responsible.

If she took back the stock, she'd have to tell Jon. They'd argue yet again about work, which would spin into the pit of despair that was their marriage. Then there was the issue of what she'd do with the used stock. Also, despite disliking Helen's frank assessment of her, Tara felt there was something inherently honest about the woman. For reasons she didn't fully understand, she didn't want Judith winning this round in what was obviously a power battle between the two women.

Her phone buzzed and Zac's name lit up on the screen. Suddenly her decision was easy. After all, what was one more secret in the growing number between her and Jon.

'Fine, but don't mention the maize crop to Jon.'

Helen smiled and shot out her hand. 'Deal.'

Noise barrelled through Tingledale—children shrieking, music blaring and numerous conversations tumbling over each other—the usual chaos that occurred when three families with young children got together. Ninety minutes into the evening, Tara was avoiding Rhianna as much as possible yet knowing exactly where she was in the house and who she was with. Added to that stress, she was biting her tongue and sitting on her hands so she didn't pluck Kelly's damn phone from her fingers and throw it in the pool.

And then there was Jon. With a longneck in hand, eyes overly bright and cheeks flushed, he was leaning against the wall chatting to Chris. One leg jiggled and his left thumb constantly rolled over the tips of his fingers as if he was preparing to run away. Like so many things with Jon lately, it made little sense.

Earlier in the evening, just before their guests arrived, he'd thanked her for organising the gang gathering in the exact same way he'd thanked her for coming to the staff meeting—polite and infuriatingly paternal. In fact the kiss he'd dropped onto her cheek was reminiscent of Ian's greetings and farewells. It seemed that as long as she was a good little wife making no demands on him—sexual or otherwise—he was happy. It had taken most of her self-restraint not to scream and her thoughts had immediately strayed to Zac. It was taking all of her restraint *not* to convert her fantasies and her outrageous flirting into something tangible and real. With the way things were between her and Jon, was her restraint even worth the effort?

'Is everything okay?' Shannon asked.

'Sorry?'

Shannon's gaze flicked between Tara and Jon. 'Are things between you and Jon okay?'

Tears of gratitude prickled her eyes at her friend's perspicacity and her words rushed out on a roll of relief. 'Things are—'

The sudden tinkling sound of a spoon on glass silenced the room almost as fast as gunshot. Shannon muttered something about lousy timing and waddled over to stand next to her husband.

Chris set down the glass and spoon and slid his arm around Shannon's thick waist, pulling her in close. 'Seeing as I have your attention—'

'Chris and his b-b-loody speeches,' Jon slurred.

The now-permanent knot in Tara's gut tightened. *Jesus, Jon! Drunk again?* Was her husband an alcoholic? More horrifying was the realisation she lacked the energy to care.

'You're up against Tara's trifle so get on with it,' Al called.

'First I want to thank Tar and Jonno for their constant and generous hospitality,' Chris said. 'It's fitting that they've inadvertently thrown us a farewell party.'

Farewell party? Tara glanced around the room, seeking confirmation of Chris's words, but everyone's faces were blank.

'What are you talking about?' she said.

Shannon held up Chris's hand, her face a combination of pride and delight. 'Chris has been offered a fellowship. Two years working and studying in New York. I'm being induced on Tuesday and the five of us leave in three weeks!'

'I'm making a table and chairs for the Thadley family,' Chris said. 'They're huge supporters of the arts in the city.'

'The city?' Jon pushed himself off the wall and, with a sloppy action, threw an arm over Chris's shoulders. 'L-listen to him. He s-sounds like a New Yorker w-wanker already.'

Tara battled shock at the unexpected news and her fury at Jon's drunkenness. She finally found her voice. 'Oh my God! That's amazing! Congratulations. What an opportunity!'

She hugged Chris and Shannon. But not even her happiness for them could alter the reality that her best friend was leaving her alone with two women who judged her, and in a marriage with a barely beating pulse. Standing back and watching the others give their congratulations, loneliness tightened around Tara, caging her like a net. Her chest heaved and her legs twitched, fighting the sensation of being dragged fast towards a deep black hole.

She knew the only way to avoid it and survive was to call Zac and run.

CHAPTER

18

Helen wielded a highlighter on yet another article in *The Standard* that was against the housing project. Once again, the rag that declared itself the 'voice of Boolanga' was making tenuous links between Australian values and the town's social problems.

An ache burned under her ribs. She was still reeling from the revealing conversation with Tara Hooper. In the same breath, the woman had declared she wasn't racist yet threatened to withdraw sponsorship of the garden. What devastated Helen the most was that the Hoopers were young. What hope did Boolanga have when its future leaders' views were so entrenched?

Where did this fear of anyone different come from? Why were young black men judged more harshly than their white counterparts? *Two hundred years of white colonisation, Helen.* Racism had arrived with the First Fleet.

She poured her outrage into another letter to the editor.

You write about this nebulous thing 'Australian values'. Do we as a nation truly believe in values that exclude the homeless, the unemployed and

people of colour? If we do, then those values you hold so dearly are the root
cause of the social problems you say you don't want in this town.

After *The Standard* had published her earlier letters, Helen had
received a dozen emails from people she didn't know telling her in
no uncertain terms that Boolanga needed progress not socialism.
The milder ones said if she loved communism so much she should
go and live in China. Others were so brutally offensive she'd reflex-
ively hit the delete key, needing the horrifying words gone.

This week, the emails had risen exponentially. Initially, she'd
replied to the polite ones, offering up an alternative point of view
in the hope of changing their minds. When it became obvious her
replies encouraged more vitriolic responses, she'd stopped.

How had these strangers even got her email address? The shire
had strict privacy rules about sharing information, and the only
other people who had her email address were Con and the members of the garden. None of them had any reason to give out her
details.

Judith and Sharon do.

Did they hate the refugee women so much it prevented them
from seeing the bigger picture?

Helen's phone rang and Vivian's voice echoed down the line,
sounding like she was speaking underwater. 'Great letter in the
paper again this week, Helen.'

'Thanks, but not everyone's in favour.'

'You mean the five letters against that Granski printed? Remember I warned you that would happen.'

'I've received some negative emails about the tiny houses. People
can be pretty blunt.'

'Tell me about it. Don't let a few morons get you down. I've been
in local politics for a decade and if it's taught me anything, it's the
need to focus on the positives. Your point of view's getting airplay
and that's what we need.'

It was true. Despite the letters from Bob, Lachlan and Roxy—Cinta, Tracey, Agape and Sue hadn't wanted to write—the paper had only printed Helen's. The comment Jade wrote on *The Standard*'s Facebook page had been referenced in the print edition of Saturday's paper, but it was buried in a forest of negative comments.

Helen was glad Jade had set up a Facebook account for her, even if the process had been fraught with much sighing and arguing from them both. She was still embarrassed that Fran at the library had suggested next time they should book a meeting room if they were going to 'engage in robust discussion'.

'Robust discussion?' Jade had looked blank. 'We're having a fight.'

Fran smiled. 'No, you're disagreeing and debating your points of view. It's only a fight if you put each other down. Why don't you combine your opinions and make a banner you both like using Canva?'

Helen had watched, genuinely impressed, as Jade took the artist's impression of the village from Helen's submission, then chose a photo of lush green spring vegetables in the garden, and used them to create the perfect banner for the Boolanga Needs A Sustainable Tiny Housing Village page. It was slowly gaining likes and Helen had posted the emails she'd written to *The Standard* on the page too.

She was about to tell Vivian about the Facebook page when the deputy mayor said, 'What did you think about the mayor's press release on Riverfarm?'

'Full of mixed messages. If he wanted to put out *The Standard*'s fire, it didn't work.'

'Exactly. I'm wondering if he wants to put it out. Since he bought Ainslea Park, he's changed.'

'What do you mean?'

There was a brief silence as if Vivian was struggling to put her feelings into words. 'Geoff was always keen to hear both sides of the story, but lately—'

This time the silence was different. 'You still there, Vivian?'

'Yes, sorry. I'm on Chinaman's Creek Road. The reception's a bit hit-and-miss.'

'I didn't hear anything after "but lately".'

'I'm starting to wonder if Geoff's more interested in the prestige and business opportunities being mayor offers him rather than the public service aspect.'

'Do you think he leaked the tiny houses submission to *The Standard*?'

'Maybe ... I'd like ... think that ... want ... staffer ... Granski.'

'What? You're breaking up.'

'Sor—' The call died.

'Damn it!' Helen pressed the faded red button on her phone, then rubbed the spot under her sternum that burned each time she thought about the project's future. A few weeks earlier they'd been so confident. Damn Geoff Rayson for doing a backflip.

Prestige and business opportunities? She recalled Vivian's comment the day *The Standard* leaked the submission—something about wealthy international horse-racing people. Today was the second time Vivian had implied Geoff was putting his own business interests ahead of the shire. It was time to do some digging.

Helen walked to the library and did an internet search. Vivian was correct—it was public knowledge that a sheik from the UAE had visited Ainslea Park.

She logged into her Facebook account and brought up the page. Jade had told her that to 'get traction' she needed to add a photo to each post. Fortunately, Jade had taken plenty of the garden and the adjacent land. Helen chose a photo of Sally Atkins's two old hacks grazing—not exactly racehorses but needs must—and started typing.

Rumours are flying around Boolanga that the delegation from the UAE who visited Ainslea Park have their eyes on more than just horseflesh. Riverfarm has always been part of this community. Be far more concerned about foreign ownership than a community-based housing project.

She checked her spelling and punctuation and hit send.

Jade was on her way to the supermarket when her phone pinged. Corey! Hope and relief made her check it immediately. Her body cramped with disappointment. There was no text notification. No message saying *I'll be home on Milo's birthday.*

'I think Daddy's planning a surprise,' she told Milo. But the words hung in the warm air like empty promises.

Her phone continued pinging and it took her a second to work out what was going on. The device had automatically connected to the library's wifi when she'd walked past and she was still in range.

She opened the Facebook app. *Holy shit.* There were five hundred likes on the tiny housing page she'd set up for Helen. Yesterday when she'd checked, there'd been twenty-five—mostly friends of Bob and Lachlan. She scrolled down and saw Helen had posted something without her help. Pride shot through her that she'd taught Helen how to do it.

There were heaps of comments on the post, but only three said they supported the housing project and they were from Lachlan, Bob and Fran at the library. The rest wrote about multinational companies and global cowboys raping Australia. There was a lot of swearing about overseas ownership of cultural icons and Jade thought they'd all missed the point of the post. Then she noticed the post had been shared twenty times, including by a right-wing page calling themselves Reclaim Australia.

A new comment came through from Cohousing Australia offering their support. Jade clicked like and walked to the garden.

Helen and Bob were having what Fran would call a robust discussion—something about the best place to plant a passionfruit vine. Jade interrupted them.

'Helen, your Facebook post's gone viral.'

'What does that mean?'

'It means people are sharing it to their groups and friends.'

Bob beamed. 'That's fantastic. Well done, Helen.'

Helen didn't look convinced. 'So people in Boolanga are reading it?'

'Maybe. Probably.'

'What does that mean?'

'It's hard to tell where everyone's from. A lot of the comments aren't about the tiny houses.'

Jade passed her phone to Helen who held it a full arm's length away.

Bob took his reading glasses out of his pocket and passed them to Helen. 'I'm buying you a lanyard.'

'You are not,' she said tersely. 'Only old people use them and I'm far from old.'

Jade snorted. 'Yeah—' Bob's frantic headshaking made her swallow the word 'right'.

'Talking about old, Jade, when are you twenty?' Bob asked.

'The eighteenth.'

'Isn't that the same day as Milo?'

'Yep.'

'You were in labour on your birthday?' Helen's expression was unexpectedly sympathetic.

'It sucked big time but Milo was worth it. At least this year I get my birthday back.'

Helen's laugh sounded more like a harsh bark. 'You'll never get your birthday back. You're a mother now and—'

'I reckon this calls for a double celebration,' Bob cut in. 'We can fire up the pizza oven. What do you say?'

Jade didn't know what to say. Even before Charlene had spent six years as a Jehovah's Witness, she'd never made a big deal about birthdays.

Bob's forehead creased at her silence. 'Silly me. You've probably got your birthdays all planned with family and friends.'

Pleasure and pain twisted Jade's heart and stupid tears burned the backs of her eyes. Bloody Bob. Always so freakin' kind. She kept waiting for him to show his true colours—discover the real reason he was being so nice—but he remained the same genial and thoughtful bloke he'd been since she met him. The only thing he'd ever asked her to do was write a letter for Helen's housing project.

Usually by this time in her birthday month, she'd dropped a hundred hints to Corey—not because he forgot exactly, but sometimes he was so busy it slipped his mind. But this year each time she'd gone to text him, something unfamiliar and hard had jabbed her. For reasons she couldn't fully explain, she'd stayed silent, reminding herself that fathers didn't forget something as momentous as their son's first birthday. Except Corey hadn't made contact in weeks.

Jade gave Bob her best nonchalant shrug—the one that said she was doing him a favour, not the other way around. 'I s'pose I could do lunch. That way maybe Fiza and the others can come.'

'Great idea.'

'Can we have bubbles and balloons?'

'Too easy.'

'I think you're forgetting something,' Helen said. 'If Judith finds out the women are coming, she'll cause a scene.'

'I'm a fully paid-up member of the community garden,' Bob said. 'The bylaws clearly state I can book the shelter for a private function as long as I stump up the booking fee. Don't you worry, I'll get it sorted.'

'Can you cook pizza?' Helen asked him.

'Oh ye of little faith.'

Helen crossed her arms. 'So that's a yes?'

Bob grinned. 'All the world is made of faith and trust and pixie dust.'

Helen rolled her eyes. 'Sounds like Peter Pan's cooking your birthday pizza, Jade.'

'You two are so weird.' But she couldn't help smiling.

'Actually, Lachlan's the pizza expert,' Bob said. 'He worked at Enzo's when he was at uni. Perhaps we could ask him—if that's okay with you, Jade?'

Jade's stomach suddenly filled with butterflies. *What the hell?* That wasn't right. She had no reason to be nervous about seeing Lachlan. The dude had dork written all over him—he sang in a choir and talked to plants!

She stomped on the irritating butterflies and concentrated on the fate of the party. 'If inviting Lachlan's the only way to avoid dud birthday pizza, you better invite him.'

All Jade really wanted for her birthday was a photo of her and Corey helping Milo blow out the candle on his cake. She'd convinced herself that if she made a cake—her first ever—then perhaps it would bring Corey home. Using this week's Vodka Cruiser money, she'd bought the ingredients and followed the recipe and instructions to a T on the *Women's Weekly Food* website. Only her number one cake didn't look anything like the picture on the screen.

Her birthday was eleven and a half hours old, the cake sat on its foil-covered baking tray yelling lousy mother, and Corey hadn't texted or called.

She picked up the cake, planning to dump it in the bin, when the doorbell rang.

'Milo, it's Daddy!' As Jade ran to the door, it occurred to her that Corey never rang the bell, he just walked in, but it wasn't enough to stop her heart from breaking. 'Fiza? Why are you here?'

'We thought it might be hard for you to walk today with Milo's cake.'

Jade's face burned. Why had she told the women at the garden she was making a cake, like it was something she was good at? But they'd all been interested, wanting to know about birthday celebrations, which apparently weren't a big deal in their culture. It had felt good having their attention.

'I didn't make it,' she lied.

Fiza looked over her shoulder, her face creased in confusion. 'But I see it.'

'It's really bad.'

'Let me look.' Fiza walked in and studied the cake.

Jade fought tears. 'I wanted it to be perfect.'

'It is perfect.'

'Are you blind? It's lumpy and crooked and the icing's all streaky.'

'It is colourful and made with love. This is all that matters.'

'But—'

'I always try to give my children a cake and a small gift.' Fiza's eyes unexpectedly filled with tears. 'There were years I could not do this. It broke my heart.'

Jade thought she understood. 'Because you didn't have enough money?'

Fiza stared at her as if she was working out what to say when the twins burst through the door.

'*Om!* It's hot and—' Sammy's eyes widened when he saw the cake. 'Cool! A one cake.'

'Milo's so lucky,' Leila said. 'Can I carry it?'

'I will carry it,' Fiza said firmly. 'Come. Let's go to the party.'

Jade didn't know what to expect. After all, no bloke she'd ever known had organised a party and, going on Helen's scepticism, her hopes weren't high. Smoke puffed from the pizza oven's flue, the balloons she'd requested were tied in clusters and she saw a box of bubble bottles on the sink. Even Daisy was wearing a birthday bandana. But it was the strings of flashing coloured lights wrapped around the support poles of the shelter and criss-crossing under the perspex roof that took her breath away.

Milo squirmed in her arms, fascinated by the lights. Then he saw Bob and squealed in delight.

Bob's blue eyes twinkled. 'Happy birthday, little buddy. And to you too, Jade.'

'Thank—' The loud pop of a cork made her turn. Lachlan was holding aloft a large dark bottle.

'Happy birthday, Jade. Want a drink?'

She'd never tasted sparkling wine before. 'Sure.' She settled Milo on a picnic rug and accepted the frothing drink.

'Fiza, I've got cans of soft drink in the esky for you and the kids,' Bob said. 'Help yourself.'

'Happy birthday, Jade.' Helen walked into the shelter holding a chocolate cake with a decoration sticking out of it that looked like exploding stars. A gold 20 waved in the centre. 'Bob, the price of this cake is outrageous. I could have made it for a third of the cost—'

'Thanks for picking it up.' Bob pulled out his wallet.

Helen waved the money away. 'Oh, I didn't pay for it. I told Karina you'd be in later to settle up.'

'Right. Good. Okay, time for presents!' Despite his silver hair and craggy cheeks, Bob looked as excited as Leila and Sammy.

Lachlan gave Jade a wry smile. 'Uncle Bob loves a party. He and Auntie Pen used to have a bonfire night every June and invite half the district. When I was little, Mum would put me to bed early but Uncle Bob always snuck in and got me so I wouldn't miss out. Everyone needs an Uncle Bob.'

'This is for Milo.' Bob pushed a little wooden trolley with red wheels towards the baby. 'It's a walking toy. The blocks give it enough weight so he can stay steady and push it around.'

Lachlan bent down and built a short stack with the blocks. Laughing, Milo knocked them down. 'Is that fun, squirt?' Lachlan built them up again.

'You did exactly the same thing with the ones I made you,' Bob said.

Jade stared at him, not believing what she'd just heard. 'You made the wagon and the blocks?'

Bob nodded. 'I like to dabble in a bit of woodwork. This is for you.'

He passed her a small box wrapped in a green ribbon. Inside, a pair of earrings fashioned from three different pieces of polished wood nestled on cotton wool.

Without thinking, Jade hugged him. 'They're beautiful. Thanks.'

'No worries.'

Then Fiza gave her a card, and Lachlan mumbled something about 'not being much', which turned out to be a bar of lemon myrtle scented soap wrapped in plain tissue paper.

Helen shoved a tiny green plant in a recycled black pot towards her. 'It's a peace lily. Look after it and it'll flower eventually.'

Jade suddenly got hot and uncomfortable, which was dumb because who didn't enjoy getting presents? But she couldn't stop herself thinking how this random group of people had done more to make her feel special on her birthday than her family. Familiar hurt rose up and bit her as savagely as a pit bull. Before she could stop herself, she was saying tersely, 'Of course I'll look after it!'

'Good,' Helen said. 'Lachlan, you got those pizzas under control? People are arriving in five minutes.'

Lachlan winked at Jade. 'Halal pizza ready in ten and then I'll tie some balloon animals for the kids.'

The party rolled out across the afternoon. Although Bob had told everyone not to bring anything, the women arrived with plenty of food to share. Jade ate so much she thought she'd burst. It was a truly happy occasion, but not even her buzz from the sparkling wine or the many compliments for her cake were enough to keep despair at bay when everyone sang happy birthday to Milo.

Lachlan took a photo of her and Milo blowing out his candle, but when Jade looked at it she didn't see their smiling faces, only the absence of Corey.

Aima laughed at Milo whose cheeks were smeared with blue icing and chocolate cake. 'He likes this food. Maybe I make for my daughter.'

Jade wiped Milo's face and hands. 'A three ca—'

'Fuck, Jade. What the hell?'

The easy chatter of conversation died. All heads swung towards the angry voice.

'Corey?' Surprise and delight shot Jade to her feet. 'Everyone, this is Corey. Milo's dad.'

'G'day, Corey.' Bob stretched out his hand.

But Corey was looking past him to Milo, who was sitting on Aima's lap. Jade followed his gaze and her pleasure at his unexpected arrival vanished as wariness stalked in. She'd told him she wouldn't bring Milo to the garden.

Corey moved towards Aima, but Jade moved faster, scooping up their son. 'Look, buddy,' she said brightly. 'Daddy's here for your birthday.'

Corey threw his arm around her waist and dug his fingers into her skin. He ducked his head in close, his eyes sparking like flint, his breath all beer fumes. His words came out tight and low. 'I've been waiting two f-ing hours.'

Her heart rate picked up. Corey must have sunk more than a couple of beers while he'd waited. 'I didn't think—you didn't say you were coming.'

'I don't need to. You should be home waiting for me instead of here with stinking scum.'

Her skin flashed hot and cold. 'Shh, they'll hear you.'

'So? They're brainwashed not to have any feelings. It's why they blow people up so easily. What I care about is how you've wrecked the surprise.'

His claim tangled with the message his infrequent contact sent, but well-honed survival skills told her not to mention it. 'It's an awesome surprise. Thank you.'

She kissed him, not only to placate him but to give herself time to think of how to fix this. How to make him feel appreciated and involved. Although they'd cut and eaten Milo's cake, hers was still intact.

'Now you're here, let's sing happy birthday to Milo and get a photo to put next to the one of us when he was born.'

His grip tightened, pinching her. 'Have you lost your freakin' mind? I'm not singing happy birthday with apes or terrorist scum who don't even know the words.'

The silence behind her intensified. Jade didn't know where to look or what to do. If she told Corey to shut up, he'd go ballistic. If she told the women he was drunk and he didn't mean what he said, his reaction would likely be the same.

'Everything okay, Jade?'

She jumped at Lachlan's voice.

Corey spun around to face him. 'Who the hell are you?'

'A friend of Jade's.'

'Is that right?'

Corey was shorter than Lachlan but he took a step towards him and puffed out his chest. Some of Jade's delicious lunch rose to the back of her throat and her already highly tuned radar flicked onto high alert.

'Corey, let's go home.'

He shook off her arm and kept his gaze on Lachlan. 'Well, friend of Jade's, I'm the father of her kid, so fuck off.'

'Corey!'

'I'm not disputing who you are,' Lachlan said evenly. His gaze was fixed on Jade, his forest-green eyes full of questions. 'I was just asking Jade if she's okay.'

Her heart raced like a cornered rabbit. 'Yeah, all good. But Corey's tired after a long drive, so we should go.'

'You sure?' Bob asked. 'We haven't cut your cake.'

The kindness and concern in his eyes matched Lachlan's, but instead of circling her in caring warmth, it suddenly spiked and prickled like pity. Her spine stiffened. Sure, Corey was drunk right now, possibly stoned, but they didn't know him like she did. He'd come back for her and Milo's birthday. That was love. That was family.

'Can you drive, Jade?' Helen's voice cut across the loaded silence.

Helen could be so random. Of course she couldn't drive. She'd never had the chance to learn or a car to practise in. 'What's that got to do with anything?'

Helen inclined her head towards Corey who was jangling his keys.

Before Jade got pregnant, she'd ridden in the ute with Corey when he was high. Then it had been all about danger and exhilaration. Putting it up her mother who hated Corey. Hated her having any fun. But she still remembered the time Corey had played chicken, stopping the car millimetres from a tree. His laugh. Her terror. She wasn't that girl any more. She was a mother and she must protect Milo. Must protect Corey.

'We'll walk home,' she said firmly.

'I'm not bloody walking!' Corey said.

Lachlan opened his mouth, but Bob shook his head. 'How about I drive the three of you home? Corey, you don't want to give Denny North the satisfaction of taking your licence away, eh?'

At the mention of the police sergeant, Corey let rip a string of expletives. Surprisingly, he handed over his keys.

After Bob left the unit, Jade's cake sat on the kitchen bench looking like a woman who'd worn an evening gown to a barbecue. Milo reached for the sparkly decoration, sobbing when she whipped it out of the cake and out of his reach.

He didn't stop crying when she put his number one candle in its place and lit it. Or when she jiggled him up and down cooing,

'Shh, buddy, it's okay.' He'd tipped from tired into exhausted and nothing would placate him. The family selfie would have to wait.

Fighting disappointment, Jade took him to his room. After he was settled in his cot, she washed her hands and looked in the mirror, surprised at what she saw. She didn't usually do anything with her hair or wear make-up, but in honour of their birthdays, and so she looked half decent in the photo, she'd made an effort and styled her hair.

Corey was sitting on the bed when she came out of the bathroom. He looked happier than he had at the garden and the knot in her stomach loosened.

'You want your birthday present?'

Excitement skittered inside her. 'You got me a present?'

'Yeah.'

His hands were empty and she couldn't see a box or parcel on the bed or anywhere. 'Where is it?'

He patted his crotch. 'Right here. Come and get it.'

It surprised her how much effort it took to smile—as if the muscles in her face were fighting setting concrete. Of course he was the present. He'd come home for her and Milo. Wasn't that what she'd wanted more than anything?

After sex that was faster than usual, she left Corey sleeping, ran a bath and finished herself off. Not that she wasn't used to doing that, but doing it on her birthday sucked.

When the water began to cool, she washed herself, luxuriating in the clean and crisp scent of the soap Lachlan had given her. Her hands stalled between her legs. She dropped the bar and stood up fast, drying herself with a scratchy towel until the only sensation was pain.

When she grabbed clean clothes from the bedroom, the bed was empty. She walked into the small living space, but Corey wasn't on the couch or in the kitchen. She heard the distinctive roar of his ute and lifted the sheet that doubled as a curtain on the front window to see the vehicle disappearing down the road.

What the hell?

Even though Corey didn't leave notes she looked around for one, trying to make sense of why he'd left without telling her. She checked her phone for a text. Nothing.

Something made her open the fridge. An empty cardboard wrapper sat on the top shelf. Understanding dawned, bringing relief. He'd gone to buy beer.

She closed the fridge and noticed the cake. It looked like it had been hit by a chocolate avalanche—the fondant icing hung jagged and loose and a gaping hole existed where cake had once sat. The number one candle lay broken, snapped at its base.

She closed her eyes. Corey wouldn't have grabbed a hunk of cake like a caveman. Not when he knew how much she wanted a photo of the three of them with Milo blowing out his candle. But when she opened her eyes, nothing had changed.

'I can fix this.'

Blinking furiously, her fingers pushed the fallen cake upwards and tugged the edges of the icing together. But it wouldn't knit. It was as torn and damaged as her heart.

'Helen?' Bob's voice drifted through the screen door. 'You there?'

She had her head in the fridge organising the leftover party food and before she'd given it any real thought, she was calling out, 'Door's open.'

A second later, Bob was standing in her kitchen for the first time and holding a small bunch of sweet william.

She hauled herself to her feet and shot the flowers a suspicious look. 'Who are those for?'

'You. A thank you for clearing up after the party.'

'Give them to Lachlan. He did the lion's share.'

'He probably wanted to keep busy. Were the women okay? Something like that's pretty rattling.'

Helen sighed, understanding perfectly. 'And to think I was worried about Judith making a scene. She's got nothing on Corey.'

'I don't like him.'

'Take a number.'

'I'll take a cuppa if you're offering.' He dropped his hat on the table. 'I didn't think he was even on the scene. I've never heard Jade talk about him, have you?'

'She's twenty, Bob, and we're older than dinosaurs.' She pulled mugs out of the cupboard.

'Nah, that's ninety-eight.' He winked. 'Me, I'm still in my prime.'

'Have you always been this infuriatingly optimistic?'

He laughed. 'Yep. Only way to survive being a farmer.'

'And your wife?' God, what was she doing? 'Sorry, don't answer that. It's none of my business.'

'What happened to Pen's not a state secret. In fact, one of the first signs things weren't right was her sudden pessimism and suspicion of people.' He stirred milk into his tea. 'Alzheimer's. She died last year.'

'I'm sorry. I didn't realise your loss was so recent.'

'It's only recent in terms of her physical death. The disease swallowed my darling Pen three years ago.'

His words summoned thoughts of Nicki. Her own unrelenting grief.

'Was her illness why you sold the farm?'

'No. We'd already sold the farm and moved into town anticipating retirement. We set off with the caravan, intending to take a year to go around Australia. Wilpena Pound was the first place Pen got lost on her way back from the toilet block. We laughed, saying all the trees looked the same. But it kept happening. She'd go to the supermarket and come back with strange combinations of food, but it only occurred to me there was something seriously wrong when she navigated us into a river.

'That's when I realised she could no longer read the map. Things went down fast after that. Pen loved bushwalking but she started taking off on her own and getting lost. When she forgot to turn off the stove, I realised she was no longer safe. We couldn't get a nursing home bed in Boolanga when we needed it, but there was one in Wang, so I moved in with Debbie. Lachie's mum.'

'Did a new town worsen your wife's confusion?'

'I don't think so. I put the standard lamp she'd always knitted under and her favourite chair in the room and initially she thought she was at the farmhouse. After that, there were months when she was convinced she was at teachers' college and then, at the end, her childhood home.' He rubbed his jaw. 'She didn't recognise me for the last year.'

Too many times Helen had thought the same about Nicki.

'It pulls your heart out of your chest,' she said.

'Yep. Over and over. But believing she enjoyed my company in the moment, even if she didn't remember me, helped.' His eyes filmed as memories flooded his face.

Helen's hand rose, heading towards his, before she realised what she was doing. *Unwise. Stop.* Shocked, she pulled back fast, fisting her hand in her lap. Empathy was one thing. Physically touching him was another thing entirely.

Bob cleared his throat. 'Do you reckon we should call Jade?'

'If she wants help, she's got our numbers, but I doubt she'll call. For all that Corey's obnoxious and racist, I've never seen any signs on Jade that he's physically hurting her. And she gets around in those short-shorts and tank tops so we'd have seen the bruises.'

Bob gave her a long look. 'That's not a very high bar.'

'It's the important one.'

'Emotional abuse causes as many scars. I might pop in on my way home.'

'And what if you popping in pisses off Corey and makes things worse? Don't go using your happy marriage as the measuring stick for everyone else's relationships. Most won't come close.'

'Sounds like you're speaking from experience.'

Her empathy for him shut down fast and she stood, wishing she'd never invited him in.

'I've got an appointment. When you've finished your tea, lock the door on your way out.'

Helen's 'appointment' was at the library. She checked her email, bracing herself for negative ones, but for the first time in a few weeks it was thankfully vitriol-free. She was excited to see the Facebook page now had over fifteen hundred likes. Some of the comments made her cringe, but none of them called her a whore, bitch or worse so they were an improvement on the emails.

Jade had explained how the more likes the page received, the higher its visibility. Most people wrote messages of support for the tiny houses village, and there were three messages from successful co-housing projects offering advice and assistance. The Landcare group had messaged, wanting to talk to Helen. They were worried if a resort was built, the nature corridor along the river would be lost to the community, or worse, lost completely.

She released a slew of comments onto the page, including one that said *Geoff Rayson needs to rethink his priorities.* Then in a show of solidarity for Landcare, she wrote a post highlighting their concerns and used one of their photos of the river. She logged out and walked to the café for her shift.

When she got home four hours later, she found dishes dry in the drainer and her kitchen tidier than when she'd left. The bunch of sweet william nestled in a glass of water next to a note that looked like it had been written with a carpenter's pencil—the letters printed, solid and thick. *Thanks for the cuppa. See you at park food. Bob.*

Between the garden, the farmers' market, the food nights and his help with the campaign, she was seeing a lot of Bob. She couldn't decide if that was a problem or not.

She headed off to bed to the tunes of a cicada band, the soothing hoot of owls and the nails-down-the-blackboard screeches of the flying foxes. Exhausted after a huge day, she shoved in earplugs and fell asleep.

She woke with a start, her heart leaping into her mouth and sweat beading on her skin. Lying rigid, she tugged the earplugs out and strained to hear whatever had ripped her out of a deep sleep. Thick and suffocating silence pressed in on her. She held her breath, waiting for it to break. For the danger to reveal itself.

When it didn't, she slowly released her breath and let her head fall back on the pillow. It must have been a nightmare. The thought depressed her. After three years of stable housing, she'd thought those terrors were long gone.

Pulling up the sheet to her chin, she closed her eyes and rolled over. A jangling noise crashed around her, the sound old but familiar from her childhood—of dustbin lids being crashed together like cymbals. Wheelie bins didn't make that metallic clash.

The new shed! Bloody kids!

She lurched to her feet, grabbed her phone and bat light and dragged open the front door. Swearing at the hedge blocking her view and with her heart pounding, she forced herself to step off the safety of the veranda. In her shaking hand, the white LED beam of her torch bounced wildly as she tried to find the shed. When she did, the door was hanging open.

She arced the light again and this time caught sight of two dark shapes running into the orchard. *Bastards!*

'Keep going!' she yelled.

She counted to fifty, watching and listening keenly, but there was no more movement or human-made noise. She did another sweep with the torch, but the garden was empty.

Should she ring the police?

She trudged up to the shed to see if they'd stolen anything. They'd used boltcutters on the padlock, but a quick glance showed all the tools in place on the shadow board and shovels and forks hanging on their allotted rack. Thank goodness one of the buggers had let the door bang and she'd disturbed them before they could pilfer anything. Although why would teenagers want garden equipment?

It was probably just part of a dare. That had been Trent and Jax's motivation three years earlier.

She checked her phone: 03:51 am. There was no point waking up the good sergeant. She'd call him at eight.

After tossing and turning from four until seven, Helen was pulling on thick socks when loud and rapid thumping on the front door made her jump.

'Who is it?' she called.

'Jade. Open the door!'

Was Jade hiding from Corey? Helen half ran, half slid along the bare boards. She flung the door open, grabbed Jade and pulled her and the pram into the hall. Then she kicked the door shut so hard the slam vibrated the glass in the windows.

Milo screamed.

'Does he have a gun?' Helen asked. 'I'll ring the police.'

Jade was unbuckling Milo. 'What the hell are you doing? You've just scared the shi—shirt out of him.'

Indignation poured through Helen. 'I'm keeping you safe.'

Jade straightened, her expression confused. 'From what?'

'From who.'

Jade's eyes lit up in triumph. 'From whom.'

'Fine! But save the grammar discussion for later. Does Corey know you're here?'

Her eyes dimmed but her chin lifted. 'No.'

'Does he know you've left your place?'

'No.' Jade chewed her lip. 'And I don't know where he is. Probably halfway to God knows where.'

'Then why are you hammering down my door like the hounds of hell are on your heels?'

'Because some bastard's wrecked my flower bed! They've snapped off half my plants and stomped on the others. They pulled out the bedhead and dropped it on Kubra's chives and they ripped Fiza's tent. Some of the maize plants are broken. But the worst thing—' her voice cracked, breaking with despair, '—the disgusting deviants shat on my daisies. Who would do that?'

Helen thought about the shadowy figures running towards the orchard. Remembered the ugly words Corey had spoken at the party.

'Corey doesn't like you being here, does he?'

Jade looked at her feet. 'No.'

'So he has a reason to destroy your garden bed.'

Her head shot up. 'He doesn't even know I have a garden bed! Anyway, he's not like that. It was probably those African kids *The Standard*'s always talking about.'

'Why would they damage Fiza's tent and her plants?'

'I dunno.'

Helen made herself give Jade's shoulder a pat. 'I understand what's happened is upsetting, but the worst thing we can do is attribute blame before we have the facts.'

'A minute ago you were blaming Corey!'

'No. I was pointing out he has more reasons to hurt you than some random kids.'

'Corey wouldn't …' Jade bit her lip.

But Helen knew all about angry young men. 'I know you don't want him to have done it, but that's not always enough. Let's call the police and then we'll ring everyone else.'

Every time Jade looked at her flower bed, tears formed. Then she flushed hot with anger at herself. What was wrong with her? Who cried over a garden bed? But since finishing school and giving birth to Milo, the garden was the first activity that was just for her. She hated that some prick had stormed in to deliberately destroy it.

Helen thought it was Corey, and Jade resented her for that. Sure, he'd wrecked her cake, but everyone knew when the munchies hit they needed to be satisfied. It didn't mean he'd wrecked her garden. Hell, he didn't even know which bed was hers.

You should have been home waiting for me instead of here with stinking scum.

She tried shaking away Corey's words, but like borers tunnelling relentlessly into wood, they ate into her confidence.

Did Macca know about the garden? She'd come here straight after he'd taken the PlayStation. Had he followed her?

A flash of colour caught Jade's attention and she looked up. Fiza was rushing straight to the torn tent and snapped maize. She cried out and sank to her knees, her distress blooming like a mushroom cloud and drifting over to envelop Jade. She'd never seen Fiza other than happy and her audible wailing grief unsettled her. It was embarrassing.

Jade didn't know what to do, especially when Fiza picked up the broken plants and buried them as carefully as if they were human. That felt private—something she shouldn't interrupt.

Eventually, the need to commiserate over their joint heartache propelled Jade up the hill. Fiza was stroking the leaves on the surviving maize and murmuring something unintelligible to them. Jade itched with awkwardness. Fiza's face was wet and shiny with tears, and the droop of her usually square shoulders made her look as broken as the maize.

Something deep inside Jade ached and she didn't want to feel it. It was a path leading to a dark place she had no intention of revisiting.

'Why are you even growing maize anyway?' Her words came out harsher than she'd intended.

'For my father. For my heart.'

The prickling sensation morphed into rushing heat. Jade's father didn't give a shit about her, but Fiza's dad must have loved her if she was planting things for him on the other side of the world.

'If you miss him so much, why did you come to Australia without him?' she asked.

'I did not choose to leave him or Sudan.'

Jade thought about leaving Finley. She'd hardly chosen to do that and even though it was only a couple of hours down the road, it may as well have been a plane ride away. When she'd told Charlene she was pregnant, her mother had stormed into Jade's bedroom and taken what she'd wanted—dresses, make-up and her stash of cash—before dumping everything else, including her books, into two-dollar-shop bags and throwing them outside into the rain. She thought about how Charlene had screamed at her, calling her a slut, telling her to never come back unless she got rid of 'the brat'. How Corey had insisted they leave town.

'Did someone make you leave?' she asked.

Fiza looked at her then with strangely empty eyes. She laughed, only it was nothing like the usual tinkling happy sound that matched her colourful clothes. She stood, her beautiful face twisted and ugly, her eyes flashing with angry light.

'Who does this in Australia? Why here, where people have so much?'

Jade squirmed. 'I dunno. Amal might know?'

'No!' Fiza's yell reverberated around the garden. 'My son was at home with me. He did not do this!'

'He might know something though. Stuff like that gets talked about at school. At Tranquillity.'

But Fiza wasn't listening. She was watching Helen and a police officer Jade recognised walking up the hill. She'd met him a few times before. Not that she was going to admit to that in front of Helen and Fiza.

'Ladies, this is Constable Tom Fiora,' Helen said. 'Constable, this is Jade Innes and Fiza Atallah. Their garden beds sustained the most damage.'

'Sorry to hear that.' The police officer looked straight at Jade. 'Helen says Corey might have decided to defecate on your daisies. Is he at home for a chat?'

Corey had priors—dumb stuff from when he was a kid, like nicking a car for a joy ride and some bottles of Bundy from the Bottle-O. It marked him, so whenever the police turned up 'for a chat', Jade played dumb. At least this time she didn't have to lie.

'He shot through at six last night. Haven't seen him since.'

'Any idea where he might be?'

Macca came to mind, but if Corey was still in town the police would find him without her help. 'No.'

'Did he hurt you last night?'

'He wasn't around long enough to do that.' The words came out uncensored, shocking her. Helen pursed her lips and that was enough to light Jade's fuse. 'What? It's the truth, okay.'

But Helen remained silent.

The copper wrote something in his book, then turned his attention to Fiza. 'Anyone you know who might have done this, Mrs Atallah?'

Fiza's hands balled into fists by her sides. 'Are you talking in general or specifics? Half the town is unhappy that people like me live here.'

'Are you aware of anyone in town who might want to upset you?'

'No.'

'Anyone in your own community?'

Fiza's eyes narrowed. 'Boolanga *is* my community.'

The policeman flushed. 'I meant, any Africans.'

'Africa is a continent,' Fiza muttered. 'No.'

'You have children, Mrs Atallah?'

'You know I do.'

'What has this got to do with the vandalism?' Helen asked.

'General lines of enquiry. How are things between yourself and your eldest son, Mrs Atallah?' Constable Fiora asked.

'What do you mean?'

'Boys that age often run wild.'

'You think Amal did this?' Fiza's chin lifted as regally as a queen's. 'Amal was at home last night studying. He has exams soon.'

'You sure he didn't sneak out with his mates to let off a bit of steam?'

'Oh, for heaven's sake!' Helen said.

Jade's guts suddenly loosened like she'd eaten a bad dimmie. Oh God. She'd done the same thing to Fiza as the copper— implied that Amal might know something just because he was a black teenager. Why had she done that? It wasn't like she was unfamiliar with being targeted by the cops. They always came to talk to her first whenever they wanted information about Corey. She hated that they assumed she knew what he was up to, not only because it meant they thought she'd broken the law too, but because it reinforced how little Corey told her about his life.

'You'd be surprised how many seemingly random crimes are committed by people closest to the victim, Mrs Demetriou.' The constable wrote something in his notepad. 'Mrs Atallah, bring Amal to the station for a chat after school. Or if you prefer, we can visit him at home.'

'You only want to talk to him because he is black!'

He stiffened. 'I'm just doing my job, Mrs Atallah. I'll be talking to Corey Noonan as well.'

'Good luck with that,' Jade muttered.

'You say something, Jade?'

'Thank you, Constable.'

He hesitated as if he was about to say more, then stuffed his notebook into his pocket. He pointed to the Hoopers sign. 'Nothing's ever random, ladies. Boolanga's currently experiencing a petty crime spree and the hardware store's a target. They sponsor the garden and now the garden's been vandalised. The description of boys in hoodies seen running from the scene matches Hoopers' CCTV. The fact the perps' faces are never identified leads us to suspect they're African.'

'Or wearing balaclavas, fly nets or black stockings on their heads,' Helen said drily.

He ignored the comment and handed Fiza a card with his name printed on it. 'I'll expect you and your son at three forty-five this afternoon.'

Despite old fear fluttering inside her, Jade reached out an unsteady hand and touched Fiza's arm. 'We'll come with you to the station. Right, Helen?'

'Absolutely. Wouldn't miss it.'

CHAPTER

20

It was a pupil-free day and the kids were home. Usually Tara enjoyed these days without routine, but not today. All of her craved to run—to see Zac. Although Flynn and Clementine had no idea what was distracting her, they knew her attention wasn't fully focused on them. As a result, they'd squabbled and played up all morning.

Their contrariness wasn't helped by the fact the neighbours' children had been outside all morning. During their tennis drill, Flynn and Clem threw so many longing glances towards the Atallah twins, they'd missed most of the balls. Now they were back inside and, in a moment of desperation, Tara had suggested they all play Monopoly. Between turns, she found herself glancing out the window too.

Fiza and her three children continued to work in their garden. The eldest, a tall and skinny young man, appeared to be doing whatever his mother told him. Tara had seen him shovelling dirt or mulch out of a wheelbarrow and now he was hammering in stakes. She reluctantly conceded that the loss of the weed-infested eyesore that had flourished under Lyle's occupancy was welcome.

'Daddy!' Clementine leaped off her chair and threw her arms around her father as if it had been days since she'd last seen him instead of hours. 'Play with us?!'

'Daddy's only home for lunch,' Tara said.

'Actually, I don't think I'll go back this afternoon.' Jon sounded weary.

'You okay?' she asked automatically, sounding as if everything between them was normal.

Jon pulled his phone from his pocket. 'Chris sent this.'

It was a photo of a smiling Hegarty family rugged up in coats and standing by a lake in Central Park. Toy yachts sailed in the background and the caption read *Looking for Stuart Little.*

A combination of delight and melancholy twisted inside her. 'They look happy.'

'Yeah.' Sadness and meaning dripped from the word—like we used to be.

Fury blasted in, decimating melancholy. How dare Jon be sad? All year, she'd been trying different things to bring the joy back into their marriage. The intimacy. What had he done except blame her for their problems?

'Maybe we should invite the gang over?' he said.

This was Jon's solution to everything. Tara wanted to yell, 'That's right. Fill the house with people so you don't have to be alone with me. So you can talk to Rhianna about how awful I am. So you can fall into bed drunk and know I won't bother you.' But the children were in the room. At least they hadn't reached the low point of arguing in front of them. And if she was honest, she just couldn't be bothered having the same fight with him yet again.

'Your dad was here last night, so can we have a night off and just do something as a family?' She inclined her head towards the window and the shrieks of the twins. 'We need to get away and do something. How about a bike ride?'

'Dad's giving me a hand building Clemmie's playhouse,' Jon said.

'Yay!' Clemmie cheered. 'I want to help too.'

'Me too.' Flynn started packing up the Monopoly. 'Grandpa said he'd let me hammer in nails.'

Tara should have been disappointed that her idea of a bike ride was nuked but she saw it as a get-out-of-jail-free card.

'Sounds like you've got the afternoon sorted, so I'll go into town for a couple of hours. Vivian wants to discuss window dressings.'

The lie slid off her tongue so fast it shocked her.

In the gym's changeroom, Tara pulled on her brand-new compression running tights and crop top. The outfit had cost a bomb. Not only were both items made of high-tech fabric with moisture-wicking qualities and open-mesh panels, they made her feel sexy. If Jon was no longer interested in making her feel that way, it was up to her to do it herself. She'd ordered the new outfit the night Shannon and Chris announced they were leaving. Then she'd gone on another night run with Zac.

They were texting each other daily now—a mix of logistics, motivation, advice and unrestrained flirting. After she ran a PB not too far outside Zac's standard time, he'd messaged *you blow me away*. Tara had some very literal plans to do exactly that. Soon. Very soon.

Stowing her ordinary clothes into a locker, she picked up her water bottle and walked into the gym.

Zac let out a low whistle. 'Is that the new range from Nike?'

'Sure is. I'm hoping it'll shave off another thirty seconds.'

He laughed. 'That's a big ask, but it's already doing a great job. You look hot.'

A tiny part of her cringed at the juvenile compliment. The rest of her soaked it up greedily like a shrivelled sponge. 'Thanks.'

'Great that you could make it in after all.' He leaned over and pressed a button on the treadmill, lowering it to the starting position. 'How about you warm up and then we'll do some weights, squats and lunges.'

'Sounds good.' She stepped up onto the flat black surface, pressed some buttons to set the speed and inclination, and grabbed the pulse bar.

'Looks like you missed a tag.' Zac's fingers brushed her skin as he snapped off the offending article. 'Don't want you setting off the new security system in the supermarket.'

She laughed, but her pulse was jumping, the numbers leaping up fast on the screen. Horrified, she dropped her hands and gave full rein to the delicious tingles shimmering between her legs and melting her mind. As the treadmill increased its speed, she indulged in her fantasy of Zac's fingers trailing further down her spine until they slid underneath the waistband of her tights, skimming her buttocks and—

She stumbled. Her hands shot towards the stop button and missed.

You're falling.

She grabbed air. Her shoulder hit the belt, then her hips. A second later she was airborne and then her legs slammed into the rowing machine. Shock sucked the air from her lungs.

'Bloody hell.' Zac kneeled beside her. 'Are you okay? Have you broken anything?'

She lay dazed. 'Give me a second.'

He grabbed her water bottle. 'Here. Drink this.'

She took a sip. As she swallowed she became aware of a dull pain on the tip of her shoulder. Hoping it was only a bruise from landing on it, she raised both arms and legs. 'All good so far.'

'I'll help you sit up.'

He slid his arm around her, easing her up and positioning her against the wall. The gym swam in front of her and she dropped her head forward.

'Should I call an ambulance?'

She shook her head. 'I think I'm just a bit woozy from adrenaline overload. One minute I was running and the next I was flying, but not in a good way.'

Zac grimaced. 'Can you rotate your ankles?'

She rolled them left then right and raised each leg. 'All good. Just a few bruises.'

'Come on then.' He put one arm under her legs and the other around her waist and hoisted her up against his chest.

'What are you doing?'

'Taking you upstairs to lie down.'

She didn't protest. This scenario, minus the bruising, was one of her favourite fantasies.

Upstairs screamed bachelor pad. Apart from one closed door, which Tara assumed was the bathroom, it was a big open living space. The empty base of a NutriBullet sat on the kitchen bench next to enough black and red canisters of muscle and fitness supplements to stock a store. A large television hung on one wall and Tara recognised the gaming device Flynn was pestering her to buy. There was no artwork on the walls, only a large planner surrounded by motivational quotes and a photoshopped photo of Zac crossing the finish line of the New York marathon with a time of 3:00.

He lowered her onto a large rumpled bed that appeared to double as a couch. The sheets smelled of Zac—musky with a tang of sweat. She breathed in deeply.

'Sorry, it's a bit of a mess,' he said sheepishly. 'Sheets were clean on yesterday.'

'It's fine.' Tara found his embarrassment endearing. 'I'm not here to rate your housekeeping skills.'

He pushed some pillows in behind her, then his face appeared in front of hers, his dark brows pulled down in concern. He gently brushed some strands of hair out of her eyes. 'What do you need?'

Despite the niggling sense this apartment reinforced the fact that at twenty-six Zac was barely an adult, Tara didn't hesitate. Ignoring the pain in her shoulder, she reached out, wrapped her hands behind his neck and pulled his face towards her. 'You. I need you.'

His mouth curved up into a smile. It was exactly what she needed to see.

It was over a decade since she'd had sex with anyone but Jon. Back then, she'd been younger than Zac was now and she hadn't known how to ask for what she wanted in bed. Today she knew exactly.

Closing her eyes, she blocked out the apartment and the quiet but insistent voice in her head saying, *if you cross this line, there's no going back.*

Zac's lips tasted of coffee and opened generously under hers. She tumbled headlong into wondrous, sensual heat, raiding what he offered and demanding more. She craved to consume him from tip to toe.

Her hands fluttered over his skin, glorying in the touch of muscle rippling and tensing under her palms. She whipped his singlet over his head and pressed her lips to his shoulders, his chest, then flicked his nipples with her tongue. He gasped. His heart raced, each beat slamming against her hands and matching her own.

The kiss deepened, running along her veins as fast as a flame burning a detonation cord. She was heat. She was lust. She was power. Nothing existed except the vibrating need spinning unsatiated inside her for weeks. Every muscle tightened as her body edged closer to release.

Not yet. She didn't want to come on her own—she'd been doing that for months. She needed Zac inside her.

Panting, she pushed him down on the bed and straddled him. She pulled off her top, then turned her attention to his shorts, desperate to release the gratifying bulge in his pants. She wanted to ride him until she was flung out of herself, out of this room and out of her life.

'Tara.'

Her hands gripped the elastic of his shorts, ready to pull.

His hands captured hers. 'Tara.'

The combination of his tone and the weight of his hands on hers slowly penetrated her fog of arousal. She looked down into his dark eyes. They sparkled, lit like the night sky, only instead of stars, it was need for her.

She leaned down to kiss him again, her breasts brushing his chest, and her hair fell in her eyes. She pushed it away and then she was staring into his eyes again, only now they were filled with caution. It knifed her.

'What?' she said.

His mouth pulled to one side as if he was in pain. 'Do we really want to do this?'

She opened her mouth to yell *Hell yes!* then heard the word 'we'.

He means does he really want to do this.

It was like being hit by a cascade of icy water. Rafts of goosebumps rippled across her skin—the pain of rejection overlaid with acute embarrassment. Her throat tightened, trapping her scream, and then—*damn it*—she was sobbing. Hard and ugly crying.

Desperate to run, to hide, she scrambled off him.

Zac moved too. Before she understood what was happening, she was wrapped in a sheet and in his arms. He kissed her hair. 'Please. Don't cry.'

But the floodgates had opened and couldn't be shut. 'You d-don't f-find me attractive either!'

'What? No! You're amazing. Sexy. Gorgeous and—'

'Shut up! How can I be any of those things when not even my personal trainer wants to have sex with me.'

'I didn't say I didn't want to have sex with you. I just don't think we should.'

Anger broke through her paralysing embarrassment and she twisted away from him, feeling pain in her shoulder.

'Have I misunderstood all our texting and flirting? Or is that just part of the official marathon-training handbook?'

Offence scored his cheeks. 'No!'

She had no idea what 'no' meant. 'Then why are you sending mixed messages? I thought one of the perks of your job was having sex with willing clients.'

His olive skin pinked and he dropped his gaze. 'The thing is, Tara, the clients I have sex with are women I don't care about.'

Her head threatened to explode and at the same time exhaustion pulled at every part of her. 'I don't understand.'

For a long moment, the only noise in the room was the hum of the fridge, then a long sigh shuddered out of Zac. 'Of course I'm attracted to you. You have an incredible body, but it's complicated.'

'I think you have an incredible body too, so how is it complicated?' But even as she said the words she heard her voice choking on reality.

'I really like you, Tara. You're clever and funny and you chase PBs as hard as I do. You've been amazing the way you've supported me building the business and giving me solid advice. That Tara reminds me of my big sister. My friend.'

He moved so he was facing her. 'For months, I never got a hint you were interested in me other than as a personal trainer. The few times I tried flirting, you shut me down fast, talking about your husband and your kids. I respected that. But lately, everything's changed. You've stopped blocking the flirting. I'm not proud I took advantage of that and I hate it's given you the wrong idea. Thing is, you're not like the other older women I have sex with. Makes me wonder what's going on in your life?'

What's going on in your life? Tara's eyes burned hot and dry. The only person who'd come close to noticing things between her and Jon were off was Shannon and now she was on the other side of the world. Instead, Tara's buff, goal-focused personal trainer with his limited vocabulary was asking her the question Kelly and Rhianna should be voicing. The irony wasn't lost on her. A vicious laugh rocked out of her, harsh and raw, the jagged sound bouncing around the room before coming back and circling her in pain. It took her a second to realise the agonising sensation gripping her was coming from just under her scapula.

'Ice pack,' she breathed out.

Zac stared at her. 'What?'

'Muscle. Spasm.'

He strode to the freezer and returned with a gel pack wrapped in a tea towel along with some ibuprofen. 'If it isn't too weird, I could help you get your top back on and massage the spasm.'

Could her life get any stranger? She sighed. 'Thanks. I promise not to jump you.'

'Right back at you.'

He pulled her crop top back into place, minimising movement to limit the pain. Then his strong fingers worked on the area.

'Arrgh!' The air rushed out of her lungs. 'You trying to kill me?'

'Sorry. When you fell you must have strained a paraspinal muscle. They hurt like a bitch.' He pressed the ice pack into place. 'That has to stay here for ten minutes. How about you use the time to tell me what's going on.'

The usual awkwardness Tara experienced when she tried to talk about her and Jon lessened under the weight of having been half naked with Zac and by the sincerity of his concern.

'You nailed it. Things in my life have changed. My husband no longer wants to have sex with me.'

'Wow. Okay. That's big.'

'Yeah.'

'So he's having an affair?'

'He insists he isn't.'

'It's hard to hide an affair in a small town.'

'Talking from experience, are you?' she asked, half teasing, half serious.

'Little bit. Has anyone dropped any hints that he's screwing around on you?'

'No.'

'What do your friends say?'

'They don't know. It's not exactly easy dropping "Jon doesn't want to have sex any more" into the conversation.' She thought of Kelly. 'They'd either say "lucky you" or they'd feast on the gossip that my very blokey husband can't get it up any more, then rush home and tell their husbands. As furious as I am with Jon, he doesn't deserve that.'

Zac shifted next to her. 'So, he can't … at all? He's … Has he tried Viagra?'

What was it about men and the word 'impotent'? Did they think if they spoke it out loud it might suddenly affect them?

'I tried, but he won't take it. He says he doesn't have a problem. Maybe I *am* the problem. Maybe he's right and I am totally obsessed by sex. I've obviously lost the plot completely otherwise I wouldn't have kissed you.' Gratitude rolled in unexpectedly, settling over the mess of emotions roiling through her. 'I never thought I'd say this, Zac, but thanks for stopping us. Thanks for not taking advantage of my emotional crisis.'

He gave her a wry smile. 'If it helps any, it wasn't easy. I wanted it as much as you did, but I never screw a mate.'

'Physically and metaphorically?'

'That's it.' He squeezed her hand. 'I don't want things between us to change.'

'I think that horse has well and truly bolted.'

'Nah. We caught it and led it back into the stables. We can still be friends.' Remorse wove across his cheeks. 'Please don't pull out of training.'

The thought of losing their training sessions on top of losing Jon and Shannon socked her hard. She thought back to the early months of training with Zac. He was right. They'd had an uncomplicated relationship focusing on the training with some easy conversation on the side. She'd been the one who'd pushed the change and he'd responded.

'The flirting's got to stop,' she said.

'Totally. I'm really sorry things are shit with your husband.'

'Yeah. So am I.'

He removed the ice pack. 'Go and see Doug and get some treatment for this. Ring him now. He might be able to squeeze you in.'

'Yes, Mum,' she teased. But she appreciated his concern. It was a nice change from the criticism she'd been getting from other people in her life.

'And we need to fill in an incident report,' he added.

'I'm not going to sue you, Zac.'

'Yeah, but if a customer fell in the shop, you'd insist they fill one in. I'll go and grab the form.'

As his feet thundered down the stairs, her phone rang. 'Tara Hooper.'

'Tara, it is Fiza Atallah. Your neighbour.'

Her teeth clenched. How did the woman get her number? 'I know who you are. Why are you calling?'

'It is about your husband. I am at the hospital with him.'

'What? Why?' Tara's heart slammed hard against her ribs. 'Where are the children?'

'They are safe. Amal is looking after them.'

Safe?! Her mind spun. 'Where's Ian?'

'I don't know an Ian. You must come to the hospital now.'

CHAPTER
21

As long as Tara didn't breathe too deeply her level of discomfort was tolerable, but when she saw Jon lying on the hospital trolley, she gasped. Pain ricocheted through her—not all of it muscular. His big body filled the narrow mattress, but instead of looking reassuringly indomitable, it was slumped and caved in on itself. A large pale cream bandage ran from his fingertips to his elbow, and his complexion was a close colour match with the exception of the black swelling on his forehead.

His eyes met hers—brave but scared, reminding her of Flynn.

'Hey.' She squeezed his hand. 'What happened?'

'The nail gun and I disagreed.'

This didn't make much sense. Jon was always so careful with tools.

'How? Did the kids distract you? Why isn't Ian here?'

Fiza walked in then, a bright flash of colour in the muted pastels of the emergency department. A hospital lanyard hung around her neck. 'Hello, Mrs Hooper. Mr Hooper.'

'Tara, this is ...' Jon sighed. 'I'm sorry. I've forgotten your name.'

'Fiza.' She stood tall and straight and everything about her said, *Don't mess with me, this is my patch.* 'When your husband fell, your son came for help.'

'Fell?' Tara swung her gaze back to Jon. 'What did you fall off?'

'He did not fall off anything,' Fiza said.

'I don't understand. Jon?'

But his eyes were closed.

Fiza inclined her head towards the door and Tara followed her into another room.

'When we found him, your husband was lying on the ground and he couldn't stand up. He is a big man and it took Amal and me to help him to his feet. He was very unsteady and this did not improve. I bandaged his hand and brought him here for tests.'

Tara recalled the frosty way she'd instructed Fiza to leave Tingle-dale. Embarrassment mingled with an uneasy mixture of chagrin and gratitude. 'Thank you.' It came out stiff and curt so she tried again. 'That was very kind.'

Fiza shrugged. 'No one deserves to be alone on the ground and unaided.'

Was that a shot at her? Tara searched Fiza's face for criticism but saw only pride and determination in the tilt of her chin.

'I don't want to inconvenience you any further,' she said. 'I'll call my father-in-law and ask him to collect the children.'

'There is no hurry. Perhaps it is better they are playing with friends and not worrying about their father.'

Something about the way Fiza said the words clenched something tight inside Tara. Did she speak from experience? Tara had never seen an adult male on the property. Or did she know something more about Jon than she was letting on?

'I need to speak to the doctor,' she said.

'Of course. I will tell him you are here.'

Fiza walked away and Tara headed outside to call Ian.

He answered with his usual greeting. 'Hello, love. What can I do you for?'

'I'm at the hospital. Jon's okay but he's had an accident and we still need to talk to the doctor. Can you please go to Tingledale and look after the kids?'

'Sure, but it's going to take me a few hours to get back.'

'Where are you?'

'Kangaroo Flat.'

'But Jon told me you were coming over this afternoon to help him with Clemmie's playhouse.'

'Did he? I've got that written down in the diary for tomorrow.'

She rubbed her temple as sounds of a public bar drifted down the line. When Ian drank he stuffed things up all the time. 'Are you okay to drive?'

'Been on the light stuff, love. I'll start home now. Ask Rhianna or Kelly to help you out until I get there.'

'Thanks.' She hung up and called Kelly.

'Sorry, Tara, but Al and I are on the road. We're having a weekend away.'

Tara hesitated to ring Rhianna. But the children were better off with someone they knew. Pushing past her issues, she called her but Rhianna didn't pick up.

Desperation tapped in her veins. She tried the Dusseldorps, but it seemed half the town was taking advantage of the pupil-free day and had gone away for a long weekend. Tara fought tears of frustration and despair. Why had Shannon left her?

She shoved her phone into her pocket and blew her nose. As she stepped into A&E, she met Fiza coming the other way with her handbag on her shoulder.

'Ah, Fiza?'

'Yes?'

Tara licked her lips. 'I appreciate that you brought Jon to hospital, but I think the children need to be here too.'

Fiza frowned. 'Hospitals are not good places for children.'

The need to protect Flynn and Clementine surged. 'I never leave my children with people I don't know. Especially teenagers.'

Fiza's eyes flashed—a lioness defending her cub. 'Amal is a good boy! He works hard. He wants to be a doctor. Without his strength, your husband would still be lying on the ground.'

She punched some numbers into her phone, then spoke rapidly in a language Tara didn't recognise before thrusting the device towards her. 'Speak to your son.'

'Flynn, it's Mummy. I'm at the hospital with Daddy but I'm going to come and get you and Clemmie and bring you here.'

'But, Mum! We're playing totem tennis and I'm winning.'

'Who are you playing with?'

'Amal, Leila and Sammy.'

'Is anyone else there?'

'No.'

'Are you hungry?'

Flynn sighed as if Tara was being excruciatingly difficult. 'Amal gave us cheese and apples.'

Her throat burned with tension. 'Do you feel safe?'

'Duh! Clemmie, it's not your turn! Mum, I have to go.'

'Tell Clem—' But Flynn was gone, leaving only the buzzing of static in Tara's ear. She handed the phone back to Fiza. 'They're playing a game.'

Fiza's brows rose. 'Of course. They are children. Now you know they are safe and happy, go and look after your husband. He needs you.'

Something about the command riled Tara. She opened her mouth to object, but the other woman with her air of authority was already striding towards the exit.

Jon was dozing or avoiding talking to her—these days it was hard to tell. It was a long time since Tara had just sat and watched her husband without him noticing and saying, 'What?' in an aggrieved tone. The skin under his eyes was the colour of Clemmie's HB pencils and the once faint lines around his eyes were now carved in deep. The scar on his head was still raised and livid from his last accident a few weeks earlier.

Jon was rarely sick. 'Fit as a Mallee bull' was his usual response whenever people asked how he was, but he didn't look fit now. He was a faded version of himself. It shocked her how much he looked like Ian after a bender with Gerry.

Jon's leg jerked, hitting the rails on the side of the bed, and his eyes popped open, wide and frantic. 'T?'

'I'm back. I was checking on the kids.'

He turned towards her voice, his movements stiff. 'Fiza said—'

'Hello, Tara.' Stephen Illingworth, their GP, tanned from his recent Queensland holiday, walked into the room. 'Looks like Jon's been in the wars.'

'Twice in a month.'

'So I see.' He closed the door and pulled up a chair. 'Jon, I've been reading your file and it seems the locum prescribed Viagra.'

Jon made a strangled sound.

'I'm assuming he didn't do a physical examination?' Stephen asked.

'I asked for the prescription,' Tara said. 'Things have been ... difficult.'

'I imagine they have.'

'Tara's making it out to be worse than it is,' Jon said.

Tara didn't know whether it was the sympathy on Stephen's face, the horrifying realisation that things between her and Jon were so strained she'd plumbed a new low by trying to have sex with Zac, or her frustration with Jon not admitting they had a problem, but she wasn't staying silent any longer.

'I'm not exaggerating. We haven't had sex in months. You're either gaslighting me because you're having an affair, or you're drinking too much and sticking your head in the sand.'

Jon's uninjured hand moved robotically through his hair. 'How many times do I have to tell you—I'm not having an affair!'

'Then admit to the drinking and get some help!'

'Jon, Tara,' Stephen said firmly. 'Let's focus. First up, erectile dysfunction at thirty-eight is usually a sign of other problems so the prescription for Viagra was a red flag. When I was stitching your hand, I noticed a lot of muscle rigidity. That's why I did a full physical examination. Jon, have you been feeling more tired than usual?'

'You know ...' Jon glanced away. 'Life's busy.'

Bloody men's egos! 'He falls asleep on the couch most nights around eight. Then from three, he's up half the night,' Tara said.

'What about mid-afternoon? Do you feel like you could nap then, Jon?'

'Sometimes.' Stephen's caring gaze was unflinching and Jon sighed. 'Yeah. I've come home some afternoons. Like today.'

'Fiza told me Flynn said you were using the nail gun and then you seemed to fall over.' Stephen checked his notes. '*Like a tree.*'

Panic tightened Tara's chest. 'Please tell me you weren't drinking.'

'Jesus, Tara!' Jon's leg banged against the trolley's sides. 'I'm not Dad! When have you seen me drink in the afternoon other than at a weekend function?'

The awfulness of the year ran into her need to tell Stephen the truth. Make Jon acknowledge it so he could get help. It wasn't like telling their doctor the cold hard facts could make things any worse between them.

'He's been stumbling drunk at least twice recently,' she said.

'I have not!' Jon's anguish bounced off the neutral palette of the walls. 'Stephen, tell her you breathalysed me when I arrived. Tell her I blew 00.'

'It's true, Tara. He did.'

A kernel of fear broke through the malignant resignation that had hardened in her. 'Then what's going on?'

'Based on Jon's muscle rigidity, the erectile dysfunction, the pill roll tremor—'

'The what?' Tara and Jon asked in unison.

Stephen tilted his head towards Jon's uninjured hand. 'It's what you're doing now. Rolling your thumb over your fingers. That's called a pill roll tremor.'

'I noticed that months ago. I thought it was just stress,' Tara said.

'It's not stress. It's very likely Parkinson's disease.'

Jon's mouth opened. No words came out.

The diagnosis boomed in Tara's head, not making sense. 'But that's something old people get. Jon's thirty-eight!'

'There's also a condition called young Parkinson's. The only way to accurately diagnose it is to rule out every other possible neurological condition. So I'm going to refer you to a neurologist in Shepparton.'

Tara trusted Stephen. 'But you think it's young Parkinson's?'

Empathy filled the creases on his face. 'We have to run tests and rule out all other conditions before we can categorically say yes.'

An odd sensation filled her. Not exactly relief—how could it be when Jon was so sick—but something akin to a mild version of reassurance. An explanation for the shocking year that had left them floundering in an unfamiliar marriage.

'So there's a reason Jon hasn't been himself?' she said.

'I'm still here.' Jon's voice was unsteady.

She reached for his hand. 'I know. And I haven't been myself either, but at least now there's a reason.'

'Give me some examples of what you mean, Tara,' Stephen said.

A raft of changes flooded her mind. Things that individually meant nothing, but bundled together took on huge significance.

'Jon, your handwriting's become almost indecipherable. You get these blank expressions on your face as if you don't care about what's going on around you or what we're discussing. You get frustrated faster. Those times your walking was so unsteady and your speech so slurred I thought you were drunk. The way you've cut yourself off from me. Our lack of a sex life ...'

'They're all signs of a neurological disorder.' Stephen looked at Jon. 'I imagine you've been feeling like you're wading through mud every day.'

Jon nodded. 'Pretty much. It takes everything I've got to stay upright and get through the day. By the time I get home, I'm knackered and there's nothing left. Sorry, T.'

A thousand thoughts buzzed in Tara's head and she didn't know if she wanted to weep or yell. Why hadn't he told her any of this? Had he tried? Had she been so obsessed with imagining he was drinking and having an affair that she hadn't listened?

'Did you try to tell me?' she asked.

'I didn't want to worry you.' His mouth pulled down. 'Guess that didn't work.'

She turned to Stephen, needing to find a clear path through the jungle that had tangled them in its tenacious vines. 'Now we know there's a problem, how do we fix it?'

'Let's get a definitive diagnosis first.'

'Yes, fine,' Tara snapped. 'But humour me. If it's young Parkinson's, how do we fix it?'

'We manage it with drugs and physical therapy to minimise the symptoms. We respond and adjust when things deteriorate.'

'Deteriorate.' Jon's laugh was hoarse and harsh. 'My great-uncle had it. He died a dribbling, drooling, shaking mess.' He pulled his hand out of Tara's. 'What Stephen's saying is, there's no cure. I'm going to get worse. You're not happy now, you haven't been for months. Get out while you can.'

His words eviscerated her as much as the dilemma they raised.

CHAPTER
22

'Honestly. It makes you wonder about some people.' Vivian surveyed the damage in the garden and took some photos. 'You'd better fill in an incident report.'

'I've already done it,' Helen said. 'I've also spoken to both Linda in Parks and Messina, and the police attended. I was wondering if the shire might stump up for a high fence on this side of the garden.'

'We'll have to look at Parks' budget.' Vivian glanced towards the sign. 'Why isn't the shire logo on that?'

'It's on the shelter and the tank. Plus the two plaques from back in the day when they funded the arts grant for the mosaics and the gates. Besides, they didn't give us extra funding for this section so ...'

'Helen! The garden's on shire land! Learn how to schmooze.' Vivian sighed. 'Sorry. I didn't mean to snap. But if we ever want to see tiny houses over there, we need to do everything we can to bring Geoff or one of the other councillors back on side.'

Helen wasn't sure how a logo would change things, but it was worth a shot. 'I'll get it added to the sign asap. And I'll write a letter of thanks for approving the garden extension even though the housing project is still up in the air.'

'That's the spirit.' Vivian looked up the hill and shaded her eyes. 'Who's that?'

Helen instantly recognised the gait of the man who was fast approaching. 'Bob Murphy.'

'Name's familiar.'

'He's a retired farmer, widower, member of the garden and a chronic helper.'

'He's got the grazier look.'

'What do you mean?'

'Polished RMs, moleskins, checked shirt, Akubra hat. Any money?'

For some reason, the question grated. 'I have no idea.'

'It's always worth knowing that sort of thing.'

Bob lifted his hat. 'Morning, ladies.'

Helen did the introductions and Vivian asked Bob where in the district he'd farmed. At his reply, she said, 'So you know Beckley Downs?'

Bob nodded. 'The Inchleys were our northern neighbours for thirty years.'

'Then we must have met at one of Gus's Nats' fundraisers.'

'Gus loves a party.' Bob turned to Helen. 'I picked up your mail on my way past.' He handed her an envelope printed with the shire's logo.

She thought about her normally empty letterbox. 'I never get mail.'

'Then I guess today's your lucky day.'

All Helen's correspondence with the shire was done by email so she had no idea what this could be about. While Bob answered another of Vivian's questions, she ran her thumb under the seal and pulled out the letter.

Dear Mrs Demetriou,

In regard to the recent house inspection of 17 Riverfarm Road, Boolanga: unfortunately the cottage has deteriorated over the last twelve months to the point where its condition is now considered hazardous. For your own safety, you are advised to vacate the property within seven days.

The past rose up like a spectre before Helen, laughed, then slapped her hard.

'Everything okay?' Bob asked, his blue gaze watching intently.

'No.' She pushed the letter at him with shaking hands. 'I'm being kicked out of the cottage.'

'What?!' Vivian plucked the letter out of Bob's hand before he could read it.

'It says the cottage is uninhabitable. It's in better condition than when I moved in!'

'This is outrageous,' Vivian said. 'Especially the paragraph about your caretaker role.'

'What?' Helen's panic swam to the surface. 'I didn't read past *vacate the property within seven days.*'

Vivian's fuchsia nail pointed to the third paragraph. 'It says there's no longer a need for a caretaker and funds are being redirected.'

'But that's crazy! Especially given the vandalism. It would have been worse if I hadn't interrupted them.' Helen's mind raced. 'Shouldn't something like this be discussed at a council meeting?'

'Exactly. Mind you, every department's been asked to find areas where costs can be cut, but this looks like someone in Parks has gone overboard.'

'It has to be a misunderstanding. I'll go and talk to—who signed the letter? Linda?' Helen asked.

Vivian checked the page. 'Elise Toonie.'

'I've never dealt with her. Who is she?'

'Not the person to yell at. She's too far down the food chain.' Vivian tucked the letter in her handbag. 'Leave it with me. I'll do some sniffing about, find out who the moron is behind it and get it sorted. Meanwhile, promise me you won't worry. Remember, the people who count know you're far too valuable an asset to lose.'

Relief steadied Helen. 'Thanks, Vivian.'

'Any time. I'll be in touch as soon as I know something. Nice to meet you, Bob. Let's have coffee soon.'

'Lovely,' Bob said genially.

As they watched Vivian walk towards the gate, Helen couldn't stop herself. 'You and Vivian met over conservative politics?'

'I've never met her before in my life.'

'But you just agreed to coffee.'

'She's convinced we've met. Seemed rude to correct her.'

Helen snorted at his default to manners. 'You sure you're not losing your memory?'

He jammed his hat back on his head looking decidedly—and unusually—grumpy. 'You don't believe in stroking a bloke's ego, do you?'

Something about the way he said it made her revisit what Vivian had said to her about Geoff Rayson. 'Apparently, it's an area where I could improve. In that vein, why are you looking like you stepped out of an RM catalogue?'

A teasing smile crinkled his face. 'You think I look like a model, eh?'

'I'm pretty sure they're a lot younger.' But unsettling warmth was dancing deep in her belly, trying to fan faded memories of desire. 'Why are you so dressed up?'

'Whose memory is in question now? It's the excursion to the Australian Botanic Gardens in Shep.'

'What? Tell me you're not going on that!'

He shrugged as if it was no big deal. 'I paid for it before all the brouhaha. Besides, you're always on at me about not wasting money so—'

'This isn't funny. You do realise Judith's probably behind me losing the caretaker's job?'

'Come on, Helen. Judith might like to think she wields power in the garden, but as we've proven, it doesn't extend much past the cyclone fence.'

'I'm not so sure.'

'Well, I am. Just like I'm sure I'm not a traitor to the cause.'

'How do you figure that?'

'I'm a spy.' He shot her a wink. 'I plan to sit up the back of the bus and look like I'm asleep. That's when you hear all the best gossip.'

Her laugh surprised her, lightening the tension that had gripped her since she'd read the word vacate. 'I'm holding you to that, Agent 86.'

'Good one, 99. I'll report in as soon as I step off the bus.'

'Jade!'

It was Lachlan, pushing a wheelbarrow towards her, his work shirt creased and stained with what looked like tomato sauce. Jade immediately felt better about her own clothes and the dribble patch Milo had left on her shoulder. Not that she should care about her appearance for Lachlan.

'Hi,' she said.

'Hey, squirt.' Lachlan held up his hand to Milo who swatted at it with his dimpled fingers. 'Did you just wake up?'

Milo buried his head in Jade's shoulder, suddenly shy. When Lachlan didn't say anything, Milo lifted his head, said 'Boo!' and laughed before hiding again.

Jade stared. 'Did he just say boo?'

'Sounded like it.' Lachlan grinned. 'I was playing peek-a-boo with him at your party.'

Nothing about Lachlan looked embarrassed that he'd just admitted to playing with a baby. 'Peek-a-boo?'

'You don't know it?' When she shook her head, Lachlan covered his eyes with his hand and said, 'Milo. Ahhhh, boo!' He dropped his hand. Milo squealed.

Disbelief clung to Jade's delight. 'He's playing with you. That's awesome.'

'I'm a sucker for a baby.'

'You can hold him if you want.' She thrust Milo at him, glad to give her back and hips a break from his weight.

Lachlan hoisted Milo up on his shoulders, then pointed to the plants in the wheelbarrow. 'Uncle Bob told me about the morons who wrecked your garden. I was grabbing a pie from the nursery café when I saw these. There's just enough time to get them established before the summer heat hits.'

'You bought me zinnias and alstroemerias?' She lurched between stunned surprise at Lachlan's thoughtfulness, and anger and regret that it wasn't Corey playing with Milo and being kind.

'I guessed at what you like, so don't feel you have to keep them. I get it. Flowers are personal. Emotional too.'

Emotional? Jade was wrestling with her own swinging emotions. 'What do you mean?'

'Lilacs make my grandmother happy, because when my grandfather proposed to her, he gave her a bunch. Dad loved roses. He grew over a hundred and fifty of them and between September and May there were always blooms in the house.' He grimaced. 'When Dad died, Mum suddenly hated roses. She'd burst into tears whenever she saw them. She asked me to dig them up and I did it, but I cried the whole time. It felt like Dad was dying all over again.'

'Sorry.' God, that sounded so lame.

'Thanks.'

A heavy silence settled between them so she said the first thing that came into her head. 'I wonder what flowers did to Helen? She hates all of them.'

'Apparently, there's some ancient language of flowers—'

'Floriography.'

Jade immediately sucked in a breath, realising she'd just shown him up. He'd get snarky like Corey and she braced herself.

'Floriography?' Lachlan said it as if trying the word on for size. 'Wow, thanks. I didn't realise it had a name.'

Her breath released on a stunned whoosh of relief. 'No worries. According to Wikipedia, it started in Turkey during the Ottoman Empire—apparently, they were obsessed by tulips. But it was the wacky Victorians who went mental with it. They wrote dictionaries for the meanings of each flower and they used flowers to send coded messages.'

'You'd want to hope your lover had the same dictionary.'

Jade laughed. 'Right. If a woman got white roses, they could either mean innocence and purity or piss off, we're over.'

'What flowers do you like?'

She smiled. 'I haven't met one I didn't like.'

Confusion tangled in his moss-green eyes. 'So you do want the zinnias and the alstroemerias?'

'Yeah.' She bit her lip and forced herself to apologise. 'Sorry I sounded ungrateful. It's just you surprised me. I don't do so great with surprises.'

'Too many bad ones?' Although his tone was light, his gaze was intense.

She shifted uncomfortably, busying herself with the plants. 'Did you bring some of that worm poo to give these a kickstart?'

'Sure did. I reckon I should talk to my boss about making a donation to the whole garden and getting a sign like Hoopers.'

'Fiza would give you a recommendation. Actually, can you give her some more? She's moved out of Serenity Street and planted maize at her new place.'

'Too easy. How was she when she saw the damage?'

'Pretty cut up. It didn't help that the coppers wanted to talk to Amal even though he had an alibi and was nowhere near Tranquillity.'

'That doesn't make any sense. If they suspect it was kids from the park, why didn't they talk to them?'

'They don't work that way. They prefer people to rat on their mates first, then they talk to them.'

Lachlan gave her a sideways look and she realised he'd probably never talked to the police outside of a random breath test. She didn't want him to know that the police had always drifted in and out of her life.

'That's what happens on the TV anyway.'

Lachlan laughed. 'Big fan of crime drama, are you?'

'I prefer documentaries and history stuff. And reading. I love reading. There's always something to learn. What do you like?'

'Now I know you're an intellectual, I'm not sure I should tell you.'

She snorted at his comment, but was secretly pleased. 'I'm not an intellectual. I haven't even been to uni.'

'I went to uni with a bunch of blokes whose biggest aim was to write themselves off every weekend.'

'But you went.' It surprised her how much that hurt.

'You can go too,' he said quietly.

She jerked her head towards Milo. 'You forgetting someone?'

'Nope. My mum studied social work when I was a kid. I remember how proud Dad, my sister and I were when she got her degree. When she crossed the stage in her cap and gown, we stood up and cheered.'

Jade tried to picture Corey and Milo doing the same thing, but the image wouldn't come. It was hard enough to imagine herself at uni, let alone graduating.

'What would you study if you had the chance?' Lachlan asked.

'I dunno.'

'What are your two favourite things?'

'Books and flowers.'

He rubbed his jaw. 'What about a florist who sells books?'

'You been smoking the wacky baccy.'

'Nothing wrong with dreaming, Jade. That's where the best ideas come from.'

Was it? Jade let her mind wander to flowers and books. Different baskets of flowers for each genre of books. Roses for romance—that was easy. Waratahs, bottlebrush and kangaroo paws for Australian fiction. What was the flower for crime?

'You're thinking about it,' Lachlan said.

'No.' Then she noticed he was holding Milo out to her.

Lachlan wrinkled his nose. 'He's a bit whiffy. I think he's done a dump. And I better get back to work or the boss will have my guts for garters.'

Jade's daydream fractured, turning opaque like glass and blurring the view. This was why she tried not to dream—it always left her feeling agitated and diminished. And who was she kidding? She could barely pay her rent let alone start a business. She needed a job before she needed a degree.

She lifted Milo into her arms and the dream vanished completely. She was the only person who changed his nappies. She was the only person who loved him enough to stay.

No one loves you enough to stay.

CHAPTER
23

Helen was trying her best to get on with her day, but her concentration strayed on every task. The word *eviction* beat in her veins like the call of a drum.

She waved to Fran at the library desk before logging on to computer three and checking the Facebook page. There were another two hundred likes and lots of comments about the importance of transparency in local government.

Keep the bastards honest!

Community land belongs to the community.

Councillors don't give a sh*t about anyone. They're only in it for themselves.

Riverfarm is Yorta Yorta land.

No Chinese.

Keep Australia Australian. Send the buggers back!

Helen rubbed the bridge of her nose, trying to fend off a headache. Why did people go off on tangents? She deleted the racist comments and started a post to keep the followers focused.

Boolanga has a long history of caring for all of its community.

Her fingers stalled. The Yorta Yorta would dispute that. So would some of the refugees. She pressed the backspace button and started again.

Having a home is a basic human right, but each night in Boolanga up to twenty people sleep rough, many of them women. Are you shocked? You should be.

Anxiety hovered—she might soon be adding to the statistics. She tried to banish it by concentrating on uploading photos of the river, the garden and a picture of a similar housing project on the New South Wales central coast. She hit post, logged out and turned her attention to *The Standard.*

African youths strike again. No longer content with graffiti, they've turned their attention to destroying the pride and joy of Boolanga's seniors: their garden plots. Judith Sainsbury, president of the community garden, said, 'How dare they come to Boolanga and terrorise our way of life. The garden has always been a safe haven and now it's been desecrated. We no longer feel safe in our beds.'

Helen's temples throbbed so hard she thought she'd burst a blood vessel. Judith had actively worked against the women's garden but now, when it suited her racist rhetoric, she was claiming it as part of the community garden.

She forced herself to keep reading.

Police are interviewing the usual suspects. Charges are yet to be laid.

Of course they were yet to be laid! Corey had scarpered, and for all the talk in town about an African gang on the loose, the police didn't seem able to make any charges stick.

Helen's anger at the police's insistence on talking to Amal still simmered. Of course the boy had denied all knowledge of the incident—he had a cast-iron alibi. Although his manner had been respectful during the interview, the burn in his eyes and the jut of

his jaw showed his outrage. Helen couldn't blame him. It wasn't the
first time he'd been summoned to the police station.

When she'd mentioned racial profiling to Sergeant North, he'd
pointed out the two Anglo kids waiting to be questioned. As Jade
had greeted them by name when she'd arrived at the station, Helen
assumed they were from Serenity Street. That was a perfect example of geographic and socio-economic profiling, and another reason
she'd hidden her past when she'd started over in Boolanga. If the
local police knew she'd been homeless, she'd be targeted for 'chats'
regarding any and all petty misdemeanours.

She brought up a new email and typed in: *editor@Boolangastandard*
.com.au.

As the caretaker of the community garden

Her fingers paused. Could she say that? Yes. She'd been the caretaker at the time of the event. Her fingers tapped again.

I would like to address some inaccuracies in the 9/10 report of the damage
the garden sustained. The damage occurred in the new extension, which,
unlike the original community garden, is not protected by a high fence. One
flower garden was badly damaged and two other beds sustained minor dam-
age. This is hardly an attack on our way of life. I'd be far more concerned
about the lack of rain and the impact that's having on our food production
than one garden bed being wrecked.

She added her name and address and hit send.

On her way home, Helen dropped into Boolanga Signs and asked
for a quote to have the shire's logo added to the sponsorship sign.
The figure Len came up with astonished her.

'Good God. How can it possibly cost that much?'

Len's chest puffed out. 'I can't just paint it on.'

'Why not?'

'With our heat, it'll peel off in no time.'

Helen thought it peeling off fast might be a good option.

Len pointed to a sign on the wall. 'Something like that will do the job and last for years.'

Helen glanced around the shop; it was full of examples. Most were shire signs, but there was one for Ainslea Park and another for Geoff Rayson's accounting firm.

'You seem to do a bit of work for the shire,' she said. 'You must be more competitive than Sign On.'

'I like to think so.'

She turned back to the counter and noticed a photograph of a rowing crew holding a trophy aloft. 'Is that you and Geoff Rayson?'

Len laughed. 'Back in our glory days when we were younger and lighter. Mind you, we rowed in the inaugural Boolanga Business Regatta last year and came third.'

'Not too shabby.' She picked up the printed quote. 'Thanks for this. I'll check in with Sign On and get back to you.'

'Ah, Helen …' Len leaned over the counter. 'I'm the shire's approved sign-writer so if you use someone else, Finance might not reimburse you. I wouldn't want you or the garden to be out of pocket.'

'Right.'

Except not a lot about the information seemed right at all. Helen's mind churned on the walk back to the cottage.

As she opened the gate, she heard Milo's cries. A rush of goose-bumps raised her skin and she rubbed her arms, hoping Kubra, Aima or Baseera were about. They adored Milo and often gave Jade a hand.

But when Helen came out from behind the trees, Jade was standing next to her garden bed, jiggling Milo in her arms. The rest of the garden was empty.

Plants in pots were positioned across the freshly raked bed, marking their future place in the soil. One plant lay on the ground, already out of its pot.

Helen couldn't stop herself. 'The roots will dry out.'

Jade rolled her eyes. 'Okay, boomer.'

'What?'

'You're stating the obvious. I know it's drying out, but Milo was screaming blue murder. I don't need child protection breathing down my neck on top of all the other crap!'

Self-reproach stung Helen into action and she bent down to pick up the plant. 'I'll do it.'

'No!' Jade blinked rapidly. 'I mean, no, thank you. Can you hold Milo instead? He hasn't stopped crying all day.'

Helen stood slowly and met the baby's blue-grey eyes. He looked at her pensively as if he knew she'd inevitably disappoint him. Judging her with unspoken words—*you didn't do a very good job last time.*

Every part of her screamed no. 'I don't do—'

'Please.'

Anguish carried on the plea and Helen took a closer look at Jade. Black smudges—not mascara—coloured the skin under her eyes. Her hair was greasy, pulled back in a raggedy ponytail as if it had been done in a hurry, and she was wearing the same clothes she'd worn the previous two days. The girl was strung out and exhausted.

Helen remembered what that was like. Reluctantly, she held out her arms and accepted the baby. He immediately screamed and flung himself sideways, reaching for his mother. The strength in the movement shocked her as much as his weight. When Nicki was one, she'd been half his size and had lain limp in Helen's arms like a stunned bird. She tightened her grip on Milo, worried she'd drop him.

Jade sprinkled some water-storing crystals into the hole and added water. Milo's screams competed with the screeching corellas.

Helen tensed, wondering how she could distract him. Shafts of sunlight caught a mosaic in the main garden so she walked to the fence. Milo stilled, fascinated by the dancing sparkles of light bouncing off the pieces of mirror among the ceramic tiles.

'Look at that pretty rooster,' Helen said. 'He's got a good life strutting around the herb garden.'

Milo pointed. 'Doo doo.'

Helen's throat thickened with joy and heartache at the normalcy of the child's reaction—something most people took for granted. 'Yes. Cock-a-doodle-doo.'

His mother must have taught him the sounds and, not for the first time, Helen struggled with the conundrum that was Jade. For all her defensiveness and asperity, the girl had a natural curiosity that life had thankfully not yet extinguished. Helen wondered what Jade would have done with herself if she hadn't got pregnant. Then again, how bright was she getting involved with Corey?

Unfair! Helen mentally slapped herself. IQ and EQ were two completely different beasts—she should know. It wasn't like she was unfamiliar with the overwhelming need to be loved and how it could leave a woman vulnerable. For a time, she'd lived that story. She wished Jade could fast forward to the inevitable disillusionment and heartache when the scales fell from her eyes and she realised that Corey was a self-centred prick. A user of her love and affection. That she'd be better off without him in her life. But once a child was involved, it got ever more tangled and complicated. Helen knew that with Theo, she'd held onto hope for far too long.

'Ob! Ob!' Milo flung himself towards the fence.

The Coaster bus had pulled up and Bob was disembarking with other members of the garden. Some gave Helen a wave and others ignored her—it depended on their allegiance to Judith.

Bob gesticulated that he'd walk around to them and, without second-guessing herself, Helen turned towards the cottage. She'd ply Bob with tea and fruitcake and get all the gossip.

Her phone rang. Dodging Milo's grabby hands with movements worthy of a magician, she managed to answer it. 'Hello.'

'Helen, it's Vivian. Sorry it's taken me so long to get back to you.'

'That's okay, I know you're bus—'

'It's not great news, I'm afraid. I spoke to Elise who referred me to Ryan Tippett in Engineering. He says the wiring's shot. He's adamant it's uninhabitable and for your safety, they won't budge on seven days.'

The tremble hit Helen's legs and she sat down hard on the veranda steps.

'I've been as understanding as I can, Mrs Demetriou, but I'm not a charity.'

'But what about my furniture? I haven't got anywhere I can go.'

'I'll sell it and put it towards your back rent.'

'This is Judith's handiwork, isn't it?' Helen managed.

'Judith's certainly been complaining about you to anyone who'll listen, but she's not responsible for the cottage being condemned.'

'I suppose not.'

'And she has no sway in the day-to-day running of the shire.'

Helen's mouth dried. 'So the caretaker stipend? Was it attached to the cottage?'

'Not exactly.'

Thank God. It was the first hopeful thing Vivian had said. Helen swapped her phone to her other hand and tried to distract Milo with an old boot.

'... the auditor pointed out that as there's already a voluntary management committee in place for the garden, the caretaker role is unnecessary.'

'But they've known that since I took on the job three years ago! What's changed?'

'You didn't tell me you'd started a Facebook page.'

Her skin flashed hot and cold at Vivian's accusatory tone. 'I didn't *not* tell you. It's just each time we've talked recently, we've had far more important things to discuss.'

'It's important. People live and die by social media, Helen! What were you thinking?'

'You said to argue my side.'

'Writing letters to the editor at *The Standard* is completely different from getting on social media and saying the mayor's in bed with sheiks on a land deal!'

Indignation stormed through her. 'I didn't say that. I said there were rumours. Rumours you told me about!'

'In confidence!' Vivian sighed. 'I'm sorry, Helen, but you've really stuffed this up. Why did you have to make a fool of Geoff?'

'How have I made a fool of him?'

Jade and Bob arrived at the veranda steps and Jade thankfully lifted Milo out of Helen's arms.

'You made a meme,' Vivian said.

'I've got no idea what you're talking about. Sorry, can you just hang on a second?' She muted the phone. 'I need to see the Facebook page. And what's a meme?'

'Bob, give me your phone.' Jade swapped Milo for the device and scrolled quickly, before handing the phone to Helen. 'That's a meme.'

She stared at an unflattering photo of Geoff on a horse and a photoshopped photo next to it of Geoff on a camel with the hashtag *animalcruelty*. 'The mayor thinks I made it.'

Jade laughed. 'As if.'

'Not helpful, Jade,' Bob said.

'Sorry. Maybe you were hacked.'

With shaking fingers, Helen pressed buttons to unmute the phone. 'Sorry, Vivian. I've just seen the meme. It wasn't me. I think I've been hacked.'

'I've spent the last hour pleading your case but Geoff's intransigent.' Somehow, Vivian's voice was suddenly on speaker. 'I told him everything you've done for the garden—the refugees, food for the homeless—but he wants you gone.'

'But I didn't do it. He can't just sack me! There are protocols. A warning system.'

'You're on a contract,' Vivian said.

'So?'

'Unfortunately, no warnings are required. It's buried in the fine print.'

Half-formed words flung themselves around Helen's head, inaudible over the roar of panic burning through the lining of her stomach.

'What if I take down the Facebook page?'

Jade waved her hand in front of Helen's face, mouthing *No*.

'Good idea,' Vivian said. 'It's a sign of good will, which means he might not sue.'

Helen's mouth dried so fast her tongue stuck to her palate. 'What if I apologise to him face to face?'

'An apology won't remove the meme. Once something's on the internet, it's there forever. It only takes one journalist to dig it up and it's back again to haunt you.'

'But I didn't do it.'

'The law doesn't care. Geoff's masculinity's been mocked on your Facebook page.' A long sigh crackled in the speaker. 'I'm really sorry, Helen. I'll write you a glowing reference and talk to Lee at Boolanga Real Estate. She'll look after you.'

Helen managed to push out a 'Thanks' through a tight throat.

'And don't give up, hey?' Vivian added. 'This is just a temporary setback. You'll see!'

'How? I've lost my job and my home.'

'I know it looks hopeless at the moment, but this fiasco's shown me Geoff's true colours. I'm done giving him my support. Boolanga needs a mayor who puts community first, not himself. I'm going to run for mayor.'

'But that's a year away.'

'Depending on what other stunts he pulls, it could be closer. Either way, I promise that once I'm mayor, I'll put the focus squarely back on the community and transparency.'

Helen remembered her conversation with Len at Boolanga Signs. 'Does the shire only do business with Boolanga Signs?'

'No. Jobs are open to tender.'

'So if the best quote came in from Sign On, the shire would pay for the sign?'

'That's how I understand it works. Why?'

'You might want to do a bit of digging into how many signs the mayor's rowing mate has overcharged ratepayers for.'

There was an audible intake of breath. 'My fellow councillors would be very interested in that sort of information.'

'Interested enough to bring a motion of no confidence in the mayor?'

'Hopefully! If you hear anything else, let me know. Meanwhile, stay strong.'

The line went dead and Helen looked up into Jade's eyes, surprised to see the bright light of anger.

'What a prick!' Jade said.

'You won't get an argument from me.'

'At least one good thing—'

'Don't even think about saying something like adversity is a gift.' Helen glared at Bob. 'Or an opportunity.'

'Wouldn't dare. Make you a cuppa?'

His kindness pulled at the barely holding seams of her control. 'What about one of your Irish coffees?'

'I only carry a hip flask for night fishing.'

'Lucky I've got a bottle of whiskey in the pantry for emergencies.'

They trooped inside the cottage. Jade sat at the table and put Milo at her feet, giving him Helen's measuring spoons to play with and suck on. Bob boiled the kettle and Helen retrieved the whiskey, sloshing it into a mug.

Bob frowned.

'What?' Helen snapped. 'Suddenly you're a wowser?'

'No. I've just never seen you this rattled before.'

'You ever been evicted, Bob?' Jade asked.

'Got close once during the drought in the eighties, but we managed to hold on.'

'Holding on's not the same,' Jade said.

'Holding on means there's still hope.' Helen's voice trembled despite her determination to sound calm.

'I hated it when the letter finally came,' Jade said quietly, looking nowhere in particular. 'Whenever it arrived, I'd be dumped at Gran's. It's bullshit that grandmothers are all soft and cuddly. Every time I stayed, she'd tell my mother, "You chose to have the damn kid, you look after her." If I didn't do all the chores she'd threaten to call child protection. Weeks would go by and when Mum finally turned up to collect me, Gran would give her a bill. I visited my grandmother before she died and she told me I owed her five hundred bucks.'

'But you had a roof over your head and a bed. You weren't sleeping in a car or on the streets,' Helen said.

'I did once, when Gran refused to take me.'

Bob muttered something that sounded a lot like swearing and added whiskey to his own coffee. He took a gulp. 'You're not going to be homeless, Helen.'

'And why are you so confident?'

'I've got a spare room for a start.'

'I'm *not* moving in with you!'

'Jeez, Helen. Keep your hair on,' Jade said. 'No one would care. It's not like you and Bob would be getting it on. You're too old. But if you're that worried about your reputation—'

'My reputation? Remind me what year we're in again?'

'Jade's been reading *Anna Karenina*,' Bob said.

His eyes twinkled, spinning delight around her and she laughed, momentarily forgetting that her hard-fought security had just been pulled out from under her, leaving her in a precarious situation. Old memories stirred—the addiction of attraction, the giddiness of new love—and quickly turned rancid in her belly. She dropped her gaze, berating her foolishness. What the hell was wrong with her? She was too old for this sort of nonsense.

'*Anna Karenina*? Then she knows that depending on a man only ends in tears.'

'That's a bit rough on poor Levin,' Bob said.

'Yeah. He and Kitty ended up happy.' Jade dangled the spoons in front of Milo. 'If you don't want to use Bob's spare room, I s'pose I could help.'

'I didn't realise you have three bedrooms?' Helen said.

Jade's expression turned cagey. 'You can have Milo's room for a hundred and twenty dollars a week plus half the electricity.'

Ah! The offer, under the guise of help, suddenly made sense. Jade was struggling financially—of course she was. That bastard Corey probably didn't give her much. *You don't know that.* But her gut told her it was true. Could they help each other? Could she live in a house with Jade let alone an almost toddler? She'd avoided children for so long but this would throw her right into Milo's path. Did she even have a choice?

'You want me to pay half the electricity?' she said. 'There's two of you and one of me.'

'Milo doesn't use much.'

'I bet you wash more of his clothes than your own each week.'

'Yeah, but that's at the laundromat.'

Helen ran through her finances. She could ask Con for more shifts at the café, but there were no guarantees, especially as his daughter was working as much as she could to pay for a trip to Greece.

'I'll pay a third of the electricity and bring my washing machine.'

Jade tinkled the spoons, mulling over the offer. 'Only if the extra electricity costs less than what I'd spend at the laundromat.'

'I think you're both wasting your skills,' Bob said. 'You should be working as negotiators.'

Jade looked straight at Helen. 'And you don't get to boss me around.'

Helen momentarily considered Bob's offer, then remembered the effect of his twinkling eyes. Sparring with Jade would be a lot safer.

CHAPTER

24

So much had happened, Tara could barely wrap her head around all of it. Jon had been pricked, prodded and scanned and his neurologist, Dr Jaya, had ruled out a series of other conditions. His diagnosis matched Stephen's—young Parkinson's.

Although she'd hardly thought about running or about Zac, he'd been the first person Tara called when Jon got the official diagnosis. She'd justified it as necessary. After what had happened between them, she needed to explain why she was cancelling her appointments. She didn't want Zac to think she was ghosting him, not when he'd been so kind. And honest. But mostly she'd called him because he was the only person she knew who didn't know Jon. He was the only person she could tell. And she'd needed to tell someone.

'My husband's got Parkinson's disease.'

'Shit. Sorry.' Silence buzzed down the line then Zac cleared his throat. 'I thought Parkinson's was just for old dudes.'

A wave of grief hit her and she'd leaned against the wall. 'Apparently, there's more chance of winning the lottery than getting young Parkinson's.'

'That sucks. For both of you.'

'Pretty much.' She was struck by how talking to Zac was always a combination of wise adult and man-child.

'Is that why he wasn't interested in sex?'

'It's all connected.'

'At least you know for certain he hasn't been screwing around on you. That's gotta help.'

She'd laughed, then immediately choked on tears.

'You gonna be okay?' he'd asked.

She had no idea. In many ways her and Jon's relationship was on the same road it had been for months, only they'd changed lanes. The destination, however, remained undisclosed. But despite what Jon had offered her and her split-second wobble, she was staying for the journey.

Tara and Jon had told Ian the diagnosis—they needed his help with the school run and the children's after-school activities when medical appointments kept them in Shepparton. They were yet to tell their friends or employees. Jon didn't want to be rushed into anything and Tara agreed. They both needed time to wrap their heads around not only the disease but the ramifications. How could they answer other people's questions when they didn't fully understand things themselves?

It hadn't been difficult to hide Jon's medical appointments. As Tara hadn't told Kelly or Rhianna why she'd needed childminding the day Jon fell, there'd been no reason for the women to follow up. And the Hoopers' staff were used to Jon being in and out of the store and contacting him by phone. If anything had raised their suspicions, it was Tara answering his phone and troubleshooting when Jon was having his MRI and meeting with the movement specialist.

Naively, both of them had assumed Jon could take a bunch of pills each day and everything would return to normal. It was their first misconception on a very long list.

'It's a bit of trial and error to get the dosage right,' Dr Jaya told them. 'Fine line between easing the motor symptoms and making them worse.'

There were other side effects and Jon got the nausea and vomiting almost straight away. Yet another drug got added to the mix. It was hard to tell if his drowsiness was caused by the disease or the drugs. More worrying were the possible big side effects like hallucinations and impulsive and compulsive behaviours.

When Tara asked Dr Jaya and the pharmacist what to look for, they'd explained those side effects usually occurred in activities that gave an immediate reward or pleasure, such as eating, shopping and gambling—and sex. The irony of Jon possibly experiencing increased sexual thoughts and behaviours backhanded Tara with the sting of a slap. *Be careful what you wish for.* Right now, their sex life was so far down the list of concerns, it barely registered.

She hated how she'd misinterpreted the signs of Parkinson's disease, allowing them to fuel her anxieties and frustrations about their marriage. To cloud her judgement to the point she barely recognised herself. Whenever she thought about her own obsessive and compulsive behaviours with Zac, she broke out in a rash. But there was no hiding from her stupidity. Her strained paraspinal muscle still caught her if she moved too quickly.

Now she had a new obsession—reading everything she could about young Parkinson's. Unlike the difficult months preceding the diagnosis, when she'd been flailing in the dark about why their marriage was floundering, Parkinson's was a known threat. The information she found informed and terrified her in equal measure, and she became constantly vigilant, searching for signs of Jon being obsessive or compulsive about anything.

'You're doing it again,' he'd say.

'What?'

'Staring at me as if you think it'll fix everything. It's bloody annoying.'

'Sorry.'

If medical appointments, medication and Jon's general fatigue weren't enough to deal with, their social worker had 'strongly rec-ommended' they attend a Parkinson's support group.

'Most meetings are informal,' Donna had said, 'but a few times a year they have a guest speaker. You'll find it useful. There's a lot of value in a shared experience. Remember, you're not alone in this.'

But Tara felt excruciatingly alone and she was certain Jon did too. He'd retreated into himself, avoiding the cricket club and their friends. She didn't know if he was depressed or just finding his way through the complicated maze Parkinson's had dropped them in. Either way, she wanted to do everything she could to help him. Help them both. If that meant walking into a hall full of strangers, then so be it, which was how they came to be standing outside a community hall in Mooroopna. The noise of animated conversa-tion drifted towards them.

'Ready?' she asked.

Jon didn't say anything so she took his hand and walked inside. Her feet stalled at the entrance to the room. Was there anyone here under the age of seventy?

'Jesus,' Jon muttered.

The chatter ceased and several grey-haired heads swung in their direction. Some people sat, others stood. A couple of attendees had walkers parked by their chairs.

Should they leave, Tara wondered. But a woman was waving them over.

'Welcome. I'm Jill and you must be Tara and Jon? Donna told us you were coming. Sign in and write yourselves a temporary name tag. Use big letters.' She chuckled. 'We want to be able to read it.'

'Will do.' Tara forced a smile and glanced at Jon. Since starting on the drugs, his Parkinson's mask had faded, but right now, seeing his dark brows drawn down in a Flynn-esque scowl, she wished it back.

She wrote their names in large capitals, peeled off the backing and stuck Jon's on his shirt, leaving her hand splayed on his chest. 'It can't be any worse than the bowling club concert Ian dragged us to,' she joked, hoping for a smile.

'Wanna bet.'

Jill insisted they sit in the middle of a row of chairs. As everyone looked at them, Tara felt like they were an exhibit at the zoo.

Jill read out some notices—there was a chair exercise group starting up on a Tuesday at ten in the morning; a show of hands was requested for interest in an outing to Morning Melodies; and Kas and Andy needed at least two people to play five-hundred on Wednesday afternoons. Tara wondered if they'd got the venue wrong and landed up at the Senior Citizens.

With each announcement, Jon's tension ratcheted up until it threatened to push Tara off her chair. She rested her hand on his jiggling thigh.

'Please welcome today's guest: Sandra, from Leisure Assist in Melbourne,' Jill finished, and took a seat.

There was a polite scattering of applause and Sandra, a woman in her fifties, clicked a laser pointer. The PowerPoint slide behind her declared *Embracing the Journey*.

'It must feel like getting Parkinson's is incredibly unfair, especially as you've worked hard all your lives,' she began. 'But this is your fork in the road. Your chance to take a positive from a negative. This is the time to reassess and prioritise.'

Photos of iconic travel destinations flashed up on the screen behind her.

'Stop dreaming about that trip of a lifetime. Just do it! Imagine cruising the Pacific or taking a famous train journey. Follow the old camel train route on the Ghan between Adelaide and Darwin or the exotic romance of the Orient Express. Slow travel. No need to rush. It's the perfect way to travel with Parkinson's.'

Sandra outlined the many and varied holiday options her company offered, including destinations specifically tailored for the mobility-challenged and discounts for carers. 'And if I haven't convinced you yet, let's hear from some of our satisfied customers.'

A video commenced, showing a group of happy people heading off on a bus trip; a small group being met at an airport by smiling staff before being transported to a gate lounge; an older couple kissing under the Eiffel Tower; and a man in his seventies using a cruise ship's gymnasium.

The camera panned in. 'I used to live to work,' the man said. 'Getting sick was the wake-up call I needed. Life was passing me by. This is my fourth trip with Leisure Assist. What I love about cruising is I can still exercise and the time-zone changes are slow. It makes it easier to juggle my medication.'

Three more testimonials followed with similar messages— retirement was the best thing since sliced bread. The final scene was a family group with an older couple holidaying with their children and grandchildren.

As brochures were handed out—all with Sandra's business card neatly stapled to the front and her phone number highlighted in fluoro yellow—there was some general chatter about holidays.

The woman next to Tara said, 'What do you think about that then?'

Tara didn't know where to start.

'And now for the exciting news,' Sandra said. 'We're offering an all-expenses-paid round-the-world cruise for two in a wheelchair-friendly stateroom with transportation and assistance at every port. To be in the draw, all you have to do is register on our website.'

She thrust an iPad at Tara.

'I don't think this is really for us,' Tara said.

'Of course it is. Embrace the journey. Remember, life doesn't stop for you to catch up.'

A bristle ran up Tara's spine. 'You don't under—'

'Embrace the journey?' Jon's voice boomed, silencing the room. 'Sounds more like "You're sick, suckers, let me take your hard-earned cash." Does it look like we can retire? That we can take off for three-quarters of a year? Christ! We've got a business, a mortgage and two young kids to raise.'

Sandra's mouth was opening and closing like a goldfish.

Making a scene in public, Tara, is the height of bad manners. As her mother's words crashed into her, Tara momentarily considered smoothing the choppy seas they'd just created. But what was the point? Jon would never come back to this group and she didn't blame him.

She stood and took his hand and they walked out of the hall together, letting the doors slam shut behind them.

'So, that seemed to go pretty well,' she said.

For the first time in a long time, Jon laughed. It was worth failing support group just to hear the sound.

'Yeah, we'll get a black mark for sure.' He sighed and raked his hand through his hair. 'I'm so bloody sick of driving to the hospital. I'm sick of medical appointments. Sick of being asked how I'm feeling. I just want to go home and be normal.'

Tara had no idea what normal was any more. Jon was gripping the car keys tightly and her sharpened awareness noticed the slight tremble. Was it Parkinson's or was he just over-gripping the keys?

'Let's invite the gang over Friday night,' he said. 'They're the only support group we need.'

Tara was torn. This was the first time since the diagnosis that he'd shown any interest in being social and she wanted to encourage it. But it wasn't enough to stop agitation plucking at the strings of her concern.

'Is Friday night a good idea?'

'We've always done Friday or Saturday night.'

'Yes, but you know how tired you are at the end of each day. By Friday, you're beyond exhausted.'

His mouth hardened into familiar and stubborn lines. 'I'm not giving in to this fu—freaking disease. I'll be fine.'

She remembered the previous gatherings when she'd thought he was stumbling drunk. Thought about the words of caution from the movement specialist about fatigue, and the counsellor talking to her about the stages of grief and how Jon was bouncing between anger and denial. Tara knew how stubborn he could be. How he'd push through until he literally fell over, leaving her to pick up the pieces—physically and emotionally. One of them had to be sensible. One of them had to accept this disease was in their lives and staying.

'Doing things differently isn't giving in,' she said. 'What about Sunday brunch? It's not like any of us get a sleep-in anyway. We can do eggs and bacon and pancakes on the barbecue and the kids can play. Then people can head off for the rest of their Sunday.'

'And I won't be tired.'

'That's the plan.'

He cupped her cheek, caressing her skin with his thumb. 'I'm sorry I've been so difficult to live with. I should have told you I've been shit scared for months.'

She thought about her recent behaviour. 'You don't have a monopoly on being scared. I thought you didn't love me any more and I made everything about me instead of noticing what was going on with you. I'm sorry too.'

'Like when you convinced yourself I was having an affair with Rhianna?'

'Yes.' A flash of herself straddling Zac thwacked her hard and she winced. 'Stuff like that.'

His mouth pulled down in a wry smile. 'Even if I'd wanted to have an affair, which I don't, I've been too bloody exhausted just getting through the day.'

'I know that now.'

'I love you, T.'

'I love you too.'

He pulled her in close and kissed her in a way he hadn't done in months. Long and deep, like a lover. She tasted need and desire. And relief. The world steadied. This was the Jon who'd been absent for so long. This was Team Hooper.

He suddenly sagged, his weight pressing against her, threatening her balance. She braced herself and gripped his arms. 'You okay?'

'You have a powerful effect on me,' he joked.

But when he stepped away from her, fatigue was dragging at the corners of his eyes, drooping his shoulders and hanging off every part of him like an ill-fitting coat. It was hard to know if it was the Parkinson's or a side effect of the drug treatment.

He thrust the car keys towards her. 'Can you drive home?'

The question hit with a sharp arrow of loss. Jon loved driving and hated relinquishing the wheel so Tara had stopped offering years ago unless it was a long road trip. Now he was asking her to drive a fifty-minute journey at three in the afternoon.

The weight of being a carer settled over her as tight as clingwrap.

The invitation to brunch wasn't as well received as Tara had hoped.

Kelly had screwed up her face. 'But we always do Friday or Saturday night.'

'This isn't you trying to inflict your healthy living obsession onto us, is it?' Rhianna asked. 'We don't have to go for a run too?'

Tara had counted to ten, reminding herself she was doing this for Jon. 'We thought it might be fun to mix things up a bit.'

'Maybe.' Kelly looked dubious. 'There'll be mimosas, right?'

Tara hadn't planned on serving alcohol. 'Won't that just make us sleepy?'

'Exactly,' Kelly said. 'Al can be on kid duty all afternoon.'

'Kelly's right,' Rhianna said. 'It's not brunch without mimosas.'

By the time Sunday morning arrived, Jon was looking rested but Tara felt wrung out. Protecting Jon's energy levels meant she was doing more of everything at home and at work. Jon was giving her a crash course in ordering and she was also the go-to person between one and two thirty each afternoon when he went home to rest. It was the key to him managing the workday as well as being sentient for the kids in the evening.

He was definitely better in the mornings. The medication was still being tweaked but it had improved his muscle stiffness and eased the tremors, although there was still the issue of random involuntary movements. The day before, Jon's arm had jerked at breakfast, knocking over two litres of milk. A white waterfall had cascaded from the bench onto Clementine, who'd sobbed as if she'd been scalded.

Flynn had grinned. 'Does this mean I don't get into trouble now if I spill things?'

Trying to explain Parkinson's to the children without terrifying them was difficult. As they'd both been at home when Jon fell, it wasn't possible to hide the disease from them. But Tara didn't want to upend their safe world and fill it with anxiety either. After talking with Donna and reading articles online, they'd gone with a basic explanation.

'Sometimes Daddy's hands or legs might shake. When that happens, he might not be able to catch or hit a ball.'

'Or use a nail gun or the jigsaw,' Flynn said.

'That's right, but most of the time he won't shake.' Tara had said it more as a prayer than a truth.

They'd avoided information about possible problems with swallowing and speech, hoping they wouldn't appear until far into the future. Knowing hope didn't protect them one little bit.

The children had listened, but when Tara asked if they had any questions, all they'd said was, 'Can we watch TV now?'

It was hard to know how much they'd taken in. Flynn seemed fine, but Clementine was demanding a lot of cuddles from Tara and avoiding Jon. Tara couldn't accurately recall if her daughter had been doing this before the diagnosis—kids went through phases of favouring one parent over another—or if the avoidance was connected to the Parkinson's. But she added it to her ever-growing list of things she needed to watch out for so she could act and keep her family safe.

On Sunday morning, the gang arrived on time and the children wolfed down the pancakes before running off to play in the garden. There'd been less drama with the kids than at their evening gatherings and Tara wondered if they should have done brunch years ago.

Allowing herself to relax, she watched Jon happily holding court at the barbecue in the same way he'd done for years. She noticed the occasional jerk of the spatula, but he didn't appear bothered by it. He was fully engaged in the conversation about work, cricket, the school working bee and town politics.

There was a lot of discussion about the mayor, Geoff Rayson.

'I reckon Ainslea Park's a front for something fishy,' Kelly said. 'I mean why are the Chinese visiting? They don't race horses, they just eat them.'

'I thought it was the Arabs who were interested?'

'If the Chinese are going to buy anything in this town, it's more likely the dairy. That way they can corner the baby formula market,' Al said.

'I thought they did that already. Isn't it our biggest unofficial export?' Rhianna said.

'Don't wish the Chinese on me!' Kelly said. 'Oh, wait. Do the Chinese hate the Muslims? I'm on board if they sack Fatima.'

'Talking about Muslims, how are the neighbours?' Brent asked. 'Broken into the house yet as well as the store?'

'They're not like that,' Tara said, guilt squirming in her gut. 'Actually they—' she realised if she said they were helpful, she'd have to say why, '—keep to themselves.'

'A group of six of them came into the shop the other day. I followed them so they didn't have a chance to pocket anything,' Rhianna said.

'Good for you,' Kelly said.

'Thought you kept all your electronics locked up?' Jon said.

'We do. But you of all people know what they're like.'

'They're hardly going to pocket a washing machine,' Tara said, surprising herself.

Rhianna glared at her.

'Food's up,' Jon said firmly, cutting the conversation off at the knees.

Tara reached for the spatula, but he shook his head. He served the bacon, eggs and pancakes onto the platters Tara held close to him. A couple of times his hand jerked wildly and she had to chase the spatula, but only one pancake hit the deck. No one seemed to notice.

'Bacon's the reason I'll never be vegetarian.' Al piled three crispy rashers onto his plate. 'Any chance of a light beer to wash it down?'

'Don't be such a philistine.' Kelly refilled her glass with more sparkling wine than orange juice. 'Where's yours, Jon? I'll top you up.'

'I'm all good, thanks.'

'He probably wants a beer, right, Jon?' Brent said.

'Such a comedian,' Kelly said. 'Don't give up your day job. You blokes need to expand your horizons—you don't hear French men complaining about drinking champagne.' She picked up a clean glass, filled it and held it out to Jon.

'No, thanks,' he said.

Rhianna looked up from her pancakes. 'Since when does Jon Hooper refuse a drink?'

'Did you get suckered into doing one of those fundraising things?' Al asked.

'No. I got diagnosed with Parkinson's disease.'

The sound of cutlery scraping on plates ceased and four sets of eyes zeroed in on him.

Brent laughed. 'Yeah, right, mate. Now who's the dud comedian. Everyone knows it's an old codger's disease.'

Jon shook his head. 'Twenty per cent of people who are diagnosed with it are under fifty.'

Tara looked at their friends' faces and realised they didn't believe him. 'It's real. The last few gatherings when Jon's staggered and slurred his speech, he wasn't drunk. It's young Parkinson's.'

'And you have to stop drinking? You poor bastard.' Al made it sound like that was the worst part of the disease.

'That's the least of his worries,' Tara said sharply.

'She's right,' Kelly said. 'That American actor who got Parkinson's—you know the one. When he talks, he wobbles like one of those solar hula dancers. God, what's his name?'

'When did you find out?' Brent asked.

'A few weeks ago.'

'And you're only just telling us now?' Rhianna's voice rose. 'Gee, thanks.'

Jon flinched as if he'd been hit. Tara wanted to slap Rhianna for making this about her.

'We needed time to process it before we could handle telling anyone,' she said. 'Apart from Ian, you're the first people we've told.'

Why am I justifying our choices to you?

'You don't look sick,' Al said.

Jon slid his hand into his pocket—a technique Tara now recognised hid his shaking hand. 'I'm taking medication to help control the symptoms.'

'All good then.' Brent raised his glass.

Tara looked at Jon. *Tell them how it really is. How tired you are. How your memory's not as sharp. That you're working less. Tell them your balance is unsteady.* She didn't expect him to talk about the constipation, the dizziness or the erectile dysfunction, but she hoped he might mention how tough they were both finding the diagnosis. The bad days when the black dog sat heavily on his shoulder and he didn't want to get out of bed. How they needed the support of their friends.

But Jon stayed silent, his expression a blank mask. Only this time, Tara knew it wasn't blank because of Parkinson's. It was disappointment. It was shame.

A tornado of emotions whirled through her. Heartache for Jon, fury at their friends' unsympathetic response, and a desperate desire to bring Chris and Shannon back from New York.

Later, Kelly helped Tara carry the dirty plates into the kitchen and stack the dishwasher.

'So the change to brunch,' she said. 'It's because of Jon?'

'Yes.' A tiny seed of hope opened inside her that Kelly was starting to understand. Perhaps Tara had expected too much too soon from the gang—they needed time to process the information too. 'He's better in the mornings, although not every morning. Wednesday was a shocker. After I'd tied Clementine's shoes, I had to tie his too.'

Kelly's eyes widened. 'God, that's ...'

'Yeah. It's pretty confronting for both of us.'

As Tara put a glass on the coffee machine and pressed the latte button for Kelly, Rhianna walked in carrying the tray of condiments.

'Tara, I keep meaning to ask. Are you coming to lunch on Wednesday or are you too busy marathon training?'

Tara's skin ran hot and cold at the mention of the marathon, reminding her of what she'd risked and what she'd lost.

'Sorry, I meant to RSVP but things have been crazy. I'm no longer training but I'm working longer hours. Jon takes a ninety-minute break in the middle of the day and it's easier if I'm at the store then.'

Rhianna's hand touched her décolletage in exaggerated surprise. 'That must be a shock to the system.'

Tara's back teeth locked. 'Everything about Parkinson's is a shock. We're having to rethink how we do everything.'

'Are you having the kids tested?' Kelly asked.

The coffee machine beeped and Tara passed the latte to Kelly. 'Tested? What do you mean?'

'You know, for Parkinson's. Isn't it genetic?'

'Not always. They think it's a combination of a genetic disposition and environmental factors.'

'Still. I'd want to know,' Kelly said.

'Really?' Tara's patience unravelled fast. 'How would it help? I've already got a husband who's depressed and struggling with his body that's constantly moving against his will. Imagine if he'd grown up knowing this would happen? He'd have been miserable for three decades. Or worse. I wouldn't wish that on the kids. I want them to have a normal childhood.'

'But that's not really possible any more, is it,' Rhianna said.

'Of course it is!' Tara pushed the milk-frother into the coffee machine with more force than necessary.

'You just told us he needs a nap every day. How's he going to keep up with the kids?'

'You're planning on having a nap this afternoon!'

Rhianna gave her a pitying look. 'You know that's not the same. I have a choice.'

Choice. Standing in her own kitchen with a houseful of people, loneliness cloaked and choked Tara. Was this her new life?

Every part of her ached to strap on her shoes and outrun it.

CHAPTER
25

Jade considered texting Corey that Helen was moving in, but as her name was on the lease and he didn't contribute anything to the rent, she decided against it.

And he hasn't told you where the hell he is!

Constable Fiora had dropped in a couple of times, hoping to catch her out in a lie and find Corey on the couch. He was just as disappointed as Jade was by Corey's absence.

This wasn't the first time Corey had disappeared without a word. It had happened when she'd told him she was pregnant, and again when Milo was six weeks old, screaming with hunger and feeding constantly. She'd been exhausted and strung out.

'Give him a bottle to shut him up,' Corey had said, not looking up from Tour of Duty.

Since Milo's birth, Corey had either been out with Macca working or drinking—mostly drinking—or home on the couch, gaming and complaining about the 'shit state of the place'. One afternoon, during a particularly difficult two days when Jade hadn't found time to even take a shower, could smell her own stink and there were no clean dishes in the cupboards, she'd completely lost it.

'Stop playing that fucking game and help me!' she'd screamed, snatching the controller out of his hands.

He'd jumped to his feet, grabbed her and shaken her until the room spun. 'You're useless. And stupid. You're a useless stupid bitch who can't get her kid to shut the fuck up.'

He'd let her go then and she'd slid down the wall, her legs quaking and her heart racing. Corey had slammed out of the house, the walls vibrating with his fury.

She didn't know how long she'd sat sobbing with her face buried in her knees, but at some point she'd realised the only sounds in the house were her pathetic sniffles. Milo had finally and blessedly fallen into an exhausted sleep.

She'd hauled herself to her feet, cleaned herself and the house, and made Corey his favourite spaghetti bolognaise with garlic bread. And waited.

She waited three weeks and five days. Corey didn't reply to texts or calls. Macca told her, 'I don't know where he is, but if I was him, I wouldn't want to be with a clingy slut.'

Three times she'd picked up the phone to call her mother and three times she'd stopped herself. Why give Charlene a reason to tell her she'd got what she deserved? Corey's silent absence was clear evidence Jade had brought this on herself. She shouldn't have screamed at him. She should have known that adjusting to parenthood was harder for him than it was for her—men didn't feel a baby kicking inside them for months and bond before birth like women did. And Corey had never liked being tied down and a baby lashed you tighter than a truckie's hitch. She was lucky he'd hung around this long wanting to be part of Milo's life. Part of her life.

He'd been doing his best and she'd selfishly driven him away and denied Milo the chance to get to know his father. Just like her mother had driven away her father with her constant bitching, and every bloke since. Corey was right. Jade really was stupid.

So when he'd strolled through the door twenty-seven days after he'd left, greeting her as if he'd just nicked down the shops for some ciggies, she'd known this was her last chance. Milo deserved a father and she wouldn't be the reason he didn't know Corey. She'd do everything in her power to protect her family and that meant making home a place where Corey wanted to spend time. It meant making no demands on him and giving him whatever he wanted.

Jade had done all that and Corey had left her again. Only this time, she knew she hadn't done anything wrong.

You weren't home for him. You were at the garden.

Why was she expected to stay at home just in case he turned up? *Because he's working.*

But the once loud and defending voice wasn't as convincing, especially as Jade didn't see any of his money. This was why she'd struck the deal with Helen.

The irony wasn't lost on Jade that Helen losing the cottage was the answer to her holding onto the unit, even if it did mean a massive reorganisation. Milo's cot was now in Jade's room and she'd stowed his clothes in storage bins under her bed. As long as she kept things tidy she had a narrow but clear path between her bed and the door. Milo didn't seem bothered by the move and he'd gone down for his nap without any fuss.

Today, Saturday, Bob and Lachlan had loaded their utes with Helen's stuff and been ferrying boxes all morning. Helen had accepted Bob's offer to store some of her furniture and Jade had offered to swap couches. She'd felt bad when Bob insisted he take her old couch to his shed and was disappointed she couldn't tag along. For weeks, Bob had been producing things from his shed and she'd built it up in her mind as a mysterious treasure trove. She wanted to see exactly what was in it and hear the stories behind each item. Mostly she wanted to watch Bob tinkering at his workbench and see the tools he'd used to make Milo's trolley and her earrings.

Jade was creating room for Helen in some kitchen cupboards when Lachlan walked out of the laundry. He was wearing old green shorts, a black T-shirt that said *Boolanga Bards* on the front and *Urinetown* on the back along with a list of names. Apparently it was a musical. Who knew? What she did know was that the soft cotton shirt was too small for him, clinging to his shoulders and flat stomach like a second skin. It made her look, then look away and wish he was wearing his work clothes.

But right now it wasn't the T-shirt that was racing tingles along her skin and heating her cheeks. It was the way he was holding a large silver shifter. Her attraction flipped into overdrive.

'The washing machine's good to go,' he said. 'I saw you had a load in the basket so I put it on. Should be ready to peg out in about fifty minutes.'

'You know how to use a washing machine?'

His face creased into easy laugh lines. 'You think my work clothes get washed by magic or by Dame Washalot?'

'You know *The Magic Faraway Tree*?' It had been the only children's book at her grandmother's house.

'It was one of Auntie Pen's favourites. Uncle Bob built her a shelf so she could store her favourite childhood books. He decorated it with characters from *Peter Pan* and it was in the room my sister and

I used when we slept over. I think it was supposed to have been for the kids they never had. Tiff and I loved it.'

'That's sad. Bob would have been a great dad.'

'Yeah. He's ten years older than Mum so he was kind of a dad to her. And now my dad's gone, he's great for advice. Tiff and I spent a lot of our school holidays on the farm and I loved those books almost as much as the animals.'

'What else was on the shelf?' Jade asked.

'All the Narnia books, *The Hobbit, Storm Boy, The Min-Min.*' He grinned. 'Tiff was horse mad so she loved *The Silver Brumby.* Uncle Bob added the Harry Potter books saying it was for Tiff and me, but really it was for him. He's a huge fan. He took us to all the movies and Auntie Pen made us wizard cloaks. Whenever I pick up a Harry Potter book, I get a warm feeling, you know?'

No. She didn't know. Jade's hunger to learn more about Lachlan was suddenly replete. His childhood was unrecognisable.

'What about you?' he asked.

'What about me?'

He blinked at her snappish tone, wariness clouding his usually open expression. 'We were talking about kids' books ...' He trailed off.

She had an overwhelming urge to shock him so he'd stop being so nice. Expose the chasm of different experiences that lay between them so she wasn't tempted to like him any more than she already did. Men like Lachlan didn't slum it with the likes of her.

She stared him down. 'My Harry Potter experience isn't quite as heartwarming as yours. My mother wasn't a fan of me reading. She thought it was a waste of time when I could be earning money. When she found out I'd bought the Harry Potter box set, she sold it and kept the money.'

Lachlan opened his mouth a couple of times before closing it again, but she didn't miss the pity in his eyes. She hated it, even though she'd deliberately put it there so he'd know his world was shiny and hers was all banged up.

The door opened and Helen walked in with Bob. He had a bunch of daffodils tucked under his arm and he carried two Acropolis Café bags full of food and drinks.

'Hello, you two. Grab some plates and glasses for us, will you, Jade? We've brought you a late lunch.'

'Do you have any serviettes, Jade?' Helen asked.

'Yeah. I keep them next to the silver.'

Helen pursed her lips and rummaged through a box. She ripped off some paper towel squares and put them on the table.

Jade didn't have a vase, but she found a tall glass for the daffodils and arranged them evenly before placing them in the middle of the table. When they all sat, she realised it was the first time she'd had guests and immediately saw the table through their eyes. Only three of the plates matched and none of the glasses. She suddenly wished for six identical plates and yellow serviettes to match the flowers. But by the time she got her next Centrelink payment, the flowers would be dead and she couldn't afford a dinner set.

Fighting resentment, she bit into the souvlaki, savouring the treat. 'This is amazing. Thanks, Helen.'

'Thank Bob. If it was up to me, we'd have made sandwiches.'

'Thanks, Bob, for wasting your money on me.' Jade grinned at him as Helen huffed. 'And thanks for the flowers.'

'You're welcome,' Bob said. 'Thought we should mark the occasion.'

'It's only temporary,' Helen said. 'When the mayor's forced to stand down …'

'What are the chances?' Lachlan asked.

'Not sure,' Bob said. 'I popped in to have a chat with Aki and Craig, but they're both playing their cards close to their chests.'

'I reckon we go on Facebook and tell everyone what a bastard Geoff Rayson is so no one votes for him,' Jade said.

'The public don't vote for the mayor,' Helen said.

'But what he's doing isn't fair!'

'You still believe in fair?'

Sometimes Jade wondered if Helen was inside her head. 'I think you need to fight for—what do they call it when you lose your job just 'cos they want to sack you for no good reason?'

'Unfair dismissal?' Lachlan said.

'Yes. That. And Helen didn't make the meme.'

'How do you prove it?' Bob asked.

'Even if she did, there's worse stuff out there,' Lachlan said. 'Right, Jade?'

'Oh, yeah.' Jade looked at Bob and Helen. 'You two don't want to go looking too deep on the internet. It'd shock you.'

Helen snorted and drink shot out of her nose. 'Thanks for the warning, Jade.'

Jade didn't know if Helen was taking the piss or not.

'I reckon something's up,' Lachlan said. 'I was at a Landcare meeting last week and they were promised a grant ages ago so they could finish the last section of planting. But every time they ask when the money's coming, they're told a different story. Maybe all those rumours about the mayor doing a land deal really are true.'

'How would we find out?' Jade asked.

'I don't know. It might be time to go along to a council meeting and ask some questions,' Helen said.

'He's hardly going to admit to it there, is he?' Lachlan said.

'No, but we can report on Facebook what's said every time we ask about the land,' Jade said.

'Hang on,' Helen said. 'I asked you to take the Facebook page down.'

'I think we should keep it. When you offered to take it down, Vivian said it wouldn't make him change his mind about the cottage or the job, so I say stuff 'em. Don't let him silence you.'

'Jade's got a point,' Bob said. 'This way we have a voice.'

'I can't afford to be sued,' Helen said.

'If we stick to reporting exactly what the mayor says, we can't be sued. And we'll do the moderating together so Helen doesn't post any more memes.'

'Ha ha. Very funny.'

Jade grinned, happiness fizzing in her gut. The conversation reminded her of Mrs Kastrati's pop debates, which she'd usually won.

Helen refilled her drink. 'Sometimes the truth lies more in what's not said.'

'Where'd they get the money for that?' Bob said in a squeaky voice.

Helen laughed. 'God, I'd forgotten that.'

'What?' Jade and Lachlan asked simultaneously, exchanging glances.

'It was an ad from the eighties for a credit company,' Bob explained. 'It had cartoon rabbits driving past iconic buildings like the Coliseum asking, "Where'd they get the money for that?" Pen and I adopted it as a joke. We'd say it whenever we drove past an impressive house or walked into a fancy public building.'

'And?' Jade asked.

'And Geoff and his wife bought Ainslea Park, which was a massive leap up from their previous home. It just makes you wonder where they got the money for it.'

'That's what Vivian implied,' Helen said.

'So we ask some questions,' Bob said.

Helen nodded. 'And we do some digging. I'll talk to Fran at the library. She's got the back issues of *The Standard*.'

'How will that help?' Jade asked.

'Sometimes the social pages tell you more than the council minutes.'

Clutching her sponge bag, Helen surveyed the chaos in the bathroom—sodden bathmat, grey bath water in the tub, bottle of baby shampoo oozing its contents down the tiles, a pile of dirty clothes and a neatly folded but whiffy nappy. She rested her forehead on the doorjamb and breathed deeply, hoping to stall the fast rise of her blood pressure towards the red zone. Since moving in, she and Jade had been involved in a series of skirmishes involving the common areas.

Helen turned towards the lounge room and pain exploded behind her eyes. She hopped, rubbing her foot, and saw the offending block on the floor. How could a baby who didn't walk manage to spread toys into every corner of the unit? Then again, he could commando crawl with lightning speed that amazed and distressed her all at the same time.

Jade was sitting on the couch with a clean and cherry-cheeked Milo, his damp curls starting to spring back. Helen's heart tore a little and she put the block on the coffee table with more force than intended.

'Toys don't belong in the hall.'

'Jeez, Helen, take a chill pill.'

'I stepped on it and it bloody hurt! And the bathroom's a tip.'

Jade reached for a board book. 'I'll clean up after I've put him to bed.'

Helen was now familiar with the 'put Milo to bed' routine. It took at least half an hour. After a busy shift at the café she stank of fried food. All she wanted was to soak in a warm bath and wash the day away.

'I want to use it now,' she said.

Jade huffed. 'Okay, fine. You read to him.'

Helen had spent the last ten days avoiding reading to Milo. Each time she sat on the couch or a kitchen chair, he pulled himself up and deposited a book on her lap. Then he'd stare up at her with those huge blue eyes of his full of hope. She blamed Bob. The day she'd moved in, he'd read to Milo every time he'd produced a book. Now Milo thought she was fair game and the kid was annoyingly persistent. Like his mother.

Like you.

'You need to clean as you go,' she said.

Jade's mouth hardened. 'I'm doing you a favour letting you live here.'

'I'm paying rent. This is just as much my house as yours. I'm respecting you by keeping things clean and tidy and you need to do the same.'

The moment the words shot out she regretted them.

'Stop bossing me around!' Jade said. 'All you've done since you moved in is criticise me. You don't have to live here, you know!'

Helen stomped to the bathroom, pulled out the plug, flung towels into the laundry hamper and mopped up the slick trail of shampoo that could make her slip and break a hip. She should have accepted Bob's invitation to rent his spare room. Not that she had any idea if Bob was neater than Jade, but she had a hunch he had two bathrooms.

Rubbing furiously, she removed the ring of grime then ran the bath, feeling her anger ebb. As the water rushed around her, it brought reluctant memories rising to the surface. Snapshots of what living with a baby was like—the constant interruptions, the never-ending claims on her time. The overwhelming feelings of inadequacy.

Back then, Theo's income had meant money wasn't something Helen needed to worry about too much, but he'd been raised in a Greek household—men didn't do housework. Helen had struggled to keep the house neat and clean, to cook and put meals on the table when Nicki cried non-stop for weeks. Despite the years that separated her from those dark days, a shudder wove through her. Jade didn't have the luxury of a secure income to offset the worries of raising a child. She was doing it all on her own.

Pangs of conscience poked Helen and she slid under the water, seeking absolute quiet. God, how she craved quiet. And space. She'd lived alone for years and she was too old to share a house with anyone, let alone with a girl who was young enough to be her daughter.

You don't have to live here, you know.

Her breath rushed out of her lungs and a flotilla of bubbles boomed around her ears. She sat up fast, thinking about Roxy and her cycle of moving in with her daughter and grandchildren and inevitably landing back living in her car within two weeks. Roxy always sounded so positive when she moved in, but the arguments started within two days, straining an already fraught relationship and quickly snapping fragile bonds.

I'm doing you a favour. You don't get to boss me around.

If she and Jade continued along this path, things would break down fast and Helen's options were limited. The thought of being beholden to anyone, let alone Bob, terrified her. At least she and Jade were close to a level playing field financially and Helen's rent was helping to improve Jade's quality of life. Bob didn't need extra money—she'd be his charity case and would likely have to fight him to pay rent. She didn't need that power dynamic.

That left making things work with Jade. But how? In her post-grad studies, Helen had learned some conflict resolution techniques. She'd only ever thought of them in terms of advising others on how to use them. She sank under the water again, fighting the uncomfortable truth. She had to use them herself.

By the time Helen had finished her bath and tidied the bathroom, Milo was in bed and asleep. She walked into the kitchen and rummaged through her food cupboard, pulling out her bottle of Jack Daniels.

'Jade, I've got some JD and you've got a bottle of Coke. I thought we could have a drink if you're happy to share the Coke?'

Jade put down *Year of Wonders*. The girl read voraciously, reminding Helen of herself at the same age. 'I s'pose.'

Helen bit off, 'Don't do me any favours,' and lifted two glasses out of the cupboard. After quickly mixing the drinks, she carried them into the lounge. 'Here you go.'

Taking a seat on the couch next to Jade, she took a fortifying slug of her drink, enjoying the burning heat of the whiskey. 'Been a bit of a rocky week, hasn't it?'

'Little bit.'

'Sorry I lost it over the bathroom. I get a bit grumpy when I'm tired.'

'I noticed.'

Instead of jumping on the criticism, Helen took another sip and forced herself to let the silence hang. 'I've lived on my own for a long time. Have you ever shared with anyone before?'

'I lived with Mum until she kicked me out.'

That answered one question about why Jade was virtually on her own.

'That's not exactly sharing though, is it? There's the whole mother–daughter dynamic.'

Jade grimaced. 'You mean being told what to do all the time? Like you're doing even though it's my house?'

'I haven't been—' She took a deep breath. 'That's the thing, Jade, it's *our* house. We're supposed to be sharing. But right now we're two individuals living under one roof and doing our own thing. That's why we're fighting.'

'I'm not a kid.' Jade held up her drink as if to reinforce the message.

Helen took in Jade's unlined face, the faint remains of a pimple, and saw a child. She reminded herself that Nicki wasn't that much older than Jade, but Nicki was forever a child. Was that part of the problem? What did Helen know about young adults?

Memories stirred and she was suddenly back in the weatherboard house in East Bentleigh with her hand on the timber and glass front door. *Where are you going?* She was twenty-one and financially independent, but her parents still insisted on a curfew. Jade was a young mother without any family support who'd managed to live independently on a very limited income. It was a sobering thought.

'I know you're not a kid,' Helen said. 'Just like I'm not your mother.'

'Hell, no.' Jade took a deep draught of her drink. 'You can be a pain but you're nothing like Charlene.'

Questions spun in Helen's mind but she didn't ask them. 'Is that a compliment?'

'Yeah.' Jade's lips twitched into a cheeky smile that lightened her often dour expression. 'You're okay.'

'Thank you.' Helen made a decision. 'I really want to make this work because ...' Her chest cramped and she sucked in a deep breath. 'Because there was a time a few years ago when I lived in my car. I don't ever want to do that again.'

Jade stared at her, eyes wide. 'You were homeless?'

'For six long and terrifying months.'

She expected a barrage of questions about why and how, but then she remembered Jade's stories about childhood evictions and her grandmother.

'So that's why you're so passionate about the tiny houses,' Jade said. 'Makes sense.'

'Exactly. And I'm thinking that as Corey's AWOL—'

'A what?'

'AWOL. It's an army term meaning absent without leave. Anyway, at the moment he probably isn't giving you any money so my rent's helping you balance your budget, right?'

Jade grimaced. 'Corey doesn't give me much even when he's here.'

Helen bit down on her automatic criticism of the rat bastard. 'I was thinking, instead of fighting each other on everything, let's be a team.'

'What do you mean?'

'At the moment, the only thing we're sharing is the rent. I think it will work better if we share more. You know, like a kitty?'

'I don't want a cat.'

Helen smiled. 'I meant why don't we both put money into a shared purse, a kitty, to buy food? We can plan our meals together, shop together and share the cooking. We'll save money.'

'You mean like a family?'

'I suppose I do.'

'But you don't like Milo.'

Air rushed out of her lungs as if she'd been punched. 'I don't dislike him.'

Jade's gaze narrowed. 'If you don't dislike him, why do you ignore him?'

'I don't ignore him.'

'You pretty much do.'

'You're his mother. I didn't want to stand on your toes.'

Jade snorted. 'You've told me how to do everything else, so why'd you stop there?'

Helen's heart raced. It was one thing to admit to being homeless to a young woman who understood hardship. It was another thing completely to talk about why she found dealing with young children difficult.

'You do a great job with Milo, Jade.'

The shock on the young woman's face tore a piece of Helen's heart.

'Thank you,' Jade said eventually. 'It's the hardest job I've ever done.'

Helen thought of Nicki. 'And it always will be.'

CHAPTER
26

Tara slowed at the sixty sign on the outskirts of Boolanga and her phone, denied access to mobile reception for the last fifteen minutes, buzzed incessantly. She sighed as the bonds of responsibility tightened around her. A year ago, she'd have thought a spa day was an escape from her life. Now it was a solo drive to and from an appointment with Lorraine, the counsellor Donna had suggested she talk to about the challenges of being a carer. 'It's a safe environment where you can be honest about your feelings without any fear of upsetting Jon,' she'd said.

Only instead of discussing carer issues and Parkinson's, Tara had found herself talking about the gang and how much she missed her mother. She couldn't tell if it had helped or just made her sadder. She wasn't sure she'd return. Her life already seemed like a continuous round of appointments without adding in one that unsettled her.

She pulled into the supermarket car park and switched off the ignition before picking up her phone. There was a new excursion form for Flynn on the school app. Jon had emailed the agenda for the staff meeting, and there was a calendar reminder for the book group book she hadn't read and the meeting she didn't want to attend.

The phone beeped again and the sender's name bubbled agitation in her veins before spreading surprise, embarrassment and regret. She hadn't shared any communication with Zac in weeks—not since Jon's diagnosis. Why was he contacting her now? Her finger moved cautiously over the text as if she expected it to explode in her face.

Hey, Tara. Hope you and your husband ROK? I get you're not training ATM. If you want to run with a friend, just text. Your mate, Zac

A droplet of water hit the screen and she wiped it away before realising it was a tear. She didn't know if she was crying because Zac had been thinking of her and Jon, or if it was the invitation to run. Either way, he was the first person outside of their medical and allied health care team to offer her anything, even if finding time to run was now impossible.

She blew her nose and called Jon. 'Hi. How are things?'

'You checking up on me?'

'No,' she lied.

'Good. Because I'm good.'

Her heart ached at his flat and weary voice. Since the disastrous brunch, he'd gone very quiet. Too quiet. It was as if he didn't want to discuss what had happened in any detail. She assumed, like her, he was grappling with their friends' apparent lack of understanding of how their lives had not only been turned upside down, but would never return to what they'd previously known as normal. Neither the Stevensons nor the Kvants had requested any further information about Parkinson's, although Kelly had sent a couple of messages to the WhatsApp group with a vague enquiry about the date of their next get-together. Tara wasn't putting her hand up for that any time soon.

'I thought we could have early dinner tonight,' she said. 'Can you be home by five thirty?'

'Why? I told you I'm fine.'

'And I heard you. This is about the kids. They need a normal night at home with both of us, so I thought early dinner then games.'

It was true, but it also got Jon home so he didn't get overtired.

'Good idea. Do we have any C batteries for Uno Attack?'

'I'm at the supermarket so I'll grab some. See you soon.'

'Love you, T.'

'Love you too.'

She slid her phone into her handbag and walked into the supermarket, grabbing mince to make the kids' favourite—spaghetti bolognaise with garlic bread. Not that she felt like cooking, but between the barrage of medical appointments and her working full-time, they'd eaten too many frozen dinners and takeaway food. It was time to find a new normal, whatever the hell that was.

When she arrived home, she carried the shopping bags straight to the kitchen and was met by the aroma of onions, tomatoes and spices. Her stomach rumbled and she glanced around, seeking the source of the delicious tang. The stove top was empty as was the oven, then she noticed an unfamiliar slow cooker on the bench. Ian had been a great help with the kids, but he didn't enjoy cooking so this was an incredible piece of thoughtfulness.

'Hello, love.' Ian stuck his head through the sliding doors that led to the deck. She could hear the children playing in the pool. 'All good this end.'

'And you've cooked dinner too.' Full of gratitude, she kissed him on the cheek. 'Thank you.'

He laughed. 'You know I only barbecue so I can't take credit for that.'

Tara's anger at their friends dissipated on a wave of guilt—Rhianna or Kelly had finally come through for them. She remembered Lorraine's suggestion: 'Give them time, Tara. They're in shock too.' She'd been so tied up in her own grief, she'd expected too much of them too soon.

Tears of appreciation welled and she blinked them away. 'Was it Kelly or Rhianna who dropped it off?'

'Neither. Fiza brought it over.'

Every muscle tightened with a jerk. 'What?'

Ian looked sheepish. 'Yeah, about that. The kids have been playing together a bit after school. With everything that's going on, love, they need a bit of fun. Flynn really wants to perfect his somersaults.'

'So you gave in to pester power?'

'I figured you wouldn't mind. Not after the way Fiza and Amal helped Jon. I gotta tell you, they're the politest kids I've ever met. To be honest, it's easier all round when they're here.'

Tara's head spun. 'How are the Atallah twins playing over here connected to Fiza bringing a casserole?'

'When she picked up the kids the other day, she asked me how you were. I said you were running around like a chook with its head cut off trying to do everything.'

'Ian!' Tara hated that the statuesque woman with the critical demeanour knew she was struggling.

He clicked his tongue. 'Well, it's true, love. The only thing I feel bad about is that Fiza went to the trouble of cooking something no one's going to eat. But I plugged it in to be polite.'

'Grandpa!'

A ball flew past Ian's ear and he turned his attention back to the children.

Go and look after your husband. Fiza's terse words rang in Tara's head despite the fact she hadn't seen her since they'd both stood at the entrance of A&E on the afternoon of Jon's accident. Now a tangled mix of emotions battered her. Why did it have to be Fiza who'd cooked her a casserole? Why couldn't it be Kelly or Rhianna?

She reluctantly lifted the slow cooker's lid. White beans lay nestled in a thick tomato-based sauce. Ian was right—the kids would likely turn up their noses and refuse to eat this. Jon, never a fan of vegetarian food, probably wouldn't want it either. It would end up languishing in a plastic container at the back of the fridge, slowly going mouldy, and she'd throw it out in a week's time. May as well dump it now.

The tomato sauce plopped slowly, taunting her with unwanted obligation.

'Fine!' She ripped off the end of the baguette and dragged it through the contents before putting it in her mouth.

At first, all she was aware of was the heat of the sauce, but then the subtle flavours emerged—lamb stock, tomatoes, herbs and pepper. *Damn.* Why did it have to taste so good?

A thank-you note and a small gift of appreciation. The many lessons about manners drilled into her by her mother were never far away. Normally, Tara didn't need reminding of her social obligations in or outside of work. She'd been the driving force behind Employee of the Month at the store, acknowledging hard work, innovation and kindness. Once, she'd given Kelly a voucher to Bathroom Pizazz just for taking Clementine to the movies. Now, guilt chafed against her reluctance and her tardiness in thanking Fiza. She'd justified not doing it by hiding behind the excuse of a blur of appointments and trying to make sense of what Jon's diagnosis really meant for them as a family.

And because the woman always left her feeling wrong-footed.

Is that because you are?

She transferred the contents of the slow cooker into one of her casserole dishes and washed the large ceramic bowl. Then she riffled through her stash of cards, finally settling on a Royal Flying Doctors charity one covered in a mass of callistemon. She scrawled a brief note, which when she re-read it sounded stilted and polite rather than heartfelt, but she shoved it in an envelope anyway. Then she wrapped a small tube of hand cream, stuck the card to it and headed to the door. Halfway across the room she hesitated, doubled back to the gift cupboard and picked up a music voucher.

Calling out to Ian, 'Back soon,' she walked the length of the drive and around to the front door of the orange eyesore. Except it wasn't an eyesore any more. The grass was mown, the garden beds were weed-free and the porch was swept.

Sucking in a deep breath, she rang the bell.

Heavy footsteps sounded and then a very tall and very black young man answered the door.

Tara swallowed, battling every previous reaction she'd ever experienced when she'd seen groups of black teenagers in town. She tried hard not to stare, but the darkness of his skin was luminous and hypnotising. He looked down at her from his impressive height, his expression neutral and his eyes wary.

'Amal?' He gave a slight nod of his head. 'Hi. I'm Tara. Tara Hooper. From next door.' She licked her dry lips. 'I believe I have to thank you for helping my husband when he fell.' She pushed the voucher at him. 'And for looking after Flynn and Clementine.'

He stared at the rectangular piece of plastic with its distinctive logo, turning it over slowly in his hands as if he couldn't quite believe what he was seeing. Then his face lit with a smile, his teeth a dazzle of white. 'Thanks. Is he better?'

'Jon? He's—'

'Amal, who are you talking to?' Fiza walked up the hall, her feet bare.

'Mrs Hooper.' Amal turned away from Tara. 'Look what she gave me!'

'Where are your manners! Invite Mrs Hooper inside.'

The teenager ducked as if Fiza was going to clip him on the back of the head. 'Sorry, Mrs Hooper. Please. Come in.'

'No. Really. It's okay. I just wanted to return your slow cooker.'

Tara held out the bag but neither Fiza nor Amal reached to accept it. She could either lower it onto the stoop and walk away or step inside.

You have to thank her.

She crossed the threshold and almost tripped on all the shoes just inside the door. Toeing off her sandals, she followed Fiza and Amal into the kitchen that still had the original 1960s' laminate benches and lime green tiles. Feeling out of place, Tara placed the bag on the bench and lifted out the slow cooker before resting the card and hand cream on top.

'Thank you for the casserole. It was kind of you, but not at all necessary.'

Fiza switched on the kettle, then lifted two glasses out of the glass display cabinet above the island bench. Her silence unnerved Tara.

'I really should get back to the children,' she said.

'They are safe. Your father is with them.'

Damn! Fiza could see Ian's car from the kitchen window.

'Father-in-law,' Tara corrected weakly. 'Jon's dad. My father's no longer alive. Or my mother.' *Shut up! You don't have to tell her anything.*

'I am sorry for your loss.' The words carried genuine sympathy.

'Thank you, but it was a while ago now.'

'This doesn't mean you don't miss them.' Fiza poured tea into a glass and pushed it towards her. 'Your husband's father says things are difficult for you.'

It was enough that Fiza had insisted Tara come inside and drink tea. All she wanted to do was the bare minimum of polite. Discuss the weather.

'Ian exaggerates.'

Fiza's brows rose fast towards the band of her turban. 'He is worried for your family.'

'He should be more worried about his own health.'

'Older people accept health challenges are part of ageing. But his son is a young man with a disease that will only get worse.'

A flash of anger flared from fear. 'We don't need your pity!'

'You don't have it. Pity is useless.'

The words hit Tara so hard she startled and knocked her tea. They both watched the line of amber fluid roll across the speckled bench, as if it promised them answers to impossibly difficult questions.

'I appreciate you gave Amal a gift.'

Something about the soft way Fiza said it made Tara squirm. Guilt? Shame? In her heart, she knew she should have acknowledged their help much earlier than this.

'It's nothing,' she said.

'No! It is a lot.' Fiza jerkily wiped a cloth across the spilled tea. 'It means you see the truth.'

'The truth?'

Fiza raised her gaze to Tara's. 'That my son is a kind and caring boy. I thank you for that.'

But the compliment sat like a stone in Tara's gut, rubbing against the sharp edges of long-held beliefs.

The following day, Tara's thoughts were still a jumbled mess as she pulled a wagon filled with punnets of seedlings down to Helen's cottage. Given the last time she and Helen had talked it had hardly been cordial, she wasn't certain of her reception. But during this morning's stocktake of the garden section, she'd immediately thought of the community garden.

You're really thinking of Fiza not Helen.

It was true. The night before, all through dinner, then Uno Attack and supervising the bedtime routine, Tara kept hearing her neighbour's words—*it means you see the truth.* What truth?

She couldn't shift the question, so when everyone was finally in bed and she had some time to herself, she'd googled Sudan. According to Wikipedia, it was in north-eastern Africa, bordered by Egypt, Libya, Chad, the Central African Republic, Ethiopia, Eritrea, the Red Sea and South Sudan. That was news to her. She'd thought South Sudan was just a geographical reference. She'd never even heard of the Central African Republic, and the little she knew about Eritrea and Ethiopia she'd learned years ago from watching a horrifying World Vision documentary about starving children.

She'd scrolled past the prehistoric information and read about the Egyptian then British rule in Sudan and how they'd administered the north and south separately. How the north was predominantly Muslim and the south Christian and Animist, and how the country had been ravaged by drought, floods and civil war, and the enormous numbers of displaced persons in and outside the country.

She'd just started reading that the legal system in Sudan was based on Islamic Sharia law when Clemmie wandered out, rubbing her eyes and wanting a glass of water and a cuddle. This was a nightly occurrence since Jon's diagnosis and Tara was on alert for other signs of stress in the children. By the time she'd resettled Clemmie, it was late and she'd tumbled exhausted into bed.

Now, standing in front of the deserted cottage, she was struck by its air of ennui. 'Has Helen moved?' she asked one of the Hazara women she recognised from the morning tea weeks earlier.

'She lives with Jade now.'

Tara momentarily considered leaving the plants with the women. They certainly knew how to grow things—their beds were lush with herbs and vegetables. But for reasons she didn't fully wish to acknowledge, she wanted to give the plants directly to Helen.

As soon as she walked through the decorative gates of the community garden, Judith rushed over.

'Tara! You poor girl! Ian told me. And the children are so young. What a tragic thing to happen to you all. I can't imagine ...'

Tara stiffened in the woman's unwelcome embrace. As word trickled out around town about Jon's Parkinson's, people's reactions to the news seemed to fall into one of two camps. They either completely ignored it or were overly dramatic with cloying sympathy. She got a sudden flash of Fiza's proud face. *Pity is useless.*

Extricating herself from the hug, Tara straightened her shoulders. 'Jon's not dead.'

'Of course, and you're so brave.' Judith patted her hand, then noticed the wagon. 'What have you got there?'

Desperate to change the subject, Tara blurted, 'Plants we can't sell because they're not perfect. I wondered if the community garden might like them?'

Judith frowned at the selection, which was a mixture of overgrown seedlings—some slightly yellow—along with some established plants that needed repotting or immediate planting. She clicked her tongue. 'We're not miracle workers, dear.'

Tara's grip on the handle tightened so fast her hand cramped. 'So that's a no?'

'Perhaps these.' Judith picked up the healthiest punnets of strawberries and lettuces. 'Any chance of some Seasol to go with them?'

Only Judith would infer Tara was giving away dead plants and then expect a donation of fertiliser.

'Actually, it's part of our catalogue sale,' Tara said sweetly. 'Pop in to the store this week and you'll save a few dollars.'

'Judith!' A woman waved from the shade of the shelter. 'Quick chat before the meeting?'

'Coming.' Judith turned back to Tara. 'Sorry, dear. I need to go. Bit of a committee crisis.'

As Judith hurried away, Tara pulled out her phone. Bypassing a forest of non-urgent text messages from the school and the store, she brought up Helen's number.

'Tara?' Helen was walking towards her dressed in her usual flannel shirt and work boots, but this time she carried a compendium instead of a trowel.

'Hi, Helen. I was just about to ring you. I called in to the cottage but you've moved.'

'To be precise, I was moved out. The official line is the cottage is uninhabitable.'

'It could do with some love but uninhabitable's a bit of a stretch, isn't it?' Tara remembered the solid bones of the cottage and the original features. 'Is the shire going to renovate it or sell it?'

'I don't know.' Helen's gaze drifted to the wagon. 'What have you got there?'

'I wondered if you or the women in your garden might be interested in rescuing these plants?'

Helen's eyes lit up. 'They don't look like they need too much rescuing, just a bit of love. Thanks for thinking of us.'

'You're welcome.' Warmth replaced the chagrin instilled by Judith. 'I can't believe how well all the garden beds are doing. The women have green thumbs.'

'Have you told your husband about the garden yet?'

Tara hesitated. The truth was no, but the reason behind her not telling Jon had changed. Parkinson's had cast a new light on many things. 'Things have been a bit hectic ...'

If Helen thought the answer odd she didn't press for more details. 'Things have been a bit hectic here too. A few weeks ago some morons did some damage next door.'

Tara looked through the cyclone fence at the healthy beds and saw tall straight leafy stalks. 'Fiza's maize looks unscathed.'

'You've met Fiza since the morning tea?'

Tara would have needed to be deaf not to hear the surprise in Helen's voice. 'Yes. She's our neighbour.'

Helen's brows hit her hairline. 'What does your husband think of that?'

Despite the unforgiving kernel of truth that neither she nor Jon had wanted the Atallahs as neighbours, Tara bristled. 'Actually, we both appreciated Fiza and Amal's help when Jon injured himself recently.'

'Is he okay?'

'Not exactly.'

Why did you say that? But the genuine concern woven into the deep lines on Helen's face reminded her of her mother. If Jane was still alive, she would have been the first person Tara told.

'Jon's been diagnosed with young Parkinson's disease. We're ...' *Gutted? Angry?* 'Adjusting.'

'I imagine getting the diagnosis was the equivalent of being knocked off your feet by a rogue wave, inhaling water and being spat onto the sand gasping for air.'

It was the first time anyone had come close to describing exactly how Tara was feeling and she couldn't completely stifle the sob rising in her throat. 'How did you know?'

Sadness clung to the corners of Helen's eyes. 'I've been around the block a few times, Tara. Life can sucker punch you hard.'

'It's done that. I mean, don't get me wrong—Jon's not so bad yet that he needs round-the-clock care or anything—but ...'

'You're doing things for him you never expected,' Helen said.

'On the bad days, yes. But even on good days he's exhausted by seven, so I'm doing more of everything at work, at home and with the kids.'

'I'm sure you've got family and friends falling over themselves to help.'

The dull ache under her ribs twisted sharply. 'Actually, we're a little short on family. I've always thought we were surrounded by friends, but ...'

'When a crisis hits, it's never the people you expect who step up,' Helen said sagely. 'How did Amal help?'

'I was out and Jon fell. He's a big man and when he couldn't stand up, Amal helped. Then he looked after Clemmie and Flynn while Fiza took Jon to hospital.'

'That sounds like Amal. He's often here in the garden helping Fiza. Like most refugee kids, he's had to grow up fast.' Helen's fingers fiddled with the zip on her compendium. 'Did you know the police interview Amal every time something's stolen in this town?'

'They're just doing their job,' she said firmly, thinking about the times the police had been called to the store.

'Even when the kid has an alibi? Fiza moved out of town so the police would stop associating Amal with Tranquillity Park, but it hasn't changed a thing. The night of the garden damage he was at home studying for his exams.'

'So why would the police interview him if they knew that?'

'You once told me that African kids are running wild in this town.'

'Just because Amal has an alibi doesn't prove there aren't other kids behind the break-ins.'

'That's true, but it doesn't prove those other kids are black. The police target them first. I'm worried for him, Tara. I was with him at the police station when he was being harassed—'

'Harassed? Really? Surely that's an exaggeration. We live in a democracy.'

Helen's mouth flattened into a hard line. 'We live in a country where some people are afforded more rights than others, often based around an accident of birth. Of course the police don't call it harassment, they call it interviewing. Following up leads. How would you feel if those leads brought the police to your door every time something was stolen?'

Tara heard an accusation. 'Jon and I didn't ask the police to target anyone. We just want them to find the culprits and stop the break-ins.'

'So does Amal. Right now the young man who responded to a plea for help is being unfairly treated. He needs a break or he'll end up doing something stupid because no one other than his mother believes in him.'

Amal is a good boy! The memory of Fiza furiously defending her son at the hospital rushed back. At the time, Tara had been indignant that Fiza was criticising her right to question whether a teenage boy she'd never met was capable of minding her children. But it wasn't only that Amal was a teenager or a boy.

Tara had stood in this garden once before and told Helen she wasn't racist. But now she couldn't hide from the uncomfortable truth that if Amal had been white, she probably wouldn't have questioned the children's safety quite so vigorously. Fiza had reacted to her casual racism and why wouldn't she? If Amal was always assumed guilty and needed to prove his innocence even when he was ten kilometres away from the scene of the crime, it would jaundice their view of the world.

A need to make amends prompted her to say, 'Based on our experience, Jon and I could go to the police and give him a character reference.'

'You could do that.'

Tara squirmed under the intensity of Helen's gaze, just as she had under her mother's. The sensation was the same—she was coming up short. Very short.

'We will do that,' she said.

'What about showing him trust and demanding responsibility?'

'I don't follow?'

'Give him a part-time job.'

Tara's chest tightened. The annual tradition was to give summer jobs to the children of their employees. 'We usually only give jobs to people we ...' *Know.* She hardly knew Amal, but unlike most of the teenagers they employed through the long-standing system of nepotism, she'd actually met him.

'I'll talk to Jon about the possibility of a Christmas job, but I can't promise anything.'

Helen smiled and squeezed her shoulder. 'Thank you. And thanks for the plants. Sorry, I have to dash to a garden committee meeting. See you soon.'

As Tara watched Helen walk away, sadness dumped over her like thick tar, weighing her down. She desperately missed pre-Parkinson's Jon—the physically strong and indomitable version of

her husband who'd grabbed her by the hand and taken her with
him on life's adventures, easing her way. Now she was easing his
way, but who was easing hers?

She missed Shannon so much. If her friend was still here Tara
knew she'd be in her corner, like Helen was in Amal's, cheering
and going in to bat for her. She ached for the loss of her mother too.
Jane had always been a good listener and given sage advice, even
though there'd been times Tara hadn't wanted to hear it. She'd give
anything to hear it now.

Her phone pinged and a slew of messages came in.

Two appointment reminders for Jon and a *your prescription is ready*
from the pharmacy.

*Tara, Vivian's chucking a hissy fit about the bathroom tiles. I told her
you'd sort it out. Samantha*

*Hi, Tara, I need those vouchers you promised for the preschool fete today.
Can you drop them off to me? I'm at work. Ta. Kelly*

*PFA meeting tonight. Be good if you could make this one. Need your
support on the car boot sale idea. Rhianna*

*Thought I'd go to cricket training. Dad wondering if it's the usual roast
tomorrow? Be good if you can manage it. #operationnormal Jon x*

*Felix is overdue for his annual vaccination. We value your pet's health.
Please make an appointment today at Boolanga Veterinary Clinic*

God! Was it too much to ask to go ten minutes without someone
needing her?

The barrage of messages pummelled her like waves pounding on a break and she switched off the phone before another one
arrived. Before someone else was demanding something of her.
Needing her.

The future with all its known and unknown terrors rose up like
a spectre. The low-grade panic that had been quietly simmering

since Jon's diagnosis hit boiling point, racing her heart, shortening her breath and lifting her chest in short sharp jerks.

She couldn't do this.

She couldn't be the person everyone depended on to support them when she had nothing underneath supporting her.

Tears filled her eyes, blurring her vision. She half ran, half walked to the car.

Helen hurried towards the shelter for the committee meeting, excited about the unexpected donation of plants from Tara. She'd been holding her breath for weeks, fully expecting the Hoopers to pull the pin on the sponsorship, but now Tara was entertaining the idea of employing Amal. Few shocks were good shocks but this one was brilliant. It had gone a long way to restoring Helen's battered faith in human nature. The mayor might be a self-promoting bastard prepared to bulldoze anyone who stood in his way, but some people still considered others.

The thought snagged. At the thank-you morning tea, Tara Hooper had struck Helen as a privileged and self-centred bigot. She couldn't help wondering if her act of considering the women instead of throwing the plants into landfill might be connected to her own changed circumstances. When she'd heard about Jon's diagnosis, she'd wanted to hug Tara. She knew all about the challenges of being a carer and the inevitable toll it took on hopes and dreams, not to mention the unrelenting daily grind. Right now, Tara had the preoccupied air of someone overwhelmed by massive change.

Faint strands of guilt circled Helen that she'd pushed the already stressed woman about a job for Amal. But sometimes a chance only came around once and it was dangerous not to grab it and hold on tight. Next week she'd call Tara and invite her to take photos of the garden for the Hoopers Facebook page. That way she could check if Tara had lost the deer-in-headlights look.

Helen stifled a yawn, knowing she needed a coffee to get her through the committee meeting. Last night, she and Bob had attended the council meeting pumped and ready with a list of questions for the mayor, only to be disappointed when he was an apology. He was apparently out of the country on a supposed fact-finding mission.

Helen hadn't seen the point of staying, but Bob had convinced her it set a precedent. 'If we ask the questions this time, we'll be able to compare Geoff Rayson's answers and expose any discrepancies.' So they'd stayed until stumps.

The flip side of Helen's disappointment had been a quick chat with Messina and Cynthia, and seeing Vivian in action running a tight council meeting. It was a huge job keeping rambling councillors and ratepayers on track. Had Helen any doubts about Vivian's ability to be mayor, they'd been vanquished by nine o'clock when the meeting closed.

Now, as Helen stepped into the garden's shelter, she was surprised by the lack of people milling around chatting and drinking tea and coffee. Instead, everyone was seated around the wide table where Judith was holding court and Sharon was scribbling the minutes.

Helen checked her watch. It wasn't quite ten thirty and Bob was yet to arrive.

'Morning, everyone.' She took a seat at the end of the table.

Murmurs of 'Hello, Helen' greeted her from most people. Dot gave her a wide smile.

She unzipped her compendium. 'Did I miss the memo about the time change?'

Judith pursed her lips. 'Everyone was here so we started.'

The slap was obvious but Helen refused to bite. 'Bob's not here.'

'Bob's an apology,' Sharon said.

The last thing Bob had said to her last night was, 'See you tomorrow'. Was he sick? The thought bothered her.

'Did he say why?' she asked.

'No. It was just a short text saying he was unavailable.'

Sharon's words stung Helen with unwanted hurt. She briskly reminded herself that Bob wasn't required to text her if he wasn't coming—they didn't have that sort of friendship.

She glanced around the table and did a headcount. Everyone else was here.

'Did you receive an apology from me, Sharon?'

Sharon looked between her and Judith and chewed her pen. 'Ah, no.'

Helen met Judith's combative gaze. 'The agenda clearly states the meeting starts at ten thirty and not everyone was here at ten twenty-five.'

'Everyone who is a member of this committee was present.'

'I'm a member of this committee, Judith.'

A triumphant glint flashed in the president's eyes. 'Your position on the committee was attached to your job as the caretaker. As you've been stripped of that role, you're no longer entitled to serve on the committee.'

Helen's hands fisted in her lap. 'As a paid-up member of the garden, I'm very much entitled to serve.'

'The constitution states that the committee consists of a president, vice president, secretary, treasurer and no more than five ordinary members.' Judith stretched out her arm to indicate the other people. 'All the positions are filled. You'll have to wait until the AGM before you can nominate. That's if you're still a member.'

'I have no intention of resigning.'

'You may not have but the committee's looking at disciplinary action.'

If power was an aphrodisiac then Judith was experiencing her first orgasm in a very long time.

Sweat broke out on Helen's hairline. 'Disciplinary action? On what grounds?'

'Engaging in conduct prejudicial to the association.'

'How have you come to that conclusion?'

Judith jerked her thumb towards the boundary fence. '*That* garden. It's lowered the tone and impacted on the garden's good name and reputation.'

Anger streaked through Helen's veins, then boiled over. 'I find that hard to believe given the purpose of the garden.' She pulled a copy of the model rules from her compendium and flicked to a page. '*To involve a wide range of members from the broader community regardless of age, gender or background.*'

'But we've had people drop off the waiting list,' Sharon said.

'People join and drop off the waiting list all the time! If they're not joining because of the garden extension that can only be a good thing. This garden doesn't need any more racists.'

'That sort of offensive remark is why we're pursuing disciplinary action,' Judith said tartly.

Helen opened her mouth to say she could think of far more offensive remarks made by the committee, but stopped. *Discretion is the better part of valour.* Bloody Bob and his expressions. Now he had her thinking them.

She looked around the table. Everyone, including Dot, had their heads down studiously avoiding eye contact, either too scared of Judith to speak up or not caring enough to defend Helen. After all, this was volunteering—a supposedly enjoyable and feel-good activity. Most people came along for the company and the cake.

She knew this fight was really only between her and Judith. Of course the despot had chosen today to act—Bob was absent. Helen wasn't stupid. She knew a war of words with Judith would only annoy the rest of the committee and give the woman more power. She took another tack.

Glancing around at the bowed heads, she said, 'Has Judith mentioned that if you decide to pursue disciplinary action, you'll need to form a subcommittee? I have the right to take this to mediation and that will involve at least one full day in Melbourne. Possibly two.'

Murmurs whipped around the table. A couple of heads rose, brows furrowed.

'I look after the grandkids. I can't take off to Melbourne for two days,' Vin said.

'I can't afford accommodation in Melbourne,' Ann said.

'And if mediation is unsuccessful,' Helen continued, 'I can seek my own legal action against the garden and individuals.'

She wouldn't—she couldn't afford to—but they didn't know that.

'As can we,' Judith said. 'Helen, you're no longer on the committee. You need to leave.'

'I may not have voting rights, but as a member I can attend any meeting as an observer.'

Judith looked to Sharon, who riffled through the model rules. 'It doesn't mention whether a member can or can't observe a meeting.'

Helen could see the cogs of Judith's brain turning. She instinctively knew a new agenda item would be added—a call for a special meeting to close this particular loophole.

The gloves were well and truly off. Judith could try, but Helen was ready for a fight and she'd start now by refusing to leave.

Tara stood on the river bank staring at the sun-dazzled water, watching the light play across its tranquil surface. She wasn't sure how long it was since she'd left the garden or how long she'd been standing here, only that she'd needed to see the river and breathe in the eucalypt-scented air. The hum of insects buzzed and a large tree branch floated past on the brown-blue water. It was rolling along as if it had all the time in the world and nowhere in particular to be except where it was right this minute.

Come with me. Float away.

The river pulled at her, promising tranquillity. Its water would fill her ears and silence all the noise in her world—the insects, the shrieking gang-gang cockatoos, her phone, people asking her for things and the never-ending to-do list on repeat in her head. There'd be peace and quiet in the river. Freedom.

She instinctively took two steps forward towards the promise.

Every nerve ending sparked. Spiralling pain tingled from her scalp to her toes. She looked down, shocked to see her sandals glinting under cold water.

What are you doing?

This wasn't Riverbend Park. Floating here in an inner tube was dangerous. This section of river was notorious for snags and hidden currents that swirled and dragged, pulling anything that passed under the water. Trapping it in the dark.

Heart pounding, she jumped back. She didn't want to die.

God, no! She wanted to see her kids grow and thrive. Do things with Jon while he was still active. She had so much to live for, but at the same time she craved some peace to be Tara—her own person. Some time just for her. Some time when she could take a short break from being the wife, the mother, the carer and the employer.

The river winked in the sun and she turned, keen to get away from its hypnotic pull. Back at the car, she reached for her water bottle, but it was empty so she opened the hatch to grab a spare from the cold bag that lived in the car. As she reached for it, her hand hovered over her gym bag. Even though she hadn't used her running kit in weeks, she hadn't been able to bring herself to remove it from the car.

Holding onto the past won't help you embrace this new future.

'Shut up, Lorraine.'

She unzipped the bag and fingered the almost new gear she'd bought when Shannon and Chris had left for America. Her mind tried hard to lurch away from what had happened the last time she'd worn it.

Kissing Zac.

Fiza's phone call.

Jon in hospital.

She caressed the laces of her running shoes and more distant memories stirred. The breeze on her face, the sweat in her eyes, the sensation of flying. Without really thinking, she was reaching down and unbuckling her wet sandals and shoving her feet into the runners.

The moment the light fabric skimmed the tops of her toes and the foam support snuggled under her soles, she wanted to run. Was desperate to run. Knew she had been for weeks.

With no one around to watch her, she changed clothes and set off along the track. Soon, her chest was heaving and her heart racing, and the only noise in her head was the blessed reverberation of her pulse. Her full focus was zeroed in on putting one foot in front of the other and avoiding tripping on raised river gum roots.

She ran.

Time receded.

Nothing existed except her and the track.

'Tar-ra!'

No! She picked up her pace, determined not to stop. She didn't want to talk to anyone and lose the bliss of the zone.

'Tara! Wait!' The voice called again, closer this time. 'It's me.'

Zac. She didn't turn, but then he was running beside her, breathing hard.

'Why … are … you … sprinting?'

The zone fractured into a thousand pieces and the world rushed back.

'Can … you … slow … down.'

No. But her muscles screamed, on fire with red hot pain. Her lungs craved air and silver spots spun in front of her eyes.

She slowed and glanced around for her bearings, recognising Riverbend Park where Zac held his boot camps. Bending over, she gripped her thighs until her vision steadied and her ragged breathing smoothed.

'How far have you run?' Zac asked.

'From Warrabeen Lagoon. It's the first time I've run since we …' She dodged the embarrassing memory. 'Since I last saw you.'

She lay down on the ground, not caring about the dust and the dirt of tree litter, and stretched her arms wide, trying to catch a hint of a breeze.

'That's ten kay.' Zac spun the cap off an energy drink and handed it to her. 'Here.'

'Thanks.' She chugged it down, relishing the cold.

'If you haven't run in ages, why did you decide to do it in thirty-three degrees?'

It was a fair question. Running in the middle of the day between October and March was stupid. 'I didn't plan it. I'm supposed to be at work but ...'

'But what?'

She sighed. 'I think I was running away.'

His dark brows drew down. 'Running away? From what?'

She rolled the bottle over her hot skin, welcoming the cooling droplets of condensation. Thought about the river and the fright she'd given herself.

'Mostly from myself.'

'Should I be worried about you?'

Her heart squeezed at his concern. 'Maybe. Before I started running like a maniac, I was worried about me.'

'And now?'

'My head's quieter. I feel more like me.'

'The power of exercise.' He stared at the river for a bit, then turned back to her. 'Did you get my texts?'

'I did. Thanks.'

'But?'

'But ...'

'Is it because of what happened?' Distress twisted his mouth. 'Please don't make it about a stupid kiss that won't ever happen again.'

Her already hot skin burned with old embarrassment, but she realised he was right. It wouldn't ever happen again. She'd already sat next to him for ten minutes without a single strand of lust stirring inside her.

'I appreciated the texts, but I don't have time to run any more,' she told him.

'You need to run, Tara. Not just for exercise, but to help you deal with your husband—'

'Jon.' It suddenly seemed really important that Zac called Jon by name. 'His name's Jon.'

'You need to run so you can deal with all the stress and shit that comes with Jon's Parkinson's.'

'Stress and shit?' She laughed so hard she snorted.

'What's funny?' He sounded offended.

'The counsellor talked about "challenging moments" and "unexpected life events", but stress and shit are way more accurate.'

He grinned. 'And my English teacher said I was crap with words. So how's Jon dealing with it?'

She chewed the inside of her cheek. 'He was always the life of the party and now he's quiet, fighting depression.'

'Apparently that's common with Parkinson's.'

'How do you know that?'

'Been doing a bit of reading.'

She stared at him, utterly flummoxed. Zac only read stuff about exercise and nutrition. 'What sort of reading?'

He shrugged. 'Stuff about the disease and the drugs. There are some pretty sick side effects.'

'Tell me about it. They scare Jon and me rigid.'

'But he needs to take them, yeah?'

'Oh, yeah. It's like doing a deal with the devil. You can only get the good effects if you risk the bad. Jon gets shirty if I ask him how he is, so I feel like I'm an undercover cop searching for clues. It doesn't go down well if he catches me watching him, but I'm terrified he mightn't notice he's being obsessive.' She pulled at the wrapper on the bottle. 'I read an article about a man with young Parkinson's who gambled all his family's savings. Just the thought of it makes me want to hide and rock.'

'You know, exercise is important for Jon too. If he wanted, I could do some sess—'

'Thanks, but he's got cricket.' The thought of Zac and Jon together sent a chill across her skin. Not that Zac would say anything, but even so, it was two worlds best not colliding.

Zac's usually relaxed demeanour stiffened. 'I wasn't cadging for business, Tara.'

Guilt kicked her. Cutting him off was everything to do with her shame.

'I know you weren't. I'm sorry. It's a very kind offer, but Jon's never been one for workouts. He's a rusted-on footy and cricket player.'

'Fair enough.'

He still sounded hurt and she rushed to change the topic. 'How's the marathon training going?'

'Okay.'

'Just okay?'

'I'm finding it hard to stay motivated without a training buddy.'

'Sorry.'

'God, Tara. Don't be sorry.' He drew circles in the dust. 'You know, running's not just about training for a marathon. It sounds like you need to do it for the headspace stuff.'

'You're right. I'm definitely calmer than I was an hour ago.'

'But you need to do it safely. Not in heat like this, yeah?'

'Yes, Mum.'

'I meant what I said in the text.'

'I know. I just don't know where I can squeeze it in.'

'You don't squeeze it in. You make it a priority.'

Irritation dug at her. She knew he meant well, but Zac's entire life revolved around working out.

'You have no idea what my life's like now.'

'Maybe. But what will it be like for Jon and the kids if you reach a point when you can't cope?'

She closed her eyes as the image of the water over her sandal-clad feet rushed back. With it came the fear that she'd unthinkingly stepped into the water seeking peace and calm when the reality was it came with known risks. Zac was right—she needed to run.

She thought about the routine of each day, looking for gaps that coincided with the appropriate exercise weather. 'Maybe I need to come to one of your 6 am park classes.'

Zac laughed. 'I want to say yes, but I don't need you freaking out my ladies so they give up.'

'I'm not that competitive.'

He rolled his eyes. 'Tell yourself that. Here's an idea. I don't have an early class on Tuesdays and Thursdays or the weekends. We could run then.'

'But you'll lose your sleep-in.'

'I'm awake at five anyway. May as well run with you as lie in bed staring at the ceiling. You in?'

His kindness crashed into her and she swallowed hard, trying not to cry. 'I'm in.'

'Awesome.'

'Thanks, Zac.'

'No worries. Anything for a mate.'

CHAPTER
28

When Tara got out of the shower, she heard Jon calling out that he was home. She found him in the kitchen holding his hand under the tap, blood mixing with water.

She grabbed the first-aid kit. 'What happened?'

'The knife, the tomato and I disagreed. Don't fuss.'

'Does it need stitches?'

'No!' The word bounced around the room loaded with anger and frustration.

She tried not to take it personally. 'May I offer you a band-aid?'

His shoulders slumped and a long breath rumbled out of him. 'Sorry. A band-aid would be good.'

She dried his hand, checked the cut, confirmed it was superficial, then covered it with the dressing and binned the rubbish.

'What do you think about us buying and growing cherry tomatoes from now on?' she said lightly.

'Sounds good to me.' He bent down and pressed a kiss on her hair. 'Thanks, T. Did you get held up at the garden with another morning tea?'

She wanted to say yes, because she remembered his reaction to her exercise routine and marathon plans before his diagnosis. But if she didn't tell him she was going back to running, where would that leave them? In as much of a mess as before and she never wanted to return to that dark place.

'It was more when I was leaving the garden. My phone went crazy, mostly with messages from the store—'

'I'm not a bloody invalid!' He slammed his fist into his palm. 'I've been in the office all morning twiddling my thumbs. I hate they're bothering you when they should be talking to me.'

'I guess they got used to talking to me during the early weeks when you weren't in as much. Anyway, it wasn't just my phone that went crazy. I did too for a minute. I had a desperate need for peace and quiet where no one wanted anything from me. I wanted to run away.'

A stricken look crossed his face and she hastily added, 'It was a momentary thing. I promise you, I'm not going anywhere. I love you and the kids to bits and I'm staying no matter what Parkinson's throws at us. But that feeling scared me so I went for a run. It cleared my head and now I feel like me again.' She sucked in a deep breath. 'I need to start running again.'

'Okay.'

'Okay? I thought you hated me running.'

'I didn't hate you running.'

She raised her brows at his resigned tone and locked onto his gaze.

He lifted his hands in defeat. 'Yeah, okay. Fair call. I did hate the running. But one thing this bastard disease has given me is time to think. I think I hated what the running represented rather than the running. It got tangled up with me being sick and not understanding what the hell was going on with my body. It felt like you were running away from me even though you were pushing me to get help. I still hate the idea that you need to run because of me.'

'No, not because of you.' She slid her hand over his trembling one, pressing down to still the movement. 'I need to run because of me.'

He grimaced. 'Come on, T. Be honest. Team Hooper's got two junior players and a co-captain who spends more time on the bench than is fair. You're carrying this team and I hate that you have to.'

'But Parkinson's isn't the only stress in our lives. Even if you didn't have it, I'd still want to run. I fell in love with the buzz it gives me.' He gave her a long look, but there was a sparkle in his eyes she hadn't seen in a while. 'What?'

'Just checking for obsessive behaviours.'

'I'm not obsessive.' But the moment the words left her mouth she remembered her previous preoccupation with training. With Zac. 'Okay, I was, but this time I'm not training for a marathon. I don't have the time and it wouldn't be fair on you or the kids. I'm thinking more of a quick five kay a couple of times a week and maybe longer on a Sunday morning. I'll always be back for the breakfast rush.'

'Probably wise. Otherwise, Flynn and I might turn the kitchen into a river of milk and juice.'

'You're just trying to get out of breakfast entirely.'

'I'm only thinking of you.'

'You're still on toast duty, mate. Butter knives are pretty blunt.'

'Good to know you love me.'

He laughed then—a booming and joyous sound she didn't hear often enough and it released a pressure value. She relaxed into it, taking it as a sign things were improving. Once they'd teased each other all the time, but like so many things in the months before the diagnosis, they'd lost it. Now it was coming back, even if it was black humour. But the fact Jon was making jokes against himself had to be a sign he was coming out of his dark funk.

God, she hoped so for his sake as well as hers. If they could laugh together about Parkinson's instead of only crying, surely that would strengthen them as a couple.

His laughter died away. 'I get you need to run and that first thing in the morning works best, but I'm not too keen about you running on your own in the dark. What about that personal trainer guy?'

'Zac?'

'Yeah. Can you go back and run with him?'

His suggestion, born out of love for her, spun guilt so fast inside her that nausea hit the back of her throat. He had no clue she'd once run with Zac at midnight. Or kissed him. That she'd risked everything. And she hoped he never would.

'Already sorted,' she said quickly.

'Good.' He picked cutlery from the drawer and left her to carry the plates to the table. 'Let's sort out these work texts.'

'Do you want to deal with Vivian Leppart?'

He gave a non-Parkinson's-related shudder. 'Hell, no. She's all yours.'

'Thanks a lot.'

They ran through the other texts and Jon dictated some notes into his phone. 'I'll add this to the agenda so the staff have got clear guidelines about which of us is handling what.'

Tara dallied her fork over her coleslaw. 'About the summer casuals. What if we offer Amal a job?'

'Has he applied?' Jon sounded surprised.

'No, but I think we should ask him if he'd like to work for us.'

'Where's this coming from?'

'He helped you.'

'And I thanked him and you gave him a music voucher. Isn't that enough?'

Tara shifted in her chair, still uncomfortable about the length of time it had taken her to thank the Atallahs.

'It's something Helen Demetriou said. When the community garden got damaged, the police interviewed Amal even though he was at home at the time. Helen says he gets called into the police station every time there's a break-in. It's the reason Fiza moved out of town.' She pushed her plate away. 'I got the feeling Helen blames us.'

Jon's eyes flashed. 'I never said Amal broke into the store!'

'I know, but we've both said publicly we think it's African kids.'

'Yeah, because that's what Denny North keeps telling us.'

'And no one's been caught. My gut says it's not Amal. Does yours?'

He was silent for a long minute. 'Yeah. I find it hard to imagine the kid who talked footy statistics to me for ten minutes to keep me from freaking out would rip me off.'

'I didn't know he'd done that. Does he play footy?'

'Not with the Brolgas, maybe at school? Perhaps he's just a fan? Either way, the kid's a walking encyclopedia for the Doggies. Under different circumstances, I might have held that against him.'

She smiled, but it felt forced. Discomfort tangoed with a new appreciation for Amal. Most teenage boys Tara knew could barely string ten words together in the company of adults, but Amal had not only sat with Jon, he'd found the perfect way to keep him calm.

'Isn't it wrong the police automatically assume he's involved?' she said.

'They're just doing their job, T.'

'I said that too, but how would we feel if Flynn was older and the police always treated him like he was guilty?'

'That wouldn't happen.'

'Why?'

'Because we're Hoopers and they know us.'

'Exactly. But what if Hoopers didn't have a hundred years of history in the district?' She bit her lip, toying with the truth she'd been avoiding. 'What if we weren't white?'

'The Wongs have been here almost as long as us and you don't see the police giving Jack a hard time.'

'Not these days, but read Lucy Wong's book. Apparently Boolanga's favourite Chinese family were persecuted for years. It only stopped when the Greeks arrived in town and to quote Lucy, *suddenly the chinks Boolanga knew were better than the wogs they didn't.*'

Jon laughed, but Tara fidgeted. 'I laughed when I read it too, but now ... I keep thinking about how I'd feel if no one believed Flynn. I think we should trust Amal and offer him a job. He's got all the qualities we're looking for in an employee. He's kind, caring and, going on what he does for Fiza in the garden, hardworking.' She grimaced. 'He's already better than some of the new casuals.'

'That's not saying much.'

'True.'

Tara railed at the historical precedent set by Ian that was hard to break. It meant each year they ended up hiring at least one lazy and entitled kid because their father or uncle were connected with the store or their grandfather played golf or bowls with Ian. Inevitably, one or more reluctant teenagers stood around waiting to be instructed, then did the job in a way that oozed 'massive favour'.

'By the way, I vote you have that uncomfortable conversation,' she added.

Jon's leg jerked. 'Tell me you're not thinking we sack one of the casuals to employ Amal? That won't go down well with the staff.'

'Even if it's on merit?'

'Come on, Tara. You know they won't see it that way. If you want to offer Amal a job, we have to wear the cost and add him to the team without dropping anyone. After Christmas, if he's proved himself and the others haven't, then we can talk about it.'

Tara didn't need Jon's raised brows to understand that giving Amal a job was one thing. Convincing some of the staff it was a good idea would be something else entirely.

Helen had gone straight from the garden meeting to her shift at the café, where a steady stream of tourists kept her busy. By the time she knocked off at seven, her legs ached, but she'd driven straight to the park with the leftover food and spent the evening chatting with Roxy, Cinta and three new women.

Helen told the women about the tiny houses project and asked them to 'like' the Facebook page. 'The more people who support the project, the more noise we make.'

'Any news on the Chinese resort?' Cinta asked.

'That's still an unsubstantiated rumour. The mayor maintains there are no plans for the land, but he's currently in rural France promoting cultural exchange.'

'Pah! It's a junket,' Cinta said. 'And a smokescreen.'

Once Helen would have written off Cinta's comments but these days she found herself agreeing.

'I'm more interested in his stopovers in the UAE and Hong Kong,' she said.

'Buying his wife clothes, is he?' Roxy asked.

'More like selling out Boolanga. I just need some solid proof.'

'You'll find it. They slip up every time.'

'Maybe, but I have to find it before he dazzles the rest of council and they agree to getting into bed with an overseas consortium.'

'I thought you said the three women were on side with the tiny houses project?'

'They are, but four votes is a majority and the other four are men.'

'Bastards,' one of the new women muttered.

'Talking about men,' Cinta said. 'Where's the delightful Bob tonight? It's not like him to stand us up.'

'Not sure,' Helen said. 'He must have something on.'

But the words sounded wrong. Since that wet evening when she'd run into Bob at Riverbend, he'd been at every park food night. He was usually waiting for her when she arrived to help set up. She'd assumed he was running late and had then got busy and forgotten. But then she remembered the missed committee meeting and dread upended her stomach. Had something happened?

You're being ridiculous. He's a grown man who doesn't owe you a thing or even a text message.

But the urge to call and check he was okay made her fingers itch for her phone.

Distracted, she listened to the women's chatter as they finished their drinks. When they rose almost as one to walk down to the river for their after-dinner cigarette, Helen said, 'Perhaps I'll see you next week.'

'If you wait five, I'll help you pack up after the ciggie,' Roxy said.

'Thanks, but I need to get going. It's only a couple of trips to the car.'

Helen watched the craving for nicotine win the battle over Roxy's genuine desire to help. 'Thanks, Helen,' she said, and hurried after the other women.

Faint vestiges of light played across the darkening sky, casting it in shades of lilac and violet. Helen popped the boot and slid the drinks box in before returning for the esky. The shrieking cockatoos had settled and the cicadas' song filled the fast-darkening dusk, drowning the indistinct buzz of the women's voices. She glanced around, checking she hadn't missed anything, then walked back towards the car.

On the way, she paused to gaze up at Venus shining white and bright in the now inky sky. As she brought her gaze down, something moved in her peripheral vision. She turned and peered, but couldn't make out the shape of anything other than the silhouette of trees.

Old memories of nights in the car and the cold sweat of fear rushed back.

Don't be ridiculous. She had no reason to feel unsafe. In all her years in Boolanga, nothing had ever happened here or anywhere else in town—not even a whiff of danger. The movement was probably just a possum out adventuring.

She reached the car and was juggling the esky while she opened the hatch when a loud crack sounded behind her. *Just an animal snapping a twig.*

But the thought didn't reassure her enough not to glance around, seeking the dark outline of a human. Of a man. All she saw was suffocating dark.

Trembling, she slammed the hatch shut and locked herself into the car. *Breathe.*

She rested her hands lightly on the steering wheel and concentrated on long calm deep breaths, frustrated she'd allowed that time in her life to come back and haunt her. Worse still, when there was no reason.

I am safe. I am calm. I am safe.

With her heart no longer flinging itself against her ribs, she started the ignition and drove towards the road. Lights came on and followed her. She must have taken longer than she'd realised to pull herself together and Roxy was on her way to the RSL to nurse a drink until closing.

Helen pulled onto Riverfarm Road and the car followed. At the intersection, she flicked on her left indicator then held up her hand to the rear-view mirror and waved—the RSL was in the opposite direction.

She turned. The car followed, its headlights flicking to high beam and blinding her. A tingling rush of goosebumps prickled. She squinted. Was it Roxy's car? She'd never been good at identifying vehicles and the bright lights made it impossible.

If it was Roxy, was she trying to tell Helen something? But surely she'd flash the headlights. Or call her. What if she was out of credit? Then she'd toot.

Helen sped up. The car kept pace. She slowed and it slowed, showing no signs of wanting to overtake. Agitation pummelled her, putting every cell on high alert. If she drove home, she'd be showing whoever it was where she lived. She gasped, as a streak of protection for Jade and Milo shocked her.

She couldn't go home but where could she go? The police station was in the opposite direction and there was no guarantee it would be staffed at this time of night. Still, was driving past it a message?

Her navigational skills—never great in daylight—were now overlaid by the dark and blind panic. She took random left and right turns, not recognising the streets but trying to find her way to the police station. The car followed, sticking like glue.

After her eighth turn, she was halfway down a street when she passed a ute with a distinctive worm logo parked outside a Californian bungalow. *Lachlan*. Without thinking, she turned hard left and straight into a driveway.

Hitting the brakes, she grabbed her phone, her fingers reaching for 000.

The car didn't slow. It kept driving.

Her phone fell into her lap and her body crumpled, unable to hold itself upright. What could she say to the police? *A car followed me to a destination I had no intention of coming to and then kept driving?* That wasn't following. That was a coincidence. She couldn't identify the car and she didn't even have the registration to give them.

Even in her frazzled state, she recognised how flaky the story sounded. This was Boolanga! Population 7800, with fifty per cent of residents aged over sixty-five. The highbeam lights were probably a confused octogenarian.

Except she hadn't seen any elderly people at the park. Then again, apart from the women, she hadn't noticed anyone else at the park tonight.

There was a knock on the window. She screamed.

A figure jumped back. 'Steady, Helen. It's me. Lachlan.'

She recognised his voice and fumbled with her seatbelt. With a strength of will she didn't know she had, she forced her wobbly legs to cooperate and heaved herself out of the car.

'Sorry, Helen. I didn't mean to give you a fright. It's just when I heard the car and no one knocked, I came out to see who it was.'

'Right,' she managed to stammer.

'It's nice of you to pop in and check on Uncle Bob. Come in and I'll put the kettle on.'

Daisy greeted Helen by nuzzling her hand, then shook her head as if to say 'follow me'. Soon Helen was standing at the end of Bob's bed, looking at a washed-out version of the man who was usually so full of energy.

'Grey's not your colour,' she said.

'No? I thought I could carry it off.'

'Why didn't you tell me you were sick?'

'Didn't want to worry you. Looks like that didn't work.' He winked at her.

The man was incorrigible. Even flattened by gastroenteritis he was still flirting. She opened her mouth to tell him her presence had nothing to do with being worried about him, but that opened her up to the real reason.

'I'm only here because the women at park food missed you. I figured you didn't need Cinta and her theories of deliberate water contamination visiting you.'

He pressed his hand to his heart. 'Admit it. You do care.'

'Lachlan, did you give him something more than Gastrolyte?'

Lachlan grinned. 'He's been pretty happy since I brought him home from hospital. I think they gave him a happy shot.'

'Hospital?' The evening's agitation stirred again. 'You went to hospital?'

'He couldn't keep anything inside him either end,' Lachlan said. 'When he—'

'That'll do, Lachie!' Two spots of pink stained Bob's sallow cheeks. 'Helen doesn't need to hear all about that, thanks very much.'

Helen stifled a smile, understanding completely. Age made no difference; dignity was everything.

'Sounds like you've been through the wringer,' she said. 'I'll make you some chicken soup for when you're allowed more than Gastrolyte.'

'You don't have to do that.'

'Of course I don't, but I want to.'

'Thanks.'

Bob smiled and something hard inside her softened.

CHAPTER
29

Sunshine streamed into the meeting room at the library where Jade and Helen sat scanning the social pages in back issues of *The Standard*. Initially, Jade had thought reading the social pages would be boring, but it was turning out to be pretty interesting. Not that she knew any of the people whose photos seemed to pop up every week. But whoever they were, they were busy being seen at everything from openings to awards dinners, theatre nights, shire events and fundraisers.

As the research had been Bob's idea, Jade had thought he and Helen would do it together, but over a lunch of chicken soup Bob had said, 'You're the digital native, Jade. You and Helen go to the library, and me and Milo will go to the park and feed the ducks.'

'Shouldn't you have a nap?' Helen said.

Jade had never seen Bob look anything close to grumpy, but his mouth had hardened and he'd narrowed his eyes at Helen. 'I don't need a nap!'

'You've just spent two days in bed.'

'And now I'm fine. Don't fuss.'

Jade had laughed out loud. 'Fuss? Helen doesn't know the meaning of the word.'

But for some reason, a smile had woven through the silver stubble on Bob's face, and Helen had suddenly started clearing the table, not looking at either of them.

'There's no way we'll ever be in one of these photos,' Jade said now.

Helen looked up from the iPad. 'Why's that?'

'We don't have an expensive blonde bob.'

'There is a certain look, isn't there.'

'Lucky Vivian's a councillor,' Jade added. 'Or perhaps she's the diversity shot because she's got dark hair.'

Helen's face crinkled into a sea of lines and then she was shaking with laughter. 'You've got a wicked sense of humour, Jade. You're also very astute.'

A sneaky warm feeling cuddled her. 'Thanks.'

Things had changed between them since the night Helen told her she'd been homeless. People with money never lived with that fear or breathed the utter helplessness of having nowhere to go. They didn't understand that no matter how careful you were with money, it was almost impossible to stay even the smallest amount on the black side of red. But Helen knew. Helen understood the fear that glowed inside Jade like a nightlight—low but constant— that despite her rigid budgeting and skipping lunch most days, it could still happen to her and Milo.

Not that Helen didn't still drive her nuts sometimes. The woman was a neat freak—who folded fitted sheets? But for all her mutterings about 'mess', Jade knew the older woman was trying hard to treat her as an adult and a housemate. She loved the way they planned their meals and shopped together. Helen mostly ignored Milo, but she'd bought a basket at the op shop for his toys. Milo thought it was the best joke ever to tip it over, laughing as toys spilled across the floor.

'Why are the women always better dressed than the blokes at these gigs?' Jade asked.

'I think most women have a complicated relationship with clothes and make-up.'

'But not you?' she teased, expecting Helen to roll her eyes. But the older woman gave her a long look and she braced herself for a snarky comment.

'Can you see me wearing those clothes gardening, frying food or serving food to homeless women? I do own a nice dress. I just don't have any occasions to wear it.'

Despite the crisp way Helen spoke, Jade heard the sadness and it drifted into her. If Helen had a nice dress, did it mean that back in the day she'd been invited to events like in the paper? Helen didn't say much about her life before she arrived in Boolanga, but Jade sensed it had been different.

The despondent feeling deepened. She didn't even own a nice dress—not since Charlene had sold them. And apart from the year twelve formal, she'd never been to anything swanky.

Her phone beeped with a Facebook notification and she turned it screen down so she wasn't tempted by the distraction. She returned to reading, clicking through the pages, looking for anything that might be a clue to the mayor's activities. Anything that might shine a light on how he and his wife could afford Ainslea Park. There were photos of him at the ANZAC Day service with the local veterans, with polo players at an event sponsored by Ainslea Park and at the Mad Monday parade at the end of the footy season. Jade was surprised that whoever created the meme of him on the camel had missed this photo of him wearing a Boolanga Brolgas footy jumper and a blue tutu. None of the photos linked Geoff Rayson with anyone.

Her phone vibrated and she turned it over, checking it wasn't Bob. The number of notifications on Facebook had rocketed up and she clicked through to read them.

'Jeez, Helen. Who have you upset this time?'

Helen didn't look up from the iPad. 'I've no idea what you're talking about.'

'The Facebook pages for the garden and the tiny houses are being trolled.'

'As in little men under bridges?'

Jade rolled her eyes. 'As in people who go online and make trouble. Apparently you're a communist, a bleeding heart and un-Australian.'

'Oh, is that all. I've been getting emails on and off for months saying that and worse.'

'They also called you a garden wrecker.'

'What?' Helen looked up, hurt in her eyes. 'Who said that?'

'Trolls don't use their real names. They've also called you a wog and say "go back to where you came from".'

Helen snorted. 'What, Melbourne? I was born there.'

Jade screwed up her face. 'Oh, hang on. I'm not sure that one's for you. It's written under the group photo I took in front of Fiza's maize.'

'Sometimes this bloody town …' Helen sucked in a deep breath. 'Are any of the names an anagram of Judith Sainsbury? She's determined to get rid of me and the refugees.'

Anxiety flushed agitation through Jade. 'Can she really shut down the extension?'

'She'd have to convince four councillors and, as we know, that's hard work so it's unlikely to happen. But just in case, we need to keep posting photos about the success of the garden. Show how it's not only benefitting the community but meeting the garden's objectives. Tara Hooper's putting photos up on the hardware store's page too, which will—what do you call it?—"extend our reach"?'

'Yeah, that's good because it's different people. I could write something about how the garden brings women together. I mean, I didn't even know where Afghanistan was before I met Aima and I'd never eaten bolanis. Now I love them.'

'That's a great idea, but I doubt *The Standard* will print it.'

Jade waved her hand. 'I'm thinking a lot bigger than the scummy *Standard.* Mrs Kastrati was always banging on about the power of the word. If we got some attention about our garden in Shepparton or in Melbourne, or in online spaces like *Medium* and *Mamamia*, then if that old witch Judith tries to shut us down we'll have way more support than her poxy committee.'

'You're starting to think like a lobbyist.'

'Is that good?'

'It is for the garden. It'd be great if you could mention the tiny houses project in your article.'

'Yeah, okay.' Jade still thought Helen should broaden the scope of her project and open it up to single mothers.

Helen adjusted her glasses and returned her gaze to the screen, and Jade typed some points on her phone for the article.

'Well, hello,' Helen said.

'Have you found something?'

'Maybe. Can you google Andrew Tucker.'

Jade typed in the name. 'It says he's a property developer. There's pictures of paddocks and then houses and factories. *A diversified business with successful industrial and residential development in Melbourne's south-east.'*

'What else?'

Jade clicked back to the search page. 'There's a few mentions of Sino-Austral Investments.'

'Is there a website for that?'

Jade typed in the company name and waited for the page to load. Images of emerald green golf courses slid across the screen. 'There's a hotel and golf course in Queensland and a resort on the Mornington Peninsula.'

Helen glanced at the screen and pointed to the logo of the company. 'Do Sino and Austral mean anything to you?'

Jade remembered Mrs Kastrati talking about root and stem words. 'Austral is probably something to do with Australia. All I can think for sino is it's connected to sinuses, which are holes in your skull. But that doesn't make sense here.'

'Sino is a very old name for China. It either comes from ancient Greek or Sanskrit.'

'Cool.' Jade loved a fun fact and she filed it away to tell Lachlan. 'So you reckon Sino-Austral Investments is an Australian company doing deals with China?'

'I'm wondering. The golf courses and resorts are a big flag.' Helen sat forward. 'Let's see who Andrew Tucker hangs out with when he's not in Boolanga.'

Jade clicked on images and a raft of photos appeared. Andrew Tucker dressed in a morning suit at the Melbourne Cup. Another with him standing next to a silver and black Ferrari outside Crown Casino, and one in front of a helicopter with four men with Asian features.

'Holy sh—wow! He owns a helicopter!' She looked at Helen. 'Why would he bother slumming it in Boolanga?'

'Exactly!' Helen consulted her notepad. 'He's been here four times this year. He was at the business awards, at the golf tournament, the polo match and the rowing regatta. What do they all have in common?'

Jade took a punt. 'The sleazy mayor?'

'Absolutely. And there's photos of Tucker with Geoff Rayson, Aki Rehn, Craig Dangerfield and Don DeLuca.'

Jade was now up to speed on all the councillors. 'Are there any photos of him with the female councillors?'

'There's a group photo at the business awards. Messina's standing next to him, but there's a wide gap between them. Her body language says she doesn't like him.'

'You should ask her about him.'

'I think you're right.'

Jade returned to the tab she'd been on before Helen had interrupted. When the photo loaded, she was looking at a picture of a group of men. The caption read: *The a cappella group The Boolanga Blokes, singing for their supper at the Beyond Blue fundraiser.*

Lachlan's choir. Except they didn't look anything like Jade had pictured them in her head—no robes and no one was holding music. She zoomed in on Lachlan for a closer look. He was wearing black leather pants, a black T-shirt, black jacket and a black hat—he looked like a cross between a bikie and an opera singer. A tingle shot through her and she pressed her legs together, savouring the twitching sensation.

'What are you grinning at?' Helen asked.

'Nothing.'

But Helen was already leaning over her shoulder. 'Ah.'

'What does that mean?'

'It means if I was your age I'd be grinning like a fool too. Looks like Lachlan's put sexy into choir.'

Jade's skin prickled with a mix of delight and disgust. 'Gross, Helen! You could be his grandmother.'

Helen laughed and pointed to an older man standing next to Lachlan. 'So you were grinning like a fool at this one, were you?'

'Eeeuw! No way! You can have him. I don't do old or nerdy guys.'

'I'm not sure singing makes Lachlan a nerd.' Helen took off her glasses. 'It's okay to like him.'

Her complicated knot of feelings for Lachlan tightened. 'No, it's not.'

'Why?'

'Lots of reasons. There's Corey for a start.'

Helen's mouth tightened. 'I wouldn't be starting with the man who left town without telling you where he was going and doesn't give you any money to help with the care of his child.'

Jade was used to people criticising Corey and always rushed to defend him. But as the familiar words formed in her head—*Corey works hard*; *Corey needs space*—all she heard were excuses for his abandonment of her and Milo. Anger and pain twirled on a helix, ringed by confusion. She wanted to yell 'You don't know anything!' except Helen knew stuff.

'Corey knows what it's like when your family doesn't love you,' she finally said.

Helen's hand rested briefly on her shoulder. Jade knew she should have shaken it off, but the warmth and gentle pressure felt so good.

'I'm sorry you and Corey have got that in common. But it's not a basis for a relationship.'

'Milo is.'

'Only if Corey wants to be a father. Not every man does.'

Jade's thoughts drifted to her own father, before veering sharply away from her darkest fears about Corey. Both stirred up feelings she didn't want to visit, so she zeroed in on something in Helen's voice.

'That sounds personal?'

Helen shrugged. 'I was married once. He said he wanted to be a father and we had a baby. After a few years he changed his mind.'

'Did you ever meet someone else who loved you and your kid?'

Helen pinched the bridge of her nose and breathed deeply. 'I didn't look for one, but this isn't about me. This is about you and Corey. Has he ever done anything to prove he wants to be involved in Milo's life?'

Jade didn't want to answer, because saying it out loud made it true and the truth terrified her. It meant there was no going back.

'Men get more interested in their kids when they're older,' she said. 'That's when they do stuff with them.'

'That sounds more like an excuse than a known fact. There are plenty of hands-on dads from day dot.'

Not in my family. But the words stayed trapped.

'I understand when you got pregnant, Corey didn't reject you like your mother did. That he's hung around when it suits him, and he may have even told you things you wanted to hear. None of it means he loves you or that he wants to be a dad. If you've been telling yourself that he loves you the only way he knows how, then ask yourself this. Is it enough?'

Right then, Jade wanted to hate Helen for seeing into her head. For reading her thoughts.

'He's had it tough,' she said.

'And by the sounds of it, so have you. But you're not giving Milo love and attention only when you feel like it. You're showing up every day, no matter what, even when it's bloody hard. You're intelligent, funny, kind, loving and a good mum.'

Jade wanted to bask in Helen's words, but Charlene's voice squealed like static in her head. *You're not only a lazy bitch, you're a slut!*

'Are you softening me up to pay less rent?'

Helen didn't smile. 'I mean every word. And remember, I've got the credentials to say it because I've known you for a while now *and* I live with you. You deserve better than the likes of Corey Noonan. But it won't happen until you stop settling and start believing that you deserve better too.'

Jade dropped her head, uncertain if she wanted to hear Helen's opinion or not. 'When Milo was born, we promised each other we'd do a better job than our parents.'

'Being a father's so much more than contributing DNA,' Helen said. 'It's being around. It's being involved. Does Corey ever put you and Milo first? Does he ask for and value your opinion? Does he know what's important to you? Does he share your dreams for the future? Will he help you so you can get a qualification that takes you off Centrelink? Forget his words, Jade. Words are easy. Concentrate on his actions, because that's where you find the truth.'

Helen's words stung like acid rain. There were too few moments when Corey acted like a father. He only ever touched her when he wanted sex and then it was all about his need to get off, never hers. Life with Corey didn't come close to the life she'd imagined for them, but at least she didn't have to explain why she had no money. Or why her mother had stolen from her and kicked her out. Or how her father didn't give a rat's about her. Corey's family was just as useless.

Sure, Lachlan's dad wasn't around, but the man had died—he hadn't chosen to abandon his kid. And Lachlan had Bob and he was close to his mum. The nearest he'd ever come to poverty and day-to-day survival was reading about it in the paper. It put him and Jade on either side of an unbridgeable gulf.

If her family and Corey, who were intimate with poverty, still managed to hurt her, there was no way Lachlan could avoid it. And in some deep dark place, she knew his hurt would be way worse, because hope was a bastard. It ate away at preservation, leaving her wide open to a surprise knife in her heart. And that terrified her.

CHAPTER

30

'Helen! Sorry I haven't got back to you.' Vivian's voice sounded strained. 'It's been a bit crazy here. The builder's apprentice put a backhoe through my sewer pipe, the tiler miscalculated the order and I've got double the amount of imported Italian glass tiles I need, and the supplier won't accept a return. It's taken me years to save for this renovation and now it's a nightmare!'

'Sounds like it.'

'Sorry, Helen. That was thoughtless—I shouldn't be venting to you. My only excuse is your call came in straight after the tiler's snafu. Are you settled in your new place?'

'Yes, but I miss the cottage. I don't suppose there are any plans to rewire it?'

'I talked to Ross Barret from Parks about it. He told me that for the same money, he can put a new playground into Tranquillity Park.'

Helen considered the old battered slide and swing set that were likely a tetanus risk, and how close Milo was to climbing on the play equipment. 'That's fair.'

Vivian huffed. 'I told him he was just building more hidey-holes for drug deals! That park is a disgrace and the police need to crack down on the illegal activities before we install a new playground.'

Thinking about possible deals—legal or otherwise—Helen asked, 'What do you know about the property developer Andrew Tucker?'

'Handsy Andy? Other than he's pally with Geoff Rayson, not much. Why?'

'Handsy' explained the distance between the women and Tucker in the photo.

'He's been in town a bit this year,' Helen said.

'Once. At the business awards. Cynthia, Messina and I didn't want him there because the sleazebag can't keep his hands to himself, but Geoff Rayson made a captain's call.'

'He's been in town more than once. I've done a bit of digging and he attended the opening of duck shooting and the Mad Monday celebrations. Don't you remember?'

'Duck shooting and football? Even if I hadn't been on retreat in Bali, I avoid both.'

'According to photos in *The Standard*, Aki, Don and Craig were at both events.'

A tapping sound came down the line and Helen could picture Vivian thinking with her fingers on the steering wheel.

'Really? What about Messina and Cynthia?' Vivian asked.

'There weren't any photos of them.'

'That sneaky bastard!'

'Tucker or Rayson?' Helen asked.

'Both!'

Helen paced under the shade of the oak. 'I know you said council would never agree to a resort, but doesn't this point towards it being a definite possibility?'

'More than anything, I want you to be wrong,' Vivian said slowly.

'But?'

'Geoff knows exactly how Messina, Cynthia and I feel about Tucker's behaviour towards women. But it looks like he's been inviting that weasel up here for events we avoid and giving Tucker carte blanche access to the voting block of male councillors. Christ!'

A horn blared. Vivian swore and then there was silence.

'Vivian? You okay?'

'I'm ropeable.'

'Maybe you should pull over.'

'Good idea.'

'Anyway, I've been thinking that between the rorting of tenders and now this Andrew Tucker connection, surely—'

'Alleged rorting,' Vivian said.

'What?'

'For all of Geoff's affable muppet persona, he's a clever political animal. I've looked into it and Boolanga Signs got seventy per cent of the tenders and they were a mix of dollar amounts. It's not enough to prove a rort.'

Helen fumed, remembering Len's nod and a wink when she asked for the garden sign quote. 'At the risk of you accusing me of drinking the Kool Aid, what if the cottage's wiring is just an excuse to kick me out? Is the community garden next? What if the mayor's quietly freeing up the land in preparation for sale?'

'I know you're visualising the land around the cottage as the bridge between the community garden and the old farm, but they're on different titles and a public road runs between the two.

Before it can be sold or leased as a resort, they'd have to do some legal legwork and build another road.'

'So I am being paranoid?'

'No, I'm starting to think that you might be onto something. Now the cottage is vacant and derelict, Geoff can raise a motion to consolidate the titles.' Vivian barked a laugh that hurt Helen's ear. 'That scheming prick. I didn't think he had it in him, but it's the perfect "look over there" ruse.'

'I knew the cottage wasn't derelict!' The significance rolled Helen's stomach. 'God, that probably means he's paying off someone in Engineering *and* in Parks.'

'Or Tucker is. If he's schmoozing the other councillors with Geoff's blessing, any one of them can bring a proposal to the table. That takes the spotlight off the mayor, but either way, it comes with the absolute security of a win.' Vivian sighed. 'You know what this means?'

Helen had no idea. She was starting to feel like she was in the middle of a TV show about local government. 'A protest meeting?'

'Not without concrete proof. It would show our hand far too early. If those men get a bare hint we're onto them, they'll rush a vote and then we're screwed. No, we need real information from the man himself.'

'Geoff Rayson?'

'Handsy Andy Tucker.'

'How?'

'I'll brief Messina and Cynthia. We'll set up a meeting and bring the conversation around to Riverfarm.'

'But if he's never approached you and he's already got the votes he needs, why would he even take a meeting?'

'Two reasons. Votes are never a sure thing until they're cast, so if he thinks we're interested, he'll want to court us.'

'And the other reason?'

'Men's egos are always their downfall, and rich men like to brag.'

Helen had no experience with rich men. 'I'll have to take your word for it.'

'I'll be in touch when I've got something to report back,' Vivian said. 'Meanwhile, keep me posted. Unity, Helen! The only way to fight this is to stick together.'

'Do you think she changed her mind?' Jon said. He was staring out the bay window towards the orange-brick house.

'I hardly know her,' Tara said, 'but I feel she's the type of person who'd text or call if she wasn't coming. Besides, she's not all that late.'

They'd decided it was best to talk to Fiza first before offering Amal a job, so had invited her to Tingledale.

'Yeah, but I've got cricket training,' Jon said.

Tara hesitated, caught on the horns of a dilemma. As much as she wanted Jon to socialise, if Fiza didn't arrive soon it meant she'd have to talk to the woman on her own. It wasn't that she couldn't do it, but there was something about Fiza that always made her feel she was failing in some way.

'Unless you want me here?' Jon asked when she didn't respond.

'No!' He cocked his head at her emphatic tone. 'I mean, it's more important you go to cricket than be here. But if Fiza agrees, you should be the one to offer Amal the job.'

'Too easy. The other day when Flynn dragged him over for more trampolining lessons, we got talking and he asked me to show him how to bowl.' He checked his watch. 'Talking cricket, I don't want to be late.'

'You go.' The doorbell pealed.

'Thanks.' Jon kissed her. 'I'll explain on my way out.'

Flynn and Clementine thundered down the stairs, enticed by the sound of the doorbell. Their faces lit up when they saw Fiza and fell when they realised she was on her own.

Jon apologised, kissed Tara and the kids goodbye, then disappeared, leaving Tara alone with disappointed children and a confused guest.

'Sorry I am late,' Fiza said. 'I was delayed by an emergency at work.'

'Can we go next door and play with Sammy and Leila?' Flynn asked.

'Mummy, look at Fiza's hair!'

'Clementine!' Tara scolded, utterly horrified. 'Don't be so rude.'

'But—'

'It is okay, Clementine,' Fiza said. 'It has surprised many people.'

'Mummy, can I have my hair in lots of little plaits like that?'

'Can we go next door?' Flynn repeated.

Tara's head pounded. 'I have something important to talk to Fiza about so please go back upstairs and we'll discuss visiting and hair later.'

'But—'

'Go.' She pointed to the stairs. 'Or there won't be any discussion at all.'

The children bolted and she turned back to Fiza. 'Sorry about that. Please come in.'

Fiza shrugged. 'I saw your face. Clementine said what you probably wanted to say.'

As always, Tara found her directness disconcerting. 'My mother taught me that thinking something and saying it out loud are very different things.'

'I was taught the same, but it does not stop people.'

'That's true.' Tara thought about the horrifying stories people didn't censor when they learned about Jon having Parkinson's. Did they really think her knowing about their incontinent father or demented mother was helpful to her?

Fiza followed her into the lounge room and accepted a glass of soda water with lemon. Tara sat across from her and got a sudden urge to explain her reaction to her hair.

'For the record, I got a shock seeing your hair. Not because I don't like it, but because I've never seen it before. I didn't think Muslim women were allowed to show their hair in public.'

'Just like Christians, some Muslims are more religious than others. Many things are as much a part of culture as they are religious.'

'Like Christmas and Easter?'

'Yes. I choose to cover my hair during Ramadan.'

Tara didn't know much about Ramadan. She thought it was a bit like Lent, only instead of giving up chocolate or wine, people fasted from dawn and ate at sunset. 'Wasn't that earlier in the year?'

'Yes.'

Tara waited for Fiza to explain why she'd been covering her hair recently, but the woman sat straight-backed and silent, her hair swept elegantly around her head in an impressive braid bun.

Fascinated, Tara asked, 'Does it take long?'

'To box braid? Yes, a very long time. First I drive to Shepparton. Then five hours in the chair.'

'Five hours! I ... Does ...' Tara swallowed and tried again. 'Is that all your natural hair?'

'Once it was, but long hair was too hard in the camp. Now I use hair extensions.'

The camp. Fiza said it so casually, as if it was no different from her time living in Melbourne.

'Why were you in a refugee camp?'

'My country has been at war for a long time.'

'But isn't Sudan a Muslim country?'

'It is.'

'So you were safe?'

Fiza shook her head. 'War does not care if you are a good or bad person. It does not care for people, only for its cause. My husband and I got caught in the middle of a civil war. I was born in the north and he in the south.'

'Your husband?'

A shadow crossed her face. 'Idriss. He taught at the university in Khartoum. For a long time we were safe, but when South Sudan gained independence, my husband was declared stateless. A foreigner. So was Amal.'

'But if you're from the north, doesn't that make Amal from there too?'

'The law there says mothers do not have the right to pass on citizenship. This means for all his life, Amal would not be able to get an education or a job. It meant my husband lost his job. They accused him of speaking out against the government and supporting rebel groups. All of it was lies, but in war, no one bothers to check the facts. They sent Idriss to prison for three months. During that time, whenever I left the house, I was followed. Once I was accused of public indecency for wearing trousers. The police whipped me on the street.'

Tara's hand flew to her mouth. 'That's terrible.'

Fiza shrugged. 'At the time I thought so too. Now I know there are many worse things.'

A chill ran across Tara's skin. 'You don't have to talk about it if it upsets you.'

Fiza sat a little straighter. 'If you want to hear it, I want to tell you. Most people are not interested to know. They see the colour of my skin and the scarf on my head and they tell me to go back to where I come from. And if I could, I would. I love my country. I did not choose to leave my home, but it was leave it or die. What would you do to protect your family?'

Tara thought about how a war had displaced Fiza and how Parkinson's had displaced her and Jon from the life they'd always known and taken for granted. How she was always googling 'new therapies for Parkinson's' and looking for ways to change their situation.

But apparently Fiza wasn't expecting a reply because she kept talking. 'My husband had been home for six months and I was pregnant with the twins. We were selling my jewellery bit by bit, saving our money so we could leave with more than just the clothes on our backs. I wanted so badly to visit my father and the village to say goodbye, but I did not dare. I did not want to be the cause of the village being burned.'

She took a sip of water. 'A week before we planned to leave, the police arrived at our door in the middle of the night. Idriss made me promise that whatever happened, I would take Amal and run. I had just hidden our papers and money in my *thoub* when they banged down the door. Perhaps because I was pregnant or because Amal was clutching me tightly, but they did not touch me. They beat Idriss to stillness. When they dragged him away, he did not move. If he was still alive then, prison is no place to recover. I never saw him again.'

Tara tasted the bitterness of acid and closed her eyes against the unimaginable.

Look after your husband. He needs you. Fiza's words, which she'd interpreted as a command, now sounded like a lament.

'Where did you go?' she asked.

'We had talked of Egypt then to Israel, but I heard women and children were shot at the border. I took Amal to Kenya.'

Something about the way she said it told Tara it wasn't as straightforward as catching a bus or a plane. 'So the twins were born in a tent at the camp?'

'They were born in the camp hospital.'

Relief shifted. 'And you lived in a house?'

'When we arrived, I was given plastic to build our shelter. Later I got a mud house.'

'But you had water and electricity?'

'Yes and no. I carried our water from a well. We could buy electricity for the phone and computer. We used solar lights and I cooked on briquettes made from charcoal and excrement.' She laughed at Tara's shock—a tinkling happy sound so at odds with the story. 'They are fantastic. They save trees and help with camp sanitation. They burn longer. Very efficient.'

Tara remembered the few short months she and Jon had camped at Tingledale without power or hot water and she'd cooked on a burner attached to a gas bottle. One night, it had all got too much for her and she'd lost it, screaming it was 'all too hard!' Jon had treated her to a week in a cabin in the caravan park with all the amenities and she hadn't been pregnant or trying to care for a newborn, let alone twins. Back then, she'd vowed she'd never take lights or hot running water for granted again. But of course she had, and quickly.

'How many people were at this camp?' she asked.

'It goes up and down, but about one hundred and fifty thousand.'

'But that's bigger than Ballarat!'

Fiza gave a rueful smile. 'Boolanga is much smaller. The camp has shops, schools and health centres and people run businesses just like in a normal town. The UNHCR keeps different groups separate, but still ...' Memories flared in her eyes. 'Camps are not safe places for women and children. Especially a woman without a husband.'

Tara didn't ask the awful question that crossed her mind and instead focused on the children. 'Does Amal remember it?'

'Of course. He did things I wish he did not have to. Even now I feel this way with what I have to ask him, but I had babies and no husband. We had to survive. I kept promising him everything would change when we got our new life. Even though that new life was going to be far from the thorn trees. Some people spend twenty years living in the camp, but through Allah's grace, peace be upon him, and my father's sacrifice, I was there only four years.'

Tara, whose belief in God wavered, thought it was probably more to do with Fiza's grit and determination. 'Your father's sacrifice?'

'He believed in education for women. He was a farmer and the agriculture coordinator where we lived. He scrimped and saved so I could go to university and have a more secure life. I give thanks every day for that. Without knowing French and English, my life would be so much harder. I am fortunate to be in this country and have the security of a good job.'

'And that's why you're growing maize here and in the community garden?'

'Yes. To honour my father in my new home. And to honour Idriss. I am trying hard to give our children the life we both wanted for them—one with education and opportunity. To make them appreciate how lucky we are to live in a democracy. To choose where we can go and what we can wear and who and how we can worship. It is easier with the twins. They are young and their camp memories fade. It is harder with Amal. I promised him a place where no one with guns knocks on the door in the middle of the night. A place of safety and contentment. But there are days when I feel I have swapped one warzone for another. Days when I fear for my children. Especially for Amal.'

Fiza raised her gaze to Tara's, dignity and pride radiating from the determined tilt of her chin and her tall and graceful bearing. 'I teach them to work hard, respect the laws and be good citizens, but it breaks my heart they need to prove they belong here. That they must work twice as hard for the same rewards.'

Strong women had always intimidated Tara, but she could no longer hide behind that as an excuse. As difficult as it was to accept, she knew she'd allowed Fiza's dark skin to play an extra role in her antipathy towards her. Towards her son. She wasn't proud of it, especially as from their first encounter, Fiza had only offered help and concern. Brisk help, but help nonetheless. Tara shuddered at the memory of telling her to go away, and resolved to always do better.

'The reason I asked you to come over was because of Amal. Helen told me you moved next door so he ...' Given what Fiza had just said, how did she say this without offending her? 'So he's never in town on his own at night.'

Fiza stiffened as if Tara had slapped her. 'My son has *never*, would *never*, steal anything from your shop.'

Tara met Fiza's gaze, feeling the sparks of flint but this time understanding they were survival traits that had got her safely to Australia. 'I believe you.'

'He is a goo—' Fiza stopped as if only just hearing Tara's words. 'Then what is this conversation about?'

'Before we talk to Amal, we want to ask if you're okay with him working at the store.'

Her brows pulled down. 'But he wants to go to university.'

'Not a full-time job. A casual job. Most teenagers have an unskilled job they do a few hours a week when they're in year eleven and twelve.'

'And you think Amal would do a good job for you?'

'Yes. It's why we're offering. We want casuals who are bright, reliable and work hard. If he wants the job, we'll need him weekends from early November, then pretty much full-time from when school finishes until Christmas.'

Fiza's fist flew to her mouth, pressing against her lips. Her shoulders shook.

Anxiety washed through Tara. 'Are you all right?'

She nodded wordlessly, then drew in some deep breaths. 'I want this chance for Amal very much. But I work shifts at the hospital.'

Tara didn't follow. 'And?'

'When I start at seven, Amal takes the twins to school. When I start at one, he brings them home. If I work on the weekends, he is home with them.'

Tara opened her mouth to ask if there was anyone else who could help and closed it, knowing it was a stupid question. Fiza wanted Amal to work so if there was anyone who could help out, she'd have mentioned them. She thought about the conversation she and Jon had when the children were born and their purchase of life insurance so if one of them died there would be money to employ a nanny-cum-housekeeper to look after Flynn and Clementine. Fiza didn't have that option.

Tara wondered how many seventeen-year-old boys needed to help their younger siblings get ready for school or look after them at the end of the day. The parents of teenagers she knew complained about how hard it was to get them off their devices and out of their rooms, let alone give up their time to be a stand-in parent. Not only did Amal lack a network of people to recommend him, he was being denied the chance of a job because for his family to function they needed him at home.

'Perhaps we can help?'

Take it back! You have enough to do already.

But she kept talking. 'November and December will be crazy months, but we can try to roster him around your weekends and afternoon shifts. And if that gets too difficult, I'm sure the twins could come here occasionally until he gets home from work. That's if you're okay with Ian minding them with Flynn and Clementine. He says having the twins over is easier than minding my kids on their own.'

Fiza sat perfectly still—striking and proud. Tara suddenly regretted putting herself out there only to be rejected.

Fiza's chin rose. 'I can only accept this if you allow me to help you with your children on my days off.'

'That's not really nec—'

'It is.' The words rang with self-respect.

Tara remembered Helen saying that when a crisis hits, it's never the people you expect who step up. And wasn't this the perfect example. Fiza was offering help from her precious and limited time and inferring that without Tara's acceptance she may not allow Amal to work. Even though she'd confessed how dearly she wanted him to have the job.

Did she consider Tara's offer pity? *Pity is useless.* Now, knowing what Fiza had been through, that statement was even more remarkable.

So why are you vacillating? Who else has brought you a casserole? Other than Ian, who else is offering to help you? Accept a gift from one working woman to another.

Feeling buffeted yet again by the winds of change Tara said, 'Thank you. My kids would love that.'

'So it is settled?'

'Almost.' Tara smiled. 'This time I have a favour to ask you. Jon wants to offer Amal the job himself. Can you ask him to come to the store one night after school this week?'

'I will bring him myself. I will tell him I need tomato stakes.' An earnest expression crossed her face. 'This is true.'

Tara laughed. 'I'm sure we can organise some stakes. When you arrive, ask for Jon. He'll give Amal a tour of the store first so he understands what's involved. He may not want the job.'

'I know my son.' Fiza's smile—so often restrained—broke across her face. 'He will want it with both of his hands.'

CHAPTER
31

After Fiza left, Tara told the children that between now and Christmas there would be play dates with the twins at Tingledale and at the Atallahs' house. Flynn hugged her as hard as if she'd given him the new bike he wanted.

'Can I get my hair braided with beads like Leila?' Clemmie asked.

Tara ran her fingers through her daughter's fine silky hair, so very different from Leila's wiry strands, and knew it lacked the body for box braids. 'I don't have any beads. How about I do a French braid with a ribbon woven through it?'

'Okay. But then can we buy some beads?'

'Perhaps. Now into bed.'

She cuddled up in a Clemmie and Flynn sandwich, reading them one of her childhood favourites, *Fantastic Mr Fox*.

'Sleep tight, munchkins.'

As Jon was out, she poured herself a glass of wine. She knew he didn't begrudge her a drink, but in an act of solidarity she'd decided not to drink in front of him. Not that she was sneaking off to drink either. It turned out that giving up alcohol wasn't as hard as she'd imagined. They were working their way through a list of mocktails, surprised they weren't sickly sweet but refreshing and enjoyable.

Unable to settle on reading or television, she took herself outside and curled up in a chair to watch a dinner-plate moon rising in an aluminium sky. Her muscles twitched. It would be an awesome night for a run. But her crazy days of sneaking out to run with Zac were thankfully over. She'd barely sipped the local pinot gris when she heard the crunch of gravel and the familiar low hum of Jon's car. She checked the time, surprised he was home an hour earlier than expected. Oh, God. Was he sick?

Don't catastrophise.

Her hands gripped the arms of her chair, keeping her seated. If she rushed to meet him, he'd correctly interpret it as worry. She drew in some deep breaths, trying to channel calm, until she heard the glass door slide open and his heavy footfalls on the deck.

'Hey.' He dropped a kiss on the top of her head and squeezed her shoulder.

'Hey.' She raised her hand and touched his, aware that before his diagnosis she'd associated this familiar non-sexual kiss with him keeping her at arm's length. Now she recognised it as him trying hard to tell her how much he loved her.

They were yet to have sex or even have a conversation about it—there'd been too many other things to worry about. Not that she didn't miss sex—she did. But she'd read how important it was for anyone with a chronic illness to feel like they had some control over their condition. She'd unwittingly stolen Jon's control before the diagnosis by going into fix-it mode and she knew if she did it again, it would only make things worse. Still, knowing it didn't make it any easier to sit back and wait. She was hoping now they both knew erectile dysfunction was part of Parkinson's, he'd raise the topic without any coaxing from her. But hope was a double-edged sword.

Jon dropped into the cane chair, weary but thankfully not grey with fatigue. 'Great moon.'

'Gorgeous. How was cricket?'

'I arrived just as they were packing up.' His mouth tweaked up in a rueful smile. 'Must have missed the email about the time change so I only stayed for one drink. People were scattering as they had things on. Stretch and Solly were going to some community meeting about Riverfarm. Do you know anything about that?'

'Sure it wasn't Landcare? They're both involved with that.'

'Might have been.'

'Actually, Helen Demetriou from the community garden was asked to move out of the old manager's cottage. The shire told her it was uninhabitable.'

'She's the woman writing all the letters to *The Standard* and pushing for a tiny houses village, right?'

'Is she?' Tara hadn't read the paper in weeks. She suddenly sat forward, propelled by the idea she'd jettisoned during her dark, angry and self-indulgent days. 'I've been inside that cottage. It's got the original pressed-metal dados, wallpaper and fireplaces. I doubt the shire wants to spend a cent on it, but they might sell it to us.'

'Why would we want to buy it?'

'It's a piece of Boolanga history that needs preserving. If we approached the historical society and they provided a space for it, we could restore it to its former glory. Just think, it could be Hoopers Hardware's very own *The Block*.'

He smiled his old smile—one she rarely saw since Parkinson's had blanked it out—and she gave thanks the drugs were restoring it. With the help of hindsight, she now realised how much its absence had tied into her insecurities about the state of their marriage. Then the smile faded.

'What?' she asked.

He rubbed his jaw. 'Before I got Parkinson's, a project like that would have been a challenge to juggle with work and the kids.'

'I'm thinking bigger than just us. More like a twist on *The Block*. We'd decide on all the fittings, exterior work, paint and interior designs, but we'd coordinate the project. You'd be Scotty and I'd be Shelley. We can invite the best local tradesmen in to do the work and have volunteer labourers. That way we get to advertise how Hoopers can source anything anyone needs for a renovation, the tradies get free advertising, and the volunteers can learn a new skill. It can be a community project and we'll video bits of it and throw it up on Facebook as well as making a big display instore.'

Jon was quiet, but she could see his mind working, clicking the idea over and trying it on for size. It just about killed her not to ask *What do you think?*

'We'd be giving back to Boolanga and generating goodwill. And if Bunnings comes after us, we'll have another finger in the community pie and loyalty from the tradies involved.' He grinned at her. 'I love the way you think.'

Warmth spread through her. 'So will I contact the shire and see if they're interested in selling while you do some initial costings?'

'Sounds like a plan.' He shifted in the chair. 'What made you change your mind?'

'What do you mean?'

'Months ago I suggested you set up an interior design consulting service and you didn't want to do it. Now you want to spearhead a reno.'

She swallowed and dug deep, honouring the silent pledge she'd made the day after his diagnosis when she'd revisited her marriage vows. *In sickness and in health.* Making that promise when she'd been head over heels in love with a man whose height and breadth declared him invincible had been easy. She'd spoken the words glibly when not even a hint of trouble was on the horizon and any thought of it was such a foreign concept she couldn't fathom what it might mean. The 'in health' part was straightforward. Sickness was a totally different beast, taking control and pushing them away from each other. If they were going to make it, they needed to be honest with each other.

'Back then, I thought you only wanted me as a business partner and a mother to your children.'

His shoulders sagged and the tremor started in his fingers, racing up his right arm. 'How close did I get to losing you?'

She sucked in her lips, knowing instinctively that this particular truth would only damage their new and still fragile way of being together. The wife part of the relationship she had down pat. The carer part was like tiptoeing through a minefield of Jon's pride and independence and her own overzealousness and reluctance. As for the lover part, it was absent.

She shuffled her chair in close and placed her hand over his. 'I understand now why we stopped having sex.'

'Yeah, but it's still not happening.'

'No.'

He heaved in air. 'You're not the only one who misses it, T.'

'I'm glad.'

'What's that supposed to mean?'

'It means there's hope.'

'Glad you think so.' He grimaced. 'I've been reading the stuff the clinic gave me on ED. It's freakin' terrifying. There's stuff they suggest that I only ever thought was kinky.'

She noticed he couldn't even say the words *erectile dysfunction*. 'Like what?'

'Pumps.' His Adam's apple bobbed. 'Cock rings.'

'Like from sex shops? Seriously?' Tara had never got past reading about Viagra.

'Yeah.' He rubbed his face. 'And it's not just me not getting it up. There's no spontaneity. It's all about planning. I can take Viagra or I could pump myself up—' he shuddered, '—but then there's the issue of my coordination, or to be accurate, my lack of it.'

She remembered some of their disastrous attempts before they knew what was going on with his body. 'But since the drugs, you've been much more coordinated.'

'Right up until I'm excited or stressed. And sex ticks both those boxes and anything close to resembling rhythm goes out the window.'

'Should we go and talk to someone about it?'

He flinched. 'Jesus, no. I'd clam up with a stranger. It's hard enough talking to you about it. We never had to talk about it. We just did it and it was amazing.'

She ached for him and for herself. Why did Parkinson's have to impact on every single part of their lives and force them to adapt? Why couldn't one thing be free of change?

'What do you want me to do?' she asked.

'Nothing. Something. I don't know.' His leg jiggled up and down, jerking wildly. 'I don't want to ask you to do anything that makes you feel uncomfortable.'

'Jon,' she said softly. 'In the last year, I've offered you almost everything in the playbook that I'm comfortable with. You hated it.'

'I didn't hate it. I hated what it meant. I gave you orgasms with my tongue, but you don't think it's enough.' His guttural words sounded like they'd been wrenched out of him. 'That I'm not enough.'

She hated that she'd made him feel less of a man and rushed to reassure him. 'That's not true—'

'Come on, T. Be honest! We've been having sex for ten years. I know what turns you on and you've always liked it best with your legs up around my waist and me in buried deep.'

It was true. An orgasm from oral sex and masturbating was perfectly enjoyable, but she'd always considered it the prelude as it left her vagina twitching to be filled by him.

'You're right. I do.'

'And now I can't do that with any guarantee of success. I might get hard but not have the rhythm, or the other way round.' He gave a wry smile. 'So basically, we're screwed.'

She groaned at the joke. 'Metaphorically anyway.' She climbed into his lap and wrapped her arms around his neck. 'I'm sorry I made you feel bad when you gave me oral sex, but that was before either of us knew exactly what was going on. I thought when you rolled away from me, you were rejecting me.'

'I was trying to be close to you. I should have told you I was having problems, but jeez, T. Admitting to not being able to get it up is soul-destroying. I hate that it nearly broke us. That it still might.'

She gripped his shoulders. 'It's not going to break us if we talk about how we're feeling.'

He rolled his eyes. 'And I just love doing that. If you ever doubt my love for you, remember this conversation.'

She laughed and stroked his cheek. 'I don't want to put any pressure on you. When you're ready we can try Viagra. Or I could get involved with a pump? Make it part of foreplay.'

'What? Like a sex toy?'

'Why not? Just because we've never used them together doesn't mean we can't try.'

His eyes narrowed. 'Did you buy a vibrator and not tell me?'

'Maybe.'

'And you didn't tell me because you didn't want to upset me?'

She sighed. 'I bought it months ago when you—' *lost it* '—got upset about the Viagra. And about that—I'm sorry. Lorraine's made me understand that I shouldn't have asked for the prescription. It's your body and your decision.'

'Yeah, but my ED affects both of us and I was sticking my head in the sand. We both did things we probably shouldn't have.' He was silent for a bit. 'Won't it seem weird using sex toys together?'

'Probably. At first. But until you got sick we always laughed during sex, remember? I mean a pump can't be any weirder than my fanny farts. The first time that happened after I had Flynn I almost died of embarrassment. You just laughed and said it was the Chinese equivalent of burping after a meal. You taught me sex can be noisy and messy and that's part of the fun. Maybe we can make a pump fun.'

'If you want to get involved with a pump, then I'll get involved with the vibrator.' He ran his hand under her hair, cupping the back of her neck. 'I hate that us not having sex made you think I wasn't attracted to you. From the moment I saw you on the resort tennis court, all long legs and cute behind, I was a goner. All I want is to make you feel like the gorgeous and sexy woman you are.'

Her heart squeezed and a rush of love thickened her throat. She rested her forehead against his. 'I know how hard it is for you to talk about your feelings, but the fact we're talking about sex makes me feel treasured and blessed.'

Shadows filled his eyes. 'Sorry I let my ego and pride get in the way.'

'Sorry I went a bit nuts, but let's leave it in the past. Today we've made a new start and we've done it without either of us yelling or getting upset so that's huge.' A thought struck her. 'Hey, maybe we need a codeword for when one of us wants to talk about sex. You know, to give each other a heads-up.'

'It would need to be something the kids didn't twig to.'

'What about James Bond?'

He grinned. 'Okay, Moneypenny.'

'During the dark days I did a lot of reading. All sex therapists say talking about sex should never be done in the bedroom.'

He stroked her hair. 'The deck seems like a good place.'

'It does. I think we need to take the pressure off each other. Why don't we sit here and channel our teenage selves.'

'We didn't know each other when we were teenagers.'

'Doesn't matter. I bet you did a lot of this.'

Shutting out everything, she pictured the first time she'd seen Jon. He'd been striding across the resort's lawn, making a beeline towards her and ignoring the protesting yells from the gardener to 'use the path!' Tall, and with the loose-limbed confidence that comes from knowing what you want and how you plan to get it, he'd kept his gaze fixed on her face and a smile on his own. With one look, he'd made her feel as if she was the only person in the world and she'd shivered with anticipation. She did the same now and lowered her head, kissing him full on the lips.

His lips were warm and he opened his mouth to hers. She took her time exploring it as if she was kissing him for the first time. At first he was passive, accepting what she offered and savouring it. Then he groaned and deepened the kiss, claiming her mouth and infusing her with his yearning and his essence. It was as erotic as it was intimate and the tiny part of her brain not flooded by lust wondered why they'd always rushed kissing and raced to sex.

Then rational thought disappeared and she immersed herself in the kiss—the touch of his hands in her hair, the pressure of his mouth on hers, the heat streaking through her and the way his tongue demanded her response. His thighs jerked underneath her, reminding her that although his body struggled to respond to her in the way they both wanted, his desire for her was as strong and urgent as it had always been.

Right now, it was enough.

CHAPTER
32

Jade rewrote the fourth draft of her article so it was legible to type up the next day. It was too big to type on her phone so she'd booked a computer at the library and organised for Bob to mind Milo. She planned to upload the article to *Medium*, then email it to the list she'd collated of online news companies and print newspapers.

Her pen stalled on a garden statistic. She wished Helen was home to check the figure, but it was a park food night so she and Bob were out feeding her homeless friends. Helen had never invited Jade to tag along, and Jade didn't want to ask in case Helen said no and took back her 'you're a good mother' compliment. Did good mothers drag their kid out to a park at night when he was tired, had a runny nose and should be in bed? Probably not. And she knew Helen would tell her as much.

The other night, Jade had pushed out Milo's bath and bed time because she was desperate to finish reading *Lost for Words*. Milo had been fractious and Jade tried fobbing him off with a DVD. Helen had muttered something about 'the importance of routine'.

All Jade had wanted was to dive under her doona with the book and hide from the world until she'd read the last page.

'I've only got fifty pages left,' she'd said. 'Can you bath him?'

Helen had given her that just-sucked-on-a-lemon look. 'I could, but he'll scream for you and then all three of us will be miserable.'

'He only yells because you don't give him much attention.'

'He's not my responsibility.'

Frustration surged. 'I thought old ladies loved children!'

'I'm *not* old!' Helen had stomped into her room, leaving Jade with a crying child.

It had been their first argument since the truce. They'd been managing cooking and cleaning together, sharing a TV and not getting in each other's face, but Jade resented how Helen just tolerated Milo. Worse, she hated that she wanted Helen to love him.

She rewrote the final sentence and chewed her pen. What would Mrs Kastrati say about the article? Sometimes her English teacher had returned her essays covered in red lines and circles, and other times the only red was *Nailed it*. Jade took a photo of the article and used some of her precious data to email it, even though she was uncertain if Mrs Kastrati still taught at Finley High.

Switching off her data, she wondered about starting a new book, but she was still mourning finishing *Lost for Words*. She was reaching for the TV remote when she heard the throb of a diesel engine. Corey? Her heart thumped but not in a good way. He didn't know Helen was living here and chances were he'd go ballistic.

It's none of his business.

Milo's his kid.

A knock shook the wire door, making her jump. Corey never knocked. Macca? She dismissed the thought. She hadn't heard from him since he'd taken the PlayStation and that suited her just fine. Perhaps Helen had forgotten her key.

Another knock followed. Worried Milo might wake up, Jade ran to the door and used the peephole. A fluttery feeling, similar to the times she'd received a school prize at assembly, danced in her belly.

She opened the door. 'Lachlan?'

He wore a yellow T-shirt, black pants, a cape and was holding a garden broom, bristles pointing skyward. Even for him, it was weird.

'Bit early for Halloween,' she said.

He grinned and picked up an esky with his free hand. 'Can I come in?'

'Ah, sure.' She stood back, giving him space to walk through the door. He smelled of sunshine, laundry powder and cologne—fresh and clean. *And sexy.* She gasped on the thought and immediately coughed.

Lachlan frowned. 'You okay?'

The coughing continued so she waved and nodded, trying to indicate she was fine. He strode to the kitchen and poured her some water.

'Drink this.'

She drank, coughed, drank again, then cleared her throat. 'Thanks.' The word came out low and husky as if she was a pack-a-day smoker. 'Want to tell me why you're dressed like a bee?'

He rolled his eyes and tapped the small logo of a badger on his chest. 'If I was a bee I'd have wings.'

It took her a moment to work out what he was talking about, but then the colours and the broom suddenly made sense. He was one of the Harry Potter characters, but in his typical left-of-centre way he wasn't wearing the house colours of Gryffindor or Slytherin, but Hufflepuff. Of course he'd chosen Hufflepuff—he was kind, hardworking and honourable. The fluttery feeling intensified.

'Well, Cedric Diggory, I hope you brought butterbeer.'

'I did actually.'

Lachlan flipped off the lid of the esky and lifted out butterscotch schnapps, vanilla vodka, cream soda, whipped cream, a packet of Bertie Bott's Every Flavour Beans, chocolate frogs and all eight Harry Potter DVDs.

'Fancy a Harry Potter night?'

Stunned, Jade stared at her kitchen bench now crowded with confectionary. She opened her mouth but words failed her. She couldn't work out if she wanted to cry or squeal in delight. Both responses unsettled her.

'Unless of course you're busy?' Worry carved lines across his forehead. 'Hell, you told me once you don't like surprises. I should have called you first or gone with a traditional date. I was going to ask you out, but I didn't want to stress you about babysitting or hear you say no. Shit, I've stuffed it, haven't I? Sorry.'

His sincerity baffled her. She wasn't used to anyone apologising to her, let alone a guy. And part of her *would* have liked him to ask her out, even though this sort of surprise was kind and thoughtful.

Lachlan put the bottle of schnapps back in the esky.

Say something!

'If I'd known you were coming, I'd have cleared my schedule and dressed for the occasion. Now I'm going to have to squeeze you in between talking to Beyoncé and finding a cure for Ebola.'

His eyes sparkled like morning dew on rainforest moss. 'In that case I feel very privileged.' He handed her a bag. 'Sorry if I got this wrong too.'

Confused, she opened it and pulled out a blue and grey scarf. 'Ravenclaw?'

'Yeah. You're always reading and spouting fun facts.'

'Thanks.' She wrapped the scarf around her neck, trying not to think about how Cho Chang from Ravenclaw had been Cedric Diggory's girlfriend. Was Lachlan trying to tell her something?

Shut up!

She got out glasses for the butterbeer. 'Did you know that The Three Broomsticks in the movie is a real pub in Oxford?'

'I did not.' Lachlan mixed the ingredients and dolloped in cream. 'Did you know they laid carpet and hung wallpaper with the Hogwarts emblem in the Princess Theatre in Melbourne just for *Harry Potter and the Cursed Child*?'

'I did not.' Tickets to the show cost more than half her fortnightly Centrelink benefit. 'Sounds amazing. Have you seen it?'

He swallowed, his Adam's apple bobbing, and she realised he didn't want to tell her. She didn't know if she was offended he didn't want to make her feel bad or annoyed with him that it had crossed his mind.

He handed her a butterbeer. 'Uncle Bob and I went to see it soon after it opened.'

'I bet it was amazing.'

'Almost as amazing as this butterbeer.'

'That's probably overselling it.'

He grinned. 'I dunno. I've spent a lot of time perfecting this recipe. Cheers.'

She clinked his glass and took a sip. At first she could only taste sugary sweetness and then the alcohol swooped through her veins. 'Oh my God.'

'Told you.'

She laughed and picked up the chocolate frogs and the box of Bertie Bott's Beans before walking to the couch. 'So are we watching *Goblet of Fire*?'

'You do realise Cedric dies in that.'

She grinned. 'Yeah, but he goes out a Triwizard champion.'

Lachlan looked unimpressed, but he slid the DVD into the player and joined her on the couch.

Jade momentarily wondered if he'd do what most men she knew would—cop a feel as payment for the food and drink. Of course he didn't. Nerd that he was, he got into the movie, quoting most of Cedric's lines and making her laugh.

When they paused to make a second butterbeer, Jade realised it was almost ten. 'I wonder where Helen is? She's usually home by now.'

Lachlan's neck flushed red and he busied himself with the vanilla vodka.

'What's going on?' she asked.

'Nothing.'

'Yeah, nah. Something.'

He sighed, his face now bright pink. 'I might have asked Helen if she'd mind going to Bob's place until eleven.'

Jade didn't know what shocked her more—that Lachlan wanted to be alone with her or that Helen had gone to Bob's when she didn't have a reason.

'I ... that's ...' But her usually quick brain was floating in a warm bath of vodka and schnapps. Before she could stop herself, she said, 'Do you want to kiss me?'

'Only if you want me to.' He met her gaze. 'Do you?'

Did she? No guy had ever bothered to ask her the question before. The men she knew just moved right on in whether she wanted them to or not. She and Corey had sex the first night they met, which she'd been fine about, but he hadn't asked if she wanted it—it had been a given. Jade fiddled with the hem of her faded T-shirt. Was Lachlan a wimp for not swooping in for a romantic kiss or was this what respect looked like? She thought about years of drunk boys and men and how their kisses were never like the movies.

'Do you always ask first?'

'Since Me Too, I do.' He gave a wry smile. 'When I was at uni, I thought I was a decent bloke who only kissed girls who gave me the vibe they wanted me to. I thought it worked right up until Grace slapped me. Turned out I'd confused friendship with something more. I know asking's not particularly romantic, but neither is being kissed by someone you don't like that way. I figure the romance starts once I've got consent.'

The butterflies that had been fluttering low in her belly since he'd arrived multiplied by ten thousand, swooping and diving. Then her breath hitched. Not once had she initiated anything with a bloke. Charlene and her Finley friends had told her only sluts make the first move and no man respects a slut—they just use her. But like many of the lessons she'd learned growing up, this was another she was starting to question.

She supposed that by asking her, Lachlan had technically made the first move, but she wasn't going to let semantics stop her. She rounded the bench and stood in front of him. His warmth filled the small space and she rose on her toes, planning to reach his lips.

He slid his hands gently along her cheeks. 'I've wanted to do this since I helped you put that bedhead into your garden.'

'You have?' Her words came out on a puff of air as anticipation softened her knees.

'Pretty much.'

The pads of his thumbs drew circles on her skin, sending wondrous sensations of pleasure and torture skating through her. 'So are you actually going to kiss me or do I need to take over?'

He laughed. 'I like a woman who knows what she wants,' he said softly, then lowered his lips onto hers.

Oh my God! There was nothing nerdy about his kiss. He didn't rush it, taking his time and gently tracing the seam of her lips with his tongue, as if exploring rather than forcing entry. She was the one left wanting more.

She opened her mouth under his and tasted caramel, chocolate and desire, and then his arms were around her waist pulling her close and the gap between them vanished.

The world stood still. All that existed was his heat, her breath and their bodies filling each other's dips and curves. Her hands slid under his T-shirt, pressing against smooth skin stretched over hard muscle. He groaned and returned the favour, his fingers running lightly up her spine. Stars spun in her head and every cell in her body screamed for his touch.

Breathing hard, Lachlan suddenly broke the kiss and then his hands were resting gently on her shoulders, holding her slightly away from him. Disappointment rushed in along with cool air.

'What?' It was the only word her fuddled brain could manage.

It took a second for his glazed eyes to focus. 'That was amazing.'

'It was. Why stop?'

'Didn't want to move too fast on a first date.'

She'd felt his body against hers and knew exactly how fast he'd moved. She narrowed her eyes at him, searching for the truth. 'You're terrified Helen's going to walk in on us.'

'You got me.' He grinned and held out his hand. 'Want to snuggle up on the couch and watch the rest of the movie?'

She swayed slightly, swamped by a barrage of emotions. Lachlan had arrived unannounced on a date he'd spent money on and planned so they could be alone. He'd told her she was gorgeous and sexy and kissed her until neither of them could think straight, but instead of sex, he was suggesting they cuddle on the couch. Jade didn't know if this was amazing, devastating or something else entirely.

Flummoxed, she laced her fingers through his and followed him back to the couch.

CHAPTER
33

Helen surveyed the freshly painted walls of Bob's open-plan living area. 'Are you sure you're okay with me sticking paper on the walls?'

'If I had a problem with it, I wouldn't have suggested it,' he said. 'But I can see you're worried, so use the windows.'

'Good idea. They're much easier to clean.'

It was Saturday morning and Bob had suggested the four of them meet at his place. Now they were seriously searching for any information that might incriminate Andrew Tucker, the mayor and the male councillors, the library was no longer a safe space. 'Anyone can walk past, glance in and relay information, which would put the kybosh on anything we find,' Bob had said. 'Plus there's more room for Milo at my place.'

Jade was now looking sceptically at an old wooden playpen that Daisy was sniffing. 'Are you sure this is safe, Bob?'

'Hey, that was mine,' Lachlan said.

'Yeah, and look how you turned out,' Jade said.

Helen hid a smile at the good-natured teasing. Not that she thought Jade and Lachlan had much of a chance given the obstacle of Milo, their very different upbringings and the fact she wasn't convinced Corey Noonan was completely out of the picture. But if in the short term Jade learned there were better men out there than Corey, Helen would do whatever it took to help that along.

'I got it out of the shed, gave it a good clean and checked all the wood,' Bob said.

'You did all that for Milo?' Jade's voice was husky.

'And I added some padding on the corners for us. Saves bruises for the less coordinated members of the team.' He winked at Helen.

She bristled. 'I'm not uncoordinated.'

'Never said you were. Lachlan's the one sporting a bruise on his neck.'

Jade kept her head down, settling Milo into the playpen, while Lachlan shot his uncle a warning look. But Bob just grinned.

Helen wondered if she should suggest he didn't tease them, especially as they'd only had one sort-of date and she and Bob had no idea if they were dating or just friends. Although going on the lovebite, perhaps friends with benefits.

Daisy settled next to the playpen, her head on her paws and watching Milo. Lachlan fired up his laptop and Jade sat next to him at the table and opened Bob's.

'Can I check my mail first?' she asked.

Helen opened her mouth to say, 'No, we've got a job to do,' but Bob said, 'You've got five minutes while I organise coffee.'

Helen was pressing butcher's paper onto the windows when Jade squealed. Helen dropped the sheet and her hand thumped her chest. 'What on earth?! Are you trying to give me a heart attack?'

'Sorry.' But Jade was grinning widely. 'The *Shepparton News* read my article and they want to send a photographer to the garden.'

Lachlan shoulder-bumped her. 'That's awesome!'

'And I'm starting to get claps on *Medium*.'

'Claps?' Helen asked.

'They're like "likes" on Facebook.'

'Ah. Well done, you. Now will you believe me and your old English teacher that it's an excellent article?'

Jade fiddled with her ponytail the way she always did whenever she was uncertain about things.

'Oh, for heaven's sake!' Helen said. 'Do you need a parade?'

Jade poked out her tongue. 'A trophy will do.'

'In that case, I'll frame Mrs Kastrati's email and highlight *sharp-shooting, insightful and worthy of publication*.'

'What about almond croissants?' Bob put a platter of the buttery treats on the table along with a coffee pot.

'You should start investigating uni courses for next year,' Helen said, excitement skittering at the prospect of helping Jade choose. 'I could—'

'I need a job, not a useless degree.'

'You *need* a degree to get a secure and well-paying job so you can provide for Milo.'

Jade's eyes flashed. 'And that worked out so well for you.'

The shot hit and stung like venom, despite Helen telling herself that Jade was only lashing out because she hated being told what to do.

'That's more to do with age than education,' she said. 'You're young. At least university offers you a place where you can argue to your heart's content.'

Jade stood abruptly and shoved the plate of croissants at Helen. 'Sorry. I know you're trying to help.'

Bob squeezed Jade's shoulder. 'How about we talk about careers after we've looked for a pot of money?'

'I guess.' Jade, who was never demonstrative, suddenly flung her arms around Bob and hugged him. 'Thanks.'

Bob threw Helen a surprised but gratified look over Jade's shoulder. Of course he was happy about a public display of affection. He was an old softie.

She rubbed at an odd empty feeling under her sternum, not certain if it was because she missed being touched or because Jade was more comfortable around Bob than she was.

She pulled the lid off a marker and wrote *Andrew Tucker* in the middle of the butcher's paper, then scrawled all the councillors' names around the edges. 'We know about the events Tucker's been to. We need to know what he's offering and to which councillors.'

'He might not be offering them anything,' Bob said, playing his usual role as the voice of reason or devil's advocate. Helen was never exactly sure.

'Going on past history, the role of "property developer" is up there with snake-oil salesman, insurance companies and used-car dealers,' she said.

'True, but Tucker's hardly going to turn up in Boolanga with a suitcase of money,' Lachlan said.

Helen snorted. 'A Chinese businessman flew into Melbourne with eight hundred thousand dollars in a bag.'

Lachlan's jaw fell open. 'Wow. Okay. I don't get out of Boolanga enough. Do we know if any of the other councillors, besides the mayor, have been splashing money about?'

'To be fair, you wouldn't notice with Craig Dangerfield,' Bob said. 'Old money.'

'Even so, the market's been down and he bought a Tesla,' Lachlan said. 'That's a triple-figure chunk of change.'

'Craig's always been a sucker for cars—he's got a shed full of them. And he probably didn't buy it, but leased it.'

'Nothing's coming up on any of them other than the events they've attended or what they've said at council,' Jade said.

'The internet's good but local gossip's better,' Bob said.

'Good. I was starting to wonder if you were on our side,' Helen said.

'Of course he's on our side,' Jade said stoutly. 'It's just you're not very good at recognising it.'

Helen opened her mouth to object, but Jade added ruefully, 'Neither am I.'

Sometimes Jade's observations astonished her. 'There might be a certain truth to that.'

Bob laughed. 'I was in Stevenson's Electrical the other day asking about sound bars. Brent mentioned that Don DeLuca's installed a home theatre with surround sound and wired the entire house for music in every room. Apparently those Bose speakers don't come cheap.'

'Where'd dodgy Don get the money for that?' Helen wrote *home theatre* under DeLuca's name.

'I also got chatting with Erica at Boolanga Travel,' Bob said. 'Told her I wanted to get away from it all and really treat myself. She recommended an exclusive island in Indonesia at seven hundred dollars a night that came highly recommended by Birdie Rehn. By all accounts, being a councillor's very stressful and Aki needed to get away and switch off.'

'Seven hundred dollars a night? Fa—far out! That's what I live on for a month,' Jade said. 'We have to nail these pricks.'

'Steady, Jade.' Bob's tone was mild. 'Remember, it's not a red flag unless we can prove this holiday was something out of the ordinary for the Rehns.'

While Jade typed furiously, her eyes darting across the screen, Lachlan said, 'Aki was in the Boolanga Bards' production of *Mamma Mia*. He teaches drama at the high school.'

'And his wife works two days a week in a gift shop,' Jade said. 'There's a photo of their kids playing in the waterpark at the All Seasons Holiday Park in Mildura earlier in the year.'

'How on earth did you find that out so quickly?' Helen asked.

Jade grinned. 'Birdie's not up to speed with her Facebook privacy settings.'

'What about the other councillors?' Lachlan asked. 'Pretty sure Mum mentioned Messina bought an apartment in Docklands for Greta to live in now she's at RMIT.'

'Messina's daughter and her two flatmates are paying rent, which covers the mortgage,' Helen said.

'Isn't Vivian renovating?' Bob asked.

'Yes, but unlike the Rehns' holiday, it's not an out-of-the-blue thing. She's been talking about those Italian glass tiles for two years.'

'What about Cynthia?'

Helen shrugged. 'She's quiet. She got onto council with a platform of motherhood statements. She tends to be more of a follower, which is fine by me because she's supportive.'

'It's the quiet ones you've got to watch,' Lachlan said. 'She has to declare who donated to her campaign, doesn't she? We should look at it and see who really got her elected.'

'Assuming she declared it,' Jade said. 'Politicians are always getting exposed for conveniently forgetting that a crime boss came to their fundraising dinner and ate lobster.'

Milo, who'd been content throwing toys over the side of the playpen, suddenly squawked. Daisy barked and picked up a toy in her mouth.

Lachlan stood and scooped up Milo, who was waving his arms. 'Jailbreak time is it, squirt?'

'I doubt Cynthia's a Tucker plant,' Helen said firmly.

'Do you want me to take him?' Jade asked Lachlan.

'No, all good. You're faster on the computer.' He sat and gave Milo the plastic hammer to hit against the table.

Helen pressed on. 'If Cynthia's a plant, why would she have told me three times that she'd vote for the housing project? The mayor's far more likely to be dabbling in bribery and corruption.'

'Or are you blinkered because you want it to be Geoff?' Bob asked.

'I don't want it to be anyone, but there's a pattern emerging and I'm facing facts.' She uncapped a red pen, circled the male names and drew lines between them. 'When I started this project, all the councillors met with me except the mayor. His secretary always had an excuse. Right from the start, the female councillors were enthusiastic and supportive, but the men vacillated saying things like "We'll certainly give it serious consideration" and "We need to think about it in the broader context of the shire's social responsibilities".

'Geoff Rayson gave Vivian a verbal "in-principle" agreement and since then he's consistently backed away from the project, removed me from my job and kicked me out of the cottage. We have photographic proof that all these men have met with Tucker and all of them have gone cold on the tiny houses project. On the other side, we have three female councillors who have only been in the same place as Tucker at the business awards and he hasn't approached any of them.

'After I told Vivian how many times Tucker's been in Boolanga this year, the three women requested a meeting with him. He told them Riverfarm was too small for his company to consider building a resort, but we think it's a smokescreen.'

'It's less hectares than across the river,' Lachlan said.

'Not if they incorporate the community garden,' Jade said. 'I know you hate Judith, Helen, but should we give the garden committee a heads-up? They might come on board if their garden's under threat.'

'Outside of this group, I don't think we should be telling anyone anything,' Bob said. 'Not until we've got real evidence.'

Helen tapped the marker against the butcher's paper. 'I know Bob thinks Craig has the money for the Tesla, whereas the other two appear to have had recent cash windfalls. But in my mind, that money shines a spotlight on the Tesla.'

'According to Google, the Tesla dealership's in Melbourne,' Jade said.

'I might take a drive,' Bob said.

Helen tried not to roll her eyes. 'You might know everyone in Boolanga, but Melbourne's a different kettle of fish. There's no way you can just walk in and find out if Craig paid cash or if someone else did.'

'People are people, Helen. If you take an interest in them, they tell you all sorts of things. Besides, I've always wanted to test-drive a Tesla.'

'I'll come.' Lachlan's eyes sparkled with enthusiasm.

'Not this time, son. I'm thinking an old duffer from the country might get a bit more information than a young buck.'

'You're nothing like a duffer, Bob,' Jade said.

Lachlan laughed. 'Yeah, but he can act the part when it suits him. He's conned me more than once.'

'We could post a photo on Facebook of the Rehns' island holiday,' Jade said. 'It's not like it's illegal. It's sitting right here unprotected on Birdie's page.'

'That would be like firing a flare and the others would scramble,' Helen said. 'Our power comes from being able to implicate all four at once. Now we've found evidence of money, we need to track it to the source.'

Milo threw the hammer for the third time, enjoying how Lachlan took him with him as he bent down then straightened up.

'Now that child's conning you, Lachlan,' Helen said. 'Might be time to wise up.'

Bob's phone buzzed. 'Oh, good, lunch is ready. Jade, Lachie, can you duck down to the bakery and pick it up? You can leave Milo here if you like.'

As soon as they'd left, Helen said, 'Don't push them so much.'

'All I'm doing is providing some opportunities for them to have a bit of time on their own.'

'A ten-minute walk to the bakery and back?'

'Magic moments.'

'It's not real though, is it? Milo exists.'

'I don't follow.'

'It's my observation that many blokes are put off by other men's kids.'

'It's not like Lachlan got to know Jade first and then discovered Milo. He knows they're a package deal.' Bob sounded as close to belligerent as she'd ever heard him.

'Yes, but does he know the deal includes Corey?'

Bob frowned. 'Lachie only made his move because he thought he was off the scene.'

'He'll always be Milo's father.'

Bob pondered that for a minute. 'The course of true love never did run smooth.'

'O brawling love, O loving hate,' Helen countered.

'That was Romeo on Rosaline, not Juliet. Don't be so bleak.'

Helen was about to say that Corey Noonan generated bleak wherever he went when Bob added, 'Can you keep an eye on the little chap for a sec? I need to use the facilities.'

Bob disappeared and Daisy followed. Milo voiced his objection from under the table.

'Don't worry,' Helen told him. 'Your biggest fans will be back soon.'

Milo crawled out with the hammer, pulled himself up and handed her the toy.

'Thank you.' She gave it a gentle toss a few feet away.

His sky blue eyes widened in surprise and then he chortled in delight before babbling what was probably, 'Do it again.'

'Go and get it.' He stared at her. 'Bring it to me and I'll throw it again.'

He babbled some more and her attention drifted back to the butcher's paper. When he shrieked, she glanced around and was surprised to see him standing on his own halfway between her and the hammer. She was used to seeing him pull himself up to stand next to objects, but never standing on his own.

'Milo, did you walk there?'

He turned at her voice and promptly sat down.

An unexpected thrill shot through her and she pulled him to his feet. When he was steady, she let go of his hands and picked up the hammer, holding it out towards him. 'Come on, Milo.'

His usually cheery face frowned in concentration and his chubby left foot moved forward, followed by his right. In two more steps, he was snatching the hammer.

'You're walking! You clever, clever kid!'

It was the most natural thing in the world to hug him and his achievement. He snuggled in, his body warm and soft against hers, his curls tickling her nose, his scent a combination of baby shampoo and banana.

Out of nowhere, her throat tightened and then she was gasping as long-suppressed hulking sobs heaved out of her.

CHAPTER
34

'Helen?' Bob's hand was on her shoulder. 'What's happened?'

She didn't dare look at him. 'M-Milo … w-walked.'

'And that's upset you?'

But she couldn't form words, let alone speak.

Bob pushed a clean and ironed hankie at her, Daisy tried to lick her and Milo struggled to be released from her overtight grip.

'Sit, Daisy!' Bob said as he reached down for Milo. 'Come on, sport, let's give Helen a bit of air.'

But the loss of the little boy's body drove through her heart like a stake, intensifying her sobs. Shaking, she fought for each breath, battling old grief that surged with renewed intensity.

Bob's arms circled her, the touch flattening her protective walls. She gave in to comfort and cried in a way she hadn't done in years.

Slowly, she became aware that Milo was banging the toy hammer on her head. The touch reset something inside her and she made a strangled sound that was part sob, part laugh.

'That's a better sound,' Bob said. 'Unless of course you're choking?'

Another laugh gurgled up and she blew her nose.

'I know you do yoga and you're used to sitting on the floor, but my hips are going to lock if I stay down here any longer.' He rolled over onto all fours and pushed himself to his feet, before extending a hand.

She accepted it and rose. When her eyes focused, she noticed the large wet patch on his shirt. Embarrassment hit her so hard she almost ran for the door.

'I'm sorry you had to see that.'

He gave her a small smile. 'Don't be sorry. People think it's the bad things that undo us. But in my experience, it's often the good stuff that trips us up, reminding us what we had and what we miss the most.'

Understanding radiated from him, offering her safety and support.

'Jade's right,' she said. 'You're not a duffer in any shape or form.'

'Can I have that in writing?'

'About Jade being right?'

'Hah! Glad you're feeling better.' He sat on the couch and she joined him. 'So Milo walked, eh?'

'He took three steps!'

As if Milo knew they were talking about him, he repeated the trick. Bob cheered and Milo grinned a gummy smile.

Helen's heart filled with joy ringed with sadness. 'I didn't expect him walking would affect me. But his little face was creased in such fierce concentration and he was so stunned and delighted that he'd done it, I got excited for him. I never expected it to release a tidal wave of emotions.'

Milo lay down next to Daisy and sucked his thumb, clearly exhausted after his mammoth milestone.

Helen kept her gaze focused on him so she didn't look at Bob. 'I had a daughter. Nicki. She never walked.'

Bob picked up her hand and squeezed it gently, but instead of making her cry, it was oddly reassuring. She knew then she could tell him.

'Nicki was born a few weeks early. The doctors told us it wasn't unusual and there was nothing to worry about. But as the weeks passed and I met other women with babies the same age, it became obvious something was going on. Her head seemed smaller than other babies, and she didn't follow us much with her eyes. Then one day she fitted. It was the first time in my life I experienced true fear.'

'It sounds terrifying.'

Helen shuddered. 'It got worse. Apparently when I was pregnant I got something called toxoplasmosis. Normally it isn't an issue and I don't even remember being sick, but it can have catastrophic effects in the first three months of pregnancy. It left Nicki severely physically and intellectually disabled and partially blind. She spent her life in a wheelchair with no verbal communication other than high-pitched shrieks.'

'Oh, jeez. I can't even imagine.'

She thought about how he'd watched Alzheimer's steal his wife from him and knew he had more of an idea about loss than most people.

'I spent years fighting the diagnosis, fighting for funding and trying every therapy under the sun. Theo gave up long before I did.'

'Your husband?'

She nodded. 'When Nicki was a baby Theo was pretty good, but as she got older and was obviously very different from other kids her age, he found it increasingly hard to accept. He'd look at her and only see all the things she wasn't instead of who she was.

I wanted another child, but he was adamant. Things spiralled and eventually he met someone and walked away from us both.'

'I'm sorry.'

'No need. It was years ago.'

'Doesn't mean it still won't bite you occasionally.'

'Nicki will always reduce me to a blubbering mess, but not Theo.' She sighed. 'To be honest, when he left it was a relief to have one less person to worry about, and the divorce inevitably followed. We'd heavily geared to buy the house, expecting I'd return to work when Nicki was one, but of course that didn't happen and there was no NDIS back then. Our costs for equipment and care were higher. Although we'd met the mortgage repayments, we'd only been paying interest and hadn't touched the principal. We had to sell the house. I came out of the marriage with less money than I'd taken into it, and without a way to earn much beyond a carer's benefit.'

'Where did you live?'

'I moved in with my mother. She was starting to fail and I looked after her and Nicki.'

'And they've both passed away?'

'Yes. Nicki lived longer than anyone expected and she died of an overwhelming infection when she was twenty-two. It broke Mum's heart. She died a few months later.'

'When was that?'

'Five years ago.'

'Did you come to Boolanga for a river change?'

She looked into his craggy face and read care, kindness and a complete lack of judgement. The fact he'd only ever been accepting of the women in the park drove her to tell him, but niggling doubt remained. In her experience, it was one thing for people to 'help the underprivileged' and feel good about it in the process. It was another thing entirely to have an underprivileged person inside your friendship group.

He's great with Jade.

He fathers her.

The thought that Bob might turn his paternalistic tendencies towards her was enough to change her mind. But was their friendship worth anything if she withheld the truth when he'd only ever been open and honest with her?

Does it matter?

For the first time in years, she knew that it did. 'It's a bit of a long story.'

He squeezed her hand again. 'I've got the time to listen.'

'Okay.' She took in a deep breath and started talking. 'I've only been in Boolanga three years. I was fifty-four when Mum died and I hadn't worked since before Nicki was born. I was excited about upskilling and I went back to uni and added a graduate diploma in community services to my arts degree. I'd had so much experience as a user of community services, I figured I was the ideal person to work in them as a provider. The study was invigorating and I really thought it was my time to shine.

'The reality hit when I tried to get a job. No one wants to hire a fifty-five year old.' She kept her gaze on his face, watching him carefully. 'If you own your own home, JobSeeker might keep you afloat, but it doesn't when you're paying rent in Melbourne. First my fridge died, then I got pneumonia and fell behind in my rent. I sold everything I didn't need but it wasn't enough to keep me in my flat.'

Bob's eyes widened and he closed them for a moment, breathing deeply. When he opened them, the same warm look he usually gave her remained, but something else had joined it. 'You're telling me you've been homeless, aren't you?'

'I slept in my car for six months, including my first few weeks in Boolanga.' She sighed. 'I'm half homeless now.'

'You're not.'

'Pfft! I am from where I'm sitting. God, I'm sharing with a baby and a twenty year old who's currently floating on air and incapable of putting anything away!'

'Exactly,' he said firmly. 'It sounds like family to me.'

'Jade and Milo are not my family.'

Bob laughed. 'You want her to go to uni—'

'So she can have a better quality of life.'

'Exactly. And in some ways you're both pretty similar so you bicker like mother and daughter.'

'It's nothing to do with a mother–daughter dynamic. You try living with a twenty year old!'

'And despite your best efforts to keep your distance, Milo's snuck into your heart. It scares the hell out of you.'

His words rained down, unwelcome and unwanted. 'Stick to gardening and cycling, old man.'

'Did you know you only get acerbic when you're scared?'

His gentle indulgence of her tantrum only made her angrier. 'I've survived sleeping rough, buster. As if a toddler's going to break me.' Except after her crying jag, the words rang hollow, stealing the oxygen from her fury. 'I really hate it when you're right.'

'Lucky it doesn't happen often then, eh?' He squeezed her hand again. 'Does Jade know about your sleeping rough?'

'Yes.' She shot him a wry smile. 'I used it as a lesson.'

He laughed. 'Classic mother move. Have you told her about Nicki?'

'Not yet. Perhaps I should.' Her heart contracted and swelled at the same time. 'Thanks for using her name. It's nice hearing it again.'

'Too easy.'

The bang of the wire door sounded and Helen pulled her hand out of Bob's before Jade or Lachlan could notice. The last thing she needed was Jade misinterpreting empathy for something else.

Hah! Good one, Helen. As if!

And thank God Bob's hand-holding was one hundred per cent empathy because it had been so long since she'd been intimate with a man, everything was probably rusted shut. An unwanted pang of regret curled under her ribs. She stiffened and blew out a long breath to move it on. It refused to budge.

Jade didn't trust feeling this happy even though she wanted to. Since the Harry Potter movie, she and Lachlan had talked every night, either in person or on the phone. Helen made herself scarce, but the fact she was in the unit and Milo was in Jade's room put the brakes on anything other than cuddling on the couch. Not that Jade had any objections to that. There was something incredibly hot about old-school pashing and restraint.

Lachlan's mouth nuzzled her neck, sending a tingle of pure desire arrowing through her. She pressed her legs together so fast the bakery box she was holding wobbled.

'We better get back before we drop lunch,' she said.

Lachlan groaned and raised his head. 'Just give me a sec, okay.'

She laughed and kissed him again.

'Not helping!'

'You know, if you invited me over to your place you might just get lucky.'

'Yeah?' His eyes lit up, then sobered. 'That means we need a babysitter, and that means we're pretty much telling Helen and Bob we're having sex, and he'll tell my mother.'

A protective streak shot through her. 'Are you ashamed of me?'

'God, no!' He gently cupped her cheeks. 'You're smart and gutsy and gorgeous. It's just most adults don't usually have their family chiming in about their sex life. It's embarrassing.'

'It's better than them not caring at all.'

He didn't look like he believed her so she moved to kiss him, but as she leaned in something flashed in her peripheral vision. Her lips grazed his as she turned her head to see a ute cruising past slowly. *Macca!*

She leaped back from Lachlan so fast the bakery box sailed into the air.

He caught it and followed her gaze. 'What's up?'

'Nothing.' It came out sharp, defiant and utterly false. More than anything, she wished she could take it back.

'Doesn't sound like nothing. The panicky expression on your face doesn't look like nothing.'

Her heart thumped so hard she heard it in her ears. 'Sorry. I thought I saw a mate of Corey's but I was just being stupid. His ute's red.'

Lachlan frowned. 'What would it matter if his mate saw you kissing me? You and Corey broke up weeks ago.'

Her mouth dried. She swallowed, trying to generate saliva.

'Jade?' His lovely eyes darkened. 'You have broken up with him, right?'

Lie. But she couldn't do it. Didn't want to do it and smudge something wonderful. 'Sort of.'

'Sort of?' Lachlan swore.

She took a protective step back, but Lachlan didn't move a muscle. 'I want to break up with him, okay. But he hasn't called or texted me in weeks.'

'You should have called him.'

She stiffened, hating that in his world people didn't just vanish then reappear when it suited them. 'Of course I called him but he doesn't pick up. I'm not doing this by text.'

The ute cruised past again, only this time the driver made a gesture then took a photo of them. Fear sliced through her.

'Hey!' Lachlan ran, but the driver floored it and the ute disappeared around the corner. He turned back to Jade. 'Did you recognise him?'

She shook her head as a tremble hit her legs.

'What about the ute?'

'I've never seen it before.'

'But you think it's connected with Corey?'

She wanted to deny it, but adrenaline was making it difficult to think let alone speak.

'Come on,' he said wearily. 'You need something to eat and then we're going to the police.'

When they reached Bob's, she walked inside to see Helen grinning at her like a clown.

'Guess what? Milo—' Helen's smile fell. 'What's wrong? You're as pale as a ghost.'

'She got a fright.' Lachlan put the bakery box on the kitchen bench. 'Some moron drove past us a couple of times on Park Street, before giving us the finger gun symbol. Then he took our photo.'

'Someone you know, love?' Bob asked gently.

Before she could answer, Lachlan said tightly, 'Jade thinks it's something to do with Corey.'

'No, I don't! Anyway, he wouldn't send someone. He'd come himself.'

She hated the way Lachlan was looking at her as if she'd let him down. God! Why had she believed him when he'd told her she was smart and gutsy? When he said stuff like that she wanted to be her best self, only look where that had landed her. Instead of staying safe and lying, she'd ignored the warning bells and told him the truth. Now he hated her for it.

You are so stupid, Jade.

Helen suddenly sat down hard on a kitchen stool, her hands gripping the bench. 'It happened to me.'

'What?' Lachlan's and Bob's voices drowned out Jade's.

'The night you had gastro. I left Riverbend and someone followed me. Every time I sped up or slowed down, he did the same.'

'He?'

'It was dark and I couldn't really see, but I assumed it was a he. Women don't tend to do that sort of thing. All I could think was I didn't want him to know where I lived and I didn't want to put Jade and Milo in danger. I made random turns and that's when I saw Lachlan's ute parked on the street. I was so relieved, I turned into the drive.'

'Helen!' Bob glared at her. 'Why are you only just mentioning this?'

'Because the car kept going and I thought I must have imagined the whole thing. It hasn't happened since.'

'Corey doesn't have a reason to follow you,' Bob said.

'I'm living with Jade.'

'Which brings us back to Corey,' Lachlan said.

'No, it doesn't,' Jade said hotly.

'Why are you defending him?'

'I'm not! But if he wanted to scare me why choose today? Why not when I'm walking alone with Milo? For all we know, the ute was following you.'

Lachlan crossed his arms, anger radiating off him. 'Yeah, right. Like I have so many reasons to be followed. I broke up with my last girlfriend a year ago.'

'You're being such a—'

'Let's all take a breath,' Bob said. 'We understand there's a possibility Corey could be behind it, but Jade's right. It's not an absolute. Who else would want to scare Helen?'

'No one, Uncle Bob! This is Boolanga.'

'Small towns aren't immune to skulduggery. Grafton and Snowtown come to mind.'

Jade had no idea what Bob was talking about but made a note to google the names later. 'That bitch Judith wants Helen gone from the garden. Hey, Bob, didn't you say Judith used to live on a farm? The ute was muddy.'

'I know the Sainsburys. It wasn't any of them,' Lachlan said.

'Most of the people on the Facebook page are supportive of the tiny houses village, but there are a couple of nutters,' Jade said. 'Maybe it's one of them.'

'Or it's Geoff Rayson,' Helen said. 'He kicked me out of the cottage, but I haven't gone away and I'm living with Jade.'

'The mayor isn't going to have you followed. That's crazy sauce,' Lachlan said.

'No, it's not.' The need to defend Helen rose up so fast it gave Jade whiplash. She thought about the many things that had been said and done to her by family and so-called friends before she'd left Finley. The memories spun into anger at herself and at Lachlan and she couldn't stop the words from rushing out. 'You live in a fluffy bubble of theatre people where everyone hugs each other and says "good job" even when it's crap.'

'I do not!' His jaw jutted. 'I work with farmers who are doing it tough, but at least they're straight with me.'

'I've been straight with you!'

'Then we've got a different definition of straight.' He picked up his keys. 'Sorry, Uncle Bob, but I should go.'

Jade's heart twisted. *I thought you were different.* But of course he was leaving. Everyone left her.

'That's disappointing, Lach,' Bob said. 'Not like you to walk away from injustice.'

'I'm going to the police station to make a statement.'

'They'll just tell you not to hang around with people like me,' Jade said. 'Oh, wait. You're already doing that.'

He walked out the door without looking back.

You're so stupid, Jade. She sucked in her lips, pressing them hard and trying not to cry.

Helen sighed, rose and unexpectedly wrapped her in a hug. Jade held herself back from the comfort on offer, waiting for the sting when Helen said, 'I told you it would never work.'

Instead, Helen said, 'Milo's a star. He took three steps.'

'What? He walked?' Her excitement was instantly slammed with disappointment. 'I m-missed it?' The tears she'd valiantly held at bay spilled over.

Helen stroked her hair. 'Bob and I made a fuss of him, and I can promise you he'll do it again and again just to hear the claps. Life just changed, Jade. You're the mother of a toddler. We need childproof locks for the kitchen cupboards and we'll have to put everything dangerous or precious out of reach.'

'Ladies,' Bob said, 'given the drive-bys, you should both move in here for a while.'

'No way!'

Helen's voice chimed in with Jade's, and Jade hugged her. She didn't care that Helen was probably saying no because she hated depending on anyone. She was just grateful Helen wasn't leaving her.

CHAPTER
35

The Chamber of Commerce was planning a Christmas kick-off, having moved the traditional Santa parade from early December to mid-November.

'It's what they do in Melbourne,' Jon told Tara when she'd complained the change meant bringing the summer casuals' training forward. 'It's a good thing. It focuses everyone's attention early that they need to buy gifts. We need to be fully stocked and fully staffed when the parade finishes and be cooking sausages and a shirt-load of onions to entice them into the store.'

'The powerful aroma of hot fat?'

He grinned. 'That's the one. Works every time.'

'Are you bumping a community group off the sausage sizzle roster?'

'No. I gave Bob Murphy a call and worded him up for peak time. He's going to have a table of produce from the community garden too. He's raising funds for an outreach food van to feed the poor and homeless in the district.'

'Do we have homeless people?'

'Apparently.'

'Have we been living in a different Boolanga?' Tara said.

'What do you mean?'

'I didn't know there was a community garden. I'd never met a refugee. I had no idea the police harassed people, and now Boolanga's got people who are homeless?'

'You make it sound like we've been completely out of touch. We've always supported the community.'

'We've supported the mainstream stuff like sport.'

He bristled. 'There's nothing wrong with that.'

The uncomfortable feeling that kept coming and going settled again in her chest. 'I don't know how to explain it. Before you got Parkinson's, we'd vaguely heard of it, but we didn't know anything about it because it didn't affect us. Now it does and it's making me notice things I've either been blind to or chose not to see.'

'I think I know what you mean. When we installed the ramp at the store entrance we did it because we got audited and it's the law. I didn't give much thought to people with movement issues. Now I look at every business I enter with new eyes.'

The big day dawned clear and bright with no sign of any rain on the Christmas parade. The children had insisted Jon take them to see Santa and then to the carnival, probably because he was a softer touch for junk food and rides. Tara battled sadness that they couldn't all go together and focused instead on making the store as festive as possible. She'd created targeted displays of gift ideas for him, her, them and kids. She'd put the casuals—Sabrina, Darcy and Amal—in charge of helium balloon inflation. Amal had suggested using some of the balloons to create a welcome arch.

As no staff members' relatives had been impacted by Amal's employment, Tara hadn't heard any official disgruntled comments, although that didn't mean there weren't any. There'd been a tricky couple of weeks after she and Jon had told the staff about Jon's illness and the changes in management style with Tara doing more, but once they'd been reassured their jobs were safe, they'd settled and been remarkably helpful. Tara wanted to believe this good will extended to Amal.

With the car park converted into a mini carnival and stage to entertain the parade crowd, there was a constant flow of customers through the store. Tara was troubleshooting and supporting the summer casuals as they found their feet.

A large man in a suit approached the counter clutching a wobbly tower of duct tape, rope, screws, a paintbrush and a punnet of lettuces. Sensing imminent disaster, Tara reached for the plant. 'Let me help you with that—oh, Mr Mayor.'

'Geoff,' he said genially. 'You're Jon's wife, aren't you? I was just chatting to him and your delightful children. Presiding over the Christmas parade is one of my favourite mayoral duties.'

Tara grabbed an unexpected opportunity with both hands. 'It's a great idea to use the car park for the kids' carnival. Of course, if it was lit, we could hold all sorts of festivals.'

He gave her a politician's smile. 'We're trialling many initiatives. It's an exciting time for Boolanga.'

Tara was about to press the point that four store break-ins weren't exciting when she remembered the cottage. She'd been playing phone lotto with the shire, being passed from Parks and Gardens to Engineering to Municipal Resources and back again, even taking a detour to Volunteer Services when someone pressed the wrong button. She was yet to talk to anyone with any authority over the cottage.

'Geoff, this might seem like it's coming out of left field, but Jon and I have been discussing the old manager's cottage at Riverfarm.

It's an important piece of Boolanga's history and we feel it needs to be preserved.'

'You won't get an argument from me. Unfortunately, we haven't been successful with any restoration grant applications. It's looking like we'll have to dismantle it for public safety.'

Dismantle? As part of their initial costings, she and Jon had snuck down and snooped around the outside of the cottage. Jon had insisted on crawling under it and she'd held her breath the whole time. Although it had taken him longer than it used to, he'd emerged filthy but with a grin that spun her heart. She knew his excitement wasn't limited to no signs of termites in the foundations.

'What if the community restored it?' she asked Geoff.

He sighed. 'That's a nice idea in principle, but we don't have any fat in the budget to run a fundraising campaign, let alone allocate a staff member to coordinate it. It's my experience that everyone's sentimental about history until they're asked to stick their hands in their pockets.'

Tara frowned. 'The war memorial was restored two years ago.'

'Yes, well, people feel differently about the war. This is a cottage that looks pretty similar to half a dozen in town.'

That was inaccurate given the cottage predated the town by twenty-two years, but Tara knew she wouldn't win any points by mentioning it.

'We feel very strongly about the cottage,' she said. 'Hoopers Hardware and Timber would happily spearhead a community restoration project and provide the building materials. We'd work closely with the historical society and the library to ensure a faithful restoration. All we're asking is for it to be relocated to the museum.'

Geoff pulled on his ear, his expression thoughtful, then slid a business card out of his wallet. 'I can't make you any promises—due process and all that—but email me a document outlining exactly what you're offering. I'll get Engineering and Parks' input and discuss it with my fellow councillors. But as community is what we're all about here in Boolanga and your idea has that written all over it, I'm pretty optimistic it will sail through.'

Anticipation buzzed, making her jumpy and excited. 'Thank you, Geoff!'

'I better get going or Sheree will have my guts for garters.' He tapped his credit card and left with his purchases.

Tara's stomach rumbled. It was two o'clock and she'd covered everyone's lunch break but not taken one herself. She texted Jon: *Meet me at the sausage sizzle tent?*

Clemmie on the teacups. Give me five

She grabbed her hat and on the way out ran into Al Kvant.

'Hey, Tara. You must be happy. Looks like everyone's doing their present-buying early.'

'A lot will be browsing for ideas with plans to order a cheaper online version on Black Friday.'

'That's gotta hurt.'

Tara had always liked Al more than Kelly—he was the kinder of the two. 'It does, but we get the win when their item arrives damaged or doesn't fit. Then we woo them with our customer service and keep them. Are you looking for something in particular?'

'Just some leather cleaner. With the bye this afternoon, I thought I'd give the Valiant some love.'

Cricket and classic cars were Al's two passions.

'Do you reckon the team can beat Numurkah next week?' Tara asked.

'It's always a bit of a grudge match, but Simmo's in good form so I reckon we're in with a chance.'

'Paul Simpson? I thought he was playing with Cobram these days.'

'He's back. Lucky really with Jon being sick and all.'

'Jon's not sick. He has a condition.'

'You know what I mean. His bowling's not what it was.'

Tara flashed hot and cold. *I arrived just as they were packing up.* 'Have you told him Simmo's back?'

'I tried the other night, but the poor bugger was already sitting there nursing soda water.' Al shifted his weight, looking uncomfortable. 'Thing is, Tara, the team's determined to wrench back the trophy from Tatura this year so we're cutting a few people.'

She hooked his evasive gaze. 'And which *few* people would that be?'

He looked at his feet and sighed. 'Yeah, okay. It's just Jon. Would you mind telling him? It will come better from you.'

Are you freaking kidding me? She breathed deeply, trying to douse the molten fury melting her control. 'No, Al.'

Genuine surprise creased his forehead. 'Why not?'

'I think you know why. The team's name is Boolanga Old Boys for a reason. None of you are twenty any more. So he bowls the occasional wide and drops a catch; most of you do that. How would you feel if you discovered the club you've belonged to all your life has replaced you without having the decency to tell you? If the team doesn't want Jon to play then the team tells him.' Her restraint slipped. 'And Jesus, Al! You're supposed to be his friend.'

'I am!' Al sounded shocked she'd questioned his friendship. 'When the committee were worried Jon might pull his sponsorship, I told them he wasn't like that.'

I am. I'll pull the sponsorship. 'I can't answer for him.'

Al frowned, disappointed not to get the reassurance he wanted. 'It's hard, Tara. I don't want to make him feel any worse.'

'I think that boat's already sailed.'

'Right.'

But there was nothing right about any of this.

'I promised the kids I'd meet them five minutes ago,' she lied, desperate to get away.

'No worries.'

Seething, she walked outside before Al suggested she host a gang get-together so he could break Jon's heart in his own home.

The melodic tones of the Boolanga Blokes rang out, singing Christmas carols—the lyrics about snow incongruous in the afternoon heat. Tara noticed Jade, the young mother from the community garden, standing off to the side and listening intently to Kelly's boss, Fatima.

The lunchtime rush was well and truly over so Tara walked straight up to the sausage sizzle serving table. She was delighted to see Helen standing behind it.

'I didn't know you were part of the—' she glanced at the chalkboard, checking the exact organisation, '—Food Rights group.' She had a sudden need to be honest. 'To tell the truth, I didn't know we had people going hungry in Boolanga. You're teaching me a lot.'

Helen smiled. 'Happy to help. Have you met Bob Murphy?'

'Mummy!' Clementine ran over clutching a red balloon and excitedly flung her arms around Tara's waist. 'Daddy bought us fairy floss.'

'I'd never have guessed.'

She glanced over Clementine's head and saw Jon walking towards her, the change in his gait so very obvious to her since his diagnosis. Fiza was walking beside him, her height a close match for his. It seemed odd to see her dressed sedately in navy hospital scrubs. The dark colour didn't really suit her and Tara suddenly realised why she always wore such bright colours—they made her sparkle.

Flynn and the twins bounced behind them on similar sugar highs to Clementine.

'Who's for a sausage?' Jon asked the kids.

'Me! Me!' four voices called.

Tara's heart sank, remembering what she'd read on Wikipedia. 'Jon, I don't think the twins are allowed to eat sausages.'

'These are halal beef snags, Tara,' Bob said. 'They suit everyone except the vegos. We've got vegan burgers for them.'

'My children love to eat a sausage in bread.' Fiza fished out some coins from her purse.

'Put that away,' Jon said. 'My treat.'

'Thank you, but that's not nec—'

'Fiza, if you hadn't taken one for the team by going on the Whizzer with the boys, I'd still be lying on the ground with the world spinning.'

'Taken one for the team?'

'Done something you didn't want to do to help everyone else,' Tara said. 'And if you went on the Whizzer you deserve a lot more than a two-dollar sausage.'

'It was fun.' Fiza's smile dimmed. 'I am fortunate to have the chance to do these things with my children.'

A shiver ran up Tara's spine as it did every time she thought of Fiza alone in the refugee camp with twin babies, a nine year old, and grieving for a husband who'd been murdered in front of her.

She shoved a twenty-dollar bill at Bob. 'Seven, please. Keep the change.'

'Thank you.' He shot her a silver fox smile. 'Can I tempt you with some fresh herbs or some cucumbers?'

'No, thanks. My garden's generously giving me more cucumbers and rhubarb than I need. Oh! Would you like some to give to people in need?'

'That's a kind thought, but cooking's a challenge when you're homeless,' Helen said. 'However, if you're able to make a rhubarb crumble or rhubarb bars, they'd be very much appreciated.'

'Oh, right. Of course. Sorry.' Her cheeks burned that she hadn't thought about how a homeless person would cook.

While Bob was handing off sausages in bread to the kids and Fiza and Jon were supervising sauce, Helen tilted her head to the side and took a step. Tara followed.

'There's no need to be embarrassed about the food offer, Tara. It's not until we're in the thick of something that it even crosses our radar.'

Helen's words unlocked a barrage of emotions that spilled out fast. 'I'm learning that. Most people don't understand what Jon having Parkinson's means to us. If he'd been diagnosed with cancer, the footy club would hold a fundraiser. If he'd died, our friends would rally around, bring over casseroles, offer childminding, and give me a spa day, knowing I'd eventually get back on my feet and there'd be an end date.

'But no one knows how to handle a chronic illness that will partner Jon for another thirty to forty years. No one wants to look at us or ask us how we are in case we tell them. These days I get "ask and answer" questions like, "How are you, all good, yeah?". It leaves me no place to go. But if I say, "Well, no actually, I'm not all good," they feel trapped and embarrassed because really, they didn't want to know in the first place.

'Part of me understands that Jon's shakes and trembles make them uncomfortable. They're terrified it might happen to them, even though we've explained Parkinson's isn't like the flu—you can't catch it from someone. I hate that they only see the tremors, because it means they're remembering how he was rather than seeing the man he is right now. He's not even bad at the moment and they're staying away. How will it be when he's worse? Don't answer that.'

Tara sighed. 'The awful thing is, I wonder if I was in their shoes, would I have behaved the same way? Outside of Jon's father, the one person who's helped us is the person with the least reason.' Her voice broke and she pulled a tissue from her pocket. 'Oh, God. I'm sorry. I didn't mean to dump all this on you.'

Helen gave her arm a gentle squeeze. 'There's nothing to be sorry about. Don't waste your precious energy whipping yourself about what you might or might not have done in the past. You've got enough to deal with now. Instead, appreciate that in the midst of chaos you've taken the time to reflect and grow.'

Gratitude poured through her, stilling some of the agitation that was now a permanent part of her. 'How did you get so wise?'

Helen gave a wry smile. 'I'm hardly wise. I tend to jump in feet first so I think it's more to do with experience. My daughter was severely disabled so I understand how people drop away when they find it all too hard.'

'I'm sorry.' Tara returned the arm squeeze. 'Are you ever free for coffee?'

'Absolutely! We have a regular group lunch with the women on Thursdays so bring some lunch to share and join in. You might enjoy it.'

'Thanks, but I work across lunch so Jon can grab a rest.'

'No problem. I'm in the garden all day Thursdays. Call in when it suits, but if you're not fond of instant coffee, bring your own.'

'Around eleven? Can I bring you one too?'

'A latte would be lovely.'

When Tara turned around, Fiza must have left for work and Jon was fifteen metres away. He pointed to the kids and the stage, indicating he was taking them closer to hear the Wacky Warblers, Boolanga's version of the Mik Maks.

Tara was making her way towards them when she passed Jade and Fatima, who were still deep in conversation.

'Hi, Tara,' Jade said, looking over. 'Thanks for those vinca seedlings. They're really taking off.'

'I'm glad they survived. How are things, Fatima?'

'Great! This time Monday, I'll be relaxing on Magnetic Island.'

'Sounds amazing.'

'But you won't be able to go to the beach, will you?' Jade asked. 'I mean not to swim.'

'Of course I can. I treated myself to one of these new Nike state-of-the-art swimmers.' Fatima swiped her phone to a photo of a magenta swimsuit with full-length pants, long-sleeved top and a head covering. 'It's super light and dries fast. I can't wait to snorkel.'

'At least you won't get sunburnt,' Jade said.

Fatima laughed. 'Or get stung by an Irukandji.'

Tara shuddered. 'Good point.'

'Don't you get sick of always having to cover up all the time?' Jade asked.

Fatima shrugged. 'To be honest, I don't think about it. Besides, my thighs don't look good in shorts, so lucky, eh?' She laughed, her dark eyes dancing. 'It's my choice to dress modestly but that doesn't mean my clothes aren't smart and fashionable.' She did a little twirl and the soft fabric of her pretty swing top rose and fell.

'Did you come here as a refugee too?' Jade asked.

'Nah! I'm second-generation Aussie. My grandparents came here from Karachi in the 1970s, but they weren't the first Badoolas in

Australia. My great-great-grandfather came here as a cameleer. He transported supplies between Kalgoorlie and Broken Hill.'

'He was a Ghan?' Tara said. 'Wow!' She and Jon had ridden the train named after the cameleers and she'd been fascinated by the story.

'And he helped build the Perth Mosque, but he was sent home when the White Australia policy came in. I often wonder if he left behind any kids. I might have family in WA.'

'You should do a DNA test at Ancestry.com,' Tara suggested.

'Great idea! I might get to freak out some Skips when they find out they have Muslim relatives,' Fatima teased.

'Or be surprised you have Aboriginal cousins,' Tara said. 'A lot of the Ghans married Aboriginal women.'

'I think it would be awesome, but my grandparents would be horrified that great-grandfather Ameer hadn't kept it in his Muslim pants.'

'So Muslims don't like mixed marriages?' Jade asked.

'Name me a faith that does. I know you hear all sorts of horrible things, but Islam is a religion of peace. But just like Christianity, there are some people who wilfully get it wrong. Mostly men.'

'I'm not sure Christians go around blowing each other up,' Tara said.

'Northern Ireland anyone?'

Tara had no response to that except to ponder the role of men in wars.

Fatima smiled. 'The world's a complicated place. If you're really interested, there's a great collection of short essays called *It's Not About The Burqa*. It's written by young UK Muslim women and they talk about everything from feminism and sexuality to their faith in the western world. There's no such thing as one Muslim woman. We're as different as any group of women be they Christian, Jewish or atheist. The book says it way better than I ever could.'

Tara thought about Fiza, who seemed to have her own interpretation of her faith that worked for her. 'It sounds interesting. If my book group read it, would you come along and give your perspective?'

Fatima cocked one very dark and well-shaped eyebrow. 'Isn't Kelly Kvant in your book group?'

Tara got the urge to both laugh and cringe at the same time. 'I take your point, but as I'm hosting the next meeting, I get to pick the book.'

'Well, if you're sure you want to go there ...'

'I am. And I might invite Fiza. She's Muslim too. Do you know her?'

Fatima shook her head. 'I don't know every Muslim in town, Tara, just like you don't know every Christian.'

'Right. Sorry. I guess me asking is like when we were in Greece and people found out we were from Australia—they'd say, "You know my brother, Costa? He lives in Sydney." Have a great holiday, Fatima. I'll talk to you when you get back.'

The gold embroidery on Fatima's headscarf sparkled in the sun as she walked away. Tara turned back to Jade and realised she'd issued the invitation and completely ignored the younger woman.

'If you'd like to come to book group too, Jade, you're very welcome.'

Jade looked at her feet, clearly uncomfortable. With a jolt of understanding and regret, Tara realised Jade considered her old and out of touch, just like the teenagers at work did.

'No pressure, but we could do with a younger woman's perspective,' she added. 'And we're pretty open. There was a lot of talk about sex when we discussed *Anna Karenina*.'

Jade's head shot up, eyes shining. 'I loved that book.'

Tara forced a smile, trying to forget how she'd used Anna as an excuse to put herself first. 'I think I should re-read it and concentrate more on Kitty and Levin. What they lacked in excitement they made up for in commitment and understanding, don't you think?'

'I s'pose,' Jade said half-heartedly.

Tara gave what she hoped was an encouraging smile. 'You don't have to agree with me. That's the fun of book group. Everyone has a different opinion.'

Jade grimaced. 'I'm not sure any bloke's worth the risk of loving.'

Tara saw faint traces of what one day might become hard lines around Jade's mouth. Combined with the antipathy in her voice, they spread a thin ribbon of melancholy through Tara. Jade was too young to be so defeatist.

Tara thought about herself at twenty. She'd been studying tourism at UTS, living in a share house in Annandale and spending her summers working on the ski fields in Whistler. Boyfriends had come and gone without too much heartache, although there'd been one stressful week living with a false positive pregnancy test after a two-week fling with a Canadian snowboarder. His reaction had been all about himself and nothing about Tara. How would her life have panned out if she'd had a baby then? The snowboarder wouldn't have supported her. Would she and Jon even have met? Tara wondered about the father of Jade's little boy.

'Sometimes men let us down,' she said.

'Tell me about it.'

'And as hard as it is to accept, sometimes we let them down too.'

But Jade didn't reply, her attention taken by Milo who was squealing and pointing to the stage. The Boolanga Blokes had joined the Wacky Warblers and were singing 'The Lion Sleeps Tonight'.

Tara smiled at Lachlan McKenzie. She got a kick out of the fact he was an agronomist during the week and a children's entertainer on the weekends. Today his face was intricately painted with lion markings and his costume came complete with a mane and a tail.

He was lying down, pretending to be asleep, then he yawned, sat up and, using his fist, pretended to clean his ears and eyes. The other performers encouraged the children to call out, 'Go to sleep,' and Lachlan did a vaudeville act of wilfully misunderstanding. The glorious sound of children giggling filled the air.

Lachlan jumped to his feet and leaped across the stage as if he was in the cast of *Cats*. The music changed and Milo clapped his hands in delight.

Tara laughed. 'Lachlan grabs any excuse to put on a costume and a show.'

'That's weird, right?' Jade said.

'No, that's finding joy in the little things. I'm a bit late to the party, but I'm learning if we can't do that, we're sunk.'

She picked out Jon's height in the crowd and saw that he and Clementine were following Lachlan's dance moves. Clementine's movements were smooth while Jon's weren't quite so fluid and his kicks were smaller, but they were both grinning. Tara caught the indecision on Flynn's face—that moment of wondering if he was too old for such public foolishness but still wanting to take part. Her heart rolled.

'Embrace the moment, Jade, and dance with your little boy. I'm off to dance with mine while he still tolerates it.'

She elbowed her way through the crowd and hip-bumped Flynn before touching her knee with her elbow and singing along with the crowd.

He grinned, kicked and joined in.

Together they yelled, 'Nutbush City limits!'

Jade didn't know what to make of Tara Hooper. The first time she'd met her at the garden, she'd written her off as yet another cool and standoffish woman with a poker up her arse. With her big flashy engagement ring, family-tree necklace and clothes that definitely didn't come from Kmart or Best & Less, she looked exactly like the ice-queen bitches from mothers' group. But lately, Jade was picking up a different vibe and it wasn't just that Tara's hair was longer than the average yummy mummy or she mostly wore the Hoopers Hardware and Timber uniform of black drill pants and a blue polo shirt. Instead of being all self-involved, she seemed interested in people—like she gave a shit. Maybe all those weeks ago she'd been having a crap day and Jade had judged her too quickly.

Tara was dancing with her family. Jade had seen photos of her and her husband in some of the back issues of *The Standard*. Back in the day, her husband had been an ace cricketer and footballer, but he sure wasn't a dancer. He stepped left instead of right, bumping into Tara, then sagging against her for a moment. She slid her arm around his waist and gave him a look that made Jade feel lonelier than she had in a long time. The next minute they were laughing so hard, as if him being unco was the funniest thing ever.

Dance with your little boy.

Jade felt stupid doing the Nutbush on her own, but she did a version holding Milo between her feet and lifting his legs. He giggled and she laughed too, right up until the moment she turned to tell Helen or Bob and Lach—

Her thoughts veered away fast. She'd been trying not to look at Lachlan on stage, but it was hard not to. He danced like he didn't have a care in the world—like he hadn't even noticed they were no longer hanging out.

He hadn't even come to hear Bob's bombshell about the Tesla— that it had been leased for Craig Dangerfield by a company that was a subsidiary of Sino-Austral Investments. The whole deal looked and stank of bribery. Jade had wanted to post the information onto the Facebook page straight away, but although Helen and Bob couldn't agree on the best way to use the information, they both agreed Facebook wasn't it. Jade wished Lachlan had been there to give another opinion.

She missed their easy months of friendship. The way they rolled their eyes together at the things the boomers said, but at the same time shared a deep affection for Helen and Bob. How Lachlan called Milo 'squirt' and took the time to say hello to him and play with him even though he could only say nine words. How he gazed at her as if she wasn't only pretty but the only person in the room who mattered. How his eyes had darkened just before he'd kissed her.

She bit the inside of her cheek until she tasted the metallic tang of blood. Why had she fallen for romantic bullshit when she knew it didn't exist in real life? And why had Lachlan organised that Harry Potter party date and told her he wanted to take the next step if he was going to get all bent out of shape about Corey in two seconds flat? She wished they'd stayed in the friend zone. At least then he'd still be around, helping to find information about dodgy councillors, and she'd have a mate who was younger than sixty.

When the music finished, the mayor walked up onto the stage wearing his ceremonial robes, the gold of the mayoral medallion glinting like a sun flare and dazzling the crowd. Vivian Leppart followed him, standing off to the side.

'Now wasn't that something?' the mayor said.

Jade was surprised his voice sounded a bit squeaky instead of deep and commanding.

'The shire's thrilled to be working alongside the Chamber of Commerce to bring you this wonderful family day. Yes, community's what we're all about in Boolanga.' A smattering of applause broke out. 'And we're excited about our new Christmas flags designed by local artist Coralie Baxter, who's drawn on her connection to country and given us a local but festive feel. We're thrilled to be supporting the arts in Boolanga and—'

'So that's why our rates have gone up! Bloody waste of money,' someone grumbled.

'Art won't fix the mess that's recycling!' someone else called out.

As murmured rumblings rolled around the crowd, Jade rose on tiptoe trying to see who was responsible. The mayor looked peeved he'd been interrupted. Jade recognised some of the other councillors with their families, shifting uncomfortably.

Vivian Leppart leaned into the microphone. 'I share your concerns, Terry, and we're working hard on finding a solution. Unfortunately, we're not immune to global forces and now China's changed its policy—'

'We shouldn't be depending on China for anything,' someone else said.

'Tell that to the government. They've given away our manufacturing.'

'Bloody yellow peril,' someone called out.

The mayor's shoulders squared and he changed from a bit of a pudgy duffer to statesman. 'Let's remember that Chinese tourists love our mighty Murray. Their enthusiasm for the district means jobs not only in hospitality but in local agriculture, horticulture and viniculture. They're a multi-million-dollar industry that pours much-needed funds into our region.'

He spread out his arms. 'We've got wide open spaces, magnificent night skies and no pollution. These are things Asia can only dream about. Ainslea Park now offers glamping so the visitors can ride, enjoy damper and billy tea and sleep under the stars. Boolanga River Boats have invested in a five-star restoration of a paddle steamer to take thirty guests into less-travelled parts of the river so they can see the wildlife and enjoy sunrises and sunsets. But there's so much more we can do. For our children's future, we must develop new and innovative ways to engage tourists before they're tempted to leave Boolanga, and cross the bridge to spend their money at the resort. The shire's keen to work with local businesses to explore ways of maximising these opportunities.'

'When you say wide open spaces, are you talking about selling Riverfarm?' Jade yelled, ducking slightly behind a tall man in front of her.

The mayor squinted into the sun. 'Not specifically.'

'But you're talking about a resort?'

'Not specifically.'

'What about social housing?'

'What about a community pool?' someone called out.

'Not specifically.'

'God, are they the only two words he knows,' a woman in front of Jade said to her husband. 'Next it'll be jobs and growth.'

The mayor mopped his forehead with a hankie. 'There are no specific plans for Riverfarm. But that said, it seems a shame for the community not to benefit more from its use. I encourage you to formally submit your suggestions for consideration.'

'Like that hasn't been happening for years and they've ignored every one of them,' a man grumbled behind Jade.

'So just to clarify "not specifically",' Jade called out. 'You may or may not have some non-specific, vague and inexact plans to lease or sell Riverfarm to a casino for the Chinese?'

There was an audible intake of breath from the crowd and heads whipped round to see who'd spoken.

The mayor leaned forward, bringing his hand up to act as a sun visor, and knocked over the microphone stand. Reverberations screeched through the speakers as it hit the stage. People pressed their hands to their ears. The mayor reached for the stand, but Vivian got to it first.

'If anyone in my ward has specific or non-specific concerns about Riverfarm or anything else for that matter, my office is always open.'

'As are all the councillors' offices,' the mayor said testily. 'As elected officials, we're here to serve.'

'Indeed we are,' Vivian said smoothly, looking cool and calm while the mayor was tugging at his collar.

'Go, Vivian,' Jade muttered. The woman would more than fill Geoff Rayson's size eleven elastic-sided boots.

'And now it's time to draw the raffle, isn't it, Mr Mayor?'

'Thank you for the reminder, Deputy Mayor.'

Only Geoff Rayson looked far from thankful—thunderous would be more apt. But Vivian snatching a PR win and showing him up was the least of his worries. Helen and Bob had information that could, and hopefully would, take him and half the councillors down.

Jade's phone beeped and she checked it, hoping it was Lachlan. It was Macca. *Thought I should help a mate out and check in on you*

The thoughtful text surprised her. *All good*, she replied.

Yeah? Corey's worried about you

A traitorous warm feeling rolled through her, quieting the question of if he was worried, why didn't he call or text himself? She typed *That's nice* and hit send.

He reckons you must be gagging for it by now. I told him I'd help a slut out

Her lunch lurched to the back of her throat. She swung around but couldn't see him. Hating that her fingers shook, she managed *Fuck you*

That's the plan

Her heart galloped and her phone beeped again. She almost didn't look. When Bob's name rolled across the screen she almost cried with relief.

Helen here. Not to be specific or anything but you were awesome.

Another text followed. *What about journalism? #uniplans*

Jade rolled her eyes, wishing she'd never taught Helen about hashtags.

Just posted a video of the mayor making a monkey of himself on Facebook #askyourcouncilloraboutRiverfarm going off!

Bob here. Just wrestled my phone off Helen. Come to tent. Am driving you and Helen home.

Jade had been grumbling all week about Bob's insistence on driving her everywhere when there'd only been one sighting of the ute all week. But with Macca's texts burning through her brain, she didn't want to be home alone this afternoon. She didn't want to be home alone ever again.

CHAPTER
36

After Tara's conversation with Al, she held her breath waiting for the cricket guillotine to fall. Should she have done what Al asked? Ripped off the metaphorical band-aid and got the job over and done with? Instead, she slept poorly, woke up tired, irritable and stressed, and spent the day stuck close to Jon.

'For God's sake, Tara. I never thought I'd say this, but go for a run.'

A geyser of panic shot through her at the thought of leaving him alone. 'I'm good. Why don't you come to the gym with me?'

Really? You, Jon and Zac in the same space?

'No.' Jon's hand jerked through his hair. 'This isn't about me, T, it's about you. Go to the gym, phone a friend, go and annoy the people at the community garden and take some new photos for the Facebook page. Visit Fiza. Just do something that gives me some breathing space!'

His frustration tore through their weeks of unity and she almost told him why she was so on edge. She wanted so badly to badmouth

Al and their friends for their lack of support, but she stopped herself, desperate to believe Al had stepped up and done the right thing.

As Fiza worked on Sundays, Tara gave Amal a break from the twins and took the kids to the community garden, joining the Hazara women and their children. If they were confused as to why she'd suddenly arrived, they didn't show it. There was something almost therapeutic about shutting out everything and only focusing on weeds. The women had insisted Tara take home some fresh coriander, and even though she had plenty in her own garden she'd accepted it, treasuring the care behind the offering.

On Monday night, she tried not to think about Jon at cricket practice. She prepared the kids' lunchboxes, sent out the book group email and sewed a button on a shirt, before going out onto the deck and watching the light fade from the sky. Her heart clogged her mouth when she heard Jon's car and it took all her resolve not to rush and meet him.

When he found her, he was clearly exhausted, but smiling.

Her heart settled back in her chest. 'How was it?'

'Yeah, good. They're having a family barbecue after the match on Saturday. You know, the usual BYO meat and a salad or dessert to share. Rhianna will text you an S or a D so we don't get all desserts like last year.' He pulled a flyer out of his pocket. 'And a Kris Kringle.'

The low-grade simmer of stress that came with keeping all the balls in the air bubbled harder. 'Kris Kringle? It's still November!'

'Kelly's idea apparently. You know how she likes shiny things. Anyway, we haven't been out much lately and this is an easy way to see everyone.'

Since the brunch, Jon hadn't suggested another gang get-together, saying he caught up with Brent and Al at the cricket club and she didn't need the extra stress of entertaining. Tara knew he assumed she was still having a weekly coffee date with Kelly and Rhianna but she'd stopped going weeks ago.

She pictured sitting on a picnic rug, sipping a fruity sauv blanc and listening to Kelly bitch about Fatima and Rhianna moan about how her mother-in-law insisted on correcting the children's table manners. She knew she'd want to scream at them, 'None of it's life and death. None of it's turned your life on its head.' The only reason she didn't say no was because the invitation meant Jon was still on the team. Al had come through. She'd go to the barbecue just to thank him.

'Sure. Sounds like fun.'

Jon stifled a yawn but he pulled her onto his lap. 'You sitting out here because you want to make out?'

They'd been focusing on kissing and cuddling and hadn't strayed beyond it. The fact he'd just suggested it combined with her jittery relief that he'd avoided another hit to his masculinity. She stroked his face.

'If you play your cards right, you might just get to third base.'

He laughed. 'When Brent, Al and I were teenagers, we spent hours trying to decide exactly what each base included. I suppose today's teenagers just google it and the art of conversation is lost.'

She spider-crawled her fingers up his chest. 'We could write our own playbook.'

'I like the sound of that. I might even try a little blue pill.'

The lover in her wanted to whoop in delight, but she knew he was exhausted. The moment he fell into bed, he'd fall asleep. Then he'd feel like he'd let her down and she didn't want all the positive steps they'd taken to be wiped out due to bad timing.

He's an adult, he has to make his own choices. You're his wife, not his mother.

But she was also his carer and far too often the lines blurred and tangled, leaving her floundering.

He yawned again. 'Or maybe not. Sorry. Bowling practice took it out of me.'

Why were they even thinking about having sex at night? Kids in bed was why. Sometimes, amid the demands of running their own business and keeping staff happy, she forgot they were the bosses.

'You know how the store survives when we have to go to Shepparton for medical appointments and Samantha runs the ship?' she said. 'Well, she's in all day tomorrow. How about we sneak home and try a home run around eleven when your energy levels are high?'

His fingers entwined in her hair. 'You'd give up coffee with the girls for me?'

'They won't even notice.'

'So a blue pill at breakfast?'

'I like the way you think.'

Helen was fast asleep when she became vaguely aware of being hot. As she threw back the doona, she heard Milo calling out. She kicked off a blanket, rolled over, adjusted her pillow and pressed her earplugs back in. Closing her eyes, she willed herself to dive back into blissful sleep.

Did she need to wee? The unwanted thought halted the dive. No. Yes. Maybe. *Damn it!*

With a sigh, she sat up. Milo had stopped crying.

As she padded towards the closed door, it opened and a bleary-eyed Jade stood there holding Helen's phone. 'Can't you hear it?'

Helen pulled out her earplugs. 'What? Is Milo sick?'

'No. It's your phone. It keeps ringing.'

She squinted at the bedside clock. 'But it's 3:17.'

'Believe me, I know.' Jade handed her the phone. 'It's rung four times in the last ten minutes.'

Fear lanced her and she stared at the device as if it was a ticking bomb. 'Only bad news comes before the dawn.'

'It's always darkest before the dawn,' Jade corrected. 'I'll have to tell Bob his quotes are rubbing off on you.'

Helen was about to say, 'Ha ha, very funny,' when the phone rang again. She prickled all over and shoved the phone at Jade. 'You answer it.'

'How?'

'Press the green button.'

'Hello? … Hello? … Who is this?' Jade pressed the red button. 'They hung up. How do I find the call log on this dinosaur?'

Helen fiddled with the phone and a list of numbers came up. Jade called the last one. It rang out.

'It's not the hospital,' Jade said. 'And the police don't ring with bad news—they turn up at your door. Would it be someone from Melbourne? Maybe your ex-husband died and his family wants to tell you?'

Helen shook her head. 'We dropped out of contact years ago. Anyway, they don't have this number. If it was someone I usually call, their name would show up—'

The phone rang again.

'Put it on speaker.' When Helen vacillated, Jade pushed some buttons. 'Okay, talk.'

'Helen Demetriou.'

'You have to stop,' an electronic-sounding male voice said.

'S-stop what?' Her heart was flinging itself wildly against her ribs.

'You know. If you don't stop, we'll stop you. You'd make great fertiliser for that precious garden of yours.'

'Who is this?' But even as she said the words, she knew the question was futile. The line beeped at her. She turned off the phone and threw it onto her bed, wanting to be as far away from it as possible. 'Oh, God.'

Jade grabbed her hand and pulled her into the lounge room. 'Sit. I'll get us a drink.'

Helen heard her rummaging through cupboards and she returned with two generous fingers of whiskey. Helen took a gulp, coughed, then cleared her throat.

'Unless Judith Sainsbury's lost her mind, I don't think it's her. Did you recognise the voice?'

'No. They probably used something to disguise it so we couldn't tell. God, I wish we could afford the internet. I want to know if they've left any threats on the Facebook page.'

Helen's mind struggled to think and she heaved in a long slow breath. 'Wouldn't that make them too easy to trace?'

'You can hide if you use a VPN, and they're probably using a burner phone they bought with a fake ID.'

Helen didn't bother asking for an explanation of the unknown terms—she'd got the gist. 'Have you had any threatening phone calls or texts from someone you don't know? I know I uploaded the video of the mayor, but you asked the questions.'

Jade shook her head. 'Nothing since those horrible texts from Macca.'

'I suppose he's worked out I'm living here.'

'Probably. And if he knows, then maybe Corey knows.' Jade twisted her fingers. 'He probably figures if he freaks you out then you'll move out, and that way—' Her voice caught.

'I'm not going anywhere.' Helen squeezed Jade's shoulder. 'If you don't want anything to do with Corey and Macca, take out an intervention order.'

'Hah! Can you imagine Constable Fiora bothering to listen?'

'I'm happy to support you with a statement. So would Bob. We saw what happened at your birthday.'

'But how do we know it's even them?'

'Men like that think they own you and they get narky when you do things they don't like or can't control. They'd hate me being here, influencing you against them.'

'Yeah, but the mayor hates you. He kicked you out of the cottage and you're still posting on the Facebook page. If he's found out we know about Tucker and Sino-Austral, he'd want to bury you.'

Jade's phone buzzed with a text and they both froze. She slowly picked it up and all the colour drained from her face.

'Who is it?' Helen said.

'I don't know the number.'

'What does it say?'

Jade blinked rapidly. *'Look out the window, bitch.'*

Helen sat up straight. 'We're not going to do that.'

The roar of a diesel engine thundered outside and the room suddenly lit up like daylight. Memories assaulted Helen. She grabbed Jade, pulling her under the table just as the deafening sound of throwdowns exploded under the window.

Milo screamed. Jade moved to go to him.

Helen gripped her upper arm, her fingers digging in deep. 'He's safe. Scared but safe. You might not be.'

The whip and crack of another round of explosions detonated around them and they clung together. Amid the explosions, two shots rang out. It was history repeating itself.

'Corey's got guns,' Jade sobbed, clinging to Helen. 'I'm sorry. I never thought he'd hate me this much.'

The gunfire was the finale—the engine roared and the lights swung away.

Milo's screams rattled the walls and an intense surge of maternal protection flooded Helen. She'd do whatever it took to keep them safe.

They crawled to Jade's room and snuggled Milo between them.

'Do you have your phone?' Helen asked.

Jade shook her head.

'I'll go and get mine.'

'In a minute.'

Helen nodded, understanding how terrifying being alone was, even for a moment. The piercing wail of a siren sounded in the distance and a strangled laugh broke out of her tight throat.

'I've got a funny feeling we won't need to ring the police after all.'

'What's happening now?' Bob asked.

Helen gripped her phone with one hand and used her forefinger of the other to barely lift the sheet off the window architrave and peek outside. Serenity Street was in uproar. The fourth-generation Australians battling poverty, and dependent on a black market of drugs and anything stolen, were clearly unsettled by the presence of the police. The Hazara families, wrenched from sleep by explosions that didn't differentiate from the sounds of war, huddled together, traumatised at being plunged back into a past they'd fought so hard to flee. They were likely questioning their safety and how this could happen in Australia. Helen was asking the same question.

Most of the residents were on the street, demanding answers from Sergeant North, who didn't look as put together as normal. Constable Fiora was rolling out blue and white crime scene tape.

'It's those bloody African kids,' a man said.

Jade rounded on the bloke, whose belly hung heavily over his pyjama pants. 'Like teenagers can afford to drive a ute fully loaded with halogen driving lights.'

'Listen, girlie, it only takes one. If I had a gun, I'd shoot the lot of them.'

'You're a racist pig!'

'That's enough,' Denny said sharply, but Helen couldn't tell if the reprimand was directed at the man or Jade. 'We'll investigate all leads.'

Helen made a mental note to call Fiza and give her a heads-up of a possible visit by the police. She dropped the sheet and returned to her phone call, thankful Bob had picked up despite the hour. She needed his advice.

Sure, that's why you called him.

Fine. She did want his advice but she'd wanted to hear his voice more. Wanted to hold onto his sunny optimism and pretend her world hadn't just spun off its axis yet again.

'Denny North's telling everyone to go home, and if they have information or want to make a statement to go to the police station after eight this morning,' she reported.

'Hopefully someone saw something.'

'This is Serenity Street. Even if they did, they're hardly going to say.' Her stomach churned. 'What am I going to tell the police when they ask if I have any idea who might want to scare me? That it's probably Corey, but it just might be someone the mayor and three dodgy councillors are paying to get me and Jade to shut up? They'll think I'm nuts.'

'Not necessarily. Yesterday *The Standard* led with an article about the mayor's passionate speech promoting tourism in the district.'

'Yes, but it didn't mention a consortium with links to the Chinese. And Granski took a crack at Vivian, saying the infighting about what's best for Riverfarm needs to stop. All that says is there's friction, not corruption. None of it points to us being terrorised.'

'But since family day, you and Jade aren't the only ones asking questions or posting on Facebook.'

'But we started the page. We need to find out if anyone else is getting nasty emails, phone calls and visits in the middle of the night.' She waited for his response but all she heard was a buzzing on the line. 'Bob?'

'I'm thinking.'

'Can you do it faster? Jade's doing a stellar job keeping the police out of the house, but she can't hold them off much longer.'

Bob sighed. 'I know we agreed to hold off until we had concrete proof of at least one more connection with Tuck—hang on, someone's ringing.'

Tinny on-hold music played and then Bob was back. 'Lachie's wheelie bin just got set alight.'

It was suddenly hard to breathe. 'Oh, God. Are you all right?'

'Quiet as the grave here.'

'Can't you find a better expression than that!'

'Sorry. But as worrying as Lachie's melted bin is, unless something happens outside my place in the next ten minutes, I think it's answered your question. I doubt the gang of four's behind it.'

Helen slumped into a chair, her relief at odds with her fear, the combination making her dizzy. She hadn't wanted to tell the police, because whether they believed her or not, they would have to appear to follow up leads and interview the councillors. It would give the gang of four a heads-up they had some incriminating information.

'So, we've got some breathing space to find out who paid for the Rehns' holiday,' she said.

'I'm not so sure. There's a council meeting coming up and I wouldn't trust them not to try to push something through when everyone's busy thinking about Christmas.'

'Vivian's already alert to that.'

'Doesn't mean she can stop it.'

'No, but we can quietly arrange a protest without anyone getting wind of it. Disrupt the meeting so they can't get into the chamber and vote.'

'Sounds like part of a plan anyway,' Bob said. 'Call me when the police leave and I'll come over and pick you all up.'

A stubborn part of Helen—the part that didn't want to depend on anyone—insisted she refuse. 'Only if Jade wants to come.'

'She texted me before you called. We need a face-to-face meeting and my place is the safest. We need to discuss how best to go public.'

'We've been through this. There's no point telling *The Standard*—their bias is clear. And I don't trust the police either. Denny North's default position is to point the finger at the usual suspects and ask questions later. He's already hinted at rounding up the African kids about tonight.'

'You won't get an argument from me about any of that. It's why I think we should make a report to IBAC.'

'What's that?'

'The Independent Broad-based Anti-corruption Commission.'

'I thought that was about police misconduct. As much as I'd like to report Denny North as racist, I don't have any real proof.'

'IBAC's also for corruption in the public sector and that's exactly what we think is happening.'

An image of a courtroom loomed large in her head. 'Can Mr and Mrs Average Citizen make a report?'

'According to IBAC's website we can. And apparently I missed the announcement that we got married. Tell me I've still got the honeymoon to look forward to.'

She fought a reluctant smile. 'You'd have no idea what to do if I said yes.'

'I think you've got that the wrong way around, Helen. I'm the one who'd know exactly what to do.'

She cut the call, unsettled by Bob being one hundred per cent correct.

CHAPTER
37

Rafts of excitement and anticipation tingled inside Tara from the moment Jon winked at her during the chaos of breakfast and she saw him pop a blue pill into his mouth along with his other medications. Ian was taking the children to school so they could both get to work early and clear the important things before they left at eleven. On the drive into town, they kept breaking into laughter.

Jon squeezed her thigh. 'I feel as nervous and excited as I did on our first date.'

'I don't remember you being nervous. You walked into the bar full of football-star swagger.'

He turned into the car park. 'Of course I was nervous. You were unimpressed by football. What the—'

The charity bin in the car park had been upended and a mess of clothes and sundry donations was scattered across the concrete.

Jon, stressed and angry, fumbled with his seatbelt latch and swore again. Tara released it and he took a moment to get his uncooperative legs out of the car.

Red, green and blue paint was sprayed across the front of the store in familiar tags they'd seen around town for months. Sometimes the tags looked phallic, sometimes not, but the letters *SUC* were always incorporated inside them.

'If they'd broken in, we'd have got a phone call from the security company,' Tara said. 'Let's take it as a win.'

Jon grunted, stepped over the rubbish and opened up the store. Everything looked untouched until they reached the doors that separated the main area from the garden section. Pots lay on their sides, their contents dumped and dying. Garden gnomes wore condoms on their hats and one of the birdbaths had something in it that looked suspiciously like excrement. But it was the pungent odour of blood and bone drifting into the store from the slashed fertiliser bags that made them gag.

'How did they get in?' Tara asked.

They looked up simultaneously. There was a clear patch of blue at the edge of the large expanse of green shade cloth that joined the wall and the ceiling.

'If they dropped in from that height, they should be lying on the floor with broken legs,' Jon said.

'They must have climbed down using that.' Tara pointed to a ladder that didn't belong in the section.

'But why?'

'No cameras? No alarm?'

'So they risked injuring themselves to wreck the place? It doesn't make sense.'

'You ring the police,' Tara said. 'I'll take photos.'

When she returned to the office, all the lightness and enthusiasm that had circled Jon at breakfast had been replaced by a mix of frustration and resignation. He was staring at the blank CCTV as if willing it to show him something.

Bastards! Their planned morning tryst was dead in the water.

'Are the police on their way?' she asked. 'We can't open until we've cleared the rubbish and they'll want to see it before we do.'

'Apparently, some lunatic was charging around town last night with throwdowns and a gun and setting bins on fire so we're low on their list of priorities. North promised someone before three. We'll clean up the front or we won't get any customers, but keep the garden section closed.'

'I'll text the casuals to come in after school. They can scrub off the graffiti and get started on the garden clean-up.'

'Oh, my God!' Samantha appeared in the doorway holding a tissue over her mouth and nose. 'What's that smell?'

'Blood and bone,' Tara said.

The other staff arrived, all recoiling at the stench.

'Surely, we're not opening? No one will want to come into the store.'

'Doesn't worry me. I'm on timber today.'

'We can't work under these conditions.'

The saleyards smelled worse, but Tara knew that comment wouldn't win her any support. 'We've got masks you and the customers can wear, and I'll get some lavender oil to put on them as well. We'll set up fans to try to limit the smell to one area, and we'll also provide morning tea and lunch from the bakery. Of course, if you wish to take an annual leave day or a day without pay, you can, but I'm hoping you'll work with us and help us trade through this inconvenience. It would be a shame to let whoever did this see us close for the day.'

'I blame the refugees and Denny North. Town's gone to the dogs since both arrived,' Chris Mancini said.

'Yeah. Funny how this happened a few weeks after Amal started working here,' Debbie Sloane added. 'Bet you regret that now.'

Tara opened her mouth, but closed it as Jon's hand rested on her shoulder.

'Tara and I have no reason to suspect Amal,' he said. 'Just like we have no reason to suspect any of our valued team members, old or new. But if anyone heard or saw something last night when they were out walking the dog, please let us know.'

'It was probably the same thugs who terrorised Serenity Street,' Samantha said. 'According to *The Standard*'s Facebook page, it sounded like a warzone. It's all very well to offer people a new life but they have to live by our rules.'

'No one is disputing living by the rules. We all have to do that,' Tara said. 'I doubt anyone who's lived in a warzone would want to recreate it.'

The long blast of a horn—the morning's timber delivery—broke up the chatter and everyone got to work.

Tara thought it might be pushing the staff a bit far by asking them to clear up the rubbish so she and Jon donned gloves and returned to the entrance. Bagging and mopping took longer than expected as a lot of rubberneckers wanted to discuss the night's events.

'Isn't that your personal trainer?' Jon said.

Tara looked up from dropping rubbish into a bag. Zac was jogging straight towards them, his tanned skin stretched over bulging muscles and slick with sweat.

Her heart kicked up—nothing to do with Zac and everything to do with Jon. A cocktail of memories was playing across Jon's face—admiration and pride stirred with sorrow. She knew Zac was reminding him of himself at the same age. He'd been just as fit if not quite as buff.

'Yes, that's Zac. I thought you met him at the Chamber of Commerce dinner?'

'Yeah, but he was wearing clothes. Should I be worried?'

Not any more. 'Absolutely.'

'Good to know.' He didn't wait for Tara to introduce them, but greeted Zac with a hearty, 'G'day. Zac, isn't it?'

Zac pulled an earbud out of his ear and wiped his hand on his shorts before extending it to Jon. 'G'day, Jon. Hi, Tara. What happened here?'

They gave him the quick version and he made all the appropriate commiserations.

'I can see why you cancelled on me this morning,' Zac said to Tara.

Jon grinned at her, then laughed. 'Yep, that was the reason.'

Tara's cheeks burned from embarrassment that Jon was joking about sex in front of Zac while being delighted he had. Much of the time he managed to laugh when his tremors caused problems, but he was still raw around the issues affecting their sex life.

Zac glanced between them. 'Am I missing something?'

'Sorry, mate. Didn't mean to be rude,' Jon said. 'Bit of a private joke.'

'Cool.' Zac nodded as if this sort of thing happened to him all the time. 'My mother reckons laughing together's the key to staying together.'

'Wise woman,' Tara managed.

'Yeah. Mum's pretty woke.' Zac shifted his weight. 'I'm starting a kickboxing class, Jon. Wondered if you might be interested?'

Surprise flashed across Jon's face at the unexpected invitation. 'Thanks, but it's not really my thing. I prefer team sports.'

'Tara said.' Zac rubbed his jaw, clearly contemplating what to say next. 'Did you know kickboxing's been proven to help with balance, tremors and stiffness?'

'You and Tara talk about me when you run, do you?'

'Nah. She runs too fast for any conversation.' Zac's grin faded. 'Tara's a mate and I wanted to help is all. She told me you wouldn't be interested, but I thought it was worth a shot. If you change your mind, call me. Or just drop by the gym.' He gave a nod, pushed the earbud back into his ear and took off.

Tara opened her mouth to reassure Jon that she didn't spend all her time with Zac talking about him when he said, 'Nice bloke.'

'Yeah. Underneath all that body sculpting there's a lovely kind-hearted guy.'

Tara was heaving the last bag into the rubbish skip when she saw Gerry crossing the car park.

'You're still a bit jittery after the shock, so to avoid spilled coffee I'll go to the bakery,' she told Jon.

He rolled his eyes. 'Commandeering my condition for your own nefarious means, are we?'

'When it comes to Gerry, needs must. Don't let him talk you into inviting him to Thursday roast. He'll want Ian to drink and your dad's been so good lately. I don't need them too drunk to play Uno and have the kids pestering us to watch something.'

'I know he's a bugger, T, but he's lonely.'

Tara hesitated, feeling yet again like she was looking at herself from a distance. It had been happening on and off since she'd gambled their happiness on her own needs. Since she'd skated to the point where the ice was so thin it had broken underneath her and she'd tumbled, only to have Zac steady her. Tara understood loneliness. She'd lived it for a large part of the year and, despite her and Jon working hard to be a team again, she was still lonely. She missed Shannon.

Gerry's not your problem. Only she knew exactly what it felt like to be lost and wandering through life.

Trying to muster grace, she said, 'Say he's welcome, but his drinking isn't? That way he can decide.'

Jon nodded and gave her a rueful look. 'Sorry about our morning matinee.'

'It's not your fault.'

'The fact we have to schedule sex is.'

An ache stirred, disrupting the earlier feel-good moment. It lifted the mute from her anger at the disease that had invaded their lives and the many ways it demeaned him.

'Again, *not* your fault. You didn't ask to get Parkinson's.'

'Yeah, but when I come to dinner or to bed, I can't leave the Parkinson's behind, can I?'

'You think I'm asking too much of Gerry?'

'I don't know. It just got me thinking. We don't invite him over because when he drinks he gets loud and obnoxious and we're embarrassed for him. Sometimes I'm a danger to china and carpet. It embarrasses me but it also embarrasses other people. I've seen it on their faces.'

'If you're talking about that rude waitress at the resort, she's not worth worrying about.' Tara hated that he'd noticed the ignorant woman and she laid her head on his chest, welcoming the vibrations of his heartbeat.

He stroked her hair. 'So instead of sex for morning tea, I guess we're forced to indulge in bakery goodness.'

'I quite fancy a long slow lick of a chocolate éclair.' She got a delicious tingle at the flicker in his eyes and walked away laughing.

CHAPTER
38

After Tara had fought through the thick plastic strips in the bakery's doorway, she was greeted by Nancy, the baker's wife. 'Oh, my God, Tara. You poor things! We heard you got attacked.'

Tara tried not to sigh at the overblown drama. 'The store got rubbish-bombed and graffitied, but no one was attacked.'

'But it's still an attack.' Nancy leaned across the counter. 'I'm petrified. I mean, this sort of thing doesn't happen in Boolanga.'

Tara was getting sick of this response too. 'This is the fifth time the store's been damaged this year. How many times has the bakery been broken into? Graffitied?'

'Thankfully none, but that doesn't mean it won't happen. We have to be vigilant and look out for each other. I'm only letting two of those African kids into the store at a time and all bags have to be left outside. Now, what can I get you?'

Tara knew she should challenge Nancy's statement, but all she wanted to do was get out of the bakery as soon as possible. She reeled off a list of coffees and pastries, then ordered the sandwiches and a selection of mini quiches and sausage rolls for lunch. She handed over her credit card.

As she stepped back from the counter, she heard someone call her name. She turned and her stomach sank. *Damn.* It was Wednesday. Rhianna and Kelly were sitting at the table she and Shannon had shared with them for years.

'Hi,' Tara said.

'Hi. Brent said you guys had another break-in last night,' Rhianna said.

'So we didn't expect to see you today,' Kelly added and gave her a tight smile. 'Not that we've seen much of you lately.'

Tara bit back a rising 'Sorry'. Instead, she said, 'It's all a bit of a mess. The staff are working under difficult conditions so I'm grabbing them food and coffee.'

'Sit while you wait.' Rhianna kicked out a chair.

'Thanks.' As Tara sat, she remembered the cricket barbecue. 'Do you want me to bring a salad or a dessert on Saturday?'

'What's easier for you?'

'A salad.' She relaxed, giving Rhianna an appreciative smile at her thoughtfulness. 'Thanks. The veggie patch is going gangbusters at the moment.'

'Ours isn't. What's your secret?'

'Worm castings.' Rhianna gave her a blank look. 'Worm poo. I heard about it at the community garden.'

Kelly snorted. 'You taking advice from Muslim peasants now?'

Tara tensed. 'Last time I looked, Lachlan McKenzie wasn't Muslim.'

'But Fatima is.' Kelly glared at her. 'I got your email. What's this shit about inviting her to book group?'

Tara tried not to flinch. 'She and I had a really interesting conversation on the weekend about feminism and religion.'

'So you're ignoring us and socialising with her now?' Kelly's belligerent words were laced with hurt.

'I'm not doing either of those things. I worked on Saturday and ran into Fatima,' Tara said wearily. 'Didn't Al tell you I saw him at the store?'

'No. Oh! Did he order the teak two-seater for the garden for Christmas?' Kelly clapped her hands over her ears. 'No, wait. Don't tell me. I want it to be a surprise.'

'My lips are sealed.' Tara wished the coffees would hurry up.

'Tara, we're worried about you,' Rhianna said, her expression its usual calm.

A hundred thoughts flitted in Tara's mind, from 'Thank you' to 'I didn't know'.

'Yes,' Kelly said. 'We were just discussing it when you walked in. You've changed.'

'No, I haven't.'

'Yes, you have! First you went all early midlife crisis on us training for a marathon, but since Jon got sick ...'

Unspoken words hung between them.

Rhianna sighed. 'We're trying hard to be there for you and Jon, but you're not making it easy.'

Incredulity pummelled Tara. 'I'm not making it easy?'

Kelly nodded. 'Every time we reach out, you block us.'

Reach out? Her mind floundered, trying to find an example of them reaching out. 'When did I block you?'

'I've been asking on WhatsApp when we're all getting together, but you ignore me. You haven't even set up an event.'

'You could have done that.'

'I'm hardly going to invite myself to your house, am I?'

It hasn't stopped you before.

Tara spoke slowly to keep her voice even. 'I meant you could have invited us over to your place—'

'You know the house isn't finished.'

The Kvant house had been in a state of permanent renovation for six years. 'The weatherboards don't have to be freshly painted for a barbecue!'

'There's no need to lash out at Kelly,' Rhianna said. 'This is a perfect example of what we're talking about.'

'And we always come to your place,' Kelly said. 'We even did brunch when it wasn't convenient.'

'I'm working.'

'We're all working,' Rhianna said. 'And to be fair, Kelly's been working more hours than you for years.'

Tara lurched between fury and incomprehension. 'Your husbands don't have a chronic illness that's changed your lives forever. You're not constantly worried their medication is going to make them binge eat or binge shop or worse. You're not doing the bulk of the cooking because sharp knives and hot pans need a steady hand. And you don't have to plan your day around the hours their energy levels are at their peak and deal with the times they can't do things everyone takes for granted.'

'Are you sure you're not exaggerating?' Rhianna tapped her spoon on the edge of her cup. 'Jon says the medication helps. He makes it sound like it's no big deal.'

And Tara both understood and hated why he did that. 'You've known him longer than me, so you know his pride is both a blessing and a curse. If you always ask him how he is in a public place, he'll always tell you he's fine, even when it's obvious he's not.'

'Well, that's not helpful,' Kelly said. 'Especially as we haven't had any private get-togethers lately. If you'd been honest with us, we'd have known you needed help. We're not mind-readers.'

Zac's voice drifted into Tara's head. *Been doing a bit of reading.* What did it say when her millennial personal trainer took the time to try to understand the impact of Parkinson's, but Jon's lifelong friends hadn't? A flare went off behind her eyes, turning everything vermilion.

'Al and Brent know Jon's coordination is unreliable,' she said. 'And that day at brunch, I told you sometimes I have to tie his laces.'

Two bright pink spots flared on Kelly's cheeks, then her nostrils flared. 'And I've told you how I feel about Fatima, but that didn't stop you inviting her to talk at book group about something none of us want to know anything about!'

'What's that got to do with you supporting me?'

Heads turned, interest clear on faces, but Tara was beyond caring. Her brain hurt from trying to fathom Rhianna's and Kelly's thought processes.

'Look, Tara, we're sorry Jon's got Parkinson's, we really are, but you're not exactly helping yourself,' Rhianna said. 'And flying off the handle at your friends doesn't help either. You're obviously not coping so the best thing for you is to go and see Stephen Illingworth. You need to get a mental health plan.'

Tara lurched to her feet. 'What I *need* are friends who can think beyond themselves. Friends who don't wait to be asked for help but actually do practical things like dropping off a meal or inviting my kids for a sleepover or a play date.'

'Tara,' Nancy called. 'Your order's ready.'

With hands shaking worse than Jon's, Tara stacked the coffee carriers and left the now silent café without looking back.

When she arrived at the store, her heart rate had slowed but she desperately wanted to strap on her running shoes and pound out ten kays.

Instead, she had to host morning tea and check the staff were coping. Jon didn't join the first tea shift and she hoped that was because the police had arrived.

Her phone rang as the second tea shift ended.

'Tara, Geoff Rayson. I've got good news about the cottage.'

'Wow, that was faster than I expected.'

'Well, with Christmas only six weeks away, if we don't act now nothing will happen until February. I'm emailing you all the details and as soon as you have them, give Ryan Tippett in Engineering a call to set up the move.'

Jon walked in just as she hung up. 'Guess what? That was—' But her excitement faded. He was pale under his tan and his big frame was hunched over as if he'd just been winded by a tackle. She closed the door. 'What's wrong? What's happened? Is it Ian? The kids?'

'Tara, breathe. Everyone's fine.'

'Then why do you look like your best friend just died?'

'I feel like part of me just died.' A long sigh rattled out of him. 'Al just called about Saturday.'

The thought of having to see Kelly and Rhianna at the cricket barbecue pumped nausea through her. 'Actually, I just saw Kell—'

'They're replacing me with Paul Simpson. I won't be playing.'

The nausea churned harder. 'Bastards!'

He shook his head. 'I've been expecting it. Hell, when I was captain, I changed the team around. The point is to win. I just didn't think they'd shaft me completely.'

'So you're not even twelfth man?'

He shook his head and she closed her eyes as the fallout of the decision battered her. Football and cricket were a huge part of Jon's life and this was yet another loss—a mighty one.

'What about coaching?' she said. 'Going on the committee? They owe you that. And if they think they're getting money from us next year—'

'I know you're trying to help, T, but I'm not up to problem-solving yet. I'm too raw.'

'Sorry.' She squeezed his hands. 'It's just I was already angry at Rhianna and Kelly. They gave me a serve at the bakery for letting them down.'

'How?'

'By stopping going to coffee. By not inviting them over. By suggesting Fatima talk at book group.' He crooked one brow. 'Yeah, okay, that one was deliberately baiting Kelly. But I'm so furious with them. Lorraine said I needed to give them time to adjust, that they're grieving in their own way for how things have changed. But compared to how our lives have changed, theirs have barely altered. I can't support them through this as well as you and the kids and work—'

'And you don't have to,' he said calmly.

She sought his gaze. 'Do you think we've only been good-time friends? If this had happened to them, would we be as self-obsessed and clueless?'

'Who knows. I'd like to think that even if we didn't fully understand, we'd have at least invited them over.'

'That's hardly a change in behaviour. You invite everyone over.'

A faint smile tugged at his lips. 'True, but we've done other stuff for them. When Kelly had Hudson you took over a few meals and ended up cleaning their kitchen and bathroom.'

'Why do you remember that?'

'Because Al thanked me for sending around a tiler to regrout the shower as a baby present.'

She laughed. 'I'd forgotten that. I think because Tingledale has the space and lends itself to entertaining, we became the social glue for the group without realising.'

He shrugged. 'All I know is that every time I catch up with Brent and Al for a drink, I miss Chris.'

'I think our best friends went to New York and left us with pale imitations.'

'I think you're right.'

'So what do we do about Saturday? If we don't go they'll call us bad sports, and if we do go, we'll have to endure them either telling us how we've failed them or have them carry on as if nothing's changed when everything has.'

'I reckon by Saturday, there's a pretty big chance one of the kids will be conveniently sick.'

She smiled. 'Well, there's a lot of gastro going around. Poor Monique had all three kids home with it.'

'There you go. Problem solved.' He kissed her. 'Let's talk about something else. What were you telling me when I walked in?'

It took her a moment to remember, then she clapped. 'You won't have time for cricket anyway. We got the cottage!'

His face brightened. 'That's awesome.'

A knock sounded on the door and it opened. 'Police are here,' Samantha said.

Sergeant North stood in the garden section surveying the damage. 'The fact we've got the same tagging and general trashing says it's the teenagers again. I hear you've employed the Atallah boy. You might think you're helping, but you're just making things harder for yourselves.'

'We were being broken into before we employed Amal,' Tara said.

'But as you've pointed out, never this way. Does Amal work in this part of the store?'

At training, Amal had asked if he could work in the garden section. Given Darcy and Sabrina didn't know a sprinkler from a shovel or a vegetable from a vinca seedling, Tara had thought it a great idea. Three customers had sought her out to tell her how helpful he'd been. She'd even sent him home with a small gardenia they couldn't sell, saying he had time to nurture it into a healthy plant for Fiza for Christmas. He'd smiled politely and she'd realised her faux pas—of course the Atallahs didn't celebrate Christmas.

Now Tara swallowed, unwilling to answer the question—not just because Denny North would give her an I-told-you-so look, but because she didn't want doubts eroding her new faith in the young man they'd trusted. 'He does but—'

'And is that ladder usually there?'

'No.'

'Have you ever seen it there before?'

She glanced at Jon who shook his head. 'No.'

'I think we can safely rule out teleporting, although there might have been some black magic involved,' Denny said.

'Amal's our best casual,' Jon said.

'And I know him,' Denny said. 'Butter wouldn't melt in his mouth, but insolence runs just under the surface. There's more than one way of being a shit and there's a pattern. Every time something like this happens he's never far away. The smart ones are the ones to watch.'

'There's nothing smart or intelligent about trashing the garden centre and sticking condoms on gnomes,' Tara said.

'I didn't say his mates were smart. I suggest you check your stock levels of previously stolen goods along with things like knives and machetes.'

'Why?'

'Look around, Tara. It would be easy to smuggle stock out here and stash it in those big pots, ready to go out and over the wall.'

'But we traded on Monday. Surely someone would have noticed if things were hidden.'

'Sell a lot of those giant glazed pots every day, do you?'

Jon swore. 'We'll do a stocktake.'

Faith fought disbelief. 'But if we find missing items, there's still no proof it's Amal.'

'I get that you want to believe that giving Amal a job is insurance he won't steal from you, but I'm the police officer. If goods are missing from the store, it's strong proof it's an inside job.' Denny put on his cap. 'Give me a call when you know.'

As soon as he'd left, Jon turned to her, his face grim. 'We need to keep a lid on this. I'm not asking the staff to check the stock. We have to do it.'

'I don't want to look.'

'Neither do I.'

The eddies of doubt swirled faster. 'He wouldn't have done it. Surely he wouldn't have done it. Not after we gave him a chance.'

'Saying it over and over won't change a thing.'

Morning tea rose to the back of her throat. 'Oh, God. You think he did it.'

'I think we're going to find things missing, otherwise there's no reason for anyone to break into the garden section.'

'I can't believe I woke up so happy and excited this morning.'

A long sigh rumbled out of him. 'Come on. Let's get this over and done with.'

They checked the spray paint first. Six cans were missing. Tara's trust shattered, falling to dust around her feet on the concrete floor.

Her phone rang and she checked the caller ID. Fiza.

My son has never, would never, steal anything from your shop.

Tara didn't know if she wanted to rage or cry. After everything Fiza had been through, now she had to break her heart all over again.

CHAPTER
39

Jade's fingers clicked Duplo blocks together but her mind wasn't on the big red barn; it kept flashing back to Serenity Street. To the terrifying moments under the table. Her heart rate picked up again, just as it had been doing on and off all day.

'Moo,' Milo said. Since Bob had unearthed the box of Duplo from the shed and spilled the contents onto the sunroom floor, he'd been clutching the cow as if it was sacred.

'Cows say moo and sheep say baa.' Jade bounced the sheep up his leg, thankful for his giggles.

She hated that he'd been alone and scared in his cot during those long and petrifying minutes. Hated that Corey had deliberately instilled fear in the son he'd told her over and over she had to protect. Hated her own stupidity of clinging to empty words when actions spoke the truth.

She thought of Lachlan. His actions and his words were unambiguous. Right now he was furious with her over something she couldn't control and she was mad right back at him. She was sick of men blaming her not only when she hadn't done anything wrong but when she was trying to do the right thing.

The police had interviewed her and for the first time Constable Fiora had been sympathetic, promising he'd call as soon as he had any news. She and Helen had applied for personal safety intervention orders against Corey and Macca and the magistrate had granted an interim order, although it hardly made Jade feel safer.

Since they'd arrived at Bob's, he and Helen had been on the computer making their IBAC report. Jade had wanted to help, but Milo was clingy and every time she tried to write something, she heard those bloody throwdowns in her head.

'Go and cuddle with Milo and Daisy,' Helen had suggested after Jade had scrunched up paper for the third time. 'It'll make you feel better.'

Jade had wondered if anything could do that. 'How can you think straight?'

'Right now I'm running on anger and adrenaline, but I'll reach a point when I fall in a heap. Hopefully by then you'll be feeling better and we can tag team.'

Bob set up a porta cot in one of his spare bedrooms and suggested Jade try to nap too. But whenever she lay down her brain sped up, so she'd retreated to the sunroom. She and Milo had snuggled up on the couch with Daisy at their feet, watching some old show on YouTube Bob had recommended called *Little Bear*. Milo loved it and it was so slow and comforting, it had sent them both to sleep for an hour.

Just as Jade snapped on the barn's yellow roof, Helen and Bob walked in, each carrying a tray.

'Bought and brought your favourite,' Bob said, indicating the pink-iced matchstick.

'Why are you being so nice when this is all my fault?' Jade savagely swiped at unwanted tears.

'Being nice is my superpower, right, Helen?'

Helen rolled her eyes. 'It's definitely not being humble.'

Bob passed Jade the tissue box. 'None of this is your fault. You're not responsible for Corey's behaviour.'

'But I chose to be his girlfriend. I thought if I loved him better than his mum, I could change him.'

'Sadly, we can't change anyone. It's a hard lesson we all learn at some point.' Helen passed her a mug. 'Here, drink your tea.'

'Thanks.' Odd how a warm drink soothed. 'I thought the coppers would have rung by now.'

'First they have to find them and if Macca and Corey share a brain, they'll be in New South Wales. That means working with their police force. When the police find them, they have to apply for an extradition order, which slows things down. It won't be any time soon.'

Jade's fingers tightened on the mug. 'So we're going home?'

'Not without getting the locks changed.'

'I can't afford that! Can you?' Panic skittered. 'And we can't do it without asking the real estate agent. I'm already on a warning because I've been late with the rent a few times. This will be their excuse to kick me out.'

'You don't have to make any fast decisions,' Bob said. 'There's room here for as long as you need it.'

Relief streaked through her and she tried really hard to say thank you, but the stupid tears came back. She shoved a piece of matchstick in her mouth.

The back door slammed.

Jade gasped, then coughed violently on pastry. She gulped tea.

'I thought you'd locked it?' Helen's voice wavered.

'I did,' Bob said.

'Uncle Bob?' Lachlan's voice called from the kitchen.

They all slumped.

Bob managed, 'Sunroom,' and Lachlan appeared in his socked feet, wearing grimy work gear. 'You gave us a hell of a fright, Lachie! Why didn't you ring the bell?' Bob demanded.

'Because I've got a key ...' He glanced around the room and suddenly his ears boiled red. 'Sorry. I didn't mean to scare you. I should have thought.'

Milo broke the taut silence. 'Moo.' He offered Lachlan his precious cow.

'Thanks, squirt.' Lachlan accepted it before sitting down next to Jade. 'How are you?'

'Rattled,' Helen said.

'How about you and I go into the kitchen and give Milo something to eat?' Bob said to Helen. He retrieved the cow, caught Helen gently by the elbow and steered her out of the room.

Jade's eyes were still streaming from her coughing fit and her wildly seesawing emotions. She wiped her eyes and sucked in a long steadying breath, and immediately coughed again. 'Oh, my God! You reek!'

'Oh hell.' Lachlan pulled off his socks and deposited them outside the room before sniffing his feet and returning to the couch. 'Sorry. I should have gone home and had a shower first, but I wanted to see you. I would have come earlier, but I got a late start because of the police interview and—shit. Sorry. None of it matters. How are you?'

'Weird. I keep crying.'

'That's pretty normal after a big fright. Do you need to see a doctor?'

'No. I just want the police to catch the bastards.' She risked looking at him. There was no sign of the tight anger of a week earlier, just sympathy etched around his eyes. Her resentment towards him softened. 'I'm really sorry they involved you.'

'I can get a new bin.'

'You know what I mean. It's a warning to stay away from me.' She twisted the tissue in her fingers. 'Maybe you were right. Maybe if I'd sent a text instead, this wouldn't have happened.'

Lachlan winced. 'I know I said you should have told him, but I didn't get it. I do now. Sorry. No matter how you did it, I think he'd have done something. I can't stop thinking that if you'd broken up with him in person, he'd probably have hurt you.'

'Six months ago I would have told you he wouldn't hurt me,' she said, 'even though he shook me once when Milo was six weeks old. I was so desperate to be a family that every time he did something that didn't fit the story I needed to believe, I made up excuses for him. I didn't want to believe the signs that he only cares for himself. Or that you and Bob, and now even Helen, take more notice of Milo than he does. Even when you said you wanted to date, I tricked myself into thinking that Corey could still be part of Milo's life. But last night changed everything. Corey doesn't care about Milo and me. But he doesn't want anyone else to care about us either.' She pressed her lips together, trying not to cry. 'It makes me too difficult to be around.'

He slid his hands into hers. 'No, it doesn't.'

'You say that now, but next time it won't just be setting your bin on fire.'

'The police will catch them before anything else happens. Besides, I have a personal protection order.'

A hysterical laugh burst out of her. 'So do I, but it means squat. People like Corey don't live by the rules. He'll be holed up somewhere and then, when we least expect it, he'll ride in one night and do some real damage. I don't want you or Helen or Bob to get hurt.'

'You have the right to live the way you want to live, Jade.'

'Yeah.' But theory bore little resemblance to her reality. 'Did you honestly expect that dating me would be this hard?'

The dart of something in his eyes confirmed the answer she already knew.

Tara and Jon sat opposite Fiza and Amal at the Tingledale kitchen table. When Fiza had called and Tara had told her Amal was a suspect, there had been a long silence on the line.

'I telephoned you to say I was sorry to learn about the break-in. I did not telephone you to accuse my son!'

The words had slammed down the line, their ferocity jostling Tara. 'I'm sorry, Fiza. We're heartsick, but the evidence points towards him.'

'I will get Amal from school. We will come and talk to you.'

'I don't think that's—'

'Please, Tara. I beg you. Talk to him before you involve the police.'

'I'm not happy about it,' Jon had said when Tara had raised it. 'It's best to leave everything to the police.'

But Jon hadn't heard first-hand about the night Fiza's and Amal's lives had changed forever. He hadn't felt the grief for a dead husband and a lost way of life. Nor had he seen the flash of a lioness in Fiza's eyes when she spoke of still needing to fight for her child even though they were twelve thousand kilometres from the warzone they'd fled. And then there was the uncomfortable brick in Tara's belly that the police were determined to pin something on Amal. She couldn't work out if it was because Amal was involved with a group of boys or if there was racism at play.

What would you do to protect your family? Fiza's lilting question wouldn't leave her. Tara wasn't contending with a war or racism, but she understood that bone-deep protective urge that went hand in hand with love and motherhood. Recognised it in Fiza. Understood it was the reason she'd pushed so hard to convince Jon to take the meeting.

'It doesn't mean I'm not furious with Amal for breaking our trust,' she'd explained. 'I want to shake him for causing his mother more anguish and pain after they've been through so much and she's worked so hard to give him a safe life full of opportunities.'

'You do realise just because Fiza said he didn't do it isn't proof, right?' Jon said.

'Yes.'

'And I'm still calling Denny North.'

'*After* we've spoken to Amal.'

Jon grumbled but he'd agreed to the delay. Now he was showing Amal photos of the graffiti, the rubbish and the garden section. 'So what do you know about this, Amal?'

His school uniform made the boy look younger than his years. 'I didn't do it. I wouldn't ever do something like this. Especially not to you and Mrs Hooper.'

Some of Tara's hard line wavered at his sincerity, but not Jon's. 'You specifically asked Tara to work in the garden section.'

'Because I love plants. Not because I want to destroy them!'

'He was home last night,' Fiza said. 'He has been home every night since we moved here.'

'Unless you check him every hour, you have no idea if he snuck out of bed and into town or not,' Jon said.

'We live ten kilometres out of town,' Amal said. 'How would I even get there?'

Jon folded his arms. 'I can think of many ways. Steal your mother's car. Get picked up by one of your mates. You tell me.'

'He did not drive my car. I put petrol in yesterday and I pressed the ...' Fiza's hands moved as she searched for a word, ' ... the number again. They were the same.'

'I'm telling the truth. I didn't go into town.' A hint of antagonism threaded through Amal's words. 'The last time I was at the store was when I watered the plants.'

'Amal, I want to believe you,' Tara said. 'You're polite, you work hard, you're always smiling and cheerful. I appreciate all those qualities.'

Gratitude crossed his face. 'Thank you, Mrs Hooper.'

'You're welcome.' She waited a beat. 'Tell me, why would boys break into the garden section last night, not the store?'

His pupils dilated fast. He looked down, staring determinedly at his hands.

'Amal?'

'I don't know.'

But the quietly spoken words didn't carry the same weighted conviction of his previous denials. For the first time he looked frightened. It niggled Tara. They hadn't told him or Fiza about the missing spray cans, the pocket knives or the jobsite radio, only the damaged plants and mess. If Amal had been lying cheerfully to their faces about his innocence up to now, the question shouldn't have thrown him.

'Amal, if you know something you need to tell us.'

He kept his head down. 'You won't believe me.'

Fiza said something to Amal in Arabic, then looked at Tara. 'I am sorry. When I am stressed, I lose English words. I beg him to tell you what he knows.'

Amal looked up then, straight at Jon, his gaze challenging. 'Aussie blokes don't dob on their mates.'

Jon winced and pressed two fingers between his eyes as if he'd just been pierced by an arrow. When he removed them, his arm trembled and he placed one hand over the other.

'What is dob?' Fiza asked.

'I know a bit about being a mate, Amal,' Jon said. 'I've got one mate who has my back no matter what. Then there are some blokes I thought were mates, but when I got Parkinson's and I needed their understanding, they couldn't manage it. You did a better job of it the day I fell, and when we played backyard cricket and some of my bowls went wide.'

A tug of emotions played out on the boy's face but he remained silent.

Jon continued. 'I want you to ask yourself this. Is someone a mate if they let you get convicted of a crime you didn't do? Are they a mate if they expect you to stay quiet to protect their illegal activities and let you lose your chance to become a doctor? I can tell you that a true-blue mate would never ask you to do those things.'

'But you don't know what it's like,' Amal muttered.

'Then please explain it to me. I want to know.'

Amal's fingers fiddled with some loose rattan on a placemat. 'They call us African. They say we're all the same, but there's no such thing as African. What do I share with a boy from Ghana? They speak English. In Sudan we speak Arabic. Ghana is Christian, Sudan is Muslim. Some food's the same but a lot's different. It's like saying Australians and the French are the same!

'If I say I'm Sudanese, they tell me I'm in Australia now. But when I say I'm Aussie, they say I'm African. I have a certificate that says I'm Australian! They say they're Australian because they were

born here, like they made it happen. Every day at school I have to
prove I'm an Aussie. Show them that I deserve to be here when
they never have to. I am Australian. I studied Australian Rules.
I watch it on TV and at the oval so I can play at lunchtime. I kick
the soccer ball. I asked you to show me cricket. I even tried—'
A horrified look flashed in his eyes and he bit his lip. He didn't look
at his mother. 'No matter what I do, they expect more and more
to prove I belong. And then the black boys, they say, forget being
Aussie, be in their gang—but they ask me to do things I know are
wrong too.'

'And have you done these things?'

He ducked his head. 'Once.'

'What did you do?'

'I drank vodka with them in the park.'

Fiza gasped and Tara reached out, squeezing her hand, hoping she
wouldn't tell Amal off when they were finally getting somewhere.

'And what happened?' Jon said.

'I threw up.'

'And?'

'And ...' The rattan was now wound tightly around his finger.
'They went to the silos. I watched them spray their tags over the
Aussies' tags, but the whole time I was scared. I kept thinking,
Om will kill me. She will cry and I hate it when she cries. So I left
and ran home. But the policeman with all the stripes on his shirt
stopped me on Serenity Street.'

'Sergeant North?' Tara asked.

'Maybe. He wanted to know where I'd been. I couldn't tell him
or he'd find the boys. If I lied and said I was somewhere, he'd go
there and ask. I said I had the right to remain silent.' Amal shuddered. 'He didn't like that. He made me empty my pockets and my
backpack. He used his torch to look for paint on my hands. When

he only found my school stuff, he ripped my chemistry homework and sprinkled it over my head. He said, "Being smart won't save you. One day I'll get you."'

Fiza said something in rapid Arabic and Amal hung his head.

'He should not have been drinking, but it is not a crime to walk at night,' she said to Jon and Tara. Her face twisted. 'When we arrived in Australia they told us we can trust the police. Hah!'

'Amal, do you know if this gang's responsible for breaking into our store?' Jon asked.

'It's not what you think.'

'Then tell us.'

Agony creased his face. 'I can't.'

'Because the black gang's threatened you?'

He shook his head. 'No. I don't spend time with them any more.'

'If someone's asking you to keep their crime a secret, they're not a friend.'

'You don't understand. They're not my friends.' Amal's shoulders drooped and he blew out a long breath imbued with resignation. 'There are three boys. White boys. They sell stuff at school and in the park.'

'Stuff they've stolen?'

'Sometimes. Mostly they ask the black kids to steal it for them.'

'Those boys should say no,' Fiza said hotly. 'Why don't they say no?'

Amal's expression was pure teenager—long-suffering forbearance. 'Because they get the spray cans for free, *Om*. They hate the way the Aussie boys make their graffiti look like they did it. It's why they paint over it.'

Jon rubbed his temples. 'Let me get this straight. There are three teenagers masterminding a stolen goods racket in town and making it look like the Af—black kids did it all?'

'Not sports equipment,' Amal said. 'Things like alcohol and spray paint. Knives. Anything they can sell. Drugs too.'

'I need you to tell the police who these boys are.'

Amal stiffened. 'No. They won't believe me. They will say I'm making it all up because these boys are well respected.'

'Jon, he might have a point,' Tara said. 'You know what Denny North said to us about smart boys. It matches what Amal just told us.'

He ignored her and kept his gaze on Amal. 'If you don't tell the police about these boys then you're still a sus—'

'Oh my God!' Tara grabbed Jon's arm and stood up. 'Please excuse us for a few minutes.'

'Tell me if you are calling the police,' Fiza said.

'I'm not. I just need to talk to Jon privately.'

Jon followed her into the study and closed the door. 'The first break-in was April, right?'

He nodded. 'During the big DIY push before Easter.'

'When did Morgan Llewelyn ask Ian about a job for Darcy?'

'Hang on, Tara. That's a leap.'

'It's as much a leap as us thinking it's black teenagers. Was there a break-in before Darcy started?'

'I'd have to check the date on his employment form.'

'Was he working when we didn't have any break-ins?'

'He had footy finals and a holiday with his family and then I said we didn't need him until last week—shit!' He ran his hand through his hair. 'You realise you're accusing the magistrate's grandson of breaking and entering?'

'Morgan's job is nothing to do with whether or not Darcy's stealing from us.'

'Yeah, but what's his motive?'

'People steal for a hundred reasons, but think about it. He's our worst casual. He's lazy, entitled and self-serving. The only reason we haven't sacked him is because Morgan's a mate of Ian's.'

Jon paced in the small room. 'It still doesn't absolve Amal. He asked to work in the garden section.'

'I know it doesn't look good, but it's only bad in retrospect. It made sense at the time, because I'd rostered Darcy to plants but he's useless. What if it was Darcy's idea to swap?'

'It would put him inside the store and give him access to what he wanted to stash ready to steal,' Jon said.

'And we were frantic on Saturday. No one would have noticed him moving between the sections, hiding things.'

'But if Amal knew that was Darcy's intention, it still makes him an accessory to the crime. North will be all over him.'

Tara's head pounded. She desperately wanted to believe Amal, but he'd confessed to trying to please two groups to fit in. If Darcy had set up the theft, not only did it take down Amal, but also the black teenagers who'd risked being caught breaking and entering. It played right into Denny North's and the town's prejudices. She readjusted her opinion of Darcy Llewelyn. He wasn't lazy—he was conniving and evil.

She gasped, struck by a thought. 'You know when you installed the CCTV, a lot of the loyal customers got stroppy?'

'Yeah. And I told them we were only using it at night to catch the thieves.'

'Exactly. Except when I arrived on Saturday, my head was so full of balloons and displays, I forgot to turn it off. It ran until Monday morning.'

Jon frowned. 'It will show us if Darcy was lifting stuff, but it won't show him stashing it in the garden section. It's not enough to clear Amal.'

'It will be if it shows Darcy carrying the stuff into the garden section after three o'clock.'

'Why three?'

'Because Fiza worked an afternoon shift and Amal finished early to mind the twins.'

CHAPTER
40

Milo had woken up early and as Helen was minding him today anyway, she took him for a walk. The pink and violet dawn spun light on the river track and the wheeling screech of galahs drowned out the frog serenade.

'Bird.' Helen pointed to a magpie on a branch. 'Can you say bird?'

She'd discovered she got a ridiculous burst of excitement each time Milo said or did something new. She'd loved Nicki, but with Milo racing through the milestones, she'd realised exactly how much Nicki's disabilities had stolen from them both.

She'd offered to mind Milo when Jade asked Bob to drive her to Shepparton to talk to a careers counsellor. Helen was disappointed Jade had asked Bob and not her, but she was tempering her reaction with quiet relief. In the middle of chaos, Jade had emerged from her blue funk no longer resisting the idea of study. This was the first step.

From the first time Helen had met Jade, the younger woman had presented with a mix of determination, dry humour and a pinch of protective pugnaciousness. Tuesday morning had shattered her don't-mess-with-me veneer, exposing how young and in need of support she was. This version of Jade worried Helen.

Each time Lachlan visited, Jade retreated to her room so he'd spent more time with Milo than with her. Helen had been about to broach the subject of Jade talking to someone when Constable Fiora had knocked on the door. Macca had resurfaced in town, with an alibi in Deniliquin to account for his whereabouts. Given the bloke who said he'd been with Macca the whole time had a history of petty crime, it wasn't strong. Macca had told the police he hadn't seen Corey in weeks, not since he'd 'gone to see a bloke about a job'. As the tyre prints on the nature strip didn't match Macca's ute, all the police could do was remind him of the intervention order. The offensive texts stopped.

A day later, Jade had announced she wanted to be a florist and asked Bob to drive her to the TAFE in Shepparton. Helen hadn't been able to completely hide her disappointment about floristry. Not that she didn't value the joy florists gave to people, but Jade didn't have support to start her own business and working as an assistant to a florist was a low-paid casual job unlikely to lift her out of poverty.

Helen cut up from the river track to the community garden, giving herself a workout pushing Milo's pram up the rise, and unlocked the gate. As she stooped to pick some strawberries for breakfast, her hips protested. Now things had finally settled down, and with Corey hunkered down somewhere for the foreseeable future, it was time to get back to her usual yoga routine. Time to get back to normal. She supposed that included changing the locks and moving back to Serenity Street. The thought didn't fill her with enthusiasm—life in a larger house was far more pleasant.

Just admit it's Bob's company.

Apprehension twisted on a helix. If she admitted that, where did it leave her? She didn't want to examine it too closely. She was closer to sixty than fifty and she hadn't been on a date, let alone had sex, in twenty years. Just the thought of either sent her blood pressure soaring. The fact she couldn't decide if that was a good or a bad thing made it spike even higher.

She firmly reminded herself that she and Bob were good friends. Nothing needed to change. It couldn't change—she'd lived on her own for too long and it was safer that way.

Except you're not living on your own, are you?

That's just temporary.

That thought didn't reassure her either.

She gave Milo a strawberry, bagged the rest and stowed them under the pram. The promise of a hot day was already delivering in the warmth of the newly risen sun. As she pushed Milo out through the main gates onto Riverfarm Road, she saw Judith and Sharon in their exercise gear, standing chatting on the street. They appeared to be looking past her, which suited Helen—chatting to Judith was at the top of her list of things *not* to do before she died.

The low vibrating grunt of a diesel engine sounded behind them and she turned. A huge Kenworth truck lumbered slowly down the road.

'Oh, look, Milo. It's got a big digger on it.'

Milo's bright eyes rounded into blue discs of wonder and when the truck finally passed, he cried out in disappointment. Helen swung the pram around so he could keep watching it until it turned right into Mill Street on its way to the highway.

'Wuck!' Milo clapped.

Suddenly there was the long hiss of air brakes and a flash of tail-lights. Milo squealed, startled by the sound.

'It's okay. The truck's just resting.'

Except it started moving again, this time turning slowly, its wheels carefully manoeuvring onto the driveway that led down to the cottage.

Unease pulsed through her and she forced herself to speak to Judith. 'Do you know what's going on?'

Judith gave her a feline smile. 'I can take an educated guess.'

Helen gritted her teeth. 'And what would that be?'

'Excavators usually dig.'

The truck was disappearing down the drive. Helen didn't waste any more time with gloating Judith. She half walked, half jogged past the women and bounced the pram through the orchard, trying to reach the garden beds before the truck. But it didn't pull off into the garden—it continued down towards the river.

Helen reached the cottage just as the driver swung out of the cab. Panting, she took a moment so she sounded calm and conversational instead of frantic and frazzled. Milo jabbered enthusiastically, pointing to the truck. It gave her an idea.

'My grandson loves any sort of heavy equipment.'

'Mine too.' The driver pulled on a high-vis vest over his blue singlet.

'That's an excavator, right?'

'Yep.'

'So what's the plan?'

He slammed the truck door closed and tapped the signage on the door. *Moore Demolitions Corowa NSW.*

Something spasmed inside her. 'You're demolishing the cottage?'

'And flattening that lot.' He indicated the garden beds.

'What about the orchard?'

'Yeah, that too.'

Her heart raced, but her sluggish mind struggled to generate the questions she needed to ask. She pointed to the cyclone fence. 'What about next door?'

He consulted a clipboard. 'No. Just this lot.'

'Who ordered the demolition?' Not that she really needed to be told. She was ninety-nine point nine per cent certain who, and why it was happening so early in the morning.

He grimaced and shoved a hard hat on his head. 'No time for twenty questions.'

'It's a pretty simple question. Whose name is on the demolition order? Who's paying the bill?'

'Look, love, if you want to stay so your grandkid can watch the show, fine. But—' he pointed to a tree, '—you need to stand back over there.'

He busied himself walking around the tray and doing things she assumed were preparations for unloading the excavator. Once it was off the truck, he'd drive it headlong into the cottage—ripping and slashing, and destroying a hundred years of history. Destroying the dwelling that had rescued her and given her a place to belong. A place to call home.

But it was much bigger than that. It meant the gang of four were making their first strike.

Without conscious thought, Helen grabbed the clipboard off the wheel hub and threw it under the pram with no consideration for the strawberries. Then she rounded the front of the truck and ran for the cottage. After hauling and bumping the pram up the worn bluestone steps, she locked the brakes and sat down hard on the veranda. With shaking hands she found her phone. It took her two attempts to get the numbers right and then it was ringing.

Please still be home. Don't have left for Shep. Be. Home.

'Missing me already?'

For once she welcomed Bob's flippant flirty greeting.

'I'm at the cottage,' she said quietly. 'There's a demolition order for the entire block.'

'What?!'

But she didn't have time to explain. 'I need chains and padlocks.'

'Go wisely and slowly,' Bob quoted. 'Those who rush stumble and fall.'

'Not now!'

'What does the sign on the fence say? There'll be a name and we'll have fourteen days to ob—'

The whine of the truck tray joined the bird song and Helen held out her phone. 'Can you hear that? It's an excavator being unloaded.'

'Bloody hell. I've got some chain and padlocks in the shed.'

'Knowing that should bother me,' Helen said, 'but good. Bring them. And bring Jade and your phone and the car charger—'

'What the hell are you doing, lady?' The truck driver stood at the bottom of the steps, booted feet wide apart, hands firmly on hips.

It went against Helen's every principle to fall back on the weaker-sex chestnut to get what she wanted. But when it came to a crooked mayor and dodgy councillors, the rulebook went out the window.

'My blood pressure's a bit up and down. I get dizzy sometimes so I thought I'd have a bit of a sit-down. I've rung a friend to come and get us. I'm Helen, by the way.'

He was silent for a moment, weighing her up. 'Daryl.'

'You don't happen to have any Panadol in the truck, do you, Daryl?'

He sighed. 'I'll get the first-aid kit.'

The moment he disappeared on the other side of the truck, she lifted her phone back to her ear. 'Hurry.'

'It's me,' Jade said. 'I'm in the shed with Bob. He says he needs better padlocks. Also, I didn't know you have blood pressure problems. You're not having a stroke, are you?' Jade sounded anxious.

'It's a ruse. I'm buying time. Tell Bob to come straight here. You go to Hoopers and buy the padlocks.'

'It's barely seven. They won't—'

'They will. It's when the tradies shop.' She saw Daryl's yellow helmet vanish from the cab. 'I have to go.'

She deliberately slumped against the veranda post and when Daryl handed her the first-aid kit, she gave him a weak smile. 'Thanks. You're very kind.'

He grunted, clearly uncomfortable with the compliment. 'Got a bit of the blood pressure meself. Makes me grumpy so the wife told me it was her or the job.'

'Oh?' She hoped the vague enquiry might gain her more information than a direct question.

'Yeah. Retiring wasn't a hard choice. Sorry about before. I'm usually fishing at this time of the morning, but me son's got a big job on. He turned this one down, but then they added twenty-five per cent so I've crossed the river for the day.' Daryl grinned, looking like a totally different man. 'We're calling it our Christmas bonus. It's taking us and the grandkids to Canada for a white Christmas.'

Helen swallowed the Panadol tablet to stop herself from swearing. If anything, it might ease the ache in her hips. 'That sounds special.'

'Yeah. Grandkids, eh? Who knew they'd be so much fun. Yours is at the age where everything's new and fascinating.'

'He's a sponge.' She had an overwhelming urge to brag. 'He parrots back Greek words as fast as English and he points to all the farm animals when I say their names.'

Daryl pulled out his wallet and showed her a family photo. 'Mine are bigger now but this is Oliver and Sienna.'

'They're gorgeous.' And she meant it. 'I see Oliver has your nose.'

'Yeah. Poor bugger.' But Daryl didn't hide his pleasure that she'd noticed. 'How you feeling? Bit better?'

Guilt thrummed at the strings of her deception. 'My friend will be here soon.'

Daryl's phone rang and he glanced at the screen. 'It's the boss so I better take it.' Helen nodded as he said, 'Hello, son.'

Come on, Bob. Why wasn't he here? He'd set up his shed in a grid pattern, naming the corridors after Melbourne city streets, and recorded the contents onto a spreadsheet. 'I can find anything in under two minutes,' he'd said proudly when he'd added her boxes and furniture to the document. She'd muttered something about OCD tendencies, but right now she'd take it all back if he turned up with the chains.

Daryl had wandered off. What was it about mobile phones, men and the need to walk and talk?

A plume of dust rose from the road and then Bob's ute pulled up between the cottage and the excavator. He jumped out, stepped up into the excavator and a moment later reappeared patting his pocket and touching his nose.

'Ob! Ob!' Milo threw out his arms and kicked his legs.

'And today he deserves all of your adoration,' Helen said. 'He's a clever man.'

Bob heaved a hessian bag from the ute, staggering slightly under the weight, and carried it to the veranda. 'Let's hope these posts aren't rotten or chaining ourselves to them won't do us much good.'

Ourselves? 'It's just me. I need you and Jade to—'

'Together we can do something great.'

'Who said that?'

'I did! Just then.' He looped chain around the veranda post four times before wrapping it around her waist.

'What about Milo?' Helen said.

'He stays in the stroller. Jade will be here soon.'

'So will Daryl.' She pointed to the large figure stomping towards them.

'He doesn't look happy.' Bob sat down next to her and pulled chain around himself, passing it under and over and then around the post closest to him. The heavy-duty brass padlock glinted in the sun as he pressed it shut. 'The key's too big to swallow.'

'Why would we—oh, right! They could get it off us.' Her fingers tapped on the old boards, helping her think. 'Give it to me. And the excavator key too.'

Ignoring the chain digging into her waist, she lay back and stretched her arm to its full length. 'Come on, come on,' she muttered, scraping the key across the boards, desperate to feel the jar up her arm when they hit the gap near the front door. 'Bingo.' She released the keys and they fell with a tinkle. 'They're with the snakes and the spiders now.'

Bob grinned at her. 'And they can stay there.'

'Aww! Fair go, Helen!' Daryl's complexion was puce and he was panting so hard she worried for his blood pressure.

'Breathe, Daryl! I promise it's not personal. I'm only doing this because I have very strong reasons to believe this demolition's illegal.'

'That's a lot of tommy rot.' Daryl strode to the truck before reappearing. 'You took the clipboard, didn't you?'

'Sorry, but not sorry,' Helen said. 'Daryl, this is Bob. Bob, meet Daryl. He retired to fish and spend time with his grandchildren.'

'Good to meet you, Daryl. I enjoy fishing myself. Nothing like sitting in the tinny and watching the sunrise.'

'Well, it sure as hell beats dealing with crap like this. And of course the job's legal.' Daryl puffed out his chest. 'Moore Demolitions have never done anything dodgy.'

Helen didn't think it would gain her anything if she reminded Daryl he was no longer running the company. She didn't want to cast aspersions on his son.

'We believe there are some dodgy councillors involved. Why else do you think they've used you instead of a local contractor? Why throw so much money at the job?'

Daryl's eyes narrowed and his mouth tightened as he considered Helen's point. 'Bloody Victorians!' He swiped at his phone and stomped away talking.

CHAPTER

41

Jade waved to Bob as he accelerated out of the empty car park at triple the speed limit. Then she turned and ran into the hardware store. She'd never been inside before and its size surprised her. Scanning the signs, she wondered if padlocks would be in homewares or building supplies. She glanced around, looking for someone to ask, but the only hint there was anyone else in the store was a flash of yellow fluoro in the distance.

She walked the length of the first aisle and came to huge glass doors that led to the garden section. Roof sprinklers misted over hundreds of plants, their foliage spread wide and flowers tilted back in joyous greeting. Her heart sang and the lush verdant green tempted her inside. She took a step.

Padlocks!

'Hello, Jade. You're out early.' Tara Hooper smiled as if she was genuinely happy to see her. 'Can I help you find something?'

Jade consulted her phone where she'd typed Bob's instructions. 'I need three eighty-millimetre heavy brass padlocks.'

'Are you sure? They're industrial padlocks and eighty-three dollars each.'

'It's what Bob told me to get. He and Helen are chaining themselves to the cottage to stop it from being demolished.'

Tara blinked. 'Helen's old cottage?'

'Yeah.'

'It's not being demolished, Jade. It's being moved.'

Jade knew she couldn't mention a possibly dodgy mayor. 'You might think that, but it's not what Helen's saying. She rang ten minutes ago from the cottage and told Bob to bring chains. He dropped me off here to buy padlocks and said to put them on his account. I'm going straight there to do a Facebook Live and let the town know what's happening.'

Tara frowned and Jade's gut squirmed. 'It's legit,' she added. 'You can ring him if you want.'

'I believe you, Jade, but it's all a misunderstanding. Tell you what, I'll drive you to the cottage and explain everything to Helen and Bob.'

Jade thought of the two-kilometre walk and the precious time saved. 'Thanks, that would be awesome. But I still need the padlocks.'

Tara laughed. 'If I was picking teams, I'd want you on mine.'

Instead of blocking the compliment and bracing for a kicker, Jade grinned and let it warm her.

'Maybe park behind the truck,' she suggested to Tara as they reached the bottom of the cottage's driveway.

'To block it in?'

'Just in case.'

She expected an argument, but Tara pulled up millimetres away from the vehicle.

Jade jumped out of the four-wheel-drive and Milo cried when he saw her, suddenly remembering they'd been separated. 'Coming, buddy.' She ran up the steps, undid the straps and picked him up.

'Got the extra padlocks, love?' Bob asked.

'Yes, but Tara says you've got the wrong end of the stick. Right, Tara?'

'Right.' Tara stood at the bottom of the steps. 'You don't have to worry, Helen. The cottage is safe. It's being moved to the historical society so we can restore it to its original condition.'

'I didn't know that was happening.' Helen rubbed her temples and sighed. 'I'm sorry, Jade. All I've done is muck up your trip to Shepparton.'

'We can still make it, right, B—'

'Hang on!' Helen leaned forward as far as the chains allowed. 'Tara, who's "we"?'

'Jon and I put in a proposal to spearhead a community restoration project. We kept it quiet in case it didn't go anywhere. You know how slow the shire can be, but in the end it's all happened amazingly quickly. I was going to tell you as soon as we got the green light, but things at work have been crazy. And that's a whole other story.' She sighed and pulled her hair back, twisting it into a knot. 'To be honest, I'm surprised the move's happening today. I thought it was next week.'

A prickling whoosh of sensation streaked along Jade's skin. She shared a look with Helen, knowing she was mirroring the same distrust and scepticism.

'Who did you deal with at the shire, Tara?' Jade asked.

'About the project or the move?'

'Both.'

'Geoff Rayson for the idea, then Ryan Tippett about the logistics of the move.'

The two men who'd turfed Helen out of the cottage. 'Bastards!'

'I've seen the demolition order, Tara,' Helen said. 'They're not moving the cottage. They're knocking it down.'

'No! That's got to be a mistake.'

'We don't think so.' Bob indicated the truck with New South Wales plates. 'It doesn't say house-moving, does it?'

Tara's face paled. 'Don't move. I'll ring Ryan straight away and sort it out.'

Jade plonked Milo on Bob's lap. 'Can you hold onto him for a minute and give me your phone, please? I'll post some photos. Helen, think about what to say on a Facebook Live.'

Bob nodded towards the truck driver, who was still talking on his phone. 'Reckon you should give me the padlocks first so we're all secure when Daryl gets back.'

'Good idea.' Jade followed Bob's instructions on where to place them and snapped them shut.

'Here you go, mate.' Bob handed Milo the keys.

'That's not a great idea. He'll lose— Oh!'

Bob grinned. 'Smart girl.'

Jade usually hated being called a girl, but unlike when others said it and she felt the sting of an insult, whenever Bob said it, it sounded like praise.

'I'm calling Fiza and I've sent out a message on the garden's WhatsApp to get the women down here,' she said. 'Will I ring Vivian?'

'I'll call Vivian, but let's do the Facebook Live first,' Helen said. 'Then we'll have some footage and you can ring WIN TV News.'

'You think they'll listen to me?'

'Of course they'll listen to you. You've had an article published in the *Shepparton News* and now you're giving them a scoop.'

Helen's confidence steadied Jade's nerves. 'Tara, do you have any lipstick Helen can use?'

'Oh, for heaven's sake. I don't need frippery.'

Jade glared at her. 'If this video goes viral or lands up on the TV news, you'll thank me for the lipstick.'

'She's right. A bit of colour suits you,' Bob said and smiled encouragingly. Helen shot him a death stare and he raised his hands. 'Not that you don't look great without it.'

Tara handed Helen the lipstick and a mirror. 'Ryan's not in the office until nine and the mayor's not picking up so I've left messages.'

'Yeah, well, they're not stupid,' Helen said. 'They planned for this to happen before business hours.'

'But why? Geoff Rayson was genuinely excited at the prospect of the cottage being saved from demolition.'

'It's all going to come out really soon.' Jade lifted Bob's phone. 'Remember—three points, Helen. Clear and concise. And in three, two, one ...'

Helen looked straight at the phone Jade was holding steady and took a deep breath. 'Something's rotten in the Shire of Mookarii and the attempt to demolish this cottage and the community garden is just the tip of the iceberg. It's time to ask some hard questions so I invite the mayor to come and talk to me here on the steps of Boolanga's oldest building. Citizens of Boolanga, please come and ask questions too.'

'Bit of *Hamlet*. Nice.' Bob's eyes twinkled. 'I must be rubbing off on you.'

'If that was true, I'd have said "a plague on both your houses". You do fall back on *Romeo and Juliet* a lot.'

'That's because I'm a romantic.'

'Well, I doubt my *Hamlet* will call Geoff out. If you had something to hide, would you be prepared to face a crowd?'

'That's the bread and butter of being a politician.'

'That was awesome, Helen! The likes are going off!' Jade's face shone with excitement and admiration. 'You're all over this. Did you protest in the sixties?'

Indignation ripped through her. 'I was barely born in the sixties!'

Bob laughed so hard tears tracked down his white-stubbled cheeks.

'Helen, Bob.' Daryl stood at the bottom of the stairs, his hard hat in his hands. 'I think it's only fair to tell you I've called the police. I didn't want to, but taking the keys from the excavator was a step too far.'

'Fair enough, Daryl,' Bob said.

Fiza hurried over, her face filled with worry. 'Oh, Helen, Bob! Is this safe for you?'

'Nothing to worry about, Fiza,' Bob said. 'We're exercising our democratic right to make our opinions heard. I just wish I'd had breakfast first.'

'I will bring you food.'

'Good idea, Fiza.' Tara got out her phone. 'Hit me with your orders. My treat. Jade?'

'Seriously?'

'Looks like you're the communications officer so we can't have you fainting from hunger. You can have anything you want as long as the bakery sells it.'

'An egg and bacon roll and a hot chocolate would be awesome, thanks. Helen, are you right with Milo? I'm going to call WIN and get some more footage. Back soon.'

'I'll pay for whatever Daryl wants,' Bob said.

'Thanks, but I've got a thermos and the wife made sandwiches.' Daryl walked back to the truck.

'Fiza and I will be back as soon as we can,' Tara said. 'I'll call you if I hear from either Ryan or Geoff.'

'I respect your optimism, Tara, but it won't happen.'

Squinting into the sun, Helen watched Tara and Fiza leave, then recognised Judith and Sharon, still in their exercise gear. They'd probably been drawn in on their walk back due to the absence of splintering timber and crushing metal.

'Seriously, Helen, you're staging a sit-in?' Judith scoffed. 'You'll just get sore hips. Nothing will save this sorry excuse of a garden.'

Given the garden was thriving, Helen considered asking if she needed her eyes tested. Instead she said, 'What did life do to you to make you so bitter and vindictive?'

Judith's mouth pursed. 'Unlike you, Helen, I have a long history in this town. It's a place where rules are valued. All our members spend time on a waiting list to get their plot. Those people are queue-jumpers.'

Helen's ire rumbled and flared. Judith was a founding member so she hadn't spent any time on a waiting list, but 'those people are queue-jumpers' meant they were no longer talking about the garden.

'Those people are women. Some witnessed loved ones being murdered. Racial and religious persecution is why they fled their country and spent years in refugee camps in Pakistan waiting their turn. They came here legally, but even if they hadn't, I'd still give them a plot.'

Judith snorted. 'Well, there's a surprise.'

'And you know why? Because it's impossible to apply for a garden bed when you're in a country that has not only banned gardens, but banned embassies from countries with gardens. So you risk your life to get to a country with a garden where you can plant, grow and harvest. Where you can live the life we take for granted. But when you arrive, you're told that because you couldn't apply before you came, you're at the very bottom of a long waiting list that never moves. You're in limbo, belonging nowhere. Your internal garden of hope and faith withers. One day you're told there will never be a garden bed for you. Go back to the country that tortured and raped you and murdered your family. No human being deserves that.

'These women came here legally and this garden has given them a place to belong. A way of connecting with Boolanga. You're quoted in *The Standard* as saying they need to adapt to Boolanga's ways of life. Well, guess what? Having your own patch of dirt and growing some vegies is quintessentially Australian. No matter our philosophical differences, Judith, I've always respected you as a gardener. How can you get excited at the prospect of watching all these healthy plants being wantonly destroyed?'

Judith stood rigid and unusually silent, although Helen was almost certain it was more to do with momentary concern for the plants, not the women.

'And by the way,' she finished, 'the orchard's going too.'

Sharon gasped.

Judith shook her head. 'Don't add lying to your list of sins, Helen. The only thing being destroyed today is your garden.'

'Why does she sound like she knew this was going to happen?' Bob said quietly. 'It's like she was planning to be here.'

'And you once said she wielded no power outside the cyclone fence,' Helen said *sotto voce*.

'Everyone's allowed one mistake.'

He nudged her shoulder and she laughed, not quite believing it was possible in the middle of this mess.

'Judith, who told you about the garden being ploughed under?' she asked.

'None of your business.'

'Well, whoever it is hasn't told you the full story. I've seen the demolition order and it clearly states everything between the community garden and the road's to be flattened.'

'You're wrong,' Judith said. But she was already pulling out her phone and dragging Sharon up the hill.

CHAPTER
42

Helen's stomach rumbled. 'I hope Tara and Fiza are back soon with food or my lie about being dizzy will be the truth.'

'Can't have that.' Bob dug into his pocket and produced a tin of mints.

As Helen popped two in her mouth, a little red Mazda drove in. Vivian must have seen the Facebook Live and come straight down.

'Helen, what on earth's going on?'

'This is our *Current Affair* moment, Vivian. Today we nail the mayor and his cronies good and proper.'

'Vivian!' Judith made a beeline for her. 'Are the other councillors coming?'

Vivian smiled her polite politician's smile. 'I'll be with you in a minute, Judith. I'm just having a private chat.'

'Yeah, Judith. No queue-jumping. Get in line,' Jade said, grinning as she filmed.

Vivian held up her hand. 'Young lady, unless you want to jeopardise everything Helen and I have been working towards, stop filming now. Helen's already risked more than she knows.'

'Didn't you see the excavator?' Helen asked.

'The orchard is heritage-listed,' Judith called out. 'It's the envy of community gardens everywhere. Helen says it's being bulldozed and I need to know it's safe. I demand Helen shows me the demolition notice.'

A long sigh rolled out of Vivian and she held out her hand. 'Obviously we're not going to be able to talk until Judith has her question answered.'

'Don't.' Bob said it so quietly Helen almost didn't hear it. But even if she'd missed it, she knew instinctively that handing over the clipboard was a bad idea.

She leaned around Vivian and called out, 'Judith, you've known Bob for years and you trust him, don't you?'

Judith's eyes narrowed as if Helen had just set a trap.

'Helen, is this really necessary?' Vivian asked.

'Judith, you and Pen were in CWA together for years.' Bob put his hand on his heart. 'On Pen's grave I swear I will read the words exactly as they're written.'

'I'm holding you to that, Bob Murphy.'

As Bob looked straight at Judith and read the demolition notice, Helen checked her phone. One missed call and one text. *Please call Jessica Szabó WIN News.* She forwarded it to Jade's and Bob's phones so Jade could respond.

'... *all structures, all trees, flatten the site and remove the debris,*' Bob finished.

'That's outrageous!' Vivian said.

Judith ran at Vivian like a bull storming a red cloth, shaking her fists. 'I told all of you it was just the garden I wanted destroyed.'

Vivian's tolerant expression hardened. 'And I've told you repeatedly that this garden is an important part of our community and it stays. If you don't stop threatening me and step away, I'll call the police.'

'Daryl's way ahead of you,' Bob said. 'I thought they would have arrived by now. We'll need them for crowd control soon.'

A constant stream of people were filling the garden. The Hazara women had arrived and Aima was glancing around looking worried. With Jade tied up filming, Helen wished Fiza was here to explain what was happening. She could see Kubra watching Milo, who was oblivious to the chaos and cheerfully pushing a toy digger in the dirt.

Aima suddenly turned, her headscarf floating in the breeze, and she crossed the garden to meet Lachlan as he walked out of the trees. Helen relaxed.

Judith was arguing with Jade, who was filming her walking towards the Hazara women. Lachlan, standing between Judith and the women, ducked and weaved like a rugby player every time Judith tried to get around him, except Helen knew he'd never played—it was dancing that made him nimble.

I told all of you. Helen rolled Judith's words around in her head. She knew Judith had spent weeks complaining about her and the garden to all the councillors. Had the gang of four thought they could shut Judith up by making her think this morning was her idea? Except they hadn't counted on Judith's passion for the orchard. And thank goodness for that fervour—it would work in Helen's favour.

'Oh, my God, that woman.' Vivian blew out a breath. 'We both know whose name is on the paperwork, don't we?'

Helen nodded. 'And I'm going to out the lot of them today.'

'It's tempting, but you risk them banding together to deny everything, sue you for slander and throw you under the excavator.

They'll promise an enquiry, which will take months and buy them time to get all their ducks back in a row. We've both worked too hard to let that happen.'

Helen thought about her and Bob's IBAC complaint that was thankfully lodged in the system and able to complement any internal investigation of wrongdoing. Part of her understood Vivian's point of view and she'd respected it up to now, but this time she was privy to incriminating information.

'I hear what you're saying, Vivian—'

'That's a relief. I know it's hard to hold the line, but today's not the day to fold.'

Bob's hand suddenly rested on Helen's back, his thumb pressing firmly on her lumbar spine. Electricity sparked, detonating tiny explosions all over her. She jerked away, stunned that her body still knew how to respond, and risked a look at him. But there was no flirting sparkle in his eyes—just serious intent—and an almost imperceptible tilt of his head towards the drive.

Three cars were winding their way to the now very crowded area in front of the cottage. Peter Granski and a photographer from *The Standard* alighted from one vehicle, Fiza and Tara from the second, and Constable Fiora from the third.

Daryl emerged from his cab and spoke to the police officer, while Judith abandoned her quest to get past Lachlan and marched down the hill towards Daryl.

Jade hurried over to the veranda. 'Judith's like a chook with her head cut off. I've got some awesome footage.'

'Put it on Facebook,' Vivian said savagely.

Fiza and Tara distributed the food.

'Sorry, Vivian,' Tara said. 'We didn't know you were part of the protest otherwise we'd have got you coffee too.'

'That's fine,' Vivian said tightly. 'But can we please focus on our plan instead of food.'

'We'll all think better on full stomachs,' Bob said.

Daryl and Constable Fiora approached the steps.

'Morning, Helen, Bob,' the police officer said. 'I need you to unchain yourselves so Mr Moore here can carry out the job he's been employed to do.'

'Not without a new set of keys, I can't,' Daryl muttered.

'With no disrespect to Daryl,' Helen said, 'don't you think, Constable, you should at least check that all the documents pertaining to the demolition of this building are legal.'

A line of sweat beaded on the young constable's brow. 'Why? Is there a heritage listing on this house?'

'There should be,' Tara said. 'And I've been told by the mayor that the building's to be moved not demolished.'

'Hah! Join the club,' Vivian said. 'Geoff Rayson's skill lies in telling you what you want to know.'

'I've rung him this morning,' Tara said. 'I'm expecting him to call back any minute.'

Vivian snorted. 'Good luck with that. He and Sheree are on their way to Toowoomba to look at horses. But even if he was here, he'd deny everything. It's what he does time and time again.' She turned to face the growing crowd. 'Who heard the mayor on family day? He couldn't give us a straight answer about Riverfarm, could he? Why? Because he was planning this the whole time.'

'Save our orchard!' Judith called out.

'Save Riverfarm!' Lachlan yelled, waving his hand like a conductor, encouraging people to join in. 'No resort! No resort!'

'That's a pretty serious accusation, Councillor Leppart,' Constable Fiora said.

'I'm just calling it like it is. Ask Helen. She's had concerns about the mayor's activities for months.'

'Concerns aren't evidence.' The cacophony of shouts behind them grew louder. 'I'm going to call the Sarge.'

Tara muttered something that sounded like 'pig' but Helen must have misheard.

Vivian cupped her hands around her mouth and shouted into the crowd, 'The Shire of Mookarii deserves better.'

'We do!' they shouted back.

'Unlike some councillors, I've always put community first.' Vivian started listing the projects and programs she'd instigated until she was drowned out mid-sentence by Judith.

'It's the mayor!'

'Ask the mayor!' Lachlan chanted, conducting the crowd.

'Ask the mayor!' they responded. 'Ask the mayor!'

'I thought he was out of town?' Bob said.

'Apparently not.' Helen craned her neck, trying to see around Vivian. 'I can't believe he came. Tara—'

But Tara was gone. Helen could see Fiza, courtesy of her height, but not much else.

'Aren't we supposed to be the centre of our own protest?' she said.

Bob patted her knee. 'A society grows great when old men plant trees whose shade they know they shall never sit in.'

'Source?'

'Greek proverb.'

'One day you'll have to tell me how the quotes started.'

'You're on.'

'Ask the mayor! Ask the mayor!' the crowd shouted.

Constable Fiora's voice blared from a megaphone. 'The mayor is not required to answer your questions here. There's a council meeting on Tuesday night. That's the place to voice your concerns.'

'We're not leaving until we know the orchard's safe.'

'Everyone please disperse,' Constable Fiora continued. 'You're trespassing.'

'No, they're not!' Helen yelled. 'This is shire land. It belongs to the community.'

The crowd roared their approval.

'Councillor Leppart, please come down off the steps. Mrs Demetriou, release yourself and Mr Murphy and be quiet or I'll charge you with disturbing the peace.'

'Come on, Helen,' Vivian said. 'Once the police start using titles you know they're serious. It's not worth getting charged over this. The only person who wins is Geoff Rayson.'

Helen knew it was true. When Sergeant North arrived, he'd organise boltcutters to break the locks, she'd be arrested and the demolition would take place. The only way to protect Boolanga's heritage, the garden that meant so much to the refugee women and the chance that one day this land would be a garden for rehoused women, was to reveal Ryan Tippett's authorisation. She'd risk time in the lock-up for that.

She glanced at Bob. His smile not only warmed her, it was full of support and care. Sliding her hand into his, she squeezed and he returned the pressure.

Helen raised her free arm and pointed at Geoff Rayson. 'Ask the mayor why he had me sacked and evicted from this cottage. Ask him why he's demolishing it along with the garden and the orchard.'

'Ask the mayor!' the crowd chanted. 'Ask the mayor!'

'Jesus, Helen! Why?' Vivian's face contorted in an agony of frustration. 'All you had to do was wait five days. *Five days* and we'd have got all four of them at the council meeting. But Rayson's an expert snake and you just gave him a way to slither out!'

Helen's heart pumped doubt as Vivian stalked down the steps to the mayor. She gesticulated widely and repeatedly pointed to Helen, but her lips moved too quickly for Helen to decipher what she was saying.

'Have I done the wrong thing?' Helen asked Bob.

But Bob was watching the mayor, who was holding his hand out to the constable. The younger man initially shook his head but after Geoff Rayson said something, he reluctantly handed over the megaphone. As the mayor raised it to his mouth, it squealed, silencing the crowd.

'Mrs Demetriou, I understand you have an unfair dismissal complaint. If you release yourself, we can discuss your concerns in private.'

Helen saw the WIN News van drive in followed by a ute. 'No, thank you. I want this conversation to be on the public record.'

The mayor's amplified sigh rumbled in the warm air. 'Until I speak with the staff in Human Resources, I can't comment on your employment issues. But I can assure you and everyone here that your eviction was far from spurious. It was made out of safety concerns. The moment our engineer, Ryan Tippett, advised the wiring could start a house fire, we acted.'

'After you made it worth his while to tell you the wiring was faulty,' Helen called back.

Rayson stood taller, puffing out his chest. 'I understand you harbour ill feelings about the termination of your employment, but that does not give you the right to make slanderous and utterly incorrect statements.'

Incensed, Helen held up the clipboard. 'They're not incorrect statements. Ryan Tippett's signature is on this demolition notice to raze the entire block.'

The crowd called for an explanation.

Geoff Rayson pleaded for calm. 'I can assure you, Ryan Tippett's signature is on a notice to relocate the house to the historical society. Mrs Hooper can confirm that.'

'I haven't seen the paperwork,' Tara said. 'But Mr Tippett and I discussed the move and agreed it would take place next Thursday. Not today.'

A murmur shot around the crowd. Helen was relieved to see Jade was still filming out of sight of the constable.

'Constable Fiora, can you please come and receive the evidence,' she called.

'This isn't a court, Mrs Demetriou.' But Fiora took the clipboard from her and walked it to the mayor and Vivian.

Geoff Rayson slid on his glasses and riffled through the papers, his brows pulled down in confusion. 'This doesn't make a lot of sense.'

Vivian, who'd been peering over his shoulder, said, 'It's an outrage! Council will investigate immediately. I give you my word we will get to the bottom of this.'

'That's more like it,' Bob said softly.

'Save our orchard!' Judith yelled.

But Helen's sense of uncertainty ratcheted up a few notches. 'Something's off. Clearly Rayson's flustered so why didn't Vivian go in for the kill and nail him? Instead, she's just suggested exactly what she told me he'd say if I accused him.'

The mayor glared at Vivian and raised the megaphone. 'The deputy mayor is jumping the gun. Everyone needs to take a deep breath. The only thing that's going on here is an unfortunate mix-up. This is the old paperwork I cancelled when the decision was made to move the cottage to the historical society. But we've had a lucky save, so let's give Mrs Demetriou a round of applause for being out early and asking the right questions.'

Helen stared at Bob. 'He can't be serious?'

'He's got that duffer persona down pat.'

'Clever bastard.'

The television crew were filming and a journalist stood next to the excavator talking to Daryl and a younger man. A man who was the spitting image of what Helen imagined Daryl had looked like thirty years earlier.

'The mayor might want to explain how he overruled a demolition order without bringing it to council?' Vivian said to the crowd.

'With a demolition order already in place and without any extra cost to the shire, I didn't need to bring it to council.' Rayson spoke through gritted teeth. 'The only people benefitting from this decision are the citizens of Boolanga.'

'Do you believe him?' Vivian asked the crowd.

The excavator's engine roared into life and everyone jumped.

Constable Fiora spoke into his radio as he strode to the excavator. While the constable talked to the driver, Lachlan led the crowd down to surround the machine.

'Surely, they won't demolish it now?' Helen asked Bob.

'I think they're just pissed off at all the hoopla. This is their way of telling us they've got a new key.'

The excavator fell silent and the crowd cheered. Denny North joined the young constable, insisting Daryl and his son climb down from the cab.

Helen cupped her hands around her mouth. 'Mr Mayor, explain how the order you're holding instructs Moore Demolitions to raze the garden.'

'You've made your point, Mrs Demetriou,' the mayor said tetchily. 'There's no need to add to the chaos by wilfully misleading people. Yes, a mistake was made and we'll definitely investigate how this order was inadvertently sent to the company—'

'There's no mistake. That paperwork's all in order.'

The crowd chatter ceased. People craned to see who'd spoken, and the TV news cameraman swung his camera away from the mayor, focusing it on Daryl and his son.

Helen squeezed Bob's hand. 'There is a God. Geoff Rayson's going down in front of a television camera.'

'And who are you?' the mayor demanded.

'Jayden Moore from Moore Demolitions. That paperwork was hand-delivered to me last night.' He suddenly glanced around as if he'd lost something.

Helen rose as far as the chains allowed, trying to increase her view. 'Have Dangerfield, Rehn or DeLuca arrived?' she asked Bob.

'It was her.' Jayden pointed to Vivian, who was no longer standing in front of the crowd but was opening her car door. 'She delivered it along with a cash deposit.'

The camera crew ran towards the car. So did the police. But Lachlan and Judith were closer.

As the Mazda roared into life and reversed, trying to manoeuvre around Tara's four-wheel-drive, Judith grabbed the back door handle—but had to let go when the car lurched forward. Lachie leaped in front of it, pressing his hands on the bonnet.

'Stay back,' Denny North yelled.

The car reversed again, pulling hard to the left, but it was blocked in by two other vehicles. It pulled forward and Lachlan jumped. Vivian tried to accelerate around him, the wheels spinning on gravel. The rear of the car fishtailed, then the sickening sound of crunching metal broke over the crowd when the Mazda slammed into the police divisional van.

A roar went up.

Denny North wrenched open the driver's door. 'Out you get, Councillor Leppart.'

Helen sat down hard, her brain scrambling to make sense of Jayden Moore's accusation. Of Vivian's attempted flight. It was Vivian who had bribed Ryan Tippett—not the mayor. Vivian who'd engaged the Moores and paid them a cash deposit, meaning she had access to a pot of money. Fury exploded in Helen like eucalypts on fire.

'You used the tiny houses project to hide a deal with Andrew Tucker!'

Vivian whirled around, eyes blazing. 'And it was the perfect plan until you stopped playing by the rules and went off-script on social media with your little friend.' She jabbed a finger towards Jade. 'Anyone else would have given up after they'd lost their job and their house. The two of you should have left town a week ago, but you're both too stupid to recognise the signs.'

'You set up the drive-by?!' Jade moved towards Vivian, but Lachlan caught her by the arm. 'You bitch! You traumatised my son!'

'Councillor Leppart, I need to warn you that anything you say can and will be used in evidence against you,' Denny North said.

As Vivian was walked to the police car, Helen called after her, 'Your blind spot was underestimating a young single mother and an older homeless woman. We don't shy away from battles. We live them every day.'

CHAPTER
43

'Oh my God!' Jade ran up the cottage steps, her face flushed. 'How come we never suspected her?'

Helen was thinking the same thing. 'She used something I was passionate about to keep everyone's eyes away from her true intentions. God, she even said once that Geoff Rayson was using the "look over there" ruse when she was the one using it. I just hope it's enough to take down Andrew Tucker as well as the councillors.'

'It means Corey wasn't involved,' Jade said quietly, almost reflectively.

'Can you take Milo?' Lachlan said, passing the toddler to Jade. 'I need to get to work.'

'Can you go to my place and get my boltcutters first?' Bob asked.

Lachlan checked his watch and looked expectantly at Jade.

'I don't drive, remember,' she said.

He sighed. 'Back in ten.'

'We'd better add driving lessons to your getting-ready-for-uni list,' Helen said to her. 'Bob can teach you. He's got the patience of a saint.'

'I'm not even sure I'm going to uni.' Jade's gaze was on Lachlan's retreating figure. 'I better check Aima understands the garden's safe.'

Sergeant North was instructing the Moores and Geoff Rayson to come down to the station. 'And, Helen, when you and Bob have released yourselves, you need to come too. Bring Jade. Oh, and I'd appreciate it if you returned the excavator's keys to the Moores. Wouldn't want to have to charge you with theft.'

Bob's shudder melded with Helen's as they pictured the keys under the house.

'Do you reckon they'd wait until Thursday when the house is jacked up and moved?' he asked Denny North.

'It's today or you're charged.'

'It's a shame Lachlan isn't still trying to impress Jade,' Helen said. 'We could have asked him to do it.' A sudden wave of exhaustion settled over her. 'Thank goodness for Daryl's son being a straight-up-and-down bloke or we'd still be suspecting the mayor. And doesn't Jayden look like his father. I reckon Daryl must have turned heads in his day.'

'Like I turn yours?' Bob said.

She laughed. 'You're never going to give up, are you?'

'Nope. Especially not now when I'm chained to you and you can't walk away.'

Instead of ignoring the simmer of delight bubbling through her, she embraced it. 'What if I told you that being chained to you isn't as bad as I thought it might be?'

His face fell into serious lines. 'I don't want you to be chained to me, Helen. Or me to you for that matter. It implies one or both of us is being held against our will.'

She fingered one of the thick and heavy silver links, thinking how they'd worked together in the garden, at park food, and more recently in their information-gathering campaign to expose corruption in the shire. How their friendship had grown to be something she held dear. How she trusted and valued him in a way she hadn't trusted anyone in years.

'I think this chain is really more of a connecting bond,' she said.

'I like the sound of that.' His thumb caressed her hand. 'Will you come to dinner with me at the Grainery tonight?'

'That's a bit fancy, isn't it?'

'Not for a special occasion.'

'What's the special occasion?'

'Our first of what I hope will be many dates.'

A skitter of trepidation fizzed inside her. 'I'm not sure that's a good idea.'

'Why not? You just said we have a bond.'

'We do. As friends.' She twisted her fingers. 'Bob, I haven't been on a date in over twenty years. I haven't had sex in almost as long.'

'Are you saying it's not so much the date you're worried about, but having sex?'

Relief filled her at his understanding. 'Yes!'

'Well, that's a good sign.'

'How?'

'It means you've been thinking about sex. And I'm hoping that means you've been thinking about it with me.'

'I'm not going to answer that on the grounds it might incriminate me.'

He laughed then and leaned in and kissed her. His lips were gentle and warm against hers, his morning stubble lightly grazing her skin. It was as natural as breathing to raise her hand and slide it along his cheek. Then she was opening her mouth under his and welcoming the kiss. Gifting him one in return.

Someone cleared their throat behind them. When they ignored it, Lachlan said, 'Are you two sure you want me to cut the locks?'

'Oh, my God!' Jade said. 'You realise we can't ever unsee that!'

Helen laughed, high on the rush of the kiss and the fact she'd done it without second-guessing herself. Hell, she hadn't thought full stop.

'Get used to it, Jade,' Bob said, winking at Helen. 'It's going to be happening a lot.'

Helen's laugh drifted into the office from the kitchen and Jade sighed. She wanted to be happy for Helen and Bob, she really did. But since their full-on kiss on the cottage's veranda, she didn't recognise either of them. And that wasn't limited to seeing Helen walking out the door on Bob's arm last night wearing a little black dress and a strand of pearls instead of a flannel shirt and work boots. This morning Helen had giggled. Helen never giggled—she was far too pragmatic and sensible. But worse than the giggling was the unwanted thought it might mean Helen and Bob had done more than just kiss.

Jade didn't know what unsettled her more—the idea of them having sex or the fact it might change everything. She knew she couldn't stay living at Bob's forever, but she'd assumed that when she left, Helen would leave with her. The worry of not knowing gnawed at her, taking the gloss off the two amazing things that had happened to her since the protest.

A journalist from *The Age* had contacted her after reading her *Medium* contributions and interviewed her as part of a bigger article about community gardens for the weekend supplement.

Even better than that, Constable Fiora had told her they'd found Corey in outback western Queensland shooting feral pigs. 'The station manager's confirmed his arrival there was four days after your birthday. We're confident Keegan McDonald and Corey Noonan had nothing to do with the drive-by.'

Jade had thought of all the texts she'd sent Corey and all the unanswered calls. Thought about her father who'd done exactly the same thing to her for most of her life.

'Did he mention why he didn't bother to tell me he'd gone north?'

The constable had grimaced. 'Sorry, Jade. According to the manager, Noonan and the cook have got a bit of a thing going on.'

A rush of emotion hit her and she hadn't known if she was laughing or crying. 'Don't be sorry. Let's hope he stays there.'

Now, she returned her attention to the computer, toggling between the TAFE website and La Trobe University's. Floristry was simple, but the number of courses available in the humanities section of the university was overwhelming. It was hard enough trying to imagine studying, let alone picturing herself in a job.

'Knock knock. Can I come in?'

Lachlan stood at the door holding a road rules booklet. She hadn't seen him since the protest, but according to Helen he'd popped in when Jade and Bob were in Shepparton with the careers counsellor. He'd stayed for a cup of tea and played with Milo.

'Sure.' She spun the office chair to face the couch where he sat rubbing his palms up and down his chinos.

'How are things?' they said in unison, then both laughed nervously.

'It's nice to see Uncle Bob and Helen so happy,' he said.

'It's weird. They keep laughing and finding reasons to touch each other.'

'You mean like we used to?'

She squirmed. 'I didn't think old people got the hots for each other. Clearly I got that wrong.'

He laughed. 'I was thinking maybe we could cramp their style and get them to mind Milo while we go for a walk before dinner.'

'I thought we agreed I was too hard to date.'

'We didn't agree. You told me.'

'You didn't disagree.'

He swallowed, his Adam's apple bouncing. 'It was more like I took it on advisement. But now I've thought about it, I disagree.'

'Even though Corey might turn up one day out of the blue and want to see Milo?'

'I'll be honest—I'm not thrilled by the thought. But that's more to do with me not wanting you and Milo to be hurt. I just want you to be happy.'

No one had ever wanted that for her before. She checked his face carefully, looking for signs that belied his words. All she read was sincerity and care.

Panic scuttled unease all over her. 'I don't know how to be in a normal relationship.'

'Is there such a thing?'

'You know there is. You grew up in a family where people loved each other and wanted the best for each other.'

'I see how much you love Milo and how you want the best for him. Isn't that a start?'

She thought about the last eighteen months waiting around for Corey to show up, waiting for money. Just waiting. After the weeks of uncertainty, everything was now surprisingly clear.

'I can't just be a girlfriend. I want to go to uni. I want a decent job like teaching or being a librarian. Something that gives me and Milo the security I've never had.'

'That sounds like an excellent plan.' He stretched his hands out towards her. 'Any chance you can extend those plans to include me too?'

'I'll be studying and there's Milo. You won't have all my attention all of the time.'

'I don't want that. I'll be working and performing and there's Milo. You'll have to share me too.'

Her heart sped up. 'You really want to try?'

'I really want to try.'

'Why?'

'I wish you could see yourself through my eyes. See how awesome you really are. Jade, you're clever and funny, you're a great mum and you make me laugh. Relationships aren't just about being together, they're about helping each other grow. I want to grow with you.'

The idea of a healthy interdependent relationship shone as bright as a Christmas bauble, tempting her to take hold of it. But her new need to be independent cautioned her.

'Can we go slowly?'

'If that's what you need, then that's what we'll do.'

She laughed. 'Don't panic, I'm not talking about sex. I'm saying I don't think we should move in together straight away. Let's learn how to date first.'

'Good plan. And while you're living here, we've got built-in babysitters.' His face sobered. 'I'm committed, Jade.'

I'm committed. Two words that had never been spoken to her, let alone been demonstrated, were now being said to her by a man who was content in his own skin. A man who'd shown her over and over that he cared for her and for her son.

And this time she wasn't running away from her life and making decisions on the fly. This time she had knowledge and information. She was making a considered choice.

'I'm committed too.'

He grinned at her and grabbed her hands. 'Looks like we're going round together.'

'You're such a dork.'

'Yeah, but I'm your dork.'

CHAPTER
44

Tara sat in the break room at the store and read out loud from *The Standard*.

What started out as an act of civil disobedience by residents Helen Demetriou and Bob Murphy to protect one of Boolanga's oldest houses from demolition escalated into accusations of alleged corruption in the Mookarii Shire. Allegations have been made against Councillors DeLuca, Rehn, Dangerfield and Leppart for accepting bribes in exchange for paving the way for an investment company to build a resort on the land at Riverfarm. The state government has stood down the entire council and appointed an administrator.

The sacked mayor, Geoff Rayson, was quick to distance himself from his deputy and the other councillors implicated in the scandal. "I'm an open book with nothing to hide and will cooperate fully with any enquiry. I've spoken to the administrator and would like to take this opportunity to reassure the people of Boolanga that the community garden, including the new extension and the orchard, are safe."

When asked about the rumours surrounding his purchase of Ainslea Park, Rayson responded that his wife's great-aunt died last year leaving Mrs Rayson an inheritance that assisted with the purchase. "It's disappointing that a private matter has now been made public when all efforts had been made to protect the sensibilities of other family members."

Mrs Judith Sainsbury has resigned as president of the community garden after ten years in the position. Ms Helen Demetriou has been reinstated as the garden's coordinator, a role she'd worked in until recently.

In other news, police have charged a youth over a spate of break-ins at Hoopers Hardware, Timber and Steel after cans of spray paint, a worksite radio, pocket knives and other items were found at his home. Investigations are ongoing.

Tara dropped the newspaper in disgust. 'I know they can't print Darcy's name because he's underage, but bloody Peter Granski hasn't addressed the fact he's a white Anglo-Australian.'

'It will come out eventually,' Fiza said. She cut three slices of the semolina and yoghurt cake she'd brought to the store and shared them with Tara and Jon.

'Yes, but if it was one of the black boys, you can be sure he'd have mentioned that.'

'This is true. And just because the police did not find any stolen goods at those boys' houses does not mean they are innocent. Like Darcy, they have lost their way.'

Frustration made Tara spear the cake with her fork. 'Except one of them has been given every opportunity while the others have had to fight for their lives.'

'Either way, they shouldn't be stealing,' Jon said.

'I agree,' Fiza said. 'And their mothers agree too. This was not what we hoped for when we arrived in Australia. The one thing that kept us going through years of loss, heartache and pain was the chance of a better life. We told our children things would be better here. Promised them. But this country makes it hard to belong and our sons suffer.'

'I keep thinking how Amal said they risked being arrested for free paint so they could spray over the decoy tags Darcy and his mates sprayed,' Jon said. 'Can any of them paint more than just graffiti tags?'

Fiza's chin lifted. 'I do not know. I want Amal to stay far away from them.' Her glare softened. 'Perhaps the art teacher at school can advise you?'

'What are you thinking?' Tara asked.

'I dunno. Maybe a mural on the west wall. They could paint things they remember or miss about where they came from—you know, like Fiza's maize or animals? Then something they love about being in Boolanga. I'm hoping there's something.'

'This is generous,' Fiza said.

'Not really. Without evidence, they can't be charged so I'm hoping this might make them think twice about stealing from us again.'

'It's a great idea,' Tara said. 'Maybe we can involve some of them in the cottage restoration. I mean, the opportunity to use power tools is a boy's dream come true, right?' She typed a reminder into her phone to follow up with the trade teacher at the start of the new year.

'Fiza, Jon and I are putting in a formal complaint against Sergeant North. We believe his harassment of Amal and his determination to find him guilty was racially driven and it stopped him directing his officers to look elsewhere to solve the break-ins. We want you to know that you have that option too.'

Fiza closed her eyes for a moment and took in a deep breath. 'I am pleased you wish to do this, but I will not complain against the police.'

'Why not? You have a case—' Tara stopped as Jon's hand slid over hers and she felt the caution.

'Constantly fighting something is incredibly exhausting,' he said. 'If Parkinson's has taught me anything, it's that sometimes you need to let someone else carry the load for a bit while you take a breather and regroup. We'll carry this one for Fiza.'

'Thank you, Jon, for understanding. I hope in the future you will allow me to carry some load for you both.'

Tara thought about the meals Fiza had provided and the child-minding. About her unflappability and straight talking. The way she listened. Their shared bond as mothers and wanting the best for their children. As unlikely as Tara would have thought it a few months earlier, theirs was a real and growing friendship.

'You don't have to hope,' she told Fiza. 'You're already doing it.'

Tara sat on the deck, gazing up at the stars and ignoring the call of a messy kitchen. After a frantic few weeks, she could hardly believe they were about to welcome a new year. Last New Year's Eve, they'd hosted the gang and her biggest concern about the coming year had been how Clemmie would transition to school. In hindsight, Clemmie starting school was the least of Tara's worries. Her daughter hadn't skipped a beat, but she and Jon had come far too close to falling apart.

'They're asleep.' Jon lowered himself onto a chair opposite her.

She swung her feet into his lap. 'Clemmie will be up soon enough.'

'I doubt it. They're exhausted after playing in the pool all afternoon with the twins.'

He pressed his thumbs into the soles of her feet, massaging them. She sighed and stretched like a cat, loving the sensation of his hands on her.

'Tonight was nice, wasn't it?'

'Yeah. But I probably ate too many of Fiza's meat pancakes.'

'You worked them off playing kick to kick with Amal. Has he given up on cricket?'

Jon grimaced. 'I have. Anyway, Amal's more interested in footy than cricket and he's got form. If he practises over the summer, I reckon he could play for the under-eighteens next season.'

'Would he want to?'

'I think so. His face lit up when I suggested it.' He ran his finger lightly up her calf and she shivered. 'If you're cold, I know a good way to warm up.'

'Do you now?' she teased, loving the glint in his eyes.

'Ah-huh.'

He pulled her to her feet. She expected him to lead her inside, but instead he walked her to the spa and tugged her T-shirt over her head.

Goosebumps rose in tingling rafts and she tossed her head, sending her hair into a soft and flirty arc. 'Exactly how does taking my clothes off warm me up?'

'Get in and you'll see.'

Laughing, she shucked her shorts and swung her legs over the edge, sliding into the warm bubbling water. Jon followed a little more slowly, his actions tinged with a mild tremor.

He pulled her onto his lap, bent his head close, and captured her mouth in a long deep kiss. Everything inside her loosened and she wrapped her arms around his neck, returning the kiss, loving the intimacy. Loving him.

She became aware of his erection pressing against her thigh. 'Did you take a little blue pill?'

'I did.'

Her heart squeezed. 'Are we bringing in the new year?'

'Well, that's the plan ...'

The plan sometimes worked and sometimes it needed extra support and modification. But tonight all she cared about was that Jon wanted her.

She stroked his face. 'I love you, Jon Hooper.'

'I love you too.' He lifted her up and lowered her down onto him. 'Happy New Year.'

EPILOGUE

Two Years Later

Carols by Candlelight was a Boolanga institution and, despite the long hours Tara had put in at the store during the run-up to Christmas, there was no way she was missing out on their traditional picnic in the park. It was the third Christmas she hadn't made all the food from scratch, just the mince pies. These days she was at peace with that—the important thing was they were all together.

The first Christmas they'd shared with Parkinson's, she'd discussed with Jon the idea of inviting all their friends—old and new—to join them at the park.

'It's a great idea,' he'd said. 'All part of embracing new traditions when the old ones don't work for us any more. Some will come, some won't. The choice is theirs. Either way, we'll have fun.'

So, she'd suppressed the voice that said, 'Lazy hostessing,' and had sent out a general invitation: *Please join us at Carols. BYO food to share. We'll supply the mince pies, drinks and picnic rugs.*

She'd hesitantly asked Fiza in person. 'I know you don't celebrate Christmas ...'

'This is true, but we enjoy the decorations,' Fiza said. 'And all the delicious cakes and biscuits.'

Now, Tara looked forward to this gathering as a time to reflect on the year that was. It also signalled the start of a few precious weeks off while the tradies enjoyed summer holidays. She planned to rest and relax, and that included a couple of fun runs. Flynn and Clemmie were joining her this year in a family five-kay run, and Jon would be at the finish line cheering them in.

'It all looks great, Tara,' Gerry said. He and Ian raised their cans of Sobah to her in a salute. It turned out that a sober Gerry was almost impossible to beat at any game that involved numbers.

'Tara!' Monique waved as she walked past with her family. 'I just finished a novel that will be perfect for book group. I'll message you the details.'

'Sounds great. Have a lovely Christmas.'

Book group didn't look quite the same as it had two years earlier. When Fatima and Jade joined, Kelly and Rhianna left. Although they and Tara managed polite exchanges at school activities, there was a tacit agreement between the three of them that they no longer shared enough in common to repair a friendship sunk by massive differences in values, beliefs and experience.

The carols didn't start until dusk, but there was plenty of diverse entertainment—from a kids' magic show to African drumming—to keep the crowd entertained.

'I loved my white Christmases in the States,' Shannon said, 'but I missed this crazy combination.'

'Jon and I missed you both,' Tara said. 'We're glad you're back.'

'We are too,' Chris said. 'Jon and I reckon it's time to give away coaching the under-eighteens and take over the under-tens. We might just keep up with them.'

'Merry Christmas.' Zac handed out stubby holders printed with the gym's logo. 'Here's something to help you with your new year's resolutions.'

He'd arrived with his girlfriend, Katie, the PE teacher at the high school. They'd been together six months, which was the longest Zac had dated anyone in all the time Tara had known him. She liked Katie—they'd run a half marathon together earlier in the year. Tara still hadn't given up on her dream to run a full marathon and had pencilled it in for the year Clemmie turned eleven.

'Zac!' Jon said. 'Come and meet Rick. He's just joined the Young Parkinson's support group and he's interested in kickboxing.'

Being kicked off the cricket team had been a defining moment for Jon. He'd battled the disappointment and depression as he did each time he faced another loss. Tara had given him a month to come out of the blue funk and then she'd driven him to the gym.

'All I'm asking is you *try* one kickboxing session with Zac. If you hate it, fine. We'll look for something else.'

It had been a turning point. Since that auspicious afternoon there'd been times she'd accused him of being obsessed with kickboxing.

'Just keeping up with you, T,' he'd say with a grin.

She had no complaints that he left work for an hour most days for a session. His strength, stamina and balance had improved and more importantly so had his mood. He was happier and that spun into their lives in ways most people took for granted. Their sex life would never be the spontaneous thing it had once been, but that didn't mean what they had now was a poor substitute. It was just different. Sometimes Tara thought she should get *Embrace Change* tattooed on her arm.

Eight months after Jon's diagnosis, Jill, the woman from the Parkinson's support group they'd vowed never to return to, had called.

'Another young couple have contacted us. I wondered if you'd like to meet up?'

For a year, Jeremy and Jon were Sun Country's Young Parkinson's support group. Now there was Leanne and Rick.

As challenging as the disease was, it felt good to share what they'd learned. More important was knowing they weren't alone—others understood the unpredictable road they travelled every day.

'Fruit *and* chicken? I'm sure one or the other would have sufficed,' Bob grumbled good-naturedly, setting down a platter groaning with strawberries and watermelon on the Hoopers' trestle table.

Helen gave him a gentle elbow in the ribs. 'Sharing food is sharing love.'

'And my marinated chicken is now a tradition, old man,' Jade teased.

'Enough of the old, thanks very much.'

'You walked right into that one, Uncle Bob.' Lachlan steadied an excited Milo, who'd just seen Clemmie Hooper and was leaning sideways off his shoulders desperate to reach her.

'How did the exams go, Jade?' Tara asked.

The relief they were over bubbled lightness in Jade's veins. 'I passed, so all good. It's hard to believe I'm halfway through my BA.'

'She more than passed.' Helen squeezed Jade's shoulder. 'She got three high distinctions and a distinction.'

'That's fantastic.' Tara raised her hand in a high-five. 'Well done, you.'

Jade's cheeks heated. It wasn't that she didn't enjoy the compliments and congratulations—she'd got used to them now. It was the support that humbled her.

'Thanks, but I only got those marks because these three looked after Milo and fed me so I could study.'

'Pfft. It's what family does,' Bob said, lifting Milo off Lachlan's shoulders. 'Besides, this little bloke gives me bragging rights with the other grandparents at the garden. Some days it's a photo fight.'

'I'm telling everyone I got an HD in English literature,' Lachie teased. 'Although I still don't get the appeal of Jane Austen.'

'Well, I'm just glad it's over until February and I can enjoy the holidays and the garden,' Jade said. 'Milo's totally into Christmas this year and it's fun cooking and doing craft with him.'

'Are you doing anything special over the holidays?' Jon asked.

Lachlan smiled down at Jade. 'We're going to see *Harry Potter and the Cursed Child.*'

'And we're staying the night at the Grand Hyatt in Melbourne,' Jade said. 'I'm a bit worried I'll find it too grand and overwhelming.'

'A good hotel makes you feel at home,' Tara said. 'Relax and enjoy it all. You've earned it.'

Jade slid her hand into Lachlan's, still slightly awed that this man was in her life. They'd learned a lot about each other in the last two years. How to be a couple and parents. How to respectfully disagree and work on compromise. At first, she'd feared the squabbles, assuming he'd walk away, but now she was confident in his love for her and no longer panicked. Neither did she put him on a pedestal or take him for granted, but she knew how fortunate she'd been to meet him and learn that not all men are bastards.

'What do you want to drink, Councillor Demetriou?' Jon asked.

A thrill zipped up Helen's spine as it did every time someone used her title. The first shire council elections since the sacking of the previous council had been held in October. Helen's family—another thrill tingled—had urged her to stand. Bob had managed her campaign, Jade ran her social media and Lachie had designed her posters. She was still pinching herself at the community support. Tara and Jon had put posters up all over the store, the members of the community garden had decorated the fences with her image, and Roxy and Cinta had handed out how-to-vote cards. Helen had expected a hard battle, but it appeared Boolanga was grateful for her role in uncovering the corruption and she'd won easily.

There were four other new councillors, Messina was mayor and Geoff Rayson was her deputy, lending his experience while she found her feet in the job. Helen and Geoff had bonded over being used by Vivian and she'd been relieved to discover he was a caring, albeit naive man who genuinely wanted the best for Boolanga. Cynthia had decided not to stand again and Vivian and her other councillor mates, along with Andrew Tucker, were all spending varying amounts of time in different Victorian prisons.

'Champagne, please, Jon,' Helen said and linked her arm through Bob's.

Tara clapped. 'You're getting married?'

'Let it go, Tara.' It never ceased to amaze Helen why the under-forties crew thought she and Bob should marry. Neither of them needed that piece of paper to convince the other of their love and commitment. And with Bob more financially secure than her, marriage would only complicate things. But she had a sneaking suspicion that after two successful years growing together, Jade and Lachlan might return from Melbourne engaged. If it happened, she'd be first in line to congratulate them.

'We're celebrating the unanimous vote for Riverfarm to be the site of a sustainable co-housing project,' Helen continued. 'The community garden will be at its heart. It's everything I've dreamed of and worked towards for the last five years.'

'Congratulations!' Tara hugged her. 'You so deserve this.'

'We still need Hoopers' sponsorship of the garden.'

'Goes without saying.' Jon passed out champagne.

Fiza arrived in a blaze of colour—blue and yellow and green and red—carrying a cake. Clementine and Flynn immediately took off with the twins and the Hegarty kids to watch Lachlan's magic show. Amal, biceps bulging, lowered an esky to the ground with a grunt.

'She's cooked enough to feed everyone, hasn't she?' Tara said sympathetically.

'There's more in the car.'

Jon slung his arm over the young man's shoulders. 'I'll give you a hand.'

Amal had just completed his first year of medicine at Monash University and was back working in the store for the summer. After his uneasy first year in Boolanga, he'd attacked his final year of high school with determined ferocity. For a break from study, he'd played football for the Boolanga Brolgas under-eighteens. Although his grasp of the rules was a bit hit and miss, his skill with the ball was enviable. There was nothing like helping a team win a grand final to fast-track community acceptance. And back in January, when Amal was the first Boolanga high school student in over a decade to be accepted into medicine and his photo and the headline *From Refugee Camp to Doctor* appeared in the Melbourne papers, the town had claimed him as their very own success story. The Rotary Club had provided a bursary. It was a bittersweet moment.

There were still troubled youths in Boolanga struggling with social dislocation and the inability to picture a future for themselves. But at least there were now some programs in the school and projects in the community helping to re-engage these young men and women. Tara was proud that two boys had secured apprenticeships with local tradesmen after working on the cottage restoration. Fiza and Jon had also worked together—Fiza acting as interpreter and Jon as a business advisor—to assist a woman from South Sudan with a successful application for a business grant. 'It is exciting,' Fiza had told Tara. 'I no longer have to drive to Shepparton to have my hair braided.'

As proud as Fiza was of Amal, Tara knew she missed him and worried about him being so far away. Just like Tara worried about Jon. When those concerns overwhelmed her, she ran and gardened. She and Fiza now shared an enormous vegetable garden on Tingledale's boundary that both families called 'Aussie Sudan'. Fiza had mastered maize and okra and Jon teased her that all she needed now was a goat.

The garden was the place Tara went to think. There was something about feeling warm dirt on her skin, freeing tender shoots from weeds and bugs, and harvesting hard-earned bounty that stilled the mind and allowed for reflection. It gave her time to grieve for losses. But most importantly, it instilled strength. Life was an unpredictable lottery. But surrounded by a community and a garden, the future was easier to face.

And Tara dared to hope.

ACKNOWLEDGEMENTS

This novel was written during the uncertain times of the COVID-19 pandemic and its huge impact on health and the world's economies. As I write these words, we are still uncertain if we will have a vaccine or how our new world will look. So rather than guess, I have avoided it completely. *A Home Like Ours* is my fifth novel in five years and each time I am struck by how many people are involved in helping me bring a book into your hands.

As always, research plays a big role in writing a novel. Many thanks to the Geelong West Community Garden and Rosemary Nugent for letting me gatecrash their AGM. Please note, GWCG functions far better than the garden in the book! Thanks also to the Diversitat Hope Community Garden and to David the gardener and Liz Young, a horticulturist and community worker, for welcoming me and answering my many questions.

Libraries have played a special part in my life since I was a child so 'Fran' is a thank you to all the librarians who bring reading into our lives. Thanks also to Ilona from the Geelong Regional Library Corporation for enthusiastically filling me in on Baby Time and other library services for the under-fives.

Thanks to the Victoria Police Film and Television Unit for their wonderful advice on extradition laws and general crime information. Thanks to Rowan Swaney for all things hardware-store-related and the entertaining stories, and to Leah Cwikel who keeps me abreast of all things current in baby land. Lara, Emily and Michelle are my 'go to' women for everything concerning the 'young twenties', and Gabi Mansfield shared her love for, and in-depth knowledge of, all seven Harry Potter books. She suggested Cedric Diggory as the perfect character match for Lachlan. Thank you!

Thanks to Susie Lukis for information on women and homelessness, and to Theatre Works' powerful production *UnHOWsed*. I drew on acquaintance connections to research this book and I wish to acknowledge Hilary, Dee and Dianne who put me in contact with some wonderful women. Thanks to Chioma, Senam and Christiana who generously shared and made me hungry with their descriptions of the foods of their homeland. I sampled a wide variety of food at Melbourne's Queen Victoria Market's African Food Festival and at Khartoum Centre in Footscray. Foodie Trails was also a valuable resource. Meg Upton answered my questions about gyros.

I want to give a huge shout-out to Kubra and Aima, who educated me on the Hazara culture, filled me with tea and spoke so enthusiastically about chives. Although I borrowed their names, the women in the book are fictitious. Special thanks go to my dear cousin Annie for sharing her life experiences.

Although Boolanga is fictitious, the area between Echuca and Wodonga on the Murray River is not. Thanks to Tania Goldman from Burramine for her lovely Airbnb and for answering questions like 'Is the internet strong enough to watch Netflix?' My husband and I took one for the team, spending a few days in the district sampling wine, local produce and the best balsamic reduction I have ever tasted. Rich Glen is worth a visit!

The team at HarperCollins do an amazing job reassuring me when story ideas won't gel, smoothing out my writing, designing wonderful covers, generating buzz and getting the books out into the world. Thanks go to Rachael Donovan, Annabel Blay, Nicola O'Shea, Adam van Rooijen, Darren Kelly and his sales team, and Lisa White for the amazing cover design.

Writers are not always easy to live with—their minds are often lost in their fictional world rather than being in touch with domestic tasks, especially on deadline. Big thanks to Norm for being the support crew, house husband and book-tour/research driver, even if me ranting at him, 'This plot won't work' takes him out on many bike rides. Thanks to Barton for all the banners, slideshows and website maintenance. Thanks to Sandon for always being happy to brainstorm book ideas and plot problems.

And thank you, dear reader, for reading *A Home Like Ours*. The choice of books is enormous and the book budget limited, so I appreciate the time and effort you expend on my books. I love meeting you on book tours, Facebook, Twitter, Instagram and email. Please stay in touch; your enthusiasm keeps me writing.

BOOK CLUB QUESTIONS

❖ Growing and sharing food as a path to understanding different cultures is a big part of *A Home Like Ours*. What are your experiences of sharing food and culture?

❖ Displacement is a big theme in the book. Discuss how each of the main characters experiences displacement.

❖ Racism comes in many forms: overt, cultural, religious, economic and unconscious to name a few. What types of racism do the women in the book experience?

❖ Research on volunteering shows that the volunteer receives more in the way of joy, fulfilment and connection than they give. If this is true, why do you think many voluntary groups struggle to fill positions? What are your experiences with volunteering?

❖ People with a chronic illness/disability often find themselves discriminated against. Does this differ from racism? In what ways?

❖ Homelessness is a human rights issue. Helen can hide her homelessness but Fiza cannot. What do Fiza and Helen share in common? Does this impact on their acceptance in the community?

❖ It's incredibly challenging to rise out of poverty and wanting it isn't enough. How many levels of support are necessary to break the poverty cycle? Do you think assumptions are made that well-educated people are protected from poverty?

❖ Tara says in frustration of her friends, 'If Jon had been diagnosed with cancer, the footy club would hold a fundraiser. If he'd died, our friends would rally around…knowing I'd eventually get back on my feet and there'd be an end date.' Why do you think chronic illness is treated differently?

Turn over for a sneak peek.

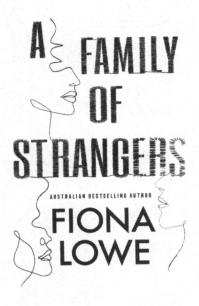

A FAMILY OF STRANGERS

AUSTRALIAN BESTSELLING AUTHOR

FIONA LOWE

Available March 2022

CHAPTER

1

Addy Topic drove off the *Spirit of Tasmania* ferry at the criminally early hour of 6:30 am and immediately found a café with a five-star coffee rating. Never a morning person, she sculled her espresso fast then sipped a latte, taking her time to savour the brew while she scanned *The Advocate*. Not a lot had changed since she'd last read it—it was still a mix of odd crimes, agriculture wins and losses, and ongoing housing issues.

'Anything to eat?' the waitress asked.

'Why not?' Moving house was why not. Addy ought to be maximising her time and getting settled before starting her new job. But knowing she should seize the day didn't touch the part of her that was in no great hurry to reach Rookery Cove. 'I'll have poached eggs with the avocado cup, thanks.'

Three hours later, after taking a detour through Penguin and dodging phone-wielding tourists snapping photos of the decorative penguins that now lined the Esplanade, she eventually drove into the cove. Then she turned away from the main drag and up the hill before pulling into her parents' driveway.

My driveway.

Addy shrugged the words away. Four years after Ivan's and Rita's deaths, the house still felt very much theirs.

She turned off the ignition, took a deep breath and got out of the car. Despite the weeds on the path, the bulging orange rose hips and the peeling paint—travesties her mother would never have allowed—she still expected Rita to step out onto the veranda, give her sadness-tinged smile and say, 'Aida, you are home.'

But Addy hadn't called the cove or the house home in twelve years; and since Rita's death, no one had called her Aida.

After her mother's funeral—six months to the day after her father's—Addy had left the fully furnished house in the care of a real estate agent and flown back to her life in Victoria. When people had asked if she'd ever live in Tasmania again, she'd replied 'possibly Hobart' while privately thinking *not the north-west coast and never the cove.* But the universe was wily and the gateway job for a long-awaited career jump had turned up two towns away.

Leaving her boxes and suitcases in the car, she walked up the steps and fished a bunch of keys out of her handbag. As she slid the old key into the front door, she got a flash of a brass key on a piece of orange wool that had once hung with great weight around her neck.

'Tell no one,' Ivan had sternly admonished each time he gave it to her.

'No, Papa.'

It wasn't until Addy was nine and had been visiting friends after school that she learned no one in Rookery Cove locked their houses. But Rita and Ivan had escaped a civil war that had turned security into something ephemeral and not to be trusted.

Turning the door handle, Addy got another flash. This time she was fourteen and standing on the porch watching Rita turning the door handle left, then right, then left, after having previously checked eight times that the windows were closed and locked. Knowing they were already late and that all eyes in the school auditorium would turn to them when they walked in, Addy had screamed, 'For God's sake, Mama! It's locked!'

The memory faded and regret tightened her chest. Addy wished she'd understood more about obsessive-compulsive disorder and post-traumatic stress when she was a teen. Although her parents had talked of their childhoods in Dubrovnik, they'd never discussed the war. Whenever she'd asked about it she'd been told, 'It's not important. We are Australian now.' But the kids at the local primary school, with their white-bread vegemite sandwiches, had disagreed when they saw Addy's lunch of salami, cheese and olives.

The glass front door swung open and the cloying artificial scent of gardenia hit her nostrils. She gagged. Beating down the nausea, she took another breath and got a lungful of the sweet smell of marijuana with a fried food chaser. So much for the reliable tenants the real estate agent had promised.

Stepping inside she girded herself for anticipated filth, but apart from the walls being brown and sticky with nicotine, everything looked much the same as it had when she'd left at eighteen eager for a different life. The same wide rust-brown velvet couch sat on its rotund feet, although minus Rita's crocheted doilies. The same framed photo of the old walled city perched on a shimmering bay hung on the wall, except instead of being fastidiously straight it tilted to the right. Addy automatically straightened it as she'd done each week as a child when it was her job to dust.

Her gaze slid to the upright piano, but with its closed lid and mahogany sheen dulled by layers of dust it lacked familiarity. Despite rising reluctance, her hands overrode her head and she pulled up the lid. She stretched her fingers, struck a chord and flinched at the off-key sound. The piano had been Rita's pride and joy and it had never been allowed to fall out of tune.

A stubborn streak of teen rebellion filled her and she played a honky-tonk riff from *The Entertainer*. The defiance evaporated and she dropped the lid.

'Sorry, Mama.'

She inspected the rest of the house. The kitchen's exhaust fan was coated in grease, the shower was host to a colony of mould, and there was a stain of unknown origin on the carpet in the master bedroom. Nothing that sugar soap, bleach, eucalyptus oil and elbow grease couldn't shift. By the end of the weekend, the house would still be stuck in its nineties-decor time warp but it would sparkle.

Addy paused in the narrow hall outside her childhood bedroom and stared at the single bed, remembering its ruffled pillowcases and detested quilt cover. At fifteen, she'd begged for a surfing design but had instead been given a grand piano cover. With it had come the full weight of Rita's expectations. From that moment, her mother's hopes and dreams, which had already cloaked Addy all through the day, became inescapable at night.

Stepping into the room, she opened the freestanding wardrobe Ivan had built for her, including a special wooden box to lock away her 'treasures'. She was surprised the tenants hadn't torn down the smiling faces of Layne Beachley and the other surfing posters she'd pinned there between thirteen and seventeen.

Was her board still in the shed? Her gaze slipped to her belly and she sucked it in. If it was, she was probably too heavy to use it.

If you lost some weight ... If you drank less ... If you were nicer to me ... tidier ... worked less ...

'Go away, Jasper.'

She released the catch on the window, threw up the sash and leaned out, stretching her arms wide. Cool salty air tingled her nostrils and she gazed down at the half-moon bay with whitecaps flashing across a moody and unwelcoming grey sea. An unexpected shaft of sunshine suddenly pierced the heavy cloud and golden rays lit a narrow band of water, taking it from steel grey to translucent tropical blue.

Addy smiled, savouring the water's familiar pull. How many times had she climbed out of this window and run to the moonlit beach? To parties at the surf club? To surf at dawn? Triple the number of times her parents had discovered her gone.

If Rita and Ivan still lived, what would they make of her return to the cove? Would they be pleased? Confused? Frustrated?

Addy was still coming to terms with it herself. When she'd accepted the teaching job at the regional vocational training and pathways college two towns away, the plan had been to live close to campus and get fit by cycling to work. After all, the point of living in a small city was to incorporate exercise with lifestyle. The plan didn't include living in tiny Rookery Cove—population three hundred—and making an eighty-minute round trip each day. But she hadn't anticipated the tenants moving out and no one else moving in. After weeks of no activity, the agent had suggested she turn the place into a holiday rental.

Although a good idea, it wasn't without on-costs. When she factored in the seasonal nature of holiday rentals, it made financial sense to live in the house for three months and redecorate it on the weekends. She could still get fit, drink less and eat better living here. She'd get up earlier and exercise with a run along the beach before leaving for work. She'd carve out an hour from her weekend redecorating schedule to prepare tasty and healthy lunches, dinners and snacks for the week ahead. She'd sleep better with the tang of salt in the air. Living here was the change she both needed and wanted.

Addy's fingers itched to crack open her first bullet journal. So far she'd only got as far as caressing the leather cover and smelling the crisp clean pages. She'd bought it, along with washi tape, markers, coloured pencils, paints and stickers, to help her plan each week so her new job, her new healthy lifestyle, the house renovations and herself all got the attention they deserved. This was her year of living intentionally. No more floundering. No more wasting time—she was taking charge of her life. But first, all the windows needed throwing open so the sea breeze could blow through and freshen the house.

She'd just reached the bedroom door when her phone rang.

'Addy, it's Grant Hindmarsh.'

Surprise tumbled with anxiety—Grant was her new boss for her new job. 'Oh! Hi! I've just arrived on the island.' Did that sound accusatory? She quickly added, 'I'm really looking forward to Monday.'

'Excellent! I'm calling to touch base and to say again how thrilled we are we tempted you back from the mainland. The students are lucky to have someone of your calibre.'

'Thank you.' A flutter of appreciation warmed her. 'I'm looking forward to meeting them.'

'That's what we want to hear. I know Lyn's already been in touch. Thanks for uploading your course work before your official start date. Others in the department could take a leaf out of your book.'

She smiled. Grant had just given her more praise in two short sentences than she'd received in three years at her previous job.

The line was suddenly silent. Given the cove's sometimes iffy mobile phone reception she said, 'Grant, are you still there?'

He sighed. 'Yes, sorry. I'm a bit distracted. Our media lecturer was in a car accident yesterday.'

'Oh, no. Are they okay?'

'Sienna's fractured her pelvis so she's off for the semester.'

'That sounds nasty.'

'It is.' Grant sighed. 'As you can imagine, it's thrown us into a spin. She teaches social media marketing and touches briefly on website design. Her class has a waiting list and it's one of our biggest earners so we're loathe to cancel it.'

Addy knew all about the pressures of funding and the appeal of courses that generated income. 'It all sounds very tricky.'

'How would you feel about taking it on?' Grant asked.

The question caught her by surprise. 'I, um ... I've never taught it.'

'But everything's new the first time, right?'

'That's true—'

'And you're a digital native so a lot of it's intrinsic,' he said.

Addy doubted it—she knew enough HTML to be dangerous and almost nothing about SEO. What she did know was that she'd spend the entire semester barely staying one step ahead of her students. She already had a full teaching load, but was saying no to her new boss the best way to start?

She sought some clarification. 'So this would be a load reshuffle? Which subject am I handing off to someone else?'

Grant sighed again. 'Ah, no, which is why I'm asking you. Going on your interview and referees, I get the impression you're the type of person who steps up. Am I wrong about that?'

She thought about her employment conditions. Three months probation, and if she aced that, permanency and a shot at the promotion she'd been chasing for a couple of years. 'Not wrong at all.'

'I didn't think so.' His tone was reassuring. 'Obviously it's not ideal and it's a big workload for you, but as we say here in the north-west, there's no "I" in "team". I promise we'll give you all the support you need. Lyn will get Sienna's teaching notes to you asap, so really it's just a matter of delivering ready-made content. So what do you say? Can you help us out?'

Addy's previous job had been fraught with never-ending budget cuts and infighting. The idea of being surrounded by a committed team all rowing in the same direction was as exciting as it was reassuring.

'Absolutely, I can help you out,' she said.

'Excellent,' Grant said. Addy heard the clicking of a keyboard as he added, 'Just be sure to send me through the unit of competency and performance criteria by four o'clock Sunday.'

Her hand tightened around the phone. 'I thought you said that had already been done.'

'I'm sure Sienna has it all ready to go. Talk to Lyn. She'll sort it. Meanwhile, thanks so much, Addy. See you on Monday at eight.'

He rang off, and an email immediately pinged onto her phone. She opened it, scanned the brief contents and rang Lyn.

'Thanks for the email,' Addy said.

'No worries,' Lyn said. 'I've sent you everything Sienna gave me.'

'Right.' Addy focused on channelling calm. 'The thing is, this reads like an ideas list rather than course content.'

'That's why the students love her,' Lyn said. 'Sienna prefers participation learning rather than setting out specific content.'

Addy's stomach clenched, but there was no point having a pedagogy discussion with the administrative clerk. 'What about the online platform? Has Sienna uploaded the learning, assessment and marking guides there?'

'I'll check.' Addy heard the click of keys and then Lyn was saying, 'As anticipated, it's not here.'

Stay calm. Breathe. 'Why not?' Addy asked.

'It's a new course,' Lyn said breezily.

What? Addy's brain froze at the full implication of four small words. She finally managed to splutter, 'That's not what Grant told me.'

'That'd be right.' Lyn sounded sympathetic. 'He probably thought it was the same as last semester. He focuses on the budget and enrolment numbers and leaves the teaching to the teachers.'

Addy knew it was a sensible management style, but it didn't help her today. 'Can you put me in touch with Sienna so I can ask her some questions about the course?'

Lyn tsked. 'The poor thing was airlifted to Hobart. She doesn't need any more stress.'

It appeared Addy's stress didn't count. 'So just to clarify, I'm devising and teaching a new course. Please tell me the first class is on Friday.'

Lyn laughed. 'You're funny. No, it's nine o'clock Monday morning, straight after the staff meeting at eight. See you then.'

The line went dead and Addy stared at her phone completely nonplussed. What the hell had just happened?

Anxiety rose in a wave, swamping all her plans for a weekend of washing walls and steam cleaning carpets. *Move!*

She ran outside to the car, grabbed her emergency supplies box, slung her laptop across her shoulder and returned to the kitchen. First, she lifted out a cloth and the antibacterial spray and wiped the sticky residue from the chunky pine table and chair. Next, she opened a large bag of almonds, popped out two protein balls, sliced an apple and refilled her water bottle. Healthy brain food and staying hydrated was key to concentration.

Bypassing the pristine bullet journal, she plugged in her laptop then transferred the documents Lyn had sent her from her phone to her computer. She reread them carefully. Calmly. Mindfully.

Addy cut and pasted Sienna's headings into a new document, numbered them, stared at them, then swore. She needed to consult the government training website.

She opened a browser, typed in the URL, then cursed the spinning rainbow ball of death as her computer valiantly tried to find her phone's hotspot. While she waited she ran through a list of her former colleagues, wondering who might be able to help her.

The internet is not available appeared on her screen.

'Are you freaking kidding me?'

She checked her phone. One bar. She walked around the house seeking a stronger signal, finally finding it in the bathroom.

Dragging a chair down the hall, she held her breath while a blue line crawled inexorably across the top of the screen. She typed in the URL and the rainbow ball appeared again. Every part of her clenched. This would take forever.

She dumped the computer on the chair and marched straight to the kitchen and her emergency box. She pulled out a notepad, pen, a plastic glass and the bottle of red she'd been saving as a treat to drink with dinner. A quick twist of her wrist and the seal broke with a reassuring click.

Addy poured half a glass, took two big gulps and refilled it.

Opening the wine early was not only easy, it was absolutely necessary.

Other books by bestselling Australian author

FIONA LOWE

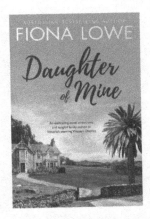
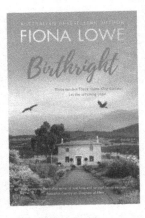
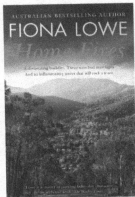

fionalowe.com